"I'm not your wife any longer."

Sophia jerked the case, throwing all her weight into the effort. "You're *not* a gentleman after all and most certainly *not* my hero, so no, I'm not inclined to thank you for *anything*."

"Not a gentleman, you say?" Claxton said in a hushed voice.

His expression dangerous, he yanked the handle *hard*, gaining possession of the valise and Sophia, who pitched forward along with it. The force of this brought her crashing against him.

"It took you until now to realize?" he said, nostrils flared.

With a downward shove, he wrenched the case from her hand, throwing it to the ground. She gasped and retreated, but he lunged, closing the distance between them to capture her face in his hands.

"Dear God, you drive me mad," he growled, his eyes alight with blue fire. His mouth fell on hers.

Stunned, she grabbed his hands to remove them, but...didn't.

He groaned, devouring her. The world around them faded into a maelstrom of desire, she only vaguely aware of the snow crunching under their feet as they danced, struggled...his hands—*her hands*—tangled in hair and wool. On skin.

Never Desire a Duke

LILY DALTON

FOREVER

NEW YORK   BOSTON

Forever
Hachette Book Group
237 Park Avenue
New York, NY 10017

www.HachetteBookGroup.com

Printed in the United States of America

First Edition: September 2013
10 9 8 7 6 5 4 3 2 1

OPM

Forever is an imprint of Grand Central Publishing.
The Forever name and logo are trademarks of Hachette Book Group, Inc.

The Hachette Speakers Bureau provides a wide range of authors for speaking events. To find out more, go to www.hachettespeakersbureau.com or call (866) 376-6591.

The publisher is not responsible for websites (or their content) that are not owned by the publisher.

*For my husband, Eric, the other half
of my romantic heart.*

*For my family—all of you—because
you mean the world to me.*

And for Cindy, who always believes.

Acknowledgments

Like all authors, I've attended my fair share of writing workshops. I remember one speaker in particular who said writers should never look at their books like their "babies." That we shouldn't be so emotionally wrapped up in them that we forget the book is business. While I see the value of such an understanding, I can't help it—each book I write is my baby. I think all good books scare the life out of the author at one point or another. Like a parent, I've fretted over the choices my characters made and lain awake at night worrying over how the story as a whole will turn out once it is grown. Now that the book is leaving the nest, I can't help but feel it's taking a piece of my heart along with it. Needless to say, I need to thank a few people for putting up with me while I go through this wonderful and awful process.

Enormous thanks to Kim Lionetti, my agent, for always believing in my writing, steering me right, and having the same taste in dark and tormented heroes as I do.

And working with an editor for the first time is sort of

like sending them naked pictures of yourself and hoping they don't call the police on you. I'm so grateful Michele Bidelspach didn't call the cops. Not only does she understand the workings of a woman's heart, she has the good sense to pull my characters back from the edge when they want to go to Crazy Town. Michele, I'm so lucky to be working with you. Thank you also to editorial assistant Megha Parekh and the rest of the Forever team, including cover designer Diane Luger and copyeditor Kathleen Scheiner, for giving this author a wonderful debut.

All writers have a supportive network of writer friends and readers. They are the most generous people on earth, and I could list pages of those who have inspired and cheered me. You know who you are, and I hope I let you know every time I see you (or Twitter or FB you!) how thankful I am for you.

Never Desire a
Duke

Prologue

"Tell me now, what has happened?" demanded Vane Barwick, fourth Duke of Claxton, tenth Earl of Renclere, as he swept through the front doors of his London residence, the frigid chill of the winter's day clinging to his greatcoat.

"Your Grace." The grim-faced butler gave a hurried bow and led him toward the grand marble staircase at the center of the house. "The Duchess of Claxton has taken a fall. The physician is with her now."

"Oh my God," he uttered, not waiting for details. Panic cut through his veins, and he took the stairs two at a time. *Sophia. Our baby.*

Having received the urgent summons while in sessions, he knew something terrible had happened. His feet couldn't carry him fast enough. His heart beat so hard and fast he thought it might explode. He had to get to her.

Several maids stood outside the duchess's door, wearing expressions of concern. Upon seeing him, they started and rushed away. He heard voices inside and entered straightaway.

"Sophia?"

In one shattering instant, he took in the scene before him. His beautiful, dark-haired wife lay curled on her bed, her face stricken and tearstained. Her lady's maid, also in tears, held her hand. The surgeon approached him, softly speaking regrets.

"No," he whispered, stunned by such a magnitude of grief, his legs nearly failed him.

"My love," he murmured, crossing the room toward her.

"Stay away," she cried. His feet staggered to a stop.

Turning from him, she collapsed again into the pillows and gave the most heartrending sob.

Certainly he misunderstood. He took several more steps, but her maid threw him a sharp glare and raised a warding hand before rushing round to the far side of the bed to soothe the duchess there.

The unexpected rejection stung, like a slap to the face. Why did Sophia turn him away when certainly she needed comfort? Not *their* comfort, but *his*.

Their baby. The reality of the moment still crashed over him in waves. Everything had been so perfect. They'd been so happy. How could this have happened? Grief cut through him, scoring his heart into shreds. Didn't she know? He needed her comfort too.

Suddenly the housekeeper was there, attempting with all discretion to lead him away.

"How did this happen?" His voice sounded as hollow as he felt.

In a quiet voice, the woman answered. "All I know, your Grace, is that after the duchess read the letter—"

"What letter?" he asked dazedly.

The housekeeper's cheeks flushed as she indicated the duchess's escritoire. An envelope and a letter lay there, beside the pearl-handled letter opener he'd given Sophia for Christmas. "After that, she was inconsolable."

Inconsolable? Because of a letter? Heartsick, he raised a hand to his head, wanting more than anything to wish the moment away, to wake up from this nightmare. "Who wrote the letter, and what does it say?"

Her eyes widened. "I don't know, sir. Needless to say, I did not read it."

Yet strangely, in the next moment, she averted her gaze.

"Tell me the rest. Where did she fall? Here in her room or the stairs—?"

He had to see the letter. To understand why this had transpired.

The housekeeper accompanied him toward the desk. "After she read the letter, the duchess packed a valise and insisted the carriage be summoned to take her to her family's home. But she was in a state, your Grace. A terrible emotional state. In her haste to quit the house, she pushed past the footman, heedless of all warnings of ice and efforts to assist her and—and I regret to inform you, she fell on the steps outside, mere feet from the front door." Her gaze fell to the carpet. "I'm so sorry, sir."

At the desk, she fell away, giving him privacy as he lifted the letter. He stared down at the words . . . and understanding washed over him in a sickening wave. *No, God, no.* The letter had clearly been intended for him.

Written in a former lover's hand—someone he'd known before they were married—the letter extended a salacious invitation and described various proposed intimacies in shocking detail. Sophia wasn't nosy. She would have opened the letter by accident. It sometimes happened and never bothered him because things were so good and happy between them. He could only imagine the moment she'd innocently begun to read.

He crumpled the page in his fist. His stomach twisted, and he thought he might retch.

While he'd been out, his past had come for a reckoning. Regret and shame thundered through him. Because of him, they'd lost their baby.

Please, let him not have lost Sophia too.

Chapter One

"The scent of gingerbread in the air!" exclaimed Sir Keyes, his aged blue eyes sparkling with mischief. Winter wind swept through open doors behind him, carrying the sound of carriages from the street. "And there's mistletoe to be had from the peddler's stall on the corner."

Though his pantaloons drooped off his slight frame to an almost comical degree, the military orders and decorations emblazoned across his chest attested to a life of valor years before. Leaning heavily on his cane, the old man produced a knotty green cluster from behind his back, strung from a red ribbon, and held it aloft between himself and Sophia.

"Such happy delights can mean only one thing." He grinned roguishly—or as roguishly as a man of his advanced years could manage. "It is once again the most magical time of year."

He tapped his gloved finger against his rosy cheek with expectant delight.

"Indeed!" The diminutive Dowager Countess of Dundalk stepped between them, smiling up from beneath a fur-trimmed turban. She swatted the mistletoe, sending the sphere swinging to and fro. "The time of year when old men resort to silly provincial traditions to coax kisses from ladies young enough to be their granddaughters."

At the side of her turban a diamond aigrette held several large purple feathers. The plumes bobbed wildly as she spoke. "Well, it *is* almost Christmastide." Sophia winked at Sir Keyes, and with a gentle hand to his shoulder, she warmly bussed his cheek. "I'm so glad you've come."

A widower of two years, he had recently begun accompanying Lady Dundalk about town, something that made Sophia exceedingly happy, since both had long been dear to her heart.

Sir Keyes plucked a white berry from the cluster, glowing with satisfaction at having claimed his holiday kiss.

"I see that only a handful remain," Sophia observed. "Best use them wisely."

His eyebrows rose up on his forehead, as white and unruly as uncombed wool. "I shall have to find your sisters, then, and posthaste."

"Libertine!" muttered the dowager countess, with a fond roll of her eyes.

Behind them, two footmen with holly sprigs adorning their coat buttonholes secured the doors. Another presented a silver tray to Sir Keyes, upon which he deposited the price of Sophia's kiss and proceeded toward the ballroom, the mistletoe cluster swinging from the lions' head handle of his cane. Together, Sophia and the dowager countess followed arm in arm, through columns entwined in greenery, toward the sounds of music and voices raised in jollity.

With Parliament having recessed mid-December for Christmas, the districts of St. James's, Mayfair, and Piccadilly were largely deserted by that fashionable portion of London's population oft defined as the *ton*. Like most of their peers, Sophia's family's Christmases were usually spent in the country, but her grandfather's recent frailties had precluded any travel. So his immediate family, consisting of a devoted daughter-in-law and three granddaughters, had resolved to spend the season in London.

But today was Lord Wolverton's eighty-seventh birthday, and by Sophia's tally, no fewer than two hundred of the elusive *ton* had crept out from the proverbial winter woodwork to wish her grandfather well. By all accounts, the party was a success.

In the ballroom, candlelight reflected off the crystal teardrops of chandeliers high above their heads, as well as the numerous candelabras and lusters positioned about the room, creating beauty in everything its golden glow touched. The fragrance of fresh-cut laurel and fir, brought in from the country just that afternoon, mingled pleasantly with the perfume of the hothouse gardenias, tuberose, and stephanotis arranged in Chinese vases about the room.

Though there would be no dancing tonight, a piano quintet provided an elegant musical accompaniment to the hum of laughter and conversation.

"Lovely!" declared Lady Dundalk. "Your mother told me you planned everything, to the last detail."

"I'm pleased by how splendidly everything has turned out."

The dowager countess slipped an arm around Sophia's shoulders and squeezed with affection. "The only thing missing, of course, is the Duke of Claxton."

The warm smile on Sophia's lips froze like ice, and it felt as if the walls of the room suddenly converged at the mere mention of her husband. It didn't seem to matter how long he had been away; her emotions were still so raw.

Lady Dundalk peered up at her, concern in her eyes. "I know you wish the duke could be here tonight, and certainly for Christmas. No word on when our esteemed diplomat will return to England?"

Sophia shook her head, hoping the woman would perceive none of the heartache she feared was written all over her face. "Perhaps in the spring."

A vague response at best, but the truth was she did not know when Claxton would return. His infrequent, impersonal correspondence made no such predictions, and she had not lowered herself to ask.

They came to stand near the fire, where a delicious heat warmed the air.

"Eighty-seven years old?" bellowed Sir Keyes. "Upon my word, Wolverton, you can't be a day over seventy, else that would make me—" Lifting a hand, he counted through its knobby fingers, grinning. "Older than dirt!"

"We *are* older than dirt, and thankful to be so." Her grandfather beamed up from where he sat in his bath chair, his cheeks pink from excitement. His party had been a surprise for the most part, with him believing until just an hour ago the event would be only a small family affair. He appeared truly astounded and deeply touched. "Thank you all for coming."

Small, gaily beribboned parcels of Virginian tobacco, chocolate, and his favorite souchong tea lay upon his lap. Sophia gathered them and placed them beneath the lowest boughs of the potted tabletop yew behind them, one that would remain unadorned until Christmas Eve, when the family would gather to decorate the tree in the custom of her late grandmother's German forebears.

Her family. Their worried glances and gentle questions let her know they were aware that her marriage had become strained. But she loved them so much! Which was why she'd shielded them from the full magnitude of the truth—the truth being that when Claxton had accepted his foreign appointment in May, he had all but abandoned her and their marriage. The man she'd once loved to distraction had become nothing more than a cold and distant stranger.

But for Sophia, Christmas had always been a time of self-contemplation, and the New Year, a time for renewal. Like so many others, she made a habit of making resolutions. By nature, she craved happiness, and if she could not have happiness with Claxton, she would have it some other way.

She had given herself until the New Year to suitably resolve her marital difficulties. The day after Christmas she would go to Camellia House, located just across the Thames in the small village of Lacenfleet, and sequester herself away from curious eyes and the opinions of her family, so that she alone could pen the necessary letter.

She was going to ask Claxton for a legal separation.

Then he could go on living his life just as he pleased, with all the freedoms and indulgences he clearly desired. But she wanted something in return—a baby—and even if that meant joining him for a time in Vienna, she intended to have her way.

Just the thought of seeing Claxton again sent her spiraling into an exquisitely painful sort of misery. She had no wish to see him—and yet he never left her thoughts.

No doubt her presence would throw the private life his Grace had been living into chaos, and she would find herself an unwanted outsider. No doubt he had a mistress—or two—as so many husbands abroad did. Even now, the merest fleeting thought of him in the arms of another woman made her stomach clench. He had betrayed her so appallingly that she could hardly imagine allowing him to touch her again. But a temporary return to intimacies with her estranged husband was the only way she could have the child she so desperately wanted.

Sophia bent to adjust the green tartan blanket over Wolverton's legs, ensuring that his lordship would be protected not only from any chill but also the bump and jostle of the throng gathered about him.

"May I bring you something, Grandfather? Perhaps some punch?"

His blue eyes brightened.

"Yes, dear." He winked and gestured for her to come closer. When she complied, he lowered his voice. "With a dash of my favorite maraschino added, if you please, in honor of the occasion. Only don't tell your mother. You know just as well as I that she and my physician are in collusion to deprive me of all the joys of life."

Sophia knew he didn't believe any such thing, but still, it was great fun to continue the conspiratorial banter between them. Each moment with him, she knew, was precious. His joy this evening would be a memory she would always treasure.

"I'd be honored to keep your secret, my lord," Sophia said, pressing a kiss to his cheek.

"What secret?" Lady Harwick, Sophia's dark-haired mother, approached from behind.

A picture of well-bred elegance, Margaretta conveyed warmth and good humor in every glance and gesture. Tonight she wore violet silk, one of the few colors she had allowed into her wardrobe since the tragic loss of her son, Vinson, at sea four years ago—followed all too soon by the death of Sophia's father, the direct heir to the Wolverton title.

"If we told you, then it wouldn't be a secret," Sophia answered jovially, sidestepping her. "His lordship has requested a glass of punch, and since I'm his undisputed favorite, at least for this evening, I will fetch it for him."

Wolverton winked at Sophia.

"I shall have the secret pried out of him before you return." With that, Margaretta bent to straighten the same portion of Lord Wolverton's blanket her daughter had straightened only moments before.

Still a beautiful, vibrant woman, Margaretta drew the gazes of a number of the more mature gentlemen in the room. Not for the first time, Sophia wondered if her mother might entertain the idea of marrying again.

Sophia crossed the floor to the punch bowl, pausing several times to speak to friends and acquaintances along

the way. Though most of the guests were older friends of
Lord Wolverton, the presence of Sophia's pretty younger
sisters, Daphne and Clarissa, had assured the attendance
of numerous ladies and gentlemen from the younger set.
Her fair-haired siblings, born just a year apart and assumed by many to be twins, would make their debut in
the upcoming season. That is, if favored suitors did not
snatch them off the market before Easter.

At the punch bowl, Sophia dipped the ladle and filled
a crystal cup. With the ladle's return to the bowl, another
hand retrieved it—a gloved hand upon which glimmered
an enormous sapphire ring.

"Your Grace?" a woman's voice inquired.

Sophia looked up into a beautiful, heart-shaped face,
framed by stylish blonde curls, one she instantly recognized but did not recall greeting in the reception line.
The gown worn by the young woman, fashioned of luxurious peacock-blue silk and trimmed with gold and
scarlet cording, displayed her generous décolletage to a
degree one would not normally choose for the occasion
of an off-season birthday party for an eighty-seven-
year-old lord.

"Good evening, Lady…"

"Meltenbourne," the young woman supplied, with a
delicate laugh. "You might recall me as Annabelle
Ellesmere? We debuted the same season."

Yes, of course. Annabelle, Lady Meltenbourne, née
Ellesmere. Voluptuous, lush, and ambitious, she had
once carried quite the flaming torch for Claxton, and
upon learning of the duke's betrothal to Sophia, she had
not been shy about expressing her displeasure to the entire *ton* over not being chosen as his duchess. Not long

after, Annabelle had married a very rich but very old earl.

"Such a lovely party." The countess sidled around the table to stand beside her, so close Sophia could smell her exotic perfume, a distinctive fragrance of ripe fruit and oriental spice. "Your grandfather must be a wonderful man to be so resoundingly adored."

"Thank you, Lady Meltenbourne. Indeed, he is."

Good breeding prevented Sophia from asking Annabelle why she was present at the party at all. She had addressed each invitation herself, and without a doubt, Lord and Lady Meltenbourne had not been on the guest list.

"I don't believe I've been introduced to Lord Meltenbourne." Sophia perused the room, but saw no more unfamiliar faces.

"Perhaps another time," the countess answered vaguely, offering nothing more but a shrug. Plucking a red sugar drop from a candy dish, she gazed adoringly upon the confection and giggled. "I shouldn't give in to such temptations, but I admit to being a shamefully impulsive woman." She pushed the sweet into her mouth and reacted with an almost sensual ecstasy, closing her eyes and smiling. "Mmmmm."

Meanwhile, a gentleman had approached to refill his punch glass and gaped at the countess as she savored the sugar drop, and in doing so, he missed his cup altogether. Punch splashed over his hand and onto the table. Lady Meltenbourne selected another sweet from the dish, oblivious to his response. Or perhaps not. Within moments, servants appeared to tidy the mess and the red-faced fellow rushed away.

Sophia let out a slow, calming breath and smothered her first instinct, which was to order the countess to *spit out the sugar drop* and immediately quit the party. After all, time had passed. They had all matured. Christmas was a time for forgiveness. For bygones to be bygones.

Besides, London in winter could be rather dreary. This one in particular had been uncommonly foggy and cold. Perhaps Annabelle simply sought human companionship and had come along with another guest. Sophia certainly understood loneliness. Whatever the reason for the woman's attendance, her presence was of no real concern. Lady Meltenbourne and her now candy-sugared lips were just as welcome tonight as anyone else. The party would be over soon, and Sophia wished to spend the remainder with her grandfather.

"Well, it was lovely seeing you again, but I've promised this glass of punch to our guest of honor. Enjoy your evening."

Sophia turned, but a sudden hand to her arm stayed her.

"What of Claxton?" the countess blurted.

The punch sloshed. Instinctively Sophia extended the glass far from her body, to prevent the liquid from spilling down her skirts, but inside her head, the intimate familiarity with which Lady Annabelle spoke her husband's name tolled like an inharmonious bell.

"Pardon me?" She glanced sharply at the hand on her arm. "What did you say?"

Annabelle, wide-eyed and smiling, snatched her hand away, clasping it against the pale globe of her breast. "Will his Grace make an appearance here tonight?"

Sophia had suffered much during her marriage, but this affront—at her grandfather's party—was too much.

Good breeding tempered her response. She'd been raised a lady. As a girl, she'd learned her lessons and conducted herself with perfect grace and honor. As a young woman, she'd maneuvered the dangerous waters of her first season, where a single misstep could ruin her prospects of a respectable future. She had made her family and herself proud.

Sophia refused to succumb to the impulse of rage. Instead she summoned every bit of her self-control, and with the greatest of efforts, forbade herself from flinging the glass and its scarlet contents against the front of the woman's gown.

With her gaze fixed directly on Lady Meltenbourne, she answered calmly. "I would assume not."

The countess's smile transformed into what was most certainly a false moue of sympathy. "Oh, dear. You *do* know he's in town, don't you, your Grace?"

Sophia's vision went black. Claxton in London? Could that be true? If he had returned without even the courtesy of sending word—

A tremor of anger shot down her spine, but with great effort she maintained her outward calm. However, that calm withered in the face of Lady Meltenbourne's blatant satisfaction. Her bright eyes and parted, half-smiling lips proclaimed the malicious intent behind her words, negating any obligation by Sophia for a decorous response. Yet before she could present the countess with a dismissive view of her train, the woman, in a hiss of silk, flounced into the crowd.

Only to be replaced by Sophia's sisters, who fell

upon her like street thieves, spiriting her into the deeper shadows of a nearby corner. Unlike Sophia, who could wear the more dramatically hued Geneva velvet as a married woman, Daphne and Clarissa wore diaphanous, long-sleeved white muslin trimmed with lace and ribbon.

"Who invited that woman?" Daphne, the eldest of the two, demanded.

Sophia answered, "She wasn't invited."

"Did you see her *bosoms*?" Clarissa marveled.

"How could you not?" Daphne said. "They are enormous, like cannonballs. It's indecent. Everyone is staring, even Clarissa and I. We simply couldn't help ourselves."

"That dress! It's beyond fashion," Clarissa gritted. "It's the dead of winter. Isn't she cold? She might as well have worn nothing at all."

"*Daphne*," Sophia warned. "*Clarissa*."

Daphne's eyes narrowed. "What exactly did she say to you?"

Sophia banished all emotion from her voice. "Nothing of import."

"That's not true," Clarissa retorted. She leaned close and hissed, "She asked you if Claxton would be in attendance tonight."

Stung at hearing her latest shame spoken aloud, Sophia responded more sharply than intended. "If you heard her ask me about Claxton, then why did you ask me what she said?"

Her hands trembled so greatly that she could no longer hold the punch glass without fear of spilling its contents. She deposited the glass on the nearby butler's tray. Within seconds, a servant appeared and whisked it away.

Clarissa's nostrils flared. "I didn't hear her. Not exactly. It's just that she's—"

"Clarissa!" Daphne interjected sharply, silencing whatever revelation her sister had intended to share.

"No, you must tell me," Sophia demanded. "Lady Meltenbourne has what?"

Clarissa glared at Daphne. "She deserves to know."

Daphne, clearly miserable, nodded in assent. "Very well."

Clarissa uttered, "She's already asked the question of nearly everyone else in the room."

Despite the chill in the air, heat rose into Sophia's cheeks, along with a dizzying pressure inside her head. The conversation between herself and Lady Meltenbourne had been shocking enough. With Clarissa's revelation, Sophia was left nothing short of humiliated. She'd tried so desperately to keep rumors of Claxton's indiscretions from her family so as not to complicate any possible future reconciliation, but now her secrets were spilling out on the ballroom floor for anyone's ears to hear.

"Trollop," whispered Daphne. "It's none of her concern where Claxton is. It is only your concern, Sophia. And *our* concern as well, of course, because we are your sisters. Someone should tell her so." Though her sister had been blessed with the face of an angel, a distinctly devilish glint gleamed in her blue eyes. "Do you wish for me to be the one to say it? Please say yes, because I'm aching to—"

"Erase that smug look from her face," interjected Clarissa, fists clenched at her sides, looking very much the female pugilist.

"You'll do nothing of the sort," Sophia answered vehemently. "You'll conduct yourselves as ladies, not as ruffians off the street. This is my private affair. Mine and Claxton's. Do you understand? Do not mention any of what has occurred to Mother, and especially not to our grandfather. I won't have you ruining his birthday or Christmas."

"Understood," they answered in unison. Her sisters' dual gazes offered sympathy, and worse—pity.

Though Sophia would readily offer the same to any woman in her circumstances, she had no wish to be the recipient of such unfortunate sentiments. The whole ugly incident further proved the insupportability of her marriage and her husband's tendency to stray. Though Lady Meltenbourne's presence stung, it made Sophia only more certain that Claxton would agree to her terms. Certainly he would prefer to have his freedom—and he would have it, just as soon as he gave her a child. Seventeen months ago when she spoke her vows, she'd been naïve. She'd had such big dreams of a life with Claxton and had given her heart completely, only to have it thrown back in her face when she needed him the most. Claxton would never be a husband in the loyal, devoted sense of the word. He would never love her completely, the way she needed to be loved.

Admittedly, in the beginning, that aloofness—his very mysteriousness—had captivated her. The year of her debut, the duke had appeared in London out of nowhere, newly possessed of an ancient title. His rare appearances at balls were cause for delirium among the ranks of the hopeful young misses and their mammas.

Then—oh, then—she'd craved his brooding silences,

believing with a certainty that once they married, Claxton would give her his trust. He would give her his heart.

For a time, she'd believed that he had. She closed her eyes against a dizzying rush of memories. *His smile. His laughter. Skin. Mouths. Heat. Completion.*

It had been enough. At least she thought it had been.

"Well?" said Daphne.

"Well, what?"

"Will Claxton make an appearance tonight?"

"I don't know," whispered Sophia.

Clarissa sighed. "Lord Tunsley told me he saw Claxton at White's this afternoon, with Lord Haden and Mr. Grisham."

Sophia nodded mutely. So it was confirmed. After seven months abroad, her husband had returned to London, and everyone seemed to know but her. The revelation left her numb and sadder than she expected. She ought to be angry—*no!*—furious at being treated with such disregard. Either that or she ought to do like so many other wives of the *ton* and forget the injustice of it all in the arms of a lover. She'd certainly had the opportunity.

Just then her gaze met that of a tall gentleman who stood near the fireplace, staring at her intently over the heads of the three animatedly gesturing Aimsley sisters. Lord Havering, or "Fox" as he had been known in the informal environs of their country childhood, always teased that she ought to have waited for him—and more than once had implied that he still waited for her.

With a tilt of his blond head, he mouthed: *Are you well?*

Of course, Lady Meltenbourne's indiscreet inquiries about Claxton would not have escaped Fox's hearing.

No doubt the gossipy Aimsley sisters were dissecting the particulars at this very moment. Sophia flushed in mortification, but at the same time was exceedingly grateful Fox cared for her feelings at all. It was more than she could say for her own husband.

Yet she had no heart for adultery. To Fox she responded with a nod and a polite smile, and returned her attention to her sisters. While she held no illusions about the pleasure-seeking society in which she lived, she'd grown up in the household of happily married parents who loved each other deeply. Magnificently. Had she been wrong to believe she deserved nothing short of the same?

Clarissa touched her arm and inquired softly, "Is it true, Sophia, what everyone is saying, that you and Claxton are officially estranged?"

In that moment, the candlelight flickered. A rush of frigid air pushed through the room, as if the front doors of the house had been thrown open. The chill assaulted her bare skin, and the hairs on the back of her neck stood on end. All conversation in the ballroom grew hushed, but a silent, indefinable energy exploded exponentially.

Both pairs of her sisters' eyes fixed at the same point over her shoulders.

"Oh, my," whispered Daphne.

Clarissa's face lost its color. "Sophia—"

She looked over her shoulder. In that moment, her gaze locked with the bold, blue-eyed stare of a darkly handsome stranger.

Only, of course, he wasn't a stranger, not in the truest sense of the world. But he might as well have been. It was Claxton.

Her heart swelled with a thousand memories of him, only to subside, just as quickly, into frigid calm. Without hesitation, she responded as her good breeding required. She crossed the marble floor, aware that all eyes in the room were trained on her, and with a kiss welcomed her faithless husband home.

Chapter Two

"Welcome home, Claxton," she murmured after placing a chaste kiss upon his cheek. And then, under the pretense of fetching her grandfather a previously promised glass of punch, she vanished into the crowd of guests.

"Welcome home, Claxton," Lord Haden, Vane's younger brother by two years, mimicked in an affected, high-pitched voice.

His cousin Rabe Grisham drolly announced what he had already surmised. "Her Grace is certainly thrilled to see you."

Vane ignored them both and set off to follow her. He was tall, and though she was not, he easily tracked the path she made as she traversed the room, because... well, she sparkled. The diamond-encrusted hair combs she wore so artfully nestled in her stylishly coiffed mink-brown hair had been a betrothal gift from him, commissioned from the jeweler Garrard.

Her hair had always fascinated him. Though current

fashion inspired many young ladies to cut theirs, hers, when set free from its pins, fell in luxurious waves to her waist. Not so long ago, he'd owned the privilege of seeing it unbound. He had touched it with all the awe and reverence of a smitten lover, and even now when he closed his eyes, he could recall its scent and the feel of it against his skin.

Upon first seeing her, his every muscle had drawn painfully tight and even now refused to relax. He had hoped time and distance would mellow his desire for her, but clearly he was a fool. He had always been a fool for Sophia.

From the brief glimpse he was granted before she fled his company, he could see his wife had only grown more beautiful in their months spent apart. But then, what had he expected? From the first moment Vane had seen her in the formal drawing room of his uncle's home, for the purpose of an arranged meeting in advance of their arranged betrothal, she took his breath away. With her green eyes and mischievous-angel smile, he even fancied that in that very moment he'd fallen in love.

He never told her, of course, even in their early days of bliss. He kept such dangerous details to himself. To do otherwise would have been to expose himself to unbelievable torment and pain.

He was twenty-eight years old, and she twenty-one, her first season delayed by her father's untimely death. He never expected to be presented with such a rare and precious gift. He didn't deserve her, but apparently his newly bestowed title, fortune, and estates did. To his shock, she seemed just as enchanted with him as he was with her. For a time.

He gave up too easily then—but not this time. He

wouldn't allow Sophia to just run away and build up more walls against him. After seeing her, he felt even more resolved than before to end the estrangement between them. As if sensing his determination, the crowd of guests parted, giving him a clear path across the floor. Just then he lost sight of Sophia and her sparkling hair, when she disappeared beneath the archway that led to Lord Wolverton's book room.

"Your Grace." A small hand gripped his arm.

Out of the corner of his eye, he glimpsed the shimmer of blonde hair and bright blue silk. With his gaze fixed on the doorway, he murmured something cordial and continued on his way. He did not miss, however, the subsequent burst of tittering and whispers he left in his wake. As heir to the Claxton title, he'd long ago grown accustomed to whispers and learned to ignore them.

He paused at the door and peered inside. Here, the air smelled of legacy and comfort, of wood, tobacco, and books. Dim light from a garden lantern streamed through the window, revealing Sophia's silhouette. She stood at Lord Wolverton's cabinet, her head tilted back on her slender neck, lowering a now-empty rummer from her lips.

He cleared his throat.

She whirled. Her skirts rustled with the sudden movement. In the darkness, her emerald velvet bodice appeared black. Its high collar served as a dramatic foil to the pale skin of her throat and décolletage.

"Claxton," she exclaimed softly. Eyes wide, she raised her fingertips to brush the moisture from her lips, no doubt oblivious to the sensual appeal of the gesture. "You startled me."

He startled a lot of people. The same had been true about his father. Whether it was his height or his dark looks or demeanor or a combination of all those things, he did not know. He knew only he did not like the way his wife flinched upon hearing his voice.

What event would drive her to seek out a bracing gulp of her grandfather's brandy, something he knew for a fact she never touched?

The unexpected return of a despised husband, of course.

He couldn't fault her for that. Looking back at himself as he existed seven months before, he despised that man as well. God, he'd behaved like an ass—but worse, a coward. He ought never to have left her. He ought to have fought harder for them.

Before his betrothal and marriage to Sophia, he'd been...desperately lost. Only he knew how completely her love had transformed him. She'd given it so freely, touching him to his very soul and blotting out the stain of his former life. He'd never burdened her with those best-buried and forgotten details of his past. Even now, in the aftermath of their tragedy, she could never understand the magnitude of the gift she'd given him when they'd learned they were expecting a child.

Yet that dreadful February afternoon, she had turned her back on him.

Now, almost a year later, she turned her back to him again. Lifting the crystal decanter, she poured a splash into a half-filled punch glass. "For my grandfather."

Capping the bottle, she lifted the glass and maneuvered toward him through the darkness. She would have walked past him if he hadn't stepped into her path. Her skirts brushed his breeches, but she stopped herself before allowing their bodies to touch. It required every ounce of his restraint not to touch her face, to kiss, inhale, and taste her. To push her back inside the room and lock the door behind them.

"Come home with me tonight," he said, his voice thick with desire.

Did she realize how difficult the words were for him to speak? That he had just given her a dagger and invited her to stab him in what was already a grievously wounded heart, one that he had made every effort to shore up in hopes that he might be worthy of her forgiveness? Of her acceptance?

She avoided his gaze. "I've already made arrangements to stay the night here."

And so stab him she did, carefully sidestepping him and going a short distance beyond before turning back.

This time her eyes met his unwaveringly. "But you could certainly extend the invitation to Lady Meltenbourne. She's here—I'm sure you know—and has already been making inquiries about you."

* * *

Sophia wended through the crowd, avoiding the myriad curious gazes fixed upon her. Her hands shook. She quaked inside to her very bones. Had she truly just encouraged her husband to spend his night in the arms of another woman? Perhaps she ought to indulge in maraschino more often.

Cheeks aflame, she slipped behind the shelter of a Corinthian column, one of six twin pairs that lined the north and south sides of the ballroom. Backed against the cool plaster, she gasped in a fortifying breath. Except for the occasional servant rushing between the teaboard and the kitchen, and two blank-eyed marble busts of famed political statesmen and adversaries, Fox and Pitt, she was alone here.

While she could not exactly claim to have shocked Claxton, his eyes *had* noticeably widened and his lips *had* parted ever so slightly. For her cool, always-controlled husband, those reactions were quite nearly the equivalent. While the gravity of their exchange did not escape her, she could not deny the satisfaction that rushed through her at having astonished him.

Come home with me tonight.

Did he truly believe it would be that simple? That after months of frigid separation she would forgive and forget? With one of his paramours presently circling the waters of her grandfather's birthday party like a hungry shark, she was in no mood to do either, nor would she ever be. What sort of husband would subject his wife to such public degradation? If she was honest with herself, she could admit she shared some of the blame.

How differently would things have turned out if she'd waited to confront him about that awful letter at home, rather than reacting like a child and running out of the house in a hysterical rush onto steps slickened with ice? Certainly there would still have been tears and angry words and hurt feelings, but maybe they would still have their child. Perhaps, even, they would still have each other.

Days later, when at last he had come to her, smelling of drink and looking like a man destroyed, he openly confessed an affair with the actress who wrote the letter, but assured her, in a most earnest and forceful manner, that the relationship ended months before their betrothal, before he and Sophia ever met. He swore that despite the unfortunate phrasing of the letter couching the affair in present terms, there had been no further dalliance, not even a spoken word.

She believed him, but still, the ugliness of the incident remained, along with a new air of mistrust between them. Seeking comfort, she withdrew to the warm embrace of her mother and sisters to grieve and to heal, never sharing with them the existence of the letter or the trouble it had caused. Claxton vacated London with Lord Haden and his gentlemen friends for his hunting lodge near Inverness. Weeks passed and he returned, but only out of obligation to his seat in the House. At her mother's insistence, she too had returned home, yet she found herself very much alone. When not in sessions, Claxton adjourned to his club, or so she thought, but Lord Havering confided to having seen him in numerous St. James's gambling hells at all hours of the night. On the rare occasions when he came home, his eyes and his manner showed the signs of increased drink and dissolution.

All that she could have forgiven. Time passed, and the heartache of losing the child was not gone, but it had eased in the same way her pain over Vinson's and her father's deaths had. She just needed him to talk to her, to say he was sorry, so that she could tell him she was sorry too. Then maybe she could have let him hold her. It was what she wanted more than anything. But then she started to hear rumors, gravely repeated to her by her closest friends at tea and cards, who thought she would want to know. He'd been seen in the company of one unsuitable woman, perhaps two.

Just the normal *ton* scandal broth, which Sophia did her best to brush off, but then early one morning when he returned home sotted after another night out, Sophia crossed paths with the maid who had retrieved his clothing. A different sort of "letter" had fallen from the pocket of his coat onto the floor between them, carefully folded inside a paper envelope. A French letter, which Sophia had only heard about, but never actually seen. The poor maid, only under duress, identified the awful thing and confirmed its purpose—to prevent a man from getting a woman with child.

Consumed by pain and rage, she hadn't been able to help herself. As he slept the sleep of the dead, she crept into his room. There, with the mother-of-pearl-handled letter opener he'd given her their first Christmas together, she stabbed the vulgar thing through and wedged the blade into his headboard so that he would awake to it dangling over his head. Relations between them only grew chillier after that.

She'd almost been relieved when in May he'd left her with barely a good-bye, sent abroad by a diplomatic appointment to Reichenbach, without so much as a suggestion that she join him later. Soon, the first letter arrived, then another. Written in his distinctive script— dark, elegant slashes and flamboyant whorls of ink— they informed her of his relocation to Töplitz and eventually Leipzig, including only the sparest descriptions of lodgings and environs, and negotiations, treaties, and battles. There had been no mention by her diplomat husband of the balls and dinners and routs he attended. Those letters came instead from a lively Hanoverian baroness, who in the manner of any social hostess worth her snuff, assured Sophia that her husband was being well entertained.

His mistress? She did not know. She did not know anything anymore.

What she did know was that in London she had awakened each day alone to the silence of Claxton's magnificent Park Lane house, to the equally magnificent attendance of his servants. His carriage had delivered her about town, wherever she wished to go. There were endless invitations. Constant callers. Every drawing room and shop welcomed her enthusiastically as his duchess. His accountants paid her bills without question.

Yet every night she went to bed feeling like a fraud, her only company the whispers that followed her everywhere, celebrating her husband of little more than a year as a connoisseur of beautiful women, a libertine, and a rogue. She'd been left to suffer it alone, managing, she believed, to keep the worst of it from her family's collective ear.

Come home with me tonight.

No, their reunion would not be as simple as that. Her breathing slowed.

Exactly how long had she stood here, behind this column? Not that she wished for Claxton to pursue her, but—

He *would* come after her, would he not?

With all discretion, she peeked through the heads and shoulders of party guests, in the direction from whence she had come. Her mouth grew dry. Claxton was gone.

Shock rippled through her, leaving her lips and fingertips numb. Did she, as his wife, matter so little to him that he would *not* pursue her? Worse yet, would he do as she had challenged him to do and spend his night with another? A sudden vision of Claxton tangled in silken sheets with the buxom, vacant-eyed Lady Meltenbourne—

"Sophia."

"No!" she exclaimed, her head turning so abruptly her curls bounced off her nose.

The devil himself stared down at her, his face mere inches from hers. Cool liquid permeated her glove, dampening her palm. His hand came beneath hers to steady the glass, a gesture so unexpected and intimate that she gasped.

"No?" he repeated, one dark eyebrow elevated in question.

"*Oh*," she insisted. "I meant, 'Oh.'"

Oh, Claxton, her inner femininity sighed in spite of everything.

Upon close inspection, Claxton had not a single perfect feature. Yet with all the imperfect pieces of him put together, what a *compelling* picture he made. He was handsome in that way, yes, but shared nothing in common with the affable, fashionable dandies portrayed in contemporary fashion plates. His attractiveness was all darkness and intensity combined with the power of uncommon height, broad shoulders, and the lean musculature of an athlete.

She stood taller and straightened her shoulders, attempting in whatever small way to match him. She hated how he always made her feel like a child.

"You've stained your glove," he observed quietly, glancing down, then again into her eyes.

She did not breathe. Could not breathe with him standing so near and scrutinizing her with such interest. With his shoulder to the column, he held her gaze with the easy confidence of a roué who feared no rebuff, which only infuriated her because in contrast she had known nothing but his disregard.

"Of course my glove is stained," she retorted. "It is your fault for startling me."

Displeasure flickered across his countenance. "For the second time tonight, it seems."

And yet in the next moment his lips slanted into a boyish half smile, one that sent her heart bounding about inside her chest like a happy hound greeting its master. Her heart had always responded in this manner at the sight of one of Claxton's smiles. Only she wasn't a sweet-tempered hound. She was a woman—and she hadn't forgotten the bitter terms upon which they'd parted.

"The third time, actually," she bit out. "The first being your unannounced arrival. You've been away seven months, Claxton. You ought to have sent word."

He deftly lifted the glass from her hand and conveyed it to the nearby ledge. "It's not my intention to be so startling."

Before she knew what he was about, he'd pinched her fingertips and stolen her dampened glove from her hand. Cool air bathed her bare skin, sending a chill down her spine. While his free hand dispatched the glove into his coat pocket, the other held hers in place with a slight upward curl of his fingertips.

His lips pursed sensually. "As for your ruined glove, it would be my pleasure to escort you to your favorite shop and purchase another pair for you."

She stared at him in bewilderment. He proposed togetherness? After months of bitterness and separation? She could only stand and stare and wonder what he was about. Her bare hand appeared small and vulnerable in his much larger one, an unsuspecting bird alighted on a wicked trap. Indeed, with a curl of his knuckles, he secured hers within his and lifted—

"Claxton—" she warned, discomfited by his sudden foray into intimacy.

"Immediately. Posthaste." He pressed his lips to the tops of her fingers. His gaze unwaveringly held hers. "Perhaps tomorrow morning?"

The warm bliss that was his mouth moved to the underside of her wrist, where he pressed his nose to her skin and inhaled, eyes closed, as if she exuded some intoxicating perfume. A mad, delicious tingling spiraled up from her toes along the back of her thighs.

His gaze captured hers. "If only you will say the word and allow it."

Say what word? Half-drunk on sensation, she didn't even recall what they were talking about.

The next kiss, placed at the center of her palm, sent a languorous pleasure into her veins, awakening long-buried desires.

Involuntarily she swayed toward him, her body a traitor that for too long had *wanted* and *ached* and *yearned* for the husband and lover she'd believed him to be. Over his shoulder, Fox and Pitt watched, two stone-faced voyeurs. From the other side of the column came the sounds of music and laughter and conversation, while she and Claxton remained just out of sight, hidden in shadows. The clandestine nature of the moment only made Claxton's kiss more thrilling.

More thrilling? What was she thinking?

Her husband had shown no care for her whatsoever since the loss of their child. He had betrayed the sanctity of their marriage and abandoned her. And now…now he sought to seduce her? Angry heat gathered in her cheeks.

She tore her hand away. "Everyone knew you'd returned to London but me."

He considered her steadily, the smile fading from his lips. "Perhaps I feared that given advance warning, you would flee."

"I don't flee," she retorted too loudly.

"Oh, but you do, Sophia." His blue eyes flashed heat. "Twice tonight, within the space of a quarter hour, which makes us almost even as far as me *startling* and you *fleeing* are concerned."

Just moments before, in the book room, she'd felt so much the lioness. For once, she'd gained the upper hand against a man who *always* held the upper hand, whether it were with his young wife or a political foe. And oh, la! Clearly Claxton believed all it required for him to erase his sins from her mind was a sensual look. An intimate touch.

"I've missed you." He leaned closer, his gaze hot on her mouth, his intention apparent. Her husband was going to kiss her, and she had but a half second to decide whether to let him.

It took her less than that.

She planted her hand against his chest and pushed. "Do you truly believe I'm that unskilled a player of the game?"

"Game?" His nostrils flared.

She stepped back. "That I am just a sad little ingenue who, at your first warm glance, will welcome you back into my life and my bed?"

Claxton's expression darkened. "No to the ingenue part, but...I am hopeful that I will be welcomed back into your life." He crossed his arms over his chest and slowly leaned closer. *"And your bed."*

Her cheeks, already warm, now went to flames.

After a long moment, he prompted, "Sophia?"

"It's just that"—her voice cracked with indignation—"I'm trying to determine *what* about our brief time spent together this evening has given you *any* cause to be hopeful on either front."

"My darling." He tilted his head and spoke in a low, patient tone, as if he need only talk her through an irrational female moment. "I'm the first to confess that when I departed England our marriage was not on the steadiest of footholds. Indeed, considering the circumstances, I assume full blame, but I had hoped that tonight we might—"

"You hoped wrong." *Roar.* The lioness had returned. She would not fall so easily. "I require more from you than *this*."

When she tried to quit him, he blocked her path, maneuvering her back into the shadows.

He did not touch her, but he might as well have for as close as he stood. "A moment ago, outside the book room, why the provoking comment about Lady Meltenbourne?

I'm not married to her." His gaze moved over her possessively. "I'm married to you."

No doubt his words and manner were intended as reassurance, foreplay for a reconciliation. Yet the presence of Lady Meltenbourne's name on his lips was like a bucket of cold water to her face, a reminder of an infuriating reality she simply couldn't forget.

"That, my lord"—she reached for the punch glass—"is precisely the problem."

He scowled, the frostiness she remembered so well returning to his blue eyes. "What are you saying?"

"Stolen kisses in shadows? Sweet words of seduction? After everything that has happened, after all this time— that is all you have to offer me?" She laughed sharply. "I'm your wife, Claxton, not some dreamy-eyed girl. Not anymore. You're going to have to do much better than that."

* * *

An hour later, Vane emerged from Lord Wolverton's study, along with the select other gentlemen who had been invited by his lordship to stay for further conversation, cigars, and spirits. The party was over, the ballroom empty of guests. During the season, balls and soirees lasted until the morning hours, but the chime of a clock indicated the hour to be just nine.

Several gentlemen donned their hats and coats and pushed out into the night, where their drivers waited to convey them home.

"Good night, Fox," Vane said to the man beside him, with all the cordiality he could summon.

He was sorely tempted, however, to plant his fist in Lord Havering's face. For the entirety of the evening, Sophia's childhood friend had submitted him to a ceaseless barrage of acidic barbs and black glares.

Without the slightest acknowledgment, Fox continued walking, unsmiling and with his gaze fixed forward. Under his breath he muttered, "It's Lord Havering to you."

Accepting his hat from the footman, he disappeared into the night.

Vane's cheek twitched, but he held himself in check. He deserved the man's disdain, but his jealous heart seethed over the idea that Havering should in any way play the part of his wife's protector. Clearly, breaking the man's face would only hinder his efforts to win Sophia back, so Vane instead turned to his wife's grandfather.

He had always admired the earl, but perhaps because of the difficult relationship he shared with his own now-deceased father, he'd never been comfortable fully expressing that respect. Though Wolverton had remained cordial throughout the evening, Vane perceived a mistrust in the elder man's eyes. Certainly, the state of his eldest granddaughter's marriage was no secret and must be a grave disappointment.

A footman approached, as if to convey his lordship to bed.

"Wolverton, if I may have a word with you," said Vane.

The earl lifted a staying hand, and the servant retreated.

He tilted his head. "What is it, Claxton?"

Vane cleared his throat, which suddenly felt as dry as

sawdust, and forced himself to speak. "I've no desire to make excuses for myself, but I've misstepped where her Grace is concerned."

"Indeed you have."

"I intend to make things right with her."

"I am an old man, Claxton, confined to my home by illness. If talk of your lack of commitment to your marriage has reached my ears, it is widely reported indeed." The earl uttered the words with withering calm. "No matter how valiant your efforts are now, they may come too late."

Age and Lord Wolverton's confinement to a chair made him no less imposing. Vane felt like a small boy who'd received a thrashing. He felt not only shamed, but ashamed.

"I pray not," Vane answered quietly. "Please know that I remain as committed as ever to the duchess, even more so today than when we first wed."

He'd never spoken truer words. Time and distance had only proved that.

Wolverton steepled his fingertips and nodded, unsmiling. "Then I recommend you put your acclaimed diplomatic skills to work and begin your groveling posthaste. I suspect this will be the most difficult accord you've ever attempted to negotiate." The earl stared into his eyes. "That is, if you're allowed through the door."

"Thank you, Wolverton."

"Don't thank me," he countered sharply. "If she decides to seek a separation from you, I'll support her every step of the way."

The air left Vane's lungs. *Separation.* Hearing the

word spoken aloud, when his mind had only ever whispered it, created a new and unpleasant reality.

Wolverton continued. "Scandal be damned. I'm too old and too stubborn to care what anyone in this town thinks. My only wish at this late stage of my life is for my girls to find happiness before I die. After my death, my title will pass to my nephew. An unworthy profligate if there ever was one. The man has no decency; he is wholly consumed with vice. I have made what arrangements I can to see that the girls' futures are secure, but life will no doubt be very different for them when I am gone." His frown deepened. "Needless to say, Claxton, I had hoped for better from you."

Claxton bowed his head. "I vow you will have it."

"She's upstairs. The third bedroom on the left."

With a gesture, the earl summoned the footman. The two disappeared down the darkened hallway. Vane ascended the stairs, preparing himself for the confrontation to come.

His knock on Sophia's door elicited no response. Turning the knob, he peered inside to find the room darkened and empty. Of course—she would seek comfort from her sisters. Never having explored the upper floor of this house, he found himself in unfamiliar territory, but he moved from one door to the next until he heard familiar feminine voices. Unfortunately, the softness with which they spoke, and the thickness of the door, prevented him from knowing whether they plotted his demise. He knocked.

"Come in."

He would not of course. They likely assumed him to be their mother or a servant.

"It is Claxton," he announced.

Frantic murmurings ensued, accompanied by several thumps, as if someone ran about the room.

A moment later, the door cracked open and he glimpsed a sliver of Daphne's nose and mouth. Her eyes narrowed. "What do *you* want?"

Chapter Three

"Miss Daphne." He nodded. "I regret to disturb you so late in the evening, but I'm looking for her Grace. Is she with you?"

"My sister doesn't want to talk to you, so go away."

"It's very important."

"Important to you, perhaps," called another voice, one he knew to be Clarissa's. "I think the duchess is past the point of talking."

He measured his response, remembering with whom he spoke. These were the two young girls who once stared at him with intense fascination and giggled delightedly at whatever he said. He and Sophia, after marrying, had taken her sisters on picnics and to Berkeley Square for pineapple ices. On quiet Sunday afternoons, they'd cajoled him into practicing the newest dance steps with them and interrogated him over what exactly men found arresting and pretty. His answer to them always: a happy smile. Never before had they spoken to him with such disrespect or dislike.

He endeavored to speak more gently. "I appreciate that you seek to protect your sister, but if that is the case, I ask that Sophia tell me herself."

Peering over Daphne's head, he spied Clarissa in a pink dressing gown, standing beside a large poster bed. Clarissa adored pink. Daphne, of course, deplored every shade of the same color.

Clarissa bent over a supine form covered in blankets, her face a portrait of sisterly concern. "Sophia. There, there, dear. Please stop crying."

Crying? His heart stopped beating or at least felt as if it did. Belowstairs, when last he'd seen her, she had shown such strength, with no sign of softer emotion.

Clarissa continued. "Claxton is here. Do you wish to speak to him?" She bent low, placing her ear near the pillow. Rising up, she glared in his direction. "I'm afraid it's exactly as I told you. She doesn't want to speak to you. Can't you see that she is overwrought? Please go away."

"Overwrought?" he repeated, stunned. "Sophia?"

His lungs constricted. Though largely responsible for creating this wide chasm between them, standing here, ten feet away, he couldn't abide that thought. "Move aside."

Daphne shoved the door, seeking to shut him out, but with steady pressure he pushed her backward, easily forcing his way inside.

Striding toward the bed, he came face-to-face with a flying pillow. With a swipe of his hand, he fended it off. "She's my wife."

"You wouldn't know it from your behavior. Stay away

from her," exclaimed Clarissa, her eyes ablaze. "Lothario!"

Daphne clutched at his coattails and skidded along behind him. "Philanderer!"

He now knew how Gulliver must have felt when attacked by the Lilliputians.

"Sophia." Arriving at the bed, he brushed past Clarissa to touch Sophia's shoulder—only to have that shoulder collapse beneath his hand. As Clarissa scrambled away, he yanked back the coverlet and found only pillows beneath.

"Where is she?" he gritted out and spun toward them.

Clarissa sneered. "We're not going to tell you anything."

"Brute!" Daphne threw a brush at him. It bounced off the center of his chest and fell to the carpet. Damn it.

"Have you both lost your minds?" he demanded.

"Perhaps so." Clarissa crossed her arms at her waist. "People often lose their minds when they care deeply about someone. Can you imagine how it feels, Claxton, when a woman takes great pride in her husband and her marriage, only to be confronted with persistent rumor and innuendo?"

"Of course he doesn't," said Daphne. "If he did, he would never submit Sophia to such humiliation. I can only pray my future husband does not commit me to the same shame and misery."

Their words troubled him more than he wished to admit. But he wasn't going to beg for their forgiveness.

He returned to the door. "I understand you are both angry with me, as you have every right to be. But I will *not* defend myself to you, not until I make things right with your sister, my wife. My confessions are for her ears only—and my forgiveness hers alone to give."

They stared at him in silence.

"Please. I beg you. I must see her. I must speak to her."

Something in his words must have broken through their feminine defenses because the sisters visibly softened and tears glimmered in their eyes.

"You're truly going to make things right with Sophia?" Clarissa asked, her green eyes pleading.

"I can only do that if you tell me where she is."

"Really, Claxton," Daphne chided softly. "What took you so long?"

"Please tell me."

"Where she thought you'd never look. She's gone to Camellia House."

* * *

Camellia House. The setting of Vane's best—and worst—childhood memories. He and Haden had lived there with their mother on the edge of London, while their father, the duke, resided a world away in a place called Mayfair.

Indeed, Vane had no memories of his father before the age of ten, when, upon the death of his mother, a tall, stern-faced man had appeared without any prior announcement and taken him and Haden away. The only reason Vane had even realized the bastard was their father was because he recognized the Claxton coat of arms on the magnificent carriage parked outside the gates of the cemetery, though the man inside the conveyance hadn't, for the entirety of the funeral, deigned to step outside.

Claxton. Vane had learned to hate the name. The very name he now bore as his own.

Snow flurries swirled outside his window, illuminated by the lamps of his carriage. In warmer months, the night streets of London would still be thick with carriages, hansoms, wagons, and pedestrians crowding the pavement. But tonight, winter ruled. Even the vendors had abandoned the streets. Anyone with a place to call home was there now, near a fire or stove until morning. Sophia had left a place of warmth and comfort, one inhabited by those she loved best. It was just more proof of her desperate need to escape him.

He had never mentioned Camellia House to Sophia. How she knew of the small estate and why she'd chosen to escape from him there, he did not know. The prospect of setting foot inside his childhood home brought a thousand memories crashing down around him, and so close to Christmas, which had always been such a special time for them there.

As each moment passed, his pulse quickened, and something akin to anxiety coiled in his stomach far greater than he had experienced on any line of battle. His nerves were already wound tight anticipating all he must say to her, all he must confess.

Philanderer. Lothario. At least there were no questions as to the allegations against him. They came as no real surprise. Only now, given the advantage of retrospect, could he look back on the darkest days of their marriage and comprehend the magnitude of rage and soul-deep hurt that had consumed him. Having lost Sophia and his child, he had for a time fallen into old vices—gambling hells, excessive drink, and yes, the company of old amours. For weeks he had danced along a dangerous edge, from which, in the end, he had stepped back. Yet…though he had not betrayed his marriage vows, he'd not particularly respected them either, allowing himself to be observed in questionable circumstances.

Perhaps, then, it was fitting that their reunion take place at Camellia House, for only by acknowledging the mistakes of his past could he hope to renew his future with her.

Vane shared more than an hour with those thoughts before his carriage concluded its passage over the Thames to trundle off the Mowbray ferry and pass through the sleeping village of Lacenfleet. At last the vehicle turned the final corner before making its way up the lawn toward the dark shadow at the top of the hill. With gloved hand, he denied his footman his duty and turned the handle, stepping down onto pavement already concealed by snow. A sudden gust caught his coat, piercing him through with frigid cold.

His footman rushed to meet him. "Your instructions, your Grace?"

"Wait for me." The rising clamor of the wind forced him to shout just to be heard. "I shan't be more than a half hour."

Though the house appeared dark, another carriage occupied the drive, its driver hunched under the burden of a thick coat and blanket. Sophia must have only just arrived. Having been shut up for some fifteen years, the residence was not regularly staffed by servants. She and her maid were likely inspecting the premises before releasing their carriage to the village livery.

Here, there were no guests to be shocked, no family

to overhear. Sophia had nowhere to escape. She would have no choice but to hear him out. Then she would either return home with him or he would depart alone. He had stopped at their London residence only long enough to change out of his evening clothes and to obtain a key, yet he stood on the steps, prepared, as a courtesy, to knock. However, with a push of the ornate brass handle, the door opened. He did not wish to startle her with his unexpected arrival, but on second thought, neither did he wish for her to bolt the doors against him. He proceeded inside.

A small oil lamp glowed on a side table. After removing his gloves and tucking them into his coat pocket, he lifted the lamp so that he might better see through the darkness. The fragrance of wood polish scented the air, whereas he'd expected mustiness and decay. Mr. and Mrs. Kettle, the married couple who'd tended the house and grounds for his mother, had remained in his employ despite their advancing years but resided in the village. He'd never expected them to actually work for their pay.

From where Vane stood, he perceived the glow of firelight in the great room. Realizing now was the time to announce his presence, he'd barely parted his lips to shout *hello* when he heard the sound of voices.

A woman's and a man's.

Every muscle in his body tensed. He approached, careful to remain out of sight from those inside.

"You're so beautiful," the man murmured. "A goddess."

"We shouldn't do this," she whispered.

Vane's blood turned to ice. In that moment he realized Sophia wouldn't be leaving Camellia House with him tonight. Not only had she come here to escape him, but she'd come with a lover. *Havering?*

"Please," she implored softly.

"Please yes, or please no?" the man whispered.

Clothing or blankets or whatever rustled loudly, evidence of sensual play. A moan, and then wet, smacking kisses.

A feminine gasp. "I don't know. I can't think."

"Don't let him come between us. Not now, not here."

Vane clenched the frame of the door, tamping down the rage, the lightning-hot instinct toward violence that clawed up from inside his chest. He had to see for himself. He would forever preserve this picture of her in another man's arms. Then and only then could he stamp out the fledgling hope he'd so foolishly allowed residence in his heart.

A long settee prevented Vane from seeing the lovers. He silently approached, the lamp shielded behind his hand. There, on the other side, the floor was a jumble of cushions. A smallish fire burned, a dot on the massive hearth, but a japanned screen dimmed its ambient glow. Still, he made out two figures struggling, with the man sprawled on top.

She gasped. "Please stop."

"You don't mean that."

"No, really, I can go no further."

"Come now, darling—"

Hearing this, Vane's composure shattered.

"*Get off her*," he roared, lifting the lantern high.

Sophia screamed. Legs and arms flailed, tangled in shirtsleeves and petticoats.

"Bloody hell," her lover shouted.

Two faces peered up at him. *Not Sophia!*

Instead, the face belonged to—

Lady Meltenbourne.

She gaped, openmouthed and wide-eyed next to his brother, her hair wildly disarrayed. Vane's first reaction was relief. Then fury.

"Haden," he thundered.

Haden stood, thrusting his shirttail into his breeches. "Good God, Claxton." He wobbled drunkenly. "Give me an apoplexy, why don't you? What in the hell are you doing here?"

"Stopping you from making a big mistake. The lady is married."

His brother rubbed a hand over his face. "So is half of the *ton*," he slurred, "who is having an affair with the other half of the *ton*...who...aren't their spouses." He blinked several times. "Zounds, that didn't exactly make sense, but...you...understand what I'm attempting to say."

His brother, Haden, had always been reckless. Having spent most of his childhood in school, growing up in the company of other boys, he still lived each day in a spirit of ceaseless revelry, leaving a trail of broken hearts, gambling debts, and halfhearted business endeavors in his wake. Having spent so many years apart, they'd been little more than strangers until seven months ago when Haden, at Vane's summons, joined him on the Continent to serve as his support attaché, assisting with matters of diplomatic minutiae Vane had no time to deal with. They'd again grown close, but God spare him, his feckless brother always knew how to put his boot right into the middle of a scandal. Vane did not know if Haden would ever settle down into a respectable sort of life.

Vane set the lantern on a small table. "If her ladyship's married status is not enough, then please understand she is also one of the most indiscreet women in all of England." No one knew that more than he.

"That's not true," Lady Meltenbourne blurted. Then she giggled. "Oh, pphssht. Perhaps it is." Throwing her arms high over her head, she collapsed back into the cushions. A bottle beside her tipped over, thunking hollowly and rolling across the floor. The lady was foxed.

When he first became duke, the *ton* matchmakers had done their best to pair him with Annabelle. Though beautiful, he found her to be vacant and insipid—the opposite of everything Sophia proved to be. Later, when his betrothal to Sophia was announced, Annabelle reacted as a woman betrayed. Though he could not ever recall having specifically encouraged her affections, she remained quite determined about attaching herself to him, heedless of how her behavior might cause disgrace to herself or her husband.

Haden collapsed onto the settee and ran his fingers through his dark hair. "Well, if it makes you feel better, we hadn't got past kissing and a bit of...er...Well, there's really no need to go into those sorts of details, is there? I didn't even know the woman before tonight, when I found her crying over some other bastard who'd broken her heart."

"It was you, Claxton," she accused from the shadows. "You broke my heart."

Haden's head swung toward him. "What? *Hell*, I hadn't realized. Claxton? I thought—"

Vane glared at his brother. "No. Just *no*. Never."

"Good. Well...whatever the case..." Haden relaxed again. "I was just trying to make her feel better."

"By taking off your breeches? You poltroon, this was our mother's house." Vane avoided looking at the portrait of his father that loomed above the mantel, one that had never been there when he was a boy. He could only assume it had been hung after his mother's death. Yes, likely by his father, claiming the one bit of territory that had belonged to her. "How could you disrespect her memory like this?"

Haden winced. "It seemed a deuced splendid idea at the moment. Confound me, I shouldn't have opened that third bottle."

On the floor, her ladyship remained flat on her back, her face covered by her hands, encircled by the puddle of her rumpled gown. "This isn't fun anymore. What time is it?"

"Time to get you home." Haden tugged on his Hessians. On the first try, however, he put the left boot on the right foot. Once the mistake was repaired, with much grunting and muttering, he took up his coat and cravat and staggered past Vane. "Come along, my lady."

"Look out for the—" warned Claxton, but too late.

His brother's boot lowered onto the empty bottle that had rolled off moments before. With a shout he upended, feet flying over his head, and crashed to the floor.

"Haden?" Claxton crouched over him and discovered him to be senseless. "Damn. Damn. *Damn.*" How like his brother to leave him to clean up his mess.

"He's dead, isn't he?" asked the countess, sitting up.

"He is not dead."

"That's too bad because if I don't get home soon, Meltenbourne will find us and shoot him. I would think that will be a much more unpleasant death. Oh, dear. It's very late, isn't it?" Lady Meltenbourne began to sniffle softly. Then cry. "I shouldn't have come. Whatever was I thinking?" She flopped back onto the floor and, with a moan, pulled her silk overskirt over her face. Her bare legs jutted out from the tangle of her petticoats.

God help him, he pitied her, but he did not have the patience for all this tonight. Where in the hell was his wife? He must return to London posthaste to find her.

"I'll return in a moment," he announced in a loud voice, hoping she heard him through her skirt. "Please make yourself decent while I am gone."

Grasping Haden by the arms, he dragged him into the vestibule and summoned a footman. Together they conveyed his unconscious brother to his waiting carriage.

Once the door was shut, he turned back to the house with the intention to retrieve Lady Meltenbourne.

"Ought we to go, my lord?" shouted the driver into the wind. Claxton spun round on his heel. Lord, it was dark. There was only the dim light from the carriage side lamps.

"No," he shouted back, making a gesture to stay with his hand.

"No?" the driver repeated.

"No."

The man nodded in understanding. Turning in his seat, he took up the reins. With a snap and a "Hee-yaw," the carriage rolled into motion.

"Wait," bellowed Claxton, lunging after the conveyance. "I said *no*, not *go*."

Yet the wind caught his voice, carrying the sound toward the house. The vehicle continued on its way, growing dimmer as it traveled into the night. Claxton skidded to a stop and shouted curses into the dark. Slowly he turned, ignoring his own servants who watched with riveted interest, and marched to the door. He fumed on the threshold, mind abuzz at the injustice of what had just occurred.

He was alone with Lady Meltenbourne.

But not for long. He'd hasten the weepy tart into his carriage, discreetly return her to her residence, and hope to find Sophia warm and safe at home—even if behind a locked door and refusing to speak to him.

Bloody hell, this had turned out to be the most miserable of nights. He was done. Exhausted. Finished. At least until morning.

Inside, he found the countess in the same position in which he'd left her, only now she snored.

Crouching over her, he shook her shoulder. "Lady Meltenbourne, please wake up."

Once he got her sitting upright, he set about collecting her things. Slippers and a cloak and a pair of clocked stockings. With a befuddled mien, she stood at last and smoothed her skirts. Disheveled curls framed her face.

She spoke, her speech slurred. "I was so very vexed with you earlier tonight for refusing to speak to me."

"My apologies. I assure you the slight was not intentional. I must not have seen you." He chose his words carefully, so as to install an appropriate distance between them. "Having only returned to London this morning, I admit to being distracted and wishing to spend the evening with my wife, her Grace. I believed her to have come here as well, or else I'd not have made the trip out."

"Oh—" Her pretty face scrunched into a scowl, and she swiped a silencing hand at him. *"Shush!"*

"I'm more than happy to shush," he muttered to himself, then urged her more loudly, "Now, come on. Fasten your dress."

Each moment ticked by in his mind, loud as cannon fire. What must the servants outside be thinking?

She shoved the hair from her face. "Your brother told me how pretty I was. I suppose I just...wanted him to be you. The two of you do look alike." She giggled, unaware or uncaring that her sleeve slipped off her shoulder, nearly baring a breast. "At least when one is drinking brandy and the light is sufficiently dim."

He gave her his back and exhaled through his teeth.

"Hurry along," he urged gruffly. "The weather is foul, and we should be off before it worsens." A glance over his shoulder provided confirmation that she worked to fasten the front of her bodice.

"I beg you, Claxton, don't tell Meltenbourne." She smoothed her hair. "You are already quite a sore spot with him—"

He gritted his teeth. "I shouldn't be."

"—and he can become overwrought over the slightest thing."

The slightest thing? Vane recalled his reaction just moments ago, when he'd believed it was Sophia he'd discovered with a lover. The emotions that had exploded inside him; yes, *overwrought* might describe how he had felt.

"I don't see what good telling Meltenbourne would do

any of us. Most especially me." He'd already been called Lothario once tonight and had no wish to incur more of the same allegations, not with matters so precarious between himself and Sophia.

"I know it may seem ridiculous for me to say it, but I really—" She hiccuped. "I really do care for my husband. Even though he is old and . . . not you."

He could not help but wonder whether it might be possible that Sophia felt a similar duality of feeling for him. Love and aversion. He knew full well, more than anyone, that such a thing was possible. If Sophia cared for him in at least a miniscule amount, then all was not lost. All he wanted was to find her. To settle this thing between them so they could move forward.

"Not me?" he muttered, closing his eyes in consternation. "You know nothing at all of me but the most superficial of details. I can't imagine what Meltenbourne has done to deserve this sort of betrayal, other than— what Annabelle, be old? You pledged your troth to him. How would you wish to be cherished when you are of a similar age?"

He peered at her over his shoulder to gauge her response. She sat very still for a moment, her expression unchanging, but with each breath she took, her breasts heaved a degree higher.

"It wasn't as if I had a choice but to marry him after you chose someone else!"

He quickly turned from the countess and again cursed Haden that he had been placed in this position. The sounds of sniffling and a strangled sob came from behind him. Pray no, he couldn't bear it if the countess began to cry in earnest.

"Let's not talk about it any longer," he suggested in a hopeful voice. "We must return you to town posthaste and with all discretion. Then we can all just forget tonight ever happened."

"Yes," she agreed. "Perhaps...perhaps Meltenbourne went to bed hours ago and does not even realize I'm gone."

"I'm certain he did." He was quickly losing his patience. "Hurry now. The carriage is waiting."

"Your Grace?" she inquired.

He turned to her. "Yes?"

She flung herself into his arms. He stumbled back, and she with him, almost falling, but he caught her under the arms. In the next moment, she gave a little jump and with puckered lips took aim for his mouth. He averted his face.

"Ah. Please don't." He laughed through clenched teeth. Laughed because he was so damn tired, and this night, which he had hoped would end so differently, had taken such a turn for the ludicrous.

"I'm not trying to seduce you. I promise," she gushed, her brandy-sweet breath filling his nostrils. Her arms came round his shoulders and her large breasts squashed against his chest. "It's just that you've been so wonderful tonight, just as wonderful as I always supposed you to be."

"*No.*"

She leapt again, springing up from her toes, trying for a kiss. "Let me say thank you, darling."

"Thanks are unnecessary. Please—"

He considered allowing her to fall to the floor, but that would be ungentlemanly. Instead, he exhaled and gathered his patience. Without a doubt, he was in for a long and cold ride home, for by apparent necessity he would be forced to ride atop with his driver. He prayed her ladyship, deprived of all companionship, would simply fall asleep inside.

"My lady, if you could please finish dressing," he urged, grasping her by the arms and trying his best to return her to the support of her own two feet. "Oh, look, how fortuitous. I've your stockings right here in my hand—"

A gasp sounded behind him.

He twisted round, the countess clinging to him like ivy on a wooden fence.

Sophia stood on the threshold, bundled in a hat, scarf, and redingote with a valise in hand.

Chapter Four

$\mathscr{S}$tay where you are," Claxton roared.

Sophia halted, the power of his voice momentarily stunning her. Throughout all of their difficulties, Claxton had never shouted at her before, and the force of his command moved through her like thunder. Slowly she pivoted toward her husband, who still had *that woman* dangling from his neck like a human necklace.

Lady Meltenbourne exclaimed, "How mortifying! Your wife."

Except the countess didn't appear one bit mortified. Rather, she looked like a naughty cat eating the evening haddock while the cook's back was turned. Sophia took in her wildly tousled hair, bare legs and feet, and the cushions everywhere. A toppled bottle of brandy. Two stockings dangled from her husband's hands. Her mind exploded all over again.

How much more sordid could the picture be?

She'd come to Camellia House for privacy. To untangle her thoughts before seeing Claxton again and making her demand for a separation. What she'd gotten instead of privacy was indisputable proof of her husband's infidelity. It hurt more than she'd expected.

Seeing them with her own eyes in each other's arms, she wanted to shriek. She wanted to break something, preferably over Claxton's head. She wanted to tear out Annabelle's hair. She wanted to retch. She wanted to wake up from this nightmare to a different reality, one in which Claxton was a different man and her heart had not been irrevocably shattered.

"In this moment it occurs to me, Claxton," she said coldly, her voice rising on each word, "that I don't have to listen to you anymore."

With an oath, Claxton pried Lady Meltenbourne from his person and thrust her shoes and stockings into her hands. One moment more and he'd retrieved her cloak and fastened it at her neck. Every move, every touch, no matter how imbued with impatience, crushed Sophia's spirit a fraction more.

He strode past, leading the countess by the arm.

Lady Meltenbourne squealed. "You're hurting me, darling."

Claxton released her. "Then, please, if you will, proceed at a more alacritous pace." He wrenched the door open. "And do not call me darling."

He turned, and with a piercing glare at Sophia, gritted out, "Do not move from that spot. You and I must talk."

"I don't want to talk." Her fingers tightened around the handle of her valise. She suffered the most overwhelming urge to throw the leather case at both of their heads. "There is nothing to be said that can resolve *this*."

She glared at Lady Meltenbourne, who leaned against Claxton's arm, her hands clutched at his wrist, her cheeks flushed and eyes bright.

Claxton's nostrils flared and he closed his eyes, visibly seething. Of course, he was very angry. Angry at his liaison being interrupted by his peevish wife. Angry at being caught. "I will return in a moment's time."

Sophia stood in place as he escorted his lover into the night. Seven months ago, he'd abandoned her. In this moment, she felt that depth of loss all over again.

The door remained open a crack. Cold air and snowflakes wafted through.

"Oh no, you won't."

Sophia rushed forward and slammed the door closed behind him.

* * *

"Yes, your Grace. We shall escort your lady home." His driver nodded in understanding.

Prior to his betrothal, his retainers had exercised the utmost discretion with regard to his private activities. They had waited in rain, fog, sleet, and snow while he enjoyed the sumptuous comforts of various ladies' company. Seeing his men now, their caps and coats covered in frost, he experienced a deep wave of regret that they should be subjected to such discomfort on the whim of their employer.

"The woman inside the carriage is not my lady," Vane felt compelled to say. "My lady—*the duchess*—is inside."

He wanted to shout that furthermore nothing untoward had occurred here tonight, at least not involving him, but it would not do to defend himself to a servant.

The man's eyes widened. "Just like old times, sir?"

Vane resisted the urge to curse. "You misunderstand, I'm afraid." He provided the proper address.

"Yes, Duke. With all due haste." The man returned the scarf to the lower half of his face and took up the reins.

As the carriage rumbled away, Vane pivoted on his heel and returned to the house, only to find the door locked. A blast of wind cut through his coat, chilling his spine.

He gripped the handle. "Sophia."

"Go away," she cried, her voice muffled by three inches of wood.

Carved into the spandrels at the upper corners of the door, two cherubs crouched above him, peering down with the most vexatious expressions of mirth. He glared back, which, admittedly, accomplished nothing.

"Please open the door."

In return she bellowed, "Take. The carriage. And *leave*."

"Not until we talk."

He could only interpret the responsive tangle of unintelligible nonsense as a rejection of his request. Turning, he stared out into the night, clenched fists resting on his hips.

From this elevated vantage point, he could not see even the slightest evidence of Lacenfleet in the vale below. A thickening, frost-laden fog made the darkness impenetrable. Old memories tugged at the corner of his mind, but he commanded himself to the present, returning his gloves to his quickly numbing hands.

For a moment, his spirit wavered. Perhaps, after all, he owned too twisted, too tangled a soul to justify claim to Sophia's respect and love. Perhaps, as Wolverton had said, his efforts came too late.

As if in answer, a vision came into his mind of Sophia on their wedding day, peering up at him during the service from beneath her headdress of feathers and lace, wearing the most astounding expression of unadulterated joy. Then another from their honeymoon in Scotland. Her eyes vivid green, her hair wet, and her chemise plastered transparent against her nymphlike body, as they'd frolicked near naked in the loch. But best of all, the look of shock on her face the moment they'd realized the visiting parson had just discovered them.

Arriving at his decision, Claxton strode toward the remaining carriage.

* * *

Sophia rubbed at the frosted pane and squinted, watching the carriage disappear into the fog and snow. Astonishingly, Claxton had actually done exactly as she demanded, which only made her feel more wretched.

Now she was alone, with only her misery and the very recent memory of finding her husband in Lady Meltenbourne's arms. Turning from the window, she faced the silent vestibule. There was nothing to do but have a good, miserable cry.

All at once, the emotion she'd held inside all evening crowded her throat, enormous and unstoppable. Hiccuping through tears, she pressed her hand to her mouth and returned to the scene of her recent trauma. Only to freeze on the threshold.

Claxton sat in a chair beside the fire, staring at her over

gloved, steepled fingertips, his hat perched on his knee. Ice crystals sparkled on the shoulders of his coat and in his raven's-wing-dark hair.

"Hello, darling," he said, with a dangerous gleam in his eyes.

His chest rose and fell as if he'd exerted himself in executing whatever trick it had taken to get inside the locked house and into his present position. If he had sent the carriage off, that left her alone with him for the night. A bubble of hysteria rose up inside her.

"Oh, *you*." From a nearby table, she snatched a figurine and raised it above her head—

"Don't." He stood, a vision of dark wool, flashing blue eyes, and utter calm. "That belonged to my great-grandmother."

Sophia almost hurled the stated heirloom, just to see if its destruction would cause a break in his dispassionate façade. It was no wonder he had been chosen by the Crown to represent England's interests abroad. Everything about him screamed of control. But she returned the figurine to its place. After all, she bore no ill will toward Claxton's great-grandmother, only Claxton. Finding nothing else within arm's reach suitable for hurling, she rounded the settee to confront him.

"Don't call me your darling," she raged, barely able to contain the impulse to leap on him and pummel him with her fists. Even now, the scent of Lady Meltenbourne's perfume clung to him. It clouded her nostrils, driving her toward the most uncontrolled madness. "You forfeited the right long ago. Why are you even here?"

He muttered something that sounded like "*because of Scotland*."

"What did you say?" Sophia demanded.

"I said, because I'm a deuced selfish bastard," he growled.

"How did you even get inside?" She glared up from beneath the brim of her velvet cap, which she still wore, in addition to her redingote and gloves.

He smiled rather like a wolf, stripping the gloves from his hands, which unnerved her further because it indicated his intention to stay. "Wouldn't you like to know?"

Though difficult to justify, even to herself, in this moment she *ached*, feeling more sadness than fury. He stood not two feet away, looking so tall and dark and dashing. Against all good sense, her heart still tried its feeble best to recognize him not as a wastrel but as the man she'd once loved.

"Vile man," she shouted. "I don't want you here."

He loomed over her, an imposing figure in the darkness. A stranger who wore the features of someone she used to know. "I came here tonight to find you—"

"And brought your mistress along for company?"

Heat flashed in his eyes, but he spoke with measured deliberation. "Good God, Sophia. Lady Meltenbourne is a bothersome gnat of a woman. She is not and has never been my mistress."

"A mere dalliance then."

"No."

"How colossal a fool do you think I am?" she cried, swiping her arm at the room, indicating the cushions and bottle. "I saw the proof with my own eyes."

"No, damn it, you didn't." With the meager fire at his back, his broad shoulders cast everything in shadows, including his face. "Your sisters informed me you would be here, but when I arrived, I found the countess here with Haden."

Oh, her sisters! They could not be trusted with the merest of secrets. How she would punish them once she returned to London. Still, the pieces of the puzzle with which she had been presented made no sense.

"With Lord Haden, you say?" Eyes wide with affected drama, she searched the room, peering into shadows and behind the settee. "Where is he? No doubt vanished in the same magical manner in which you appeared? I had not realized I married into a family of sprites."

He closed his eyes as if imposing calm. "You would have passed his carriage on your way through the village. The bloody driver misheard the instructions and left before I could get them both in the carriage." Again his eyes opened to her. "If you did not realize it, the countess was quite inebriated, as was my brother."

She trembled in reaction, wanting to believe, but so afraid of being made his fool. Perhaps there had been a carriage. The night had been so dark, and she preoccupied. She did not know Haden very well. He'd returned to London only recently, having spent the last two years abroad, the most recent seven months in the duke's diplomatic retinue. Still, he'd earned the reputation of a rakehell. Much like his brother, she supposed. Perhaps things were even more sordid than she realized, and the two brothers shared a mistress.

"I don't know what to believe," she exclaimed, turning from him, now not wanting to see his face or his seemingly earnest expression.

He came round, forcing her to do so. A sudden passion blazed to life in his eyes.

"Believe *me*." He uttered the words fiercely through clenched teeth. "Me, Sophia. Because I tell you the truth."

"I can't," she exclaimed, unsettled by the intensity of his emotion. She would not be the sort of pitiable wife who blindly believed a husband's lies.

"You need only confirm my account with your sisters."

"My sisters can't explain everything," she blurted. "If only—if only it was just Lady Meltenbourne."

He nodded, and with a turn of his wrist, he flicked his coat open to fist his hand at his hip, on the lower edge of his waistcoat. "I understand I have hurt you. It is why I followed you here tonight, in hopes of answering for myself. Please say whatever you have to say. All of it, Sophia. Because after tonight, it is done. After tonight, I will defend myself no more."

A long moment passed, wherein Sophia paced in front of the fire. Once she spoke the words, they would be impossible to retrieve. She had held them inside so long, never confiding them even to her mother or sisters.

"You are not completely to blame. If I hadn't been so naïve and had such unrealistic expectations of marriage, I wouldn't have been so wounded and hurt by it all." She closed her eyes and forced the words out. "It all started with Lady Darch."

Claxton's sudden exhalation of breath compelled her eyes open again. He pressed his lips together and looked away. A damning confession. The resulting stab of pain to her heart spurred her on.

"The morning we were married, in fact."

She lowered herself to the settee and untied the ribbon underneath her chin, removing the cap from atop her head, because suddenly the satin felt like a coarse ligature across her throat, making it near impossible to breathe.

"You remember her ladyship." Sophia scrutinized his face, wanting to observe his every reaction. "She was in my wedding party. A very beautiful widow."

He did not move. He only listened, his face several shades paler and his jaw clamped tight.

She could not stop now. "We were alone for only a few moments after the ceremony, before we all went into breakfast, but she was kind enough to assure me how fortunate I was to be wedding you." With each word spoken, her courage increased. It felt good, at last, to speak a secret she'd held inside so long.

Expressionless, Claxton closed his eyes because obviously he knew what she was about to say.

"That she knew from intimate experience how very satisfying you would be as a lover. That you were imminently talented in that regard, not only in the bedroom, but in the carriage and"—here she paused for breath, for the courage to say the rest—"in the garden. Wherever your passion might strike you."

The blood drained from Vane's cheeks. Her heart pounded so hard it hurt. But she knew if she had not died from heartache after losing their child and after he had abandoned her, she would not expire from it now.

"Sophia—" he uttered, his voice thick.

She lifted a silencing hand. "Lady Darch never stopped smiling, the whole time she spoke, but I suspect she was quite heartbroken that you and I had married." She looked Claxton directly in the eye. "Which is why I tried very hard to forget the whole unpleasant matter."

He held both of his palms open to her. "I never spoke to her again after you and I were betrothed. I swear it."

Sophia nodded, her hands working the ribbon of her cap. "I believe you, Claxton, and that's what I believed then as well, which is why I never mentioned her to you. I forgave you Lady Darch. After all, it wasn't as if I believed you to be a virgin when we married."

"Then what?" he demanded quietly. "Why tell me this now?"

Sophia blinked. "Once we married, I was very satisfied being your wife. More than satisfied. I was *happy*." Her voice failed on the word, and she had to clear her throat to continue. "I think you know that to be true. I believe you were happy as well?"

"I was, yes," he answered.

"I fear, though, her ladyship's words always stayed somewhere in the back of my mind, like an ugly little whisper, which is why I overreacted when I accidentally opened that letter from the actress."

Claxton's chin jerked.

She closed her eyes, pressing forward. "After we lost the baby, you were gone so much, especially at night. You seemed so miserable in our marriage, as if you didn't like me very much anymore."

"That's not true." He shook his head. "It was never true."

"Then that French letter fell out of your pocket."

"Received in jest from an old military friend," he provided in a controlled voice. Yet his knuckles, where they gripped the mantel, whitened. "A bawdy bit of male humor you were never intended to see."

Sophia frowned and glanced at her lap. "I'm certain

that's what every husband says to his wife upon her discovering something untoward in his pocket."

"It's the truth."

"You must understand that by then numerous rumors had already reached my ears—"

"*Rumors*," Claxton hissed.

"That you'd been seen in Hyde Park in a parked carriage, passing time with Lady Bamber."

"She is—an old friend." His lips grew thin and white, and his nostrils flared. "Passing time. Mere conversation. Nothing more—"

"Mrs. Burke. Lady Dixon."

His eyelids fluttered, and his teeth clenched. "If you would just—"

"There were more rumors, of course, and they didn't stop after you accepted your diplomatic assignment. I could recount them here for you to deny, to talk them away, but my heart and my mind are weary of it all." Sophia gave a little shrug.

"Weary of the rumors or me?"

She looked at him directly. "I only know what my old nanny, Mrs. Hudson, used to say, that to every rumor there is a kernel of truth."

"You would justify my condemnation with an . . . *an idiom*?" His eyes widened.

"A very wise idiom by my way of thinking. Perhaps I was naïve when we married, but I'm not anymore." Her voice softened. "Besides, none of that really matters. The rumors, those women—"

"They don't?" he inquired hoarsely.

"No." Perhaps it ought to make her feel good and satisfied to see him so discomposed by her words, but it didn't. She examined his face, feeling too old and too wise for her years. "What matters most is that when I needed you to be my husband, to tell me everything would be all right—"

"Yes, I know—" His blue eyes, in that moment, became black and empty. "The baby. It's just that—"

"You left me and went on to live your life without me. As if the baby and I meant nothing at all to you."

Claxton opened his mouth as if to speak.

Sophia stood from the settee. Leaving her cap there, with its shining ribbons trailing onto the floor, she walked the edge of the carpet. "I don't think I can ever forgive you for that. What a strange and terrible thing to say, being that it's almost Christmas, but it's the truth. It's wedged here, like a piece of broken glass in my heart, and I don't think the hurt will ever go away."

He moved toward her. "Sophia—"

"Please." She stepped back, shaking her head. "I'm not finished."

Now that she'd gone this far, she felt strong enough to say the rest. He'd left her no choice.

"While you were away, I passed a lot of my time alone, thinking." She straightened her shoulders to signify her resolve. "It is why I came here tonight. After seeing you, I knew I needed to make a decision, and everyone would have such different opinions, you see. My mother. My sisters. Grandfather. I needed to ruminate, to be alone and make my own decision, without being pulled in different directions."

His face hardened into stone, but at least, thankfully, he remained silent and allowed her to speak.

"And then I found you here with Lady Meltenbourne,

who had already quite humiliated me tonight in front of all my family and friends, asking everyone your whereabouts. At my grandfather's party, no less." She shrugged. "Even if she is not your lover, I don't believe I'll ever get the image out of my head. I'm not that sort of wife."

Claxton did not say anything. He only stood there, his eyes burning like cinders.

"It would only be a matter of time until there was a similar misunderstanding or difficulty to drive us apart. As things stand, I don't see that there is any way to return to the way things were before. I know what I am about to say may shock you, but I can think of no other solution."

His gaze lost its heat to be replaced with an icy gleam.

Her heart pounded so that she could barely catch her breath. He only stared at her, making each word a challenge to speak.

"If you care about me at all, Claxton, one little bit, I want ... well, I want a separation."

* * *

At hearing the words from Sophia's lips, the earth opened up and he fell through into a burning crevice of hell, a place he remembered well. Somehow, amid the flames, he heard it—his own quick inhalation of breath sharply audible in the silence.

"No."

It was all he could think. No. Goddamn it, no.

"I thought you might say that," she replied quietly, looking down at her hands. "But you see, I have something to offer in exchange for your agreement."

"Don't, Sophia—" He knew with a dark and sudden

certainty what she would say. What she would offer to gain his compliance.

"A child."

He closed his eyes. "Damn you."

She cleared her throat. "In exchange for—a child— you will grant me a separation."

For a long moment, he seethed in silence.

"A boy?" he gritted out through clenched teeth. "An heir?"

Her lashes lowered against her cheeks, something he'd always found painfully alluring. "A child," she said firmly. "Whatever its sex may be."

He'd never felt an obligation to continue the Claxton line. But yes, he had wanted children with Sophia desperately. The loss of their first had devastated him to his soul, and he had grieved each day since for that baby, just as strongly as he'd grieved the loss of his wife's affection.

Now she offered him one of the two things he wanted most in the world, a daughter or a son, in exchange for the other—herself. Instinct commanded that he go to her and fall on his knees and beg her to withdraw her abominable proposal. To carry her upstairs and make love to her until she loved him back.

Yet fear that she would still reject him paralyzed him, and he did nothing. Instead, all his hurt and anger spilled out from his throat.

"Do I have any choice?" he snapped.

"My grandfather's lawyers have assured me the separation will occur if I so wish it, regardless of your cooperation. So the choice is yours. We will separate, either with a child . . . or without."

"A *formal* separation with all the legal and binding implications," he whispered.

"A complete severance of our marital obligations."

"I shall have to think. Given the circumstances, perhaps there should be no child." He forced a casual shrug and with the next words sought to wound her just as deeply as she'd wounded him. "Perhaps, as long as we're undertaking to create a scandal, I might simply prefer a divorce. To be truly free of you. To marry and have children with someone else."

"A divorce?" she blurted, eyes widening. "But I didn't commit the adultery."

Parliament, as a rule, granted divorces only to husbands who proved adultery by their wives. There were only very rare exceptions.

"Neither did I," he ground out. "But the truth doesn't seem to signify with you. The endeavor would simply require that we make up some salacious stories about you. The more the better. Repeat them enough, and they're as good as true, eh, Sophia? Then we can have our divorce and truly be done with each other."

"*Claxton*," Sophia exclaimed, visibly mortified.

"Then a Scottish divorce, perhaps, which allows for a husband's adultery as a cause of action." He pretended to ponder the idea, tapping his finger against his lips. "We've the estate in Inverness to establish residency. I resided there for nearly a month after...well, I'm certain your investigator can find some local doxy to say she was my—"

"I believe a separation will suffice," she blurted coldly. "You're all bluster. I suspect you want a child as badly as I do, not the scandal and nastiness of a divorce."

He laughed into the shadows, a bitter sound. Of course, she was right. He wanted a child with Sophia, or no child at all. She had him by the bollocks.

This night had gone nothing at all like he had planned. It had been his intention in coming to Camellia House to confess every one of the allegations she had spoken—except for Lady Darch, which of course had occurred before their betrothal—to ask her forgiveness for giving her cause to question his commitment to their marriage. But the same sins, when described by her innocent lips, had become infinitely more indefensible than he'd allowed himself to believe. How could he have blundered so badly and caused such damage to the trust between them that she now despised him so completely? He had no idea how to take her pain away or how to return their world to center. At the same time, he felt so *angry* at her. He'd harbored such hope. He could not help but feel betrayed.

Sophia fled to the window and pushed aside the curtain to stare into the night, so she would not have to look at him anymore, he knew.

"What a miserable Christmas this has turned out to be," she announced.

Christmas. His mother had always made their Christmases special. When the duchess Elizabeth had lived within these walls, Camellia House had been draped in greenery, warmth, and light, nothing like the cold, cavernous shell that surrounded them now.

For years after her death, he'd not known a true Christmas. His father did not celebrate the occasion, finding such observances overly sentimental and gauche. Later, while an officer in the army, he had attended the occasional Christmas ball or supper, but afterward had retired to his quarters alone.

The only Christmas in recent memory where he'd felt included in a family and at peace with the world had been last Christmas, which he'd spent at Wolverton's country estate with Sophia and her family. A magical memory. How had he allowed things to fall apart so completely since that time?

He stared at her back. She stood proudly, her head erect and her shoulders back, distant and unattainable. From out of nowhere, a torch flamed into blazing life inside his chest, one born of desire so intense and hot he knew he must do whatever possible to claim her again. To ease his soul-deep need. If only for one last time.

"Very well," he muttered. "I will agree to your demand."

She did not grant him so much as a glance over her shoulder, but remained motionless. "I rather thought you would."

From outside, the sound of the wind arose, battering the house. The walls and floors creaked. The windows rattled.

"Since you seem to be holding all the cards," he said, "where do you propose we go from here?"

Chapter Five

"We'll return to London first thing in the morning. I'd prefer that you take residence at your club."

Elbow on the mantel, Vane pinched his fingertips against the bridge of his nose, an attempt to soothe the pounding inside his head. She was throwing him out of his own house?

"How do you suppose, then," he demanded harshly, "that I get you with child?"

For a long time she stood in silence, back to him. Would she turn around and tell him they could still step back from this cliff? That separating wasn't what she wanted? Did he even want her to change her mind, with the trust between them so irrevocably destroyed?

She turned, the suddenness of the motion parting her scarlet redingote below her waist to reveal a lace froth of petticoats and the pointed tips of embroidered green mules. "We will come to a mutual agreement as to when you will visit."

Though buttoned up tight, all the way to her high velvet collar, she'd never been more alluring than now. Never more beautiful and composed. He almost hated her for it.

"But first," she said, "I want the documents drawn and all agreements in writing."

Claxton blinked, dismayed. "What other agreements are there?"

"That I will retain Sylventon Place and the income from that estate, as I brought that property into our marriage—"

Claxton grunted in assent.

"And that the child, once born, will live with me to be raised by me and my family."

Her words came like a cudgel to the back of his head.

"No." He shook his head, a snarl forming on his lips. "I don't agree to that, not completely."

"You will," she answered calmly, hovering at the edge of the candlelight.

He felt dragged in the dirt. Drawn and quartered.

"You've got this all worked out in your mind already, don't you?" he growled.

She responded in a quiet voice. "I had a lot of time alone to think about it."

He shook his head. "Again, I won't agree."

"We will work out all the details then." She circled round the end of the settee.

"Whatever," he snapped.

From the cushion, she collected her valise, her cap, and the oil lamp and stood like a woman preparing for an arduous journey. "Unless there's something else, I am very tired and shall retire."

Only she didn't leave. She hovered there, staring at him.

"What do you expect?" he barked. "That I should bid you a good night?"

It was not a good night. It was a terrible night.

She looked him up and down. Her lip twitched as if she found him lacking. "I don't expect anything from you, Claxton. I haven't for a very long time."

With a glare, she disappeared down the corridor and up the stairs. The glow of the lamp dimmed with her every step, until he was abandoned to deeper darkness, with only a dying fire by which to see. Her footsteps grew faint, and at last there came the sound of a door closing.

The sound gutted him. Only in the ensuing silence did he acknowledge what he'd done. He had agreed to a legal separation from the only woman he had ever loved.

There were men on the battlefield who when faced with overwhelming force chose to blast their brains out rather than be torn apart by their enemy. In one fell moment, he'd done much the same, murdering his dreams rather than exposing himself to failure. He'd never been a coward in life or in war, but when faced with the disdain in his wife's bewitching green eyes, he had run like a callow boy.

He muttered an oath and said to the portrait over the mantel, "Are you quite happy?"

The painted countenance responded with a sneer of disdain, as his father had so often done in life. Of course, anyone else looking at the portrait would have noted only a dignified mien, the same expression emulated in countless portraits of important men. But Vane saw it. The artist had captured the dark glimmer, there in the farthest reaches of those steely blue eyes. Likely, his father had been an insufferable ass during each sitting. Oh yes, it was there. The elder lordship's general attitude of contempt for all things that breathed.

Throwing open one cabinet and then another, he searched for a bottle of something, *anything* strong and numbing. As a rule, he did not drink excessively. He mistrusted the recklessness that spirits inspired, the looseness of tongue, preferring instead to remain always in complete control.

Not tonight. Tonight he wanted to get ape drunk. His search yielded no such paradise, and the wine cellar was most certainly locked and the key in Mrs. Kettle's possession down in the village. Though less desirable in the given moment, he did, however, find another lamp and a store of oil.

With the lamp lighting his way, he followed the path Sophia had taken, noting the waning light seeping out from under the door of the ducal bedchamber, *his* rightful domain. God, he swore he could smell her fragrance and even hear the sensual brush of velvet against her skin. He felt like a feral animal, left out in the cold, when he ought to be there in the bed beside her. How would he get a moment's rest this close to her? With this shameful *need* even now burning in his blood? Instead he sullenly sought out the room he'd occupied as a boy.

Everything was familiar here, each panel and stone etched into his memory. There were his books. His drawings. Even his collection of miniature soldiers painted by his own boyish hand, waiting just where he'd left them on a table beside the window. But there were no linens or pillows. There wasn't even a mattress on the bed, just bare ropes. A glance into the other rooms—*not hers*—provided a similar result, and all hope of a comfortable night fell away. He returned to the great room.

He'd passed many a night in less gracious circumstances, on cold earth, unyielding stone, or creaking, damp boards, believing anything was better than a bed provided by his father's tainted largesse.

Though narrow and shorter than he by a good foot, the settee would more than suit for the next few hours.

* * *

Sophia stepped back from the fire she'd only just managed, after numerous failed attempts, to coax to life. Accustomed since birth to the skilled assistance of servants, she couldn't recall the last time she'd built her own. That she'd successfully accomplished the task gave her some satisfaction. If she could build a fire, she could certainly survive her future alone.

A strong wind battered the house, rattling the shutters. The cavernous room, despite its smart insulation of wood paneling, heavy draperies, and wall hangings, remained as frigid as her husband's winter-blue eyes. The fire, at least, made the chill bearable. Even so, she crossed her arms at her waist, a pitiful self-embrace, fearing she would never be warm again.

Claxton had agreed to her demand. She ought to feel triumphant or at least satisfied, but she didn't.

Behind her stood a wonderful old estate bed, made up with fine linens and thick velvet curtains, the latter of which she would not draw completely closed out of fear she would be unaware if the old house caught on fire and burned down around her. She craved the oblivion of sleep, but despite her weariness, with each passing moment, the tangle of thoughts in her head only grew more out of hand.

In some small way, she was grateful to be at Camellia House and alone in this unfamiliar room. There had never been a time in her twenty-two years when her life's biggest decisions were not decided by family committee. By her parents, or her grandfather, or the lively chattering pair that were her sisters, or some combination thereof. All her life, she'd welcomed as much as suffered the constant barrage of remarks and opinions that determined her path.

She'd rather overexaggerated to Claxton her grandfather's involvement in the matter of their separation. She and the earl had never discussed the possibility of a separation or the involvement of attorneys. When she returned to London, the news might come as a shock to Wolverton and, indeed, the rest of her family.

She couldn't even bring herself to imagine their reactions. They loved her, yes. There was not a doubt in her mind that they would support her through anything, but still, a formal separation from Claxton, even a private one, would mean some degree of social disgrace for her and the associated repercussions. If Claxton received an invitation to a party or ball or dinner, then she would not and neither would any member of her family.

Though she believed her family possessed the stature to weather such a storm, she had no wish to ruin her sisters' upcoming season. For young women whose very futures depended on a successful match, any scandal could be calamitous. No matter how lovely and charming

Daphne and Clarissa were or how besotted their suitors, if any parent or adviser caught a whiff of disgrace, no offer would be forthcoming.

Thankfully Claxton had agreed to endeavor toward having another child, which if all went accordingly, would delay their public scandal for up to a year, or... perhaps longer. A flush rose to her cheeks, imagining how many times they might have to attempt conception. Even now she could not comprehend separating herself from the emotion that their lovemaking had always inspired.

Attired in a flannel sleeping gown, Sophia filled the bed warmer with coals and after situating the brass pan, climbed onto the enormous feather mattress. The floor above her creaked, sounding almost like ghostly footsteps. In that regard, the knowledge of Claxton's presence gave her comfort.

Her heart whispered his name. Her hand curled into the linens, and a sigh broke from her lips.

No. He had forced her to this.

And yet... she'd never felt more lonely.

And on that sad little thought, the tears commenced.

The silent presence of the old house embraced her, making no judgments or efforts to dissect her thoughts, her fears, or her motivations. Nor did it chastise her when she wished, against all good sense, that Claxton—the most colossal ass on God's green earth—was lying here beside her.

* * *

Hours later, Vane sat up and rubbed his hands over his face. His breath puffed out before him, visible in the morning chill. A quick glance at the distant window showed the glass to be completely glazed with frost.

He had not slept well.

Some time before dawn, the fire burned out. Not only that, but one of the settee's damned legs, located just above his head, had abruptly failed. The sudden movement had jammed the top of his head against the armrest. Too exhausted to make any effort to repair either situation, he had passed the remainder of the early-morning hours uncomfortably cold, hovering between sleep and awareness, continually conscious of the world's lopsided slant.

Furthermore, the hellish scene that had taken place between him and Sophia the night before had played continually, even in his dreams—or rather nightmares. Nightmares, because to his horror he'd not been himself at all, but rather his father. If only he could have gotten fuddled and slept like the dead. He would have much preferred wakening to a shattering headache than this soul-deep crater in his chest.

Having slept fully dressed in all but his cravat, his foray into the world required only a push up from the settee and a brief shamble through the vestibule out the front door. There, his lungs frosted over in one breath.

A glance to his watch showed that, surprisingly, the day had gone well past noon.

Fog and snow blanketed the countryside to an extent he'd not anticipated. Only the tops of the nearby hedges remained visible, indicating an overnight fall of several feet. Having no wish to venture thigh deep into the stuff, he balanced himself at the edge of the ice-covered porch and unfastened his breeches. There, he relieved himself against a brass plaque affixed to the wall of the house, one bearing the Claxton crest. A smile curled his lips. As a boy, the same rebellious act had given him no small measure of delight.

Returned inside, he took a moment to repair the settee. He then sought out the kitchen, where he hoped to find a store of wood to renew the fire. Rounding the corner to the corridor, he came face-to-face with Sophia. The sight of her hit him like a cannonball to the chest.

She froze, her lips parting but saying nothing, as if he'd startled her as well. Her face was small and pale above the collar of her indigo gown, and weariness shadowed her eyes. Her hair fell in dark waves around her shoulders—all in all, a sight so lovely his gut twisted with want.

Sophia, *here*, in these simple surroundings that whispered his memories past, became someone else. Someone more. God, he missed her.

"Good morning," he half murmured, half growled, determined to win the first contest of the day, the one for most-civilized-spouse-seeking-a-formal-separation. After all, if they were going to proceed at some mutually negotiated point in the future to conceive a child, it might prove helpful if they remained, at the least, on cordial speaking terms.

She did not return his greeting. "The pump is frozen, but I melted some snow. There is a basin, if you'd like to wash."

She indicated the door to the scullery and continued on through the open door of the kitchen, a shadowy winter goddess. A stranger forevermore.

Vane washed, and when he was finished, he examined

himself in the small looking glass above the basin. A stark-faced man with disheveled hair and stormy eyes stared back. God, he looked frightening and so much like his father. He splashed another round of water on his face and ran the dampened fingers of both hands through his hair.

Claxton rejoined Sophia, strangely unable to stay away. Soon she would be gone from his life forever, hidden behind a wall of go-betweens and legally binding rules of engagement. To his shame, he craved with a sudden and surprising intensity whatever togetherness, whatever memories, these final hours would bring. Two narrow windows illuminated the kitchen with waning winter light. A delicious heat emanated from the stove, which he paused over to warm his water-chilled hands.

When he moved aside, she bent over the grate, peeking into a metal teapot. "There's tea. That's all, I'm afraid."

Vane granted himself the guilty pleasure of drinking her in, of committing to memory the way she looked now. The fire's glow painted red streaks in her mahogany hair. The simple lines of her unadorned gown, no doubt intended to be demure, only intrigued him, revealing the narrow column of her torso, and in alluring contrast, the high fullness of her breasts.

He remembered the body under that dress and the pleasure it had once given him in the shadowed privacy of their marriage bed. The memory of her naked, illuminated by morning's first light, was enough to awaken within him now a low, simmering madness. The understanding that he could never freely touch her again only intensified his need.

But words had been said. The decision made. He

would prove himself a better man by seeing their separation through and giving her some hope for happiness, in a world that did not include him. He owed her that much.

Bloody hell, he was such a martyr. He made himself sick.

She left the stove, making no effort to assist him. Finding a cup, he poured tea, needing something to occupy himself besides mooning after her like a love-struck idiot.

"There is no need to scowl at me," she muttered in a low voice.

The accusation startled him. "I wasn't scowling at you."

Though he ought to be, given their circumstances. Shouldn't he hate her? God help him, he couldn't. They were both wounded, the two of them.

She glanced pointedly at the cup in his hand. "I can't imagine you would be so displeased over a cup of tea, so it must be me that displeases you."

"It's not you or the tea." He rubbed a hand over his face. "I did not sleep well."

"Neither did I, but I'm not scowling at you."

He managed a smile. A small one. "Actually, you are."

Her lips parted, as if to offer some smart retort, but closed just as quickly. She sighed. Her expression softened, as did the rigidity of her posture. A bright flush rose into her cheeks.

"Oh, Claxton, let's not bicker." She exhaled morosely.

"Very well." He seated himself on a high stool. "Let's not."

"Unpleasantness between us will accomplish nothing but a loss of dignity for us both, privately and in public."

He'd always found the velvety tone of her voice soothing. He answered inanely now for the simple purpose of ensuring her response. "I am in complete agreement."

"It's not as if we are the first husband and wife to ever discover we are not well suited. This is a time for level heads and controlled emotions."

The memory came out of nowhere, shocking him. Her lips pressed against his skin, *willingly*, in a moment of passion. A shadowy glimpse of her naked body beneath his, her soft thighs outspread.

He shifted on the stool, suddenly tight in the breeches. He growled, "I shall endeavor to remain so."

"I shall as well." She let out a sudden breath—of relief or frustration, he did not know—and searched the room, her attention at last settling on the stove. "I built only a small fire. Being that we are departing shortly, it wasn't practical to make anything larger."

He crossed to the window and peered out, savoring the warmth of the earthenware mug in his hands.

"You've looked outside?" he said incredulously.

The forest encircled the back of the manse, a smudge against a white winter sky. There were outbuildings and a stable, and at the edge of the gardens, the cemetery encircled by a stone wall. All nearly obscured by snow.

The cemetery. His mother would be there. After she had died, his father had arranged for the paltriest, most shameful of monuments. As soon as he could arrange for it, Claxton had commissioned a memorial much more worthy of a duchess. Life had prevented him thus far from visiting her grave site for himself. Perhaps, more truthfully, he'd found reasons to stay away.

What would his gentle, kind mother think of him now?

Lily Dalton

He could not help but believe she would be deeply disappointed that despite her love and motherly efforts, he'd turned out much like his father.

"Of course I have." Sophia came to stand beside him, leaving a generous foot of space between them. Even so, his body reacted with awareness, with every muscle drawing tight. Feigning insouciance, he lifted his cup.

On the first sip of tea, he choked.

"What is wrong?" she asked, frowning.

"*Och*—nothing," he sputtered, unwilling to tell her the dreg plastered at the back of his throat was the worst excuse for tea he'd ever had the misfortune to imbibe. He'd found better on the battlefield and at the lowliest roadside inns.

She bit her lower lip. "It's so rare that I prepare tea myself, I'm afraid I've forgotten the proportions."

Proportions? He wasn't even certain that the contents of the cup were tea. Obviously, Sophia lacked practical skills in the kitchen, which of course was not uncommon among young women of her elevated social standing, who were expected only to plan meals with impeccable taste, with instructions to a fully staffed kitchen, not actually prepare them.

She bent over her valise. When she stood again, she held a thick gray scarf, one she proceeded to drape over her shoulders and tuck around her neck. Then she drew gloves onto her slender hands.

"What are you doing?" he asked stupidly, though her intentions were clear. Tension tightened the muscles along his shoulders.

"Going down to the village." Settling her cap onto her head, she tied its sash below her chin. "Perhaps things aren't so dire there as they appear here. Activity may have the streets cleared. Certainly someone will hire out a horse and carriage to convey us to London."

Her words incited no small amount of turmoil within him. Once returned to London, she would withdraw from him completely to the protective circle of her family. Wolverton would step in. Though inevitable, he wasn't ready yet.

Bloody hell, why not? Like a coward, he'd abandoned her, and she'd already made clear she would never forgive him. The sooner they got on with their separate lives, the better for them both. Especially him. He hadn't slept with a woman in nearly a year and intended to resolve that matter as soon as he returned to London. After all, hadn't she all but released him from their marriage vows? Once he'd relieved that particular urge, no doubt the world would become right again. If only he believed that.

Regardless, one glance outside proved they were going nowhere. Last night's storm had been uncommonly severe.

"This is Lacenfleet, not London," he said. "There will be no organized efforts funded by the municipality to clear the streets. Even if the citizenry endeavors to dig themselves free, ice floes on the river have likely rendered the ferry and any other rivercraft out of service."

"Certainly there is another route to London other than the ferry?" Her brows furrowed, and her voice took on a desperate edge. "One by land that would eventually take us to a bridge? The mail coaches would still be running."

"Not in this uncommon storm and not to Lacenfleet. It's too small and inconsequential a village to command such extraordinary efforts. Even if the roads leading northward could be discerned beneath this depth of snow, they are not paved and would be a frozen bog. Any travel, I'm afraid, would be too dangerous, not only for you but for the horses. It is doubtful you'd find anyone willing to chance the trip. People here just wait things out."

At this, her gaze dropped. Clearly the idea of spending just another moment in his company made her miserable. His heart hardened against her a fraction more.

He set the cup down. "I've no more wish to remain here than you, but we're better off staying here until the frost subsides. Certainly we can suffer each other's presence for just a day. Two at the longest."

She did not remove her scarf, but neither did she reach for her valise. "I will not spend my Christmas here with you."

"This may come as a shock to you, but I don't particularly wish to spend mine with you either." He stepped back toward the doorway. "But Christmas is seven days away. No doubt by then the weather will clear. For now, I intend to build a fire in the great room. There are books there, old, but readable, with which to pass the time."

She responded with a slight nod. "Yes. Build a fire if you wish."

* * *

Moments later, from the snow-covered front lawn, Sophia paused for one last look.

Camellia House peered back at her through broad mullioned windows, an Elizabethan fantasy of pinnacles, dormers, transoms, and chimneys. She could only imagine how in summer, the wild, terraced gardens, riotous with color, would run clear to the woods. She would have loved to explore every nook and cranny of the residence and grounds, but simply could not remain in such torturous proximity to Claxton for another minute.

Not when her sensible mind told her everything between them was finished. If only she did not cherish so many memories of their life before. They haunted her like friendly, well-intended ghosts, blurring her mind and making her forget, however momentarily, how intolerable life as his wife had become.

Instead she would rip the bandage from the wound quickly, no matter how much pain it caused her, and assume her new role as an independent lady posthaste. Her present and future happiness depended on it. Once returned to London, she would seek the comfort of her family, accept the counsel of her grandfather's attorneys—and most important, put herself into a proper frame of mind for resuming temporary intimacies with Claxton, something that even now she couldn't imagine without experiencing an unbidden rush of fever and desire. But simple attraction couldn't erase the past.

Turning, she wobbled, momentarily disoriented by the sudden give of snow under her boot and a blinding expanse of white that gave little indication of space or direction. Thankfully, a discernible, smoother swath undulated down the hill, indicating the path of the elevated private road she must follow to reach the village.

She embraced her valise with both arms and proceeded, stepping high and quick so as not to drag her hem and stockings against the snow.

All to no avail, because with each step the snow sank suddenly and gave, dropping her in above her knees.

My, it was cold, especially under her skirts. Perhaps the ladies' drawers that she had read about in *Ackermann's Repository*, fashioned of Spanish lamb's wool (and warranted never to shrink!), would not be such a terrible addition to one's winter wardrobe. But if she kept this rapid pace, she would arrive in the village easily in less than half an hour. There, she would find an inn and tea and, she felt quite sure, enough fresh, warm rolls to make her forget her insufferable husband.

Crunch, crunch, crunch. With each step, her valise grew heavier. *Crunch, crunch, crunch.* Lord, she hadn't even reached the bridge. Cold permeated her boots and wool hose, numbing her feet and, worse, her bottom. She paused, gasping for the next painful breath, and assessed her plight.

No, she assured herself, her decision to walk to Lacenfleet had *not* been an ill-conceived folly. It *wasn't* far to the village. Still, it seemed as if the private road had been laid out with the intent to provide arriving visitors with an impressive view of the house, rather than to convey a person from one place to the next in an efficient fashion.

She squinted, peering through the fog and snow. If she cut across the paddock and that little ditch, she'd join up with the public road and arrive in Lacenfleet even quicker.

Despite the snow lying deeper in the paddock than on the road, she at last arrived at the ditch, which upon closer inspection was not quite as little as she'd believed. Earthen walls cut rather steeply to a frozen, stony brook bed below. The smooth leather soles of her ladies boots, while suitable for a walk in the country, were less than ideal for such rugged terrain, especially when glazed with frost. Even so, she wasn't about to declare a retreat. By doing so, she'd increase what had become a miserable excursion by at least another ten minutes.

She dropped her valise to the stones below and gingerly began her descent.

Chapter Six

Sophia?" Vane traversed the vestibule, his mood darkening with each step.

He'd not located her in her room or the kitchen or elsewhere in the house. His wife had vanished. Not knowing where else to look, he ventured onto the porch to dispel the unlikely notion she might have ventured outside, which of course, she would not have done without telling him.

He sighted her instantly, a crimson spot in the paddock.

"Damn my eyes," he shouted, his breath clouding the air.

How reckless for her to venture off into such inclement conditions and without telling him first. Without even having the courtesy to say good-bye. Bloody hell, she provoked him, but all he could think was that he had to get her back.

He stormed half across the field in pursuit when he heard her exclamation. Flailing, she dropped from view.

A sickening terror rose in his throat, along with the unforgettable details of another fateful fall. Vane broke into a run, sliding to a halt at the edge of the ditch. She sprawled supine, eyes wide open to the sky, her redingote and skirts flipped high, revealing her stockinged legs up to her garters.

Dead. *This time* Sophia was dead. This time, in her determination to escape him, she'd broken her lovely neck.

Scrambling over, he skidded down. Ice, rocks, and earth crumbled.

By the time he slid to a stop beside her, she stood on her feet, smoothing her skirts.

"Don't say *anything*," she muttered sullenly.

Thank God for his greatcoat. Otherwise, she would see the unmistakable evidence of his heart having exploded out of his chest. He couldn't breathe. For a moment he felt certain *he* had died. He wanted to grab her by the arms and examine her body from head to toe for any sign of injury. He swallowed hard, struggling to temper his response.

"Good God, Sophia," he shouted hoarsely. "Are you certain you aren't hurt?"

"I'm perfectly well," she answered testily.

"You shouldn't have gone out in this weather."

"I walk all the time and not always in perfect weather."

He forced himself not to shout at her. "You shouldn't have gone without telling me. What if I hadn't seen you?"

"Ugh." She clasped her hands over her ears, like a naughty child suffering an unwanted lecture. "I wish you hadn't."

"Come along." With a scowl, he thrust the heel of his Hessian into the frozen earth and extended his hand.

She ignored his offer of assistance. Instead she bent to retrieve her valise, which had popped open and fallen onto its side. The open gap offered a tantalizing glimpse of something ivory trimmed with frilly violet lace. She stuffed the errant garment inside and secured the clasp. "You owe me no such courtesies."

He did not withdraw his hand. "What sort of gentleman would not offer assistance in such a situation?"

She sniffed dismissively. "You have offered assistance, and I have declined. Now go." She made small shooing gestures with her gloved hands. He could not recall the last time he'd been shooed.

"Don't be ridiculous," he said with all imperiousness.

"I'm not ridiculous." Dark lashes flared wide against pale skin. "And I require no escort, which is precisely why I did not ask you to escort me initially. Your duty is done. Isn't that what we decided on? I felt certain that's what 'I want a separation' meant, that we would go our separate ways. So go yours now and I'll go mine, at least until after the agreements are drawn. Then we will make arrangements to... well, to..." She exhaled.

"To do what?" he asked darkly, wanting to make her squirm, which to his satisfaction, she did, bristling up like a porcupine.

"Just leave me," she exclaimed, leaning toward him. "Return to the house, and I will continue on to the village."

"What happened to 'Let's not bicker, Claxton'?" He raised his voice several octaves in an imitation of hers.

"I'm not bickering." She jabbed a finger at him. "You are."

His head pounded at her obstinacy. "Did you not see

how I found you? I thought you'd broken your neck. Don't pretend as if a fall is of no concern. As if you don't remember—"

"I remember, thank you very much," she shouted. Set against the bleak backdrop of winter, Sophia's countenance blazed brilliant, with raspberry-blush cheeks and bright eyes, and just like that, desire struck him, like a kick to his gut.

"If you must know," she added testily, "I rather skated down the incline, and so as not to fall chose to deliberately slide down on my bottom there at the end. Not the most graceful move in my repertoire, but I didn't expect an audience."

Valise in hand, she carefully maneuvered the frozen brook bed, her delicate boots crunching lightly on the ice. She proceeded to the far side of the ditch, a path that would take her to Lacenfleet and away from him.

She muttered, "I'm not made of eggshells. I will not break from a mere bump or shatter from cold."

Well, good. He did not regret so much, then, the near violent urge to grab her and shake some sense into her. And then kiss her senseless again.

Damn, but he wanted to kiss her.

Something about the cold weather and the way she looked so delectable bundled up in her redingote, scarf, and hat, like a little present waved in front of his nose that he'd never be allowed to open, kindled an already smoldering fire in his chest. A consequence, no doubt, of living the life of a monk for the past seven months, two days, and five hours, trying to become a man worthy of—

He ground his teeth together. None of that mattered

anymore. He had made mistakes for which there would be no forgiveness. Now effectively set free from his vows, he would have a woman as soon as he returned to London. A pair of them, perhaps—both dark haired and green eyed and who looked like Sophia, if that was what he needed to shatter the fantasy of her and forget.

Still, he would not be dismissed. Not after he'd found her like that. She'd gone down intentionally, *his eye*. He followed her, the frost cracking loudly under his weight to a greater degree than when she had crossed.

She twisted round and eyed him like a haughty queen. She made a beautiful, regal duchess. He'd always thought so. "Really, Claxton, your *husbandly* concern is admirable. But as of last night, unless you have forgotten, I am to become an independent woman. Accordingly, I would appreciate being allowed to resolve my own difficulties from this point forward."

It had begun to snow again quite heavily. "Sophia—"

"Good-bye." She gave him her back again.

In silence he stood, observing as she climbed a few feet up the ditch wall, only to slide, scrabbling for purchase, down again. This sequence repeated numerous times until, at last, the amusement of watching her fail played out.

Vane stepped forward over the stones and grabbed the valise from her hands.

"Ah—don't!" she shouted.

He extended the case out of her reach.

"It's not that you are incapable physically of achieving the feat, dear girl." He bent, leveling his nose with hers. "Rather, the cumbersome nature of your valise undermines your efforts, as does the impractical style of your clothing. But if you haven't noticed, it has gotten colder and is snowing again. Any further delay is foolhardy."

He tossed the leather case high over the ledge, where it landed with a solid *thump*. "There. Now come along."

He reached for her.

"Not with you—" She pushed his hand away, allowing him the opportunity to capture her elbow in doing so.

"Go. Up. Now."

Leading her by the arm, he hoisted her in front of him and half pushed, half lifted her up the remainder of the ascent. Taller and heavier by far, he anchored them on the slippery slope. She blustered and protested all the way, and though he held his scowl, he could not deny taking pleasure from every touch. Even padded with layers of petticoats and wool, his estranged wife was a rare, lush confection, one he wanted to push down into the snow to taste, eat, and savor. To touch her underneath her clothes with his mouth and his hands until she couldn't even remember what the word *separation* meant.

But alas, there would be none of that. As soon as they reached level ground, where she regained possession of her valise, she stormed, pink cheeked, away from him and down the snow-laden public road.

*   *   *

Furious at his continued efforts to torment her, Sophia fumed away, but with his long legs, Claxton easily matched her pace. Wordlessly, he wrested her valise from her grasp, freeing her of its burden. This time he did not demand that she turn back, but walked beside her, his boots making easy work of the snow. For a long while, they tromped along without speaking until she could bear the quiet no longer. She had never been one for successfully brooding in silence.

"How I envy you your Hessians," she said, speaking straight from her mind. "Perhaps in the coming months, I will withdraw to the country. I'll take to wearing men's garments and boots and tromp through fields in search of adventure."

He said nothing, only continued to make easy progress over the frozen earth. Before becoming duke, Claxton had been a colonel in the light dragoons, something that had inspired romantic opinions about him among the ranks of the *ton*'s ladies, herself not excluded.

Sophia saw those physical attributes in him now, in the powerful stride of his legs and the measured breaths he took through his nose. She struggled to keep pace and appear as untaxed by the effort as he.

More words bubbled up into her mouth, any silly thing to break the uncomfortable quiet between them. "Perhaps I'll even take to smoking a pipe."

He growled, "You will *not* smoke a pipe."

"I will if I want to." She wouldn't, of course, but she liked saying so just to shock him. "Once we are separated, I'll do anything I want."

"Such as spend all your time with Havering?" he asked in a low, cutting voice.

"Of course not," she answered, startled by the accusation. "Why? Did he say something to you?"

Claxton made a sound between a grunt and a laugh. He gave her his profile and stared out over the field. Obviously Fox had indeed said something to Claxton. The knowledge did not please Sophia, but came as no surprise. Havering had always been protective, since they were children, but more so since her older brother Vinson's death four years before. He and Vinson had been best friends, sharing university and their grand tours together, not to mention the fateful trip where Vinson had been lost. Then, of course, her father had died, a man who had been more like a father to Fox than his own. Perhaps earlier in life there had been certain expectations, but she had married Claxton, and Havering had never been—and would never be—more than a friend. Looking at the duke's scowling profile, she could not help feeling badly that he might believe otherwise.

"What will you do, Claxton," she queried softly, "when you are rid of me?"

He threw her a sharp glance, but a long moment later, he answered. "I've not given the future much thought. Perhaps I will go to Jamaica, if my diplomatic duties so allow. Haden has properties there, worked by freemen, in which I've invested. I've long wanted to see them for myself."

"Jamaica sounds a world away," she observed softly. "Exotic and delightfully warm in comparison to our present circumstance."

What if he liked it there so much that he did not return? What if she never saw him again, not even in passing on a crowded London street? Her chest constricted at that thought or perhaps merely from the cold.

"Of all places, why did you come here last night?" he asked.

Ice cracked and popped on the trees. A curious jackdaw swooped beside them, flitting from limb to limb.

Sophia adjusted her scarf, bringing it higher over her

chin. "I'd seen the parish tithes recorded in the account books and inquired with the land steward about the estate. The house sounded charming and close to London and private." She shrugged. "Weeks ago I wrote to the caretakers, a Mr. and Mrs. Kettle, with instructions that I would visit the week after Christmas. Last night on impulse I decided to take residence a bit early."

That explained why the house had been in at least the early stages of readiness. Mrs. Kettle would have thrown herself into preparations immediately upon having received such word, to the best of her capability.

"You weren't there when I arrived," he noted. "Not as I expected you to be."

An image of Claxton embracing Lady Meltenbourne exploded into her mind, jagged and painful. She blinked the memory and the hurt that accompanied it away.

"I delivered my lady's maid home to spend Christmas with her family. She is newly hired, young, and quite homesick. I, for my part, wished to be alone." She steered the conversation to a less emotional topic than the events of the night before. "The property is lovely. Why has the house not been kept up?"

"No one comes here," he said quietly. "Not since my mother died."

"I thought she died in Italy."

She instantly realized she'd made a grave mistake in speaking those words. The sharpness of his glance cut her through.

"Italy," he answered in a hollow voice. "No."

Claxton had always deflected her questions about his mother and father, answering in only the vaguest of terms. Not every childhood had been as happy as hers.

Realizing this, she had respected his need for privacy and never pried. Yet before their marriage, Sophia had overheard a stodgy society matron intimate that the duchy carried a scandal in its not so distant past. Only when pressed had her mother reluctantly shared the rumor that the Duchess of Claxton had years before abandoned the duke and their young sons for a lover and subsequently died abroad in Italy.

"To my knowledge, the duchess never visited Italy." He stared ahead, his countenance stolid. "She lived here for as long as I remember, being a mother to Haden and I."

Embarrassment and shame scorched her cheeks. After all the difficulties in their marriage caused by rumor, she of all people should know better than to repeat details gleaned from a scandal, details that based on her husband's response weren't even true. She could not help but feel that she had thoughtlessly maligned the memory of an innocent woman, someone close to her husband's heart. She glanced at him to find his jaw rigid and his lips firmly set.

"I'm sorry, Claxton. I shouldn't have said it."

"It is of no consequence."

In a softer tone, Sophia sought to diffuse the tension between them with a less provocative statement. "I suppose many in the village will recognize you."

"Let's hope not." His brows rose. "My brother and I, as children, were unholy terrors. I'm certain there are still unfortunate feelings."

With that response, they returned to silence, having arrived at the edge of Lacenfleet. There, despair consumed her. From this vantage point she could see a portion of the river, the surface covered with large fragments of drifting white floes. Two barges were moored at the dock. As for the village, just as Claxton had predicted, snow buried the roads. Not a moving carriage or wagon or living person could be seen, though smoke arose from almost every chimney.

"Which way?" she said, unwilling to return to the silence and darkness of Camellia House after having come this far.

With a look of irritation, he pointed down a wide lane lined on either side by cottages with doorways almost obscured by drifts of snow.

"The inn," he answered, words clipped. "No matter the weather, the villagers will gather inside. The livery is also there, though I'm certain you will not find transport out. You can see as well as I that no one is about and that we have come all this way for nothing. Careful there. The pavement is—"

Too late. She'd stepped off and crashed in thigh-deep snow.

"—lower there."

She cried out at the discomfort, the invasion of cold where the chill had not gone before. Spanish wool drawers. Yes, she would purchase five pair upon her return to London. If she had them now, she would wear all five pair at once. Her redingote and skirts formed an unseemly puddle at her hips.

Claxton paused, his expression unabashedly *satisfied*. "Your Grace, do you require assistance?"

"Of course not," she snapped, struggling to extract her legs and proceed forward. When they did not follow the rest of her body, she toppled forward into the snow, landing on her forearms.

Gasping for air, she almost screamed from frustration, but she would not grant her husband the pleasure of seeing her fall to pieces when it was she who had insisted on coming into the village in the first place.

Large hands grasped her shoulders, righting her. Claxton thrust her valise into her arms.

"Hold this," he ordered.

Without preamble, he lifted her into his arms, crushing her to his chest. Snow fell from her skirts and boots.

"You're damnably stubborn," he said, plowing down the lane.

Frowning, sensual lips spoke the words just in front of her nose, impossible to ignore unless she shut her eyes.

"Not with most people," she answered sullenly, not closing her eyes.

He'd not shaved this morning. Dark, glossy whiskers shadowed the masculine curvature of his jaw. She remembered the pleasure during their lovemaking of having his unshaven beard dragged against her skin. Sometimes in the mornings, she'd had to hide the abrasion marks left behind from the curious eyes of her young maid.

"Is it normally so difficult for you to ask for assistance?"

"Not at all. Just from you."

He lifted a dark brow. "I don't recall you being this willful before."

His heat warmed her through his coat, a reminder of how wonderful it had once been to be held in his arms. He'd carried her in this manner before, but never on a public street. Only in the privacy of their bedroom and always toward their bed. Her heart began to beat faster, remembering how blissful things had once been—how they could never be again, because this was the man who had abandoned her in her grief, without as much as a regretful backward glance. As if neither she nor their lost baby had ever held a place in his heart.

A painted sign, encased by icicles, indicated that they had arrived at the inn. There were footprints, and the snow had been cleared from the wooden steps.

"It's called self-sufficiency." Sophia elbowed Claxton and kicked, wriggling free. She skittered away from him through the snow. Her body complained at the loss of his comfortable warmth and strength. "You were gone a very long time. I had to learn it."

"Self-sufficiency, you say?" he muttered darkly. He followed, reaching to take the handle of her valise. "You would never have arrived at this inn without my assistance." His eyes narrowed. "You're quite welcome, by the way."

Yet she held tight, seizing the case against her chest.

"You expect my thanks?" She blinked back a sudden surge of tears.

She'd been a coward at the house, sneaking out so she wouldn't have to say good-bye to him face-to-face. He'd gone and ruined that for her. Now, *this* was good-bye, and the enormity of the moment created a ball of emotion in her throat, difficult to even breathe around. They would never see each other again like this. Didn't he realize everything would change? Or was it that he just didn't care?

For Sophia, there was something devastating about the knowledge they would never spend another moment alone again until after the details of their separation—settlements and annuities and agreements—were negoti-

NEVER DESIRE A DUKE   107

ated through intermediaries and finalized. In these last moments could he not speak to her with some gentleness out of respect for the happier times they'd shared?

With all the force within her, she yanked the case back, inadvertently jerking his hand in her direction because he did not let go. His eyes flared wide with surprise.

Of course she overreacted, and in a most irrational and childish manner, but in this moment she did not care. Her mind buzzed with hurt and anger, and she didn't even feel the cold anymore. Did he not wish for them to have a decent and meaningful good-bye? They had once loved each other.

His jaw flexed. "This excursion was utter folly. Admit you were wrong in leaving the house."

That he would be so obstinate here, on the threshold of the place where she would say good-bye to him forever, upended her composure. Once she regained full possession of her case, she could go inside, shut the door on Claxton, and convince her heart to forget him.

"Of course I was wrong. I'm a foolish, silly woman. *Thank you*, your Grace, for being such a gentleman as to point out my every failing," she said archly. "And for being so much larger and stronger than me, your helpless, little wife."

She backed away in an attempt to free the handle, but still he did not release it. Indeed, he gritted his teeth and held tight.

"Sophia—" he warned.

"But I'm not your wife any longer." She jerked the case, throwing all her weight into the effort. "Not really, not for long, because you've made it clear, not just to me but the whole of England, that you prefer to be *anywhere* in the world and with *anyone* but with me." And jerked it again. "So you're *not* a gentleman after all and most certainly *not* my hero, so no, I'm not inclined to thank you for *anything*."

For a moment, there was nothing but the sound of the wind and ice cracking and the echo of her words in her ears.

"Not a gentleman, you say?" he said in a hushed voice.

His expression dangerous, he yanked the handle *hard*, gaining possession of the valise and Sophia, who pitched forward along with it. The force of this brought her crashing against him. The valise between them halted her abruptly, her face inches from his. Her heartbeat raced wildly, but not in fear. With the attraction she struggled even now, in her anger and hurt, to conceal.

"It took you until now to realize?" he said, nostrils flared.

With a downward shove, he wrenched the case from her hand, throwing it to the ground. He stepped toward her.

"Don't you touch me," she gasped, retreating toward the steps, thinking to escape him, but he lunged, closing the distance between them to capture her face in his hands.

"Dear God, you drive me mad," he growled, his eyes alight with blue fire.

She waited for the squeeze of his fingers, for him to twist off her head in the middle of the lane for being such a tiresome, troublesome wife who had ceased to bring him a single moment's peace or pleasure.

His mouth fell on hers.

Stunned, she grabbed his hands to remove them, but... Didn't.

She gasped against his lips, inhaling his breath, and in an instant remembered all she craved. His full lower lip. The bristly texture of his unshaven skin. The taste and scent that was only, deliciously Claxton. Every particle of her being exploded with need. His hands found her waist. She grasped his upper arms. He groaned, devouring her.

The world around them faded into a maelstrom of desire, she only vaguely aware of the snow crunching under their feet as they danced, struggled... his hands—*her hands*—tangled in hair and wool. On skin.

"Claxton," she breathed.

He made a guttural sound.

In a wild surge, all the anger of the past months exploded inside her, transforming the kiss into something more primal. She bit him. He nipped her back, a moment before his tongue entered her mouth to slide over hers. Consciousness blurred into a frenzy of pleasure and not-so-terrible pain.

Pain.

With a gasp, she thrust her hands against his chest and pushed.

Dazed and heavy lidded, he stared at her, his cheeks ruddy with passion, his arms bent at his sides, almost as if he'd never seen her before.

"Oh my God," he exclaimed thickly.

Touching her fingertips to swollen and tender lips, she teetered on unsteady legs and wholeheartedly concurred with his assessment. They'd shared thousands of kisses, but never anything as magnificent as that.

Just then, something appeared to draw his attention to another point of interest above her head. His face turned just a degree and his gaze intensified. For a moment, she feared they had drawn an audience, that behind her stood the whole of the village of Lacenfleet, gawking and pointing.

A strangled sound burst from his throat, something that sounded vaguely like her name. He shoved her—

The world careened.

Her shoulder, her cheek, slammed into the snow. His body smothered her in darkness.

"Claxton!" She gasped, bewildered, unable to breathe for his weight and the lapel of his coat smashed against her nose. His scent, woodsmoke and spice, filled her nostrils. Frigid cold worked through her clothes, chilling her backside. The snow numbed her skin. "What are you doing?"

He growled, "There's someone—"

A *crack* shattered the air. Atop her, his every muscle went taut.

"Someone?" Sophia strained to see if a tree branch had given way under the weight of the frost, but—

"Stay down," he growled, splaying his hand over her forehead and curling his body over hers. *Crack.* A split second later, a shower of snow covered them both.

His chest vibrated against hers as he uttered, "We're going to have to run for the wall over there."

The sudden realization came over her. A tree hadn't made the cracking noise, but a gun. Someone was shooting at them.

"Who is trying to kill us?"

"I don't know."

A door slammed, and a woman screamed, "*Claxton. Oh, Claxton, he'll kill you.*"

That voice. A familiar one. Footsteps sounded on the snow. Claxton's head went up, turning sideways toward the inn. Sophia knew that for her own safety she should cower beneath him, but curiosity compelled her to see who screamed and ran toward them. She raised up onto her elbows.

"Bloody hell," he uttered, his cheek pressed to hers.

Lady Meltenbourne bounded toward them, a vision of blue silk, bouncing breasts, and blonde hair.

"*Don't kill him,*" she screamed, arms flung high.

She hurled herself against Claxton, knocking him off Sophia. At the same time, another figure sprang into the melee. Lord Haden burst out from the front door of the inn, coatless and shirttails flapping, a pistol in each hand. Sophia scrambled around so as to watch him, keeping low. His boots thunked heavily as he descended the wooden steps on long legs. Glassy red eyes set within his lean face surveyed the courtyard. His hair, a measure longer than Claxton's, rippled in the wind, giving him a wild and dangerous appearance.

"Claxton, it's your brother," Sophia exclaimed to the struggling heap beside her. "He's trying to kill you!"

She attempted to scoot backward over the snow, but her legs tangled in layers of petticoats. The faces of villagers peeked out from the windows, wide-eyed and openmouthed, some with steaming mugs raised.

A man's voice shouted from inside, "Not the windows. Please, my lord. Spare the glass if you will."

"I'm not trying to kill Claxton," Haden bellowed, scowling.

Another shot echoed in the quiet, striking a distant patch of ground.

He whirled, aiming his firearms at the upper floor of the inn. "Lord Meltenbourne is trying to kill Claxton. Take cover."

Chapter Seven

Sophia felt herself jerked from behind and twisted round. Claxton lifted her high and carried her like a child against his chest, depositing her in the shelter of a stone wall.

"Are you hurt?" he demanded ferociously, his brows gathered and nostrils flared. His hand came to her cheek, forcing her gaze to his.

"No."

"Are you certain?" His hands roamed her shoulders, arms, breasts, hips, and legs. She gasped at the intimate touch. "Sometimes when you've been shot, you don't know it. Sometimes you don't feel the pain until later."

Again, his hand paused on her cheek, and she clasped it there. "I'm not hurt, Claxton."

He nodded, dragging the pad of his thumb across her cheek, a tender gesture that conflicted with the anger in his eyes. "Stay here, behind the wall."

But as soon as he was gone, Sophia crawled low against

the cornerstone, desperate for his safety. No matter how miserable he made her, she would never wish him dead.

At the center of the lane, Lady Meltenbourne still lay sobbing, facedown in the snow. She wore no coat or cloak, only the gown she'd worn since Lord Wolverton's birthday party the night before. Haden had backed into a position to shield her, pistols cocked and ready. He prodded her with the heel of his Hessian.

"Blast you, chit," he shouted. "Gather yourself up and get behind that wall."

Claxton, like the hero Sophia had only moments before proclaimed him *not* to be, headed straight for the countess, never breaking pace until he grabbed hold of her arms. The sight was undeniably thrilling, other than the unfortunate reality that her husband was rescuing a woman who made no secret of wanting him as her lover.

"Here the bastard comes again," Haden warned, lifting his weapons. From the shadowed interior of an upper window appeared a diminutive man wearing an old-fashioned tricorn hat and saggy trews. He wielded a pistol in one hand and an earthenware jug in the other.

"Think ye'll cuckold me, do ye?" he squalled drunkenly.

Haden pulled his trigger. *Crack.* The weapon recoiled. The earl's tricorn spiraled off, exposing his bald pate. Another shot—Meltenbourne's—sounded an instant later.

A fan of white pitched upward, inches from Claxton's boot.

"Claxton," Sophia shouted or perhaps screamed. If he died now, leaving her with the memory of that kiss, she did not know what she would do.

Lady Meltenbourne remained as limp as a child's doll. The duke hoisted her over his shoulder and carried her to the same location where Sophia crouched. Haden followed, his pistol trained on the window.

Just then a loud crash sounded from inside the inn. A mob of men, arms flailing, overwhelmed the earl. Curses echoed across the lane, loudly at first, then dimmer as they dragged their prisoner inside.

Lady Meltenbourne sobbed, throwing her arms around Claxton's legs. "You saved my life."

Haden muttered a curse and rolled his eyes.

Claxton pried the countess off him and lifted her to stand. With a firm nudge, he guided her toward Sophia as if she were a sticky-faced child with hands covered in jam to be handed off to her mother. Annabelle's teeth chattered, and she shivered. While Sophia could not bring herself to put an arm around the woman, perhaps by not stepping away, Annabelle benefited to some degree from her warmth and would not catch her death of cold.

Claxton blasted a frigid glare at his brother. "Why, may I ask, is Lord Meltenbourne trying to kill me?"

Haden shifted his stance and polished the barrel of his pistol against his cuff. "Er...well, because he believes you had a tryst with his wife last night."

Sophia's heart stopped beating, her first instinct, however fleeting, to believe what Haden said.

"How interesting." Claxton's nostrils flared. "I don't recall having any tryst with his wife."

"Mere details." Haden's chuckle carried an edge of anxiety. He holstered the firearm at his waist. "Thankfully, everything turned out well. We are all still alive."

The tension in Sophia's shoulders eased. Haden's response corroborated Claxton's story of the night before. Not that it mattered. They were to be separated soon. Weren't they? Why had Claxton kissed her like that and thrown everything into confusion?

The duke fisted his hand in his brother's cravat and slammed him against the stone wall.

"Ow!" Haden bellowed, eyes clamped shut in visible pain.

"Please," wailed Lady Meltenbourne. "Don't fight over me. You are brothers. Family."

Sophia experienced the bizarre urge to laugh.

Claxton shouted into Haden's face, "You would make light of such an untruth in front of my wife? Meltenbourne could have killed the duchess."

Haden's hands came up beside his head in surrender. "Last night, when I awakened in yonder inn with Lord Meltenbourne's pistol pointed in my face, demanding to know where you were, I felt no compulsion to immediately set the matter aright."

"It's just like you to take the easy way out, leaving the mess for someone else to clean up." Claxton released him with a snarl. "You will apologize to her Grace."

With a firm tug, Haden straightened the front of his rumpled waistcoat. Meeting Sophia's gaze, he said, "My sincerest apologies, Duchess. I intended you no disrespect. I'm sincere when I say that."

Sophia nodded, feeling it only right to acknowledge his apology, which appeared earnestly spoken.

"I've never had a pistol pointed to my face," she replied. "I imagine the experience might momentarily alter one's priorities as far as truth."

Even so, Haden's failure to set the matter straight only complicated the calamity of her marriage. Certainly the whole village, no matter how buried in snow, buzzed with the scandal.

To Claxton, Haden said, "Why are you here after all? You should have remained at Camellia House. The situation would have calmed once the brandy ran out."

They crossed the small courtyard toward the inn, Sophia at Claxton's side. Lady Meltenbourne trailed along behind, her arms embracing her own shoulders. As they crossed the threshold, the villagers crowding the windows fell back against the far wall, a silent ripple of head bobs and curtsies. What was more mortifying? That they had just witnessed a gun battle involving her husband and his brother and an earl who shouted allegations of cuckoldry, or that moments before they may have witnessed her and Claxton's unseemly kiss?

Sophia blinked, her eyesight adjusting to the dark interior, as the common room returned to its customary movement and clamor. Despite the awkwardness of their entrance, the mingled scents of burning wood, ale, and gingerbread delighted her senses, as did the room's warmth. Christmas greenery hung above the fire and over the windows. Mistletoe encircled a chandelier at the center of the room. Curiously, beneath the wooden light fixture sat the plainest girl Sophia had ever seen, wearing a mulish expression and a shapeless sack of a cloak. Though villagers crowded the floor, the circle of space around the girl spoke painful volumes, so much so that Sophia momentarily forgot her own troubles.

From the floor above came bellows and thumps, evidence of a continuing struggle to subdue Lord Meltenbourne. Claxton lowered her valise to the carpet and without further preamble disarmed Haden of his pistol.

"I'll be gone only a moment." Firearm in hand, he climbed the steps. Haden muttered something about duty and followed.

"Gor! 'E looks just like the old duke, 'e does," a wizened old man marveled.

"Eerie so," said another.

"Let's 'ope the similarities only go so far as 'is looks."

"Indeed."

A woman wearing a brisk but amiable expression emerged from the shadows and bobbed. "Your Grace?"

"Yes."

The woman smiled warmly. "I am Mrs. Stone. My husband and I, Mr. Stone, keep this humble inn. May I say what an honor it is to have the duke and your Grace visit our establishment. The whole village has waited with hopeful anticipation these past three years for the new Duke of Claxton to visit."

"Thank you, Mrs. Stone. And may I say what a fine inn you have here and smelling so delightfully of gingerbread."

The innkeeper flushed deeply, two bright apples on her cheeks. "Anything to keep old Jack Frost at the door so we might enjoy this Christmas."

"I've rarely seen such a heavy snowfall. I must admit to coming into the village to discover if travel into London might be possible today."

"Oh no, madam." She let out a wry chuckle. "There's far too much snowfall on the roads for the post chaise to make it through and great sheets of ice floating on the river. Certainly not enough for a frost fair, but enough to keep the barges in for safety. No one is willing to go out after the tragedy three years ago."

"What tragedy was this?"

Mrs. Stone's face grew solemn. "One of the local barge masters thought to bring one last load of coal over, but ice converged. Crushed the barge it did, and the vessel sank. Both him and his middle boy perished. A terrible loss for the family, and indeed, the entire village."

"Yes, I could see that it would be," Sophia murmured. "How awful."

No matter how strong her desire to escape Claxton, she would never ask anyone to endanger their life for her convenience or comfort. And so it seemed she would be lodging in Lacenfleet for at least one more night.

Mrs. Stone added, "It won't be the first time we've been snowbound here in Lacenfleet, and it won't be the last. We are as prepared as we can possibly be, if only to sit by the fire and wait for the thaw."

Her situation confirmed, Sophia allowed herself to be led to an upholstered armchair, which a luxurious blue cloak was draped over, a garment she recognized from the night before. With a mirthful little snort, Mrs. Stone tossed the cloak onto a less commodious, ramshackle chair several feet farther away from the hearth.

"The mistletoe is very festive," remarked Sophia. "And the garland hung over the fire."

The inn mistress straightened the cushion. "Some of the older folk claim it is bad luck to hang greenery before Christmas Eve, but I pay them no mind. Lacenfleet's luck can't get much worse, I say." She chuckled wryly, and at the corner of her eyes, her temples crinkled.

Sophia had the distinct impression Mrs. Stone wished

her to inquire more about Lacenfleet's luck, and so she complied.

Mrs. Stone clasped her hands in front of her apron. "Bad crops. No work. It happens to everyone. Things will improve, I vow, but it makes a dreary Christmas for some. I'll tell you one thing, though." She lowered her voice. "If his lordship decided to open Camellia House and staff her right, there'd be no shortage of qualified household help."

"I'll be certain to tell his Grace." She could always write him a letter once she returned to London, but she didn't know if her word would hold any sway.

Sophia's gaze fell again on the center of the room, where the girl still sat, arms crossed, under the chandelier. "How long has that young woman been sitting there under the mistletoe? I can only assume she is waiting for a kiss from some handsome young fellow?"

"That's Charlotte, the poor dear." Mrs. Stone sighed and shook her head. "Too old now to remain in the orphan house where she grew up, she just hasn't found her place. She's been doing a bit of scullery for Mr. Stone and me in exchange for a place to sleep in the kitchen, but I'm not certain how long we'll be able to keep her."

Fine brown hair hung limply against Charlotte's cheek, and the petticoat she wore was hopelessly frayed. Yet the girl sat in the chair proudly, shoulders back, her face a portrait of pride and determination. Everything about the girl touched Sophia's heart.

"She wants a kiss that badly?"

"Not only a kiss, I'm afraid." Mrs. Stone winked. "She wants a husband. That leggy farmer in the tall boots over there, to be exact, a widower with two young children in desperate need of a mother. Only he hasn't looked at her once in the two hours he's been here. Unfortunately, neither has anyone else."

"How disheartening for Charlotte."

Once Sophia was settled, Mrs. Stone pressed a warm mug into her hands and brought a plate of gingerbread for the side table. Sophia inhaled the tea's fragrant steam and sampled the bread, determining the blend of spices to be superior to her own London cook's recipe. Above her head, Claxton's voice thundered, incomprehensible.

Lady Meltenbourne approached, her gaze settling waspishly on Sophia. With a huff, she sank into the inferior chair and with a dramatic wave of her arm draped herself in the cloak. Taking up a small beaded reticule, from which she extracted a mirror, she stared at her reflection, pinched her cheeks, and pursed her lips. Only Sophia realized Annabelle wasn't looking into the mirror, but at her. Upon being caught, the countess looked away.

Sophia leaned forward in her chair. "You're a married woman. A countess." She kept her voice low so that only Annabelle could hear. "Don't you care what people think about you and Lord Meltenbourne? What they say?"

"Of course I do. Do you think I wanted all of this attention?" Annabelle snapped, waving a hand to generally indicate the inn and its occupants. "The earl, when he drinks, becomes the most irrational and churlish creature. He is furious with me, but I am just as furious with him—but...but...oh, I don't really want to talk about it to you."

The countess twisted away, signaling an immediate end to their conversation. That suited Sophia just as well because she had nothing more to say to the woman, at least nothing an inn full of villagers should overhear. Instead she contented herself with sipping her tea, fuming silently, and listening to the villagers' lively talk.

"Don't matter if 'e's an earl. Can't have 'im goin' about shootin' at people," said one young woman, counting out several stacks of playing cards.

"Right so," agreed her partner in the game. "We can't 'ave murder in the streets. Not this close to Christmas."

Sophia sighed morosely, at last acknowledging that which she ought to have acknowledged from the start. Her rash decision to escape Claxton by coming to Lacenfleet had indeed been folly. With her grandfather's health being so precarious, she simply could not miss Christmas. What if this was his last? What if even now he had taken a turn for the worse? She couldn't bear the thought. She had six days to get home. Certainly this winter storm would not imprison her here until then.

"The poor duchess," whispered one of the women, but loudly and plain enough for Sophia to hear. "So young and pretty, forced to abide 'is lordship's strumpet sitting *right there*."

Someone shushed her sharply.

Sophia's hand tightened on the cup. *The poor duchess.* That would be her. Annabelle, seemingly oblivious, murmured something to the woman beside her. The woman glared at her and with a huff moved to the opposite end of the table.

Unaffected, Annabelle queried the room in general. "Does anyone know how to properly dress a lady's hair?"

It took all the strength Sophia owned to remain seated. She had the sudden, overwhelming urge to "dress" Annabelle's hair with a good, savage tug.

Boots sounded on the stairs. Again, the villagers fell

into rapt silence. Haden appeared first, then Claxton, two lithe giants emerging from shadows.

The duke's gaze searched the room, but stopped upon finding her. Her pulse leapt and her mouth went dry.

How would she ever forget their kiss? She feared that, like a mortal sickness, that moment of passion had gone into her blood. How else could she explain the jumpy excitement that overtook her body the moment he'd reappeared—not to mention the feverish flush that rose to her cheeks and...other parts of her body, she felt quite certain. Without a word, Claxton returned the pistol handle-first to his brother.

A cluster of men emerged from the shadowed stair-way behind the duke. Sophia recognized them as their carriage drivers and footmen. They escorted a churlish Lord Meltenbourne, whom they deposited in a corner chair, and two of them remained to stand guard. Each retainer bore the rumpled clothing and weary expression of a difficult night passed. Apparently no one who had undertaken the trip to Camellia House the evening before had ever made it out of the village.

Meanwhile the countess had found a sympathetic friend, an old village woman who held a large hearing trumpet to her ear.

"Last night I had to sleep here in my ball gown." Annabelle lifted a length of her silk overskirt now hopelessly crushed and streaked by melted snow. "Without even a maid to assist me."

"Pardon?" shouted the woman, leaning in closer, thrusting the open end of the metal tube nearer to Annabelle's mouth.

From his chair in the corner, her husband squawked,

"Then you ought to learn to stay home, where you belong."

Annabelle sagged and lifted her hand to her forehead. She issued a low, suffering moan.

Claxton spoke to the most senior of his drivers. "I take it, then, by your presence here that the river is frozen and the ferry out of service?"

Sophia sank an inch in her chair, having no desire to hear her unfortunate circumstances once again confirmed.

"Indeed, sir." The elder man nodded, his face weary beneath his cap. "Lord Meltenbourne's conveyance came over last, with none the rest of us granted return passage for fear the ferry barge would be confined midway by ice. We all slept with the horses in the stables last night, save Lord Haden and Lord and Lady Meltenbourne, of course, who took rooms above stairs on account of their elevated personages. The innkeepers have been most kind."

"Well, then." Claxton nodded, throwing a darkly satisfied look at Sophia. "There is nothing more to be done than to wait out the frost. For now, I would like to see the stables, if you please, and view the horses' accommodations for myself." To Sophia, he said, "You'll be well here until I return?"

She nodded over her raised mug. "Oh yes. I have gingerbread."

In fact, she'd be very well here in Mr. and Mrs. Stone's inn until tomorrow or the next day if necessary.

If the kiss they'd shared outside in the snow was any indication of what could occur when they were alone together, without question, she must not allow such a thing to happen again. Kisses like that enslaved, and there would be nothing worse than being enslaved to a man like Claxton, who could never be enslaved back. Hadn't she learned well enough the first time? She'd fallen so desperately in love with him, but in the end, her love had not been enough to hold him. She wouldn't be so foolish as to make the same mistake again.

Knowing she had better confirm her arrangements before he returned, she set aside her cup and stood. Across the room sat a man who wore an apron that matched Mrs. Stone's. It was to him she made her request.

The innkeeper looked at her with no small amount of surprise. Doubtless he could not imagine any circumstances under which the Duchess of Claxton would prefer a smoky, overcrowded village inn to the grand-by-comparison manse on the hill.

"I regret, your Grace, that we've only three rooms and all of them occupied. Unless Lady Meltenbourne will agree to share accommodations—"

"That won't do, I'm afraid," Sophia answered. She turned away, at a loss as to what to do.

Annabelle stood in front of Sophia. "If you're so set on staying here, you can have my room." One of her narrow eyebrows lifted. "I'll go to the house with Claxton."

Sophia's mouth popped open, and the skin of her scalp prickled with fury. She glanced around to be certain that no one had heard the countess's brazen suggestion. While she didn't think they had, everyone in the room appeared to be watching them and waiting for a fight.

"You go too far, Annabelle," she hissed.

The young woman blinked prettily. "I've never met a

duchess with a healthy sense of humor. Do you forfeit it when you marry, or are you born and bred that way?"

Mr. Stone suddenly appeared and gave a little bow. "I beg your pardon, your Grace, for interrupting, but Lord Meltenbourne has offered to sleep in the common room tonight so that your Grace may have his quarters. Madam, would that be agreeable to you?"

Sophia glanced across the room toward the earl. He tilted his head and smiled. "It would be my pleasure, Duchess."

The two footmen who acted as his guards chuckled in amusement.

A sudden presence blocked the light from the hearth, casting them in shadows.

"Those arrangements are most certainly not agreeable," said Claxton, his voice low and dangerous. "Not to me. The duchess will accompany me to Camellia House."

"Yes, your Grace," rasped Mr. Stone, giving a little bow and backing away from them as quickly as his legs could take him.

The heat in Claxton's stare left Sophia breathless but also angry that he should intercede in the conversation so brutishly.

"I am not your chattel to be claimed and ordered about," she hissed.

He bent low so that his breath touched her cheek. "Until the papers are drawn up and signed, I am still your husband in every sense of the word. You will not humiliate me by taking a room in this inn."

"If it's humiliation you were hoping to avoid," she choked out, "I'm afraid it's far too late for that."

Moments later, nearer to the door, the innkeeper's wife

pressed a basket containing bread, cheese, and two roasted guinea fowls into Sophia's hands. Once Claxton returned from speaking with Mr. Stone about the continued room and board of his male servants, they would be on their way. Sophia felt like crying, what with the inn being so warm and she'd only just begun to feel her legs and feet again.

Only then did she see that Charlotte no longer sat beneath the mistletoe. Instead the girl occupied the chair Sophia had vacated just moments before. Lady Meltenbourne stood behind her, a little comb in her hand.

"So you see, dear Miss Charlotte, I will dress your hair in pins and curls, and once you understand how it is done, you can dress mine. Every young lady deserves to have pretty hair for the holiday, and we two are no exception."

Charlotte's face reflected a degree of emotion somewhere between terror and delight. "Thank you, my lady. I'm certainly willing to try my best."

Annabelle combed out a section of her hair. "When I was young, my father refused to hire a lady's maid for me and my three sisters, proclaiming it to be a frivolous expense, so we all learned how to dress each other's hair. Now I'm such a spoiled woman I have not only one lady's maid, but two, one to attend to my hair and daily toilette, and the other, my clothes and my dogs. My dogs! I can't think about Diamond and Pearl now, or I will start to cry." She dabbed at her eyes. After a moment in which she appeared to calm herself, she said, "Hair is very easy— really it is—once you learn how to section everything properly. I only hope I have enough pins."

Claxton joined Sophia and Mrs. Stone.

"A moment please," said Sophia, handing off the basket to Claxton. She bent over her valise. A moment later she approached the countess and Charlotte.

"Lady Meltenbourne, I overheard you say you might not have enough." She extended the little case toward Annabelle, who paused in her combing and sectioning to stare at her, wide-eyed and mouth agape. "I have plenty to spare."

Charlotte gave a happy little gasp and her face lit up like a Christmas candle.

"Thank you, your Grace," she gushed. "You and the countess have been more than kind."

Annabelle reached for the case, her gaze fixed on Sophia. Her eyes welled with tears.

"Yes," she smiled tremulously. "More than kind."

Sophia rejoined Claxton, and he led her toward the door, his hand at the small of her back, for all outward appearances an attentive husband. Yet one glance confirmed the taut line of his jaw, evidence his anger remained over her request for a room at the inn.

Haden followed, twisting a scarf round his neck.

"Where are you going?" Claxton retrieved her valise.

"With you," Haden said, "to Camellia House. There's more room there, and no one who wants to shoot me unless you're angrier than I thought. I promise not to be a bother."

"You already are a bother. You'll stay here and deal with the consequences of your own mess."

Haden sputtered, but Claxton pulled the door firmly closed on any argument before it began.

Outdoors, he released her, his hand coming away from her arm as if he'd only just realized she were a piece of rotten fruit.

"I don't believe my eyes," he bit out. "Now you are on happy terms with Lady Meltenbourne? Truly, Sophia? Are the two of you in collusion to humiliate me? And taking a room at the inn?"

"Taking a room seemed the reasonable thing to do, given our present circumstances."

"Our 'present circumstances' indeed. We wouldn't want those to improve, would we?" He returned his hat to his head and with an air of disdain descended the snow-encrusted steps. "Whatever it is that you fear will happen again when we are alone, don't worry, it won't."

"What do you mean?"

"You know what I mean," he muttered fiercely, boots sinking into the snow with each step away from her.

And she did know. He would not kiss her again.

"Suits me perfectly," she called after him. "All for the best. I didn't enjoy it anyway." But her turncoat heart shouted out apologies for having betrayed him.

He barked out a laugh but did not slow in pace.

Snow fell at a slant across the lane, carried on a sturdy wind. With a deep sigh, she set off to follow in the plowed-out rut Claxton's boots had created, dreading the night to come, for certainly the coming hours would be spent in frozen silence, sequestered in her room.

Only when Claxton reached the end of the lane did he pause to wait for her, impatience twitching his jaw.

Just then, a man driving an old-fashioned sledge drawn by an enormous black draft horse came into view from the direction of Camellia House. Bells jangled musically with each step the animal took. With a "Ho!" to Claxton, the man tugged the reins and circled round. After exchanging words, Claxton came for Sophia.

"This is Mr. Kettle. He informs me that after learning of our arrival in Lacenfleet, he and Mrs. Kettle went to the house. He came looking for us and has kindly offered to convey you up the hill."

Drawing nearer, Sophia saw that the sledge had only room for one.

"What about you?" She looked at Claxton.

"Go, please," he answered, stone-faced. "I'd rather prefer the time alone."

Stung, she instantly regretted her concern.

A moment later, with Sophia tucked warmly under a blanket, Mr. Kettle tapped his cane and the sledge lurched forward to glide through the snow. Vapor streamed from the horse's nostrils. Under any other circumstances, she would have found the experience charming, but she had never felt more dejected and alone.

At the bend in the road, Sophia leaned out to search behind for Claxton but saw only a dark shadow amid a veil of falling snow. She hated this confusion! If she truly didn't want to be near him, then why did leaving him behind make her feel so miserable?

Chapter Eight

$\mathcal{V}$ane had not long with his thoughts because Mr. Kettle returned in the sledge immediately after safely delivering her ladyship. Not that he had accepted the ride. To do so would require a person of his stature to sit awkwardly with his knees knocking his ears for the sole purpose of sparing himself a quarter-hour walk. So instead of fuming over his wife's humiliating request for a room at the inn—and after she'd bloody well kissed his Hessians off, no less—Mr. Kettle provided welcome distraction, traveling along beside Claxton to discuss matters related to the property.

After that brief passage of time, Vane entered the vestibule.

Over the previous twenty years, there had been moments when he had faced the worst mankind had to offer, in life and on the battlefront, with barely an increase in pulse. Yet now, as he stamped the snow from his boots on the threshold of the old house, he struggled to calm the low thrum of trepidation in his blood, one that urged him to immediately turn and run.

Just as he knew she would, a small woman rushed toward him out of the shadows and out from his past, her hands clasped to her plump cheeks.

Eyes full of tears, she exclaimed, "Your Grace. It is you." Her bright gaze took him in admiringly, head to toe. "A man full grown."

A thousand memories crushed in on him with such force he immediately drew up his defenses lest he be overwhelmed.

It was, of course, Mrs. Kettle, a woman who, like so many pieces of his shattered childhood, he had left behind. Only he hadn't ever forgotten her.

Since he had last seen her, her hair had grayed and she had almost certainly shrunk by a foot. For a terrifying moment, he feared she might actually embrace him, and if she did, he would most certainly fall to pieces and cry like a child.

"Oh!" she exclaimed, her face going instantly serious. "Sir, I do forget myself."

With the utmost gravity, she curtsied, then winced and wobbled, her discomfort at executing the gesture all too apparent.

His mother's household had never been one for strict formalities. Vane suspected the woman who had acted as the Duchess of Claxton's housekeeper, and indeed, her maid of all work, had not only been a loyal servant, but also in the end her closest friend. Though he required the utmost in decorum from his retainers in town, he considered Mrs. Kettle and her husband exempt from such strictures.

He gently assisted her up. "How pleased I am to see you as well."

Mr. Kettle appeared behind his wife, having insisted on driving the sledge round back and entering the house as he always did through the servants' door. The stooped old fellow, who had once towered like a giant, acted the part of footman, taking Vane's coat, hat, and gloves. Sophia, now absent her hat and redingote, joined them as well.

"His Grace was sixteen years old last time I saw him," Mrs. Kettle said to Sophia. In that moment two avenues of his life collided, his past and his present, leaving him breathless. The housekeeper sniffled and snorted into a handkerchief.

Sixteen years old. Vane could barely remember that boy. He felt a thousand years older now.

Quickly recovering, Mrs. Kettle smiled. "Mr. Kettle and I have waited all this time for his lordship to return. We long ago took residence in the village, but these last few years have kept the house in readiness, as much as two old souls could, with a bed made up in clean linens, in hopes you would return. We were thrilled to receive her Grace's missive indicating she would visit, but did not expect her—nor you—until after Christmas. I pray these simplest of accommodations have met with your approval."

"They are more than enough," he assured.

She sighed in relief. "Our apologies for not having come sooner. I've two confined mothers on opposite ends of the village. Within a space of mere days Lacenfleet will have not only one, but two new citizens, perhaps in time for Christmas."

Mrs. Kettle had acted as the village midwife in the past and apparently still did. That service had always held a certain poignancy, as she and Mr. Kettle had never been blessed with children of their own.

She clasped her hands together, leaning forward. "Which is why Mr. Kettle and I only just learned of your arrival. We had passed the night at the Martindale home, you see, believing the babe would arrive last night, but it was not to be."

Mr. Kettle chuckled. "They come in their own time."

"Indeed they do," Vane agreed, though he knew little of the subject.

He caught Sophia smiling at him. He knew what she believed, that this was a happy reunion between the lord of the manor and dutiful servants, a time for joy and re-membrances. Though very much true, his homecoming involved more complicated emotions than that. There were reasons why he hadn't returned before now.

"This way, my lord." Mrs. Kettle extended an arm. "My lady."

Mrs. Kettle led them into the great room, where a small table had been laid out beside the hearth, and upon it, several covered dishes. Here, a fire warmed the air, as well as the fragrance of something tantalizingly delicious.

"What is all this?" Vane asked.

Sophia came to stand beside him. "Mrs. Kettle has brought us supper."

As a soldier, he had long ago grown accustomed to go-ing days without food. It was only now, upon inhaling such marvelous scents, that he realized how ravenous he was. When *had* he eaten last? The day before yesterday, upon disembarking in Dover, he'd been too filled with anticipation about reuniting with Sophia to seek out a meal, and he'd remained so. Then last night in London the whole world had gone to hell, leaving food the last thing from his mind.

"And look," added Sophia. "She's even decorated in honor of the season."

Indeed, she had. A garland of greenery now adorned the mantel top. Sprigs of the same stuff sprouted from atop the portraits and art hung about the room. A scraping sound came from behind them. Vanc turned to see Mr. Kettle climbing onto a chair beneath the chandelier. A sphere swung from the chain in his hand, formed of holly, red apples, ivy, and damnably, mistletoe.

"It just wouldn't feel like Christmas without the kissing bough, now, would it?" Mrs. Kettle clapped her hands in delight.

"The kissing bough."

Vane's eyes widened, and he blurted, "You mustn't trouble yourself.

"Nonsense," said Mr. Kettle. "It's good to have young people in the house again. Oh—" He wobbled atop the chair and waved his arms for balance.

"Help him," urged Sophia.

"Careful there." Vane lunged forward, steadying the chair, and took hold of his elbow. "But again, you really shouldn't have bothered yourselves."

"Claxton," Sophia chastised softly, lifting a finger to her lips.

Once the chain was fastened, he assisted the old fellow down.

"Success!" Mr. Kettle grinned. After an extended period of silence where they all looked at one another, Mr.

Kettle said, "Don't tell me I went through all that trouble for naught."

Mrs. Kettle glowed with expectation.

Then suddenly, Sophia moved toward him, her dark hair shining like silk in the candlelight. The color of her cheeks had deepened to dark pink and her eyes sparkled brilliant and bright.

"Claxton can be so prudish," she declared in a teasing voice.

He stared at her hard, raising one eyebrow at her taunt, unable to contain the fiery combustion inside his chest. Prudish? If she only knew the decidedly *un*prudish thoughts presently forming in his mind. She shouldn't play with him. Not now, after kissing him so passionately outside the inn, only to show him and the rest of the world the kiss had meant nothing. Not after he'd come a breath from losing her to a drunken man's bullet. A low growl rumbled from his throat. "It's just a kiss," she whispered tersely.

Vexatious termagant.

She did this for the Kettles, in an effort to please the endearing couple who had already won her heart. Not for him who had lost it.

His gaze dropped to her mouth, so soft and plush, to the feminine curve of her collarbone, just visible above the high neckline of her winter dress. She couldn't know that their kiss in the snow outside the inn had awakened a raving beast inside him, one that at this moment bayed with need. If she did, she wouldn't ask this of him. She wouldn't stand so provokingly close, within the circle of his shadow.

Blood pounded in his ears. The muscles along his

spine tightened. He grazed her cheek with his fingertips, the barest caress. Lifting her chin, he bent, touching his lips to hers in a kiss so different from the one before. Controlled and respectable and torturously sweet—

And over almost before it began.

Sophia stepped back, laughing and smiling as if they'd done nothing but cordially shake hands. While wearing gloves.

"Thank you, Mr. and Mrs. Kettle," she exclaimed. "You thought of everything."

"Wonderful!" The housekeeper sighed. "So romantic."

"A most merry Christmas," declared Mr. Kettle.

Vane watched Sophia drift away and exhaled through his nose. His body raged in complaint at being so cruelly denied. If not for the Kettles' presence, he would reach out and pull her back into his arms.

"Sir and madam, please sit at the table." The older woman smiled. "Since reading the announcement of your marriage in the papers, it has been my greatest wish to prepare a meal for you and your duchess."

She lifted the covers from two plates set close together, side by side, in what could only be described as romantic proximity.

"I had something finer in mind, but this will have to do." She folded her hands and glanced downward in self-deprecation. "While certainly not the extravagant fare of your fancy town cook, a rabbit stew will warm your stomach and see you through until the morrow. Please sit, your Grace."

Vane looked at Sophia to find her peering back at him.

She whispered, "I think the only polite thing to do is to enjoy the meal Mrs. Kettle has prepared."

"For once, we are in agreement." Vane gestured, indicating that she should sit, and followed her. The heat from the fire warmed his back and shoulders, relaxing him instantly. He did not miss, however, when Sophia discreetly scooted her chair so as to add several more inches of space between them.

The old woman straightened the tablecloth, fussed over the dishes, and issued orders to her husband to fill their glasses with claret.

"And a cup of negus, as well, for you both." Mrs. Kettle settled two more glasses onto the table.

"Mrs. Kettle, you ought not to have gone through all of this trouble." Even as Vane said it, his cheeks flushed with pleasure. The housekeeper's did as well, pleased by his compliment. Mrs. Kettle had always been a marvelous cook and her meals the stuff of his non-Sophia-related fantasies.

Beside him, Sophia sat small and elegant. His blood thrummed, his every sense heightened with her nearness. But that was not all. He felt pride that she was his wife, that she sat beside him so appreciative of the Kettles' simple gift.

When her small hand touched his arm, something in his gut twisted, bending him to her will before even hearing her request. With a tilt of her head, she directed his attention to the window, with its intricate tracery of frost, where Mr. Kettle silently fretted.

"It will be dark soon," she murmured intimately. "Tell them to go home."

Ah, yes. He ought to have noticed.

Vane stood. "I've been so distracted by the gift of this wonderful meal that I've forgotten the time and circumstances of the weather outside. I really must insist that the both of you return to the village."

That would leave him alone with Sophia again, an inevitability that should not fill him with such wicked anticipation, but did.

Mrs. Kettle clasped her hands at the front of her apron in the pose of a dutiful servant. "Sir, we are more than prepared to remain in residence to attend you for the duration of your stay."

Though her eyes remained warm, a faint tension worried her brow and thinned her lips. He read her expression easily, recalling it from his youth.

"Nonsense," he answered. "Those young women and their unborn babes need you more than we do. And I insist, you must take the sledge."

"Oh, sir." She bent her head in servile deference. "How kind of you to think of them, but my primary duty and loyalty lies here with you and with the memory of your dear mother. Their families will come for me if needed—"

"Dearest, don't argue with his Grace," said Mr. Kettle quietly from his place at the window.

For a moment, the housekeeper appeared to take offense at her husband's rebuke, but then she broke into a wide smile.

"What was I thinking? You and her ladyship are still newlyweds and by nature crave your privacy. That is why you came to Camellia House, is it not? To be alone."

Vane suffered a heated flash of regret that things were not so between him and Sophia. Sophia, for her part, bit her lip and focused renewed interest on the bounty of the table.

"Before I forget." From under her apron, the house-keeper produced a small ring, selecting a narrow brass key from the others. "This one for the linens, and the one beside it"—her smile held a flash of wickedness—"is for the cellar, if you'd care for another bottle of claret, or perhaps, Madeira. The attic, and so on." Though Claxton extended his hand, she gave the keys to Sophia.

And just like that, Vane found himself alone again with his estranged wife.

For the longest while, they ate in silence, each cutting their food into ridiculously small bites, chewing without the slightest sound and displaying the utmost in culinary manners, as if they sat in the presence of His Royal Highness, the Prince Regent himself.

"This stew is delicious," she murmured.

"Indeed."

"And the silence between us completely ridiculous," Sophia said, cutting two portions from a small plum cake.

Vane paused, midchew. "Pardon?"

She deposited the larger of the two slices on his plate. "Even if we plan to separate, we ought to be able to talk with each other."

Separate. The word became no less offensive with repeated use. He flinched as if she'd struck him with the flat of her knife.

"What sort of talk? Inconsequential and meaningless talk?" The question came out sounding surlier than he intended.

He examined her face, always so expressive. She had never hidden anything from him. Never stretched the truth or told him only what he wished to hear. When they'd lost their child, he had shunned that honesty, not wanting to face what she must think of him, for certainly her sentiments could be no worse than his own. But in recent months, he'd come to crave that honesty. He wanted it now—an authentic conversation between them.

She tilted her head and then nodded. The firelight reflected off her dark hair and the softly rounded curve of her cheek. "There is value in polite conversation."

"Not to me."

She drew back defensively and sniffed. "Very well. If you don't want to talk—"

His first instinct at having offended her was to grab her hand and pull her closer for another kiss as the last had been cut so appallingly short. But he had no right, not after what they'd decided last night.

"I did not say that," he said. He shifted toward her and rested his arm along the upper frame of the chair. "I only said I don't want to talk nonsense."

"Well," she began hopefully. "I like horses and know you do as well. Why don't we talk about horses?"

"No."

Sophia scowled and her green eyes flared. "No need to be peevish. You choose the topic."

Amazing how a delicious meal and a glass of good wine could bring focus to one's perspective. He'd been so certain until now that he'd somehow fail as a gentleman or fail Sophia by not following through on her demand for a separation. There had to be another way. An arrangement that could serve both their needs and purposes. He did not want to lose her, and certainly his proper little wife did not want scandal. What sort of negotiator simply walked away, relinquishing territory he so passionately desired to keep?

"Let us talk about our marriage."

Dark lashes lowered against her cheeks, shuttering her eyes. He loved when she did that. She couldn't know how seductive that small movement was. She poked her fork at the center of her cake. "I don't know what else there is to say."

His heart clenched on the finality of her words. There *was* so much more to say. He had only to compel himself to say it.

Tomorrow morning could very well bring a break in the frost, and they would be back where they started this morning, barreling toward separation. Though he might be a fool, he wasn't stupid. If he wanted to diffuse the present situation and preserve Sophia as his wife, it was he who must make the sacrifice. The cavalry did not win the day by refusing to take the field.

Vane exhaled. Cleared his throat, which had tightened with nervousness. "I feel as if I owe you some explanation of myself. Not excuses, mind you. I don't believe in making excuses for imprudent decisions or behavior. But I feel as if last night our conversation ended prematurely and that you as my wife deserve something more."

"I would not disagree." Her shoulders remained rigid and her gaze guarded.

"Mind you." He smiled thinly. "Explanations are not something I'm in the habit of offering. They do not come easily. You see, I have had several years to become quite obnoxiously full of myself."

Sophia let out a laugh, a quiet little sound, and appeared surprised by his humor. Yet her gaze met his only fleetingly.

Her smiles. How he'd missed them. Like sunshine,

they'd once fed his soul. When she'd stopped smiling, his soul had withered. He wanted nothing more than to be the reason she smiled again. He wasn't an idiot. If he wanted to return to her good graces, he would have to regain her trust.

"As an officer in the army," he said, "one's orders are carried out, not questioned."

She lowered her fork to the plate. "Yes."

"And then of course, once I became duke, every sycophant in London came calling, endeavoring to be my new closest friend."

"I know they must have."

He surveyed the room about them. Every familiar panel and beam. "It seems so long ago that Haden and I lived here—"

"You never told me much about your mother or your father," she responded, rather tentatively, it seemed. "You didn't seem to want to."

He nodded. Touching crystal to his lips, he drained the glass of negus and sat silent for a long moment, allowing the resultant languidity to suffuse through his limbs until he felt numbed enough to continue.

"My mother, Elizabeth, had a gentle and loving spirit." Just speaking his mother's name reopened a wound that had only scarred over, but never fully healed. "Her illness came upon her suddenly. In a matter of days, she was gone. The Kettles were a great comfort to my brother and me, and very naïvely, I expected that life would go on with them acting as our surrogate family." He grinned, seeking to assign a lightness that did not exist to the memory. He turned the empty glass in his hand so that the cut crystal caught the firelight and reflected like an illuminated diamond against her skin. "They had always been here, you see, every day, and had no children of their own."

"It's obvious that they hold you very dear." Speaking of the Kettles, her demeanor softened.

He rubbed a hand over his upper lip, bristly from a day's growth. "I ought to have come back before now. It was wrong for me to have waited so long."

"Go on," she urged quietly.

"On the morning of my mother's funeral a conveyance came up the drive. There were footmen and outriders and, of course, a driver, all in full, glorious livery. They were the most magnificent things I'd ever seen. I remember Haden shouting that the king himself had come to pay his respects to our dear mother." Vane glanced at the portrait over the mantel. He breathed through his nose, subduing a low tremor of rage. "But, of course, it wasn't the king."

Beside him, Sophia straightened in her seat, her hands curling into fists upon her lap.

"It was your father," she whispered.

Claxton was silent for several moments before he continued. "What I wouldn't discern until later was that Camellia House, the home I considered a happy paradise, had been intended as my mother's prison. He'd exiled her here years before as punishment for some perceived betrayal. He was like that, you see, his behavior marked by constant paranoia, always accusing those closest to him of offenses and treachery where there were none. Forgiveness was a word of which he had no comprehension. As my mother had no family or protector to prevent this, she remained here at his discretion, virtually imprisoned in near poverty for the remainder of her life."

Sophia whispered, "What could she have done to deserve that?"

"He told Haden and me before the carriage ever left the property that she was a whore."

Sophia's face flushed with sudden fury. "No child should have to hear such an ugly accusation about his mother, especially when the mother is no longer there to defend herself."

"You must understand that she was not a—" he said, his voice suddenly thick.

"Of course she wasn't," Sophia assured.

"She was kind and loving and devoted to Haden and me. The rumor about her running away with a lover and dying in Italy all started with my father. I heard him repeat the same contrived story, over and over, to anyone who would listen. When I contradicted him—well, I did not contradict him again."

That particular whipping had sent him to his bed for three days.

Sophia's face paled. As if she knew. As if she could read the truth of his father's cruelty on his face. How he'd always admired her softer nature and her caring sympathies toward those less fortunate. He did not, however, rest comfortably as a beneficiary of those sentiments himself.

"You were just a boy," she murmured.

He could not stop there. He had to explain himself. Not his father. It's just that one explanation could not come without the other.

"Not for long. Needless to say, having been raised by this so-called whore, I was considered by my father to be completely and utterly lacking in every way. Within days after our being collected from Lacenfleet, he sent Haden to Eton, and I did not see my brother for some years after that."

"What happened to you?"

"The duke preferred that I travel with him from estate to estate, or wherever else his whim took him, and that I learn from private tutors, hand selected by himself. I received an immaculate education worthy of the duchy. But my father took upon himself the duty to educate me to be a man. His sort of man."

"His sort of man," Sophia repeated with a frown and dread in her eyes. "What did that mean, Claxton?"

Vane chose his words carefully, wanting Sophia's understanding but not wishing to reveal the true magnitude of darkness his sire had instilled inside him.

"It means that my first visit to a brothel occurred when I was not yet eleven."

"Vane."

He could not look into her eyes until he was done, not yet. "It means that because violence and the shedding of blood so amused him, he paid the largest and meanest of his servants to challenge me in pugilistic matches, for the enjoyment of him and his friends. I got the living hell beat out of me until I grew strong enough and angry enough to beat the living hell out of them instead."

Sophia shook her head.

Now her hand did go to his arm. He stood from the table, as if unable to bear her touch, not wanting it this way.

"It means that when he discovered I was sneaking away to Lacenfleet to visit the Kettles, he whipped me for, as best as I can determine, humiliating him by preferring the company of lowly country servants to his unquestionable magnificence. To punish the Kettles, he terminated their employment and shuttered this house."

The fire shifted. Sparks burst out, fledgling embers. Realizing the room had grown colder, he took up the poker and with its curled tip pushed the smoldering mass to the center of the grate. Before he stepped away, he added another log.

"That's why you haven't come back before now, isn't it?" said Sophia. "You felt responsible. Claxton, it wasn't your fault."

"Don't pity me," he answered in a low voice. "By that time, I'd already become just like him."

"I don't believe that."

"If I told you the rest"—he lifted his gaze to hers— "you would."

"Then tell me."

Claxton felt the blood drain from his face. He poured the remainder of the claret into his empty glass. "No."

Sophia stared at him with wide, somber eyes.

He eased back into his chair. "Living such a...debauched life, at some point shocking things cease to shock. Things that once had meaning became meaningless. When I think back, I can barely remember my time here. Those days when I was a child. A boy. He is someone I don't know anymore."

"You're the same person. It's just that he hurt you—"

"What I'm trying to explain in the most delicate way possible is that after leaving Camellia House, my occupations, whether in study or recreation, even later after I went into the army, were those of a man without thought of the future or concern for who my way of life might hurt."

"*Oh*," she said simply and looked down at her hands, which were folded in her lap.

He emptied the glass of claret. "It is that reckless past that intruded upon our marriage, or the remnants of it. For that, I am sorry."

A long moment of silence passed.

"Thank you," she said.

He flinched. "God, don't thank me. That isn't why I told you—"

"But I *do* thank you," she said solemnly. "I want to understand and now I believe I do." He did not like her expression, the one that pitied the person he used to be. He wanted her understanding, her forgiveness. Not her compassion.

Frustration fueled impulse and he grasped her hand, leaning close. "My past is enough to get me into hell a thousand times over, but I swear by all that is holy, indeed, on my mother's name, that I have never shared intimacies with another woman after marrying you. And goddamn it, I do not want a separation and certainly not a divorce."

Sophia's eyes widened, and she inhaled deeply, clenching his hand as tightly as he clenched hers.

"I want us to remain married and have another child."

His words echoed in his ears, so he knew he'd gotten them out. God, he'd never talked so much at one time in his life, let alone revealed so much of his soul. He felt naked and ugly and exposed. Would she recoil? Would she throw it all back in his face?

She released him and stood suddenly, going to the window, where she grasped the drapery and peered out.

"I need more time to think."

His soul shrank back into darkness. It was not the response he'd expected.

"Why, when this seems the perfect solution for both of us?" he demanded.

"I'm not certain, not anymore." Sophia walked past him toward the fire and stared into the flames. "While I am grateful that you shared these details with me, because they help me to understand and to forgive, I'm not naïve enough to believe they change our future."

The wounded creature inside him gnashed its teeth. Anger and humiliation warmed his blood. "I bared my soul to you for nothing."

"No," she breathed, turning to him, her hands open at her sides. "Please no. Don't say that. But, Claxton, please understand. I grieved the death of my marriage last night. It is *gone* in my mind and a piece of my heart with it. I don't know if I can go back to the place where we were. There are no guarantees things would be different. I would love to believe our lives hold no more tragedies or trials, but that would be naïve. I just...I just wouldn't be able to survive it all a second time."

"I would not repeat the same mistakes twice. I wouldn't leave you again."

"You say that now. I think you even believe yourself, but I don't know."

Again, despite everything said, they hovered on the edge of good-bye. Regardless of her assurances to the contrary, very likely by his confessions he had pushed her even further away.

Sophia could not read Claxton's expression. Gone were the emotions she'd glimpsed in him moments before. He'd once again become the dispassionate diplomat, seeking to secure a treaty. The quiet ease with which he made the transition from one self to the other unnerved her, but it served as a reminder that she must do the same and fiercely represent her interests.

"But everything is different now," he challenged calmly, his blue eyes piercing her through. "We are speaking like rational people, and I for one acknowledge my mistakes in allowing our marriage to fall into such early disorder. I won't allow things to return to the way they were before. I want to be there."

"Be there? What do you mean?"

"In his—or her—life. I understand you wish for your family to be involved in the child's upbringing—but know this, Sophia—" His voice lowered into a dangerous hush. "I will not be excluded."

Sophia bristled at his tone. He shouldn't be issuing edicts. After all, it was she who continued to hold the cards. If she so wished to proceed with a separation, she would have one whether or not he agreed. But if she wanted a child, she needed his cooperation.

Lord, things were not so confusing when he was on the other side of the Channel and not sitting in front of her, looking at her in a way that stole her breath and blurred all her reasons for wanting a separation in the first place.

"So…" His gaze narrowed. "What can I do to convince you to withdraw your demand for a separation?"

Something in his voice sent a shiver down her spine— the determination of a man who had made the decision to fight for his marriage and who would not waver from that course until he emerged the victor. The realization did not displease her, but she also realized they had two very different ideas of what composed a successful marriage. She wanted a love story, two hearts forever entwined, through good and bad times. Claxton, instead, offered his fidelity and good behavior in hopes of making her stay... which weren't quite the same thing. She couldn't help but ache for more. Of course, in the context of their society, she was the one being unreasonable.

One certainty remained. She wanted a child. A child would bring her some sense of belonging in this partnership and give her ownership of the name she would continue to bear by marriage, separated or not. And perhaps... perhaps she owed it to their future child to try harder to make the marriage work so that he or she might have the benefit of a father's interest and guidance.

What *could* the duke do to assure her, short of falling to his knees and issuing a declaration of love? She knew that would never happen. If it ever did, the words would be misguided and offered only to appease her.

She turned and announced with conviction, "I need to know their names."

Claxton's brows went up. "Whose names?"

"The names of your lovers. Your paramours from before our marriage. And every woman you *kept company* with afterward."

His lips twisted, and his eyes widened. "I can't imagine why. I told you I never broke our vows."

"And I believe you, but as you said, those remnants of your past still affect our future. My request for their names isn't about suspicion or jealousy or so that I can behave vindictively. It's just that if I am to drop my demand for a separation, I don't want to be surprised again. Ambushed. You can't know how it feels. Why, it's sickening. One's head fills with thunder, one's face goes numb, and everyone in the room, even those that didn't hear what was said, knows something is terribly wrong because the Duchess of Claxton looks as if she's been kicked in the stomach." Her hands clenched against the wool of her skirts. "Then there is the whole miserable aftermath of silence. Whispers and pity and *ugh*—even laughter. There are those who take pleasure in the whole scene."

"I do understand." He spoke quietly. "The same took place each time I accompanied my father into a room. He destroyed countless marriages, not just his own." He drew his thumb along his upper lip, a pensive gesture. "Only people never laughed. They did not dare."

"I am clearly not as terrifying as you and your father."

He scowled. "But to tell you their names?"

Claxton wore a rather menacing face now, but she wasn't going to back down. Of course, the idea of learning the names of his old lovers made her squeamish, but she would not enter any agreement with him to continue their marriage and bring an innocent, blameless child to life unless she gained the power and confidence to defend the two of them against attack.

Claxton wouldn't always be there to ducally glare everyone into silence. He would be off again on some diplomatic duty or the other, or in Jamaica or elsewhere, leaving her alone with the same hungry sharks as before. She refused to return to London and the society she knew under the same terms as before.

"I don't want you to say the names aloud." She went to the small escritoire in the corner and rummaged in the drawer until she came away with a quill pen, ink, and paper. "Write them."

She moved aside several of the dishes on the table and placed the writing implements in front of him.

"I don't want to write them," he answered obstinately. He crossed his arms over his chest, refusing to take possession of the quill.

She drew back. "Then things will proceed no further between you and me."

"This is the only way?" he demanded, incredulous, glaring down at the blank page.

"The only way."

He snatched the quill from her hand.

"Very well. As you wish." Lips pressed thin, he extracted a penknife from his coat pocket and expertly trimmed the pen's nib. Sophia shook the bottle of ink and after several efforts managed to twist the lid free.

"You're certain this is what you want." He scrutinized her.

"I am."

"This is highly irregular," he seethed. "I can think of no civilized circumstance wherein any lord of the realm would ever agree to comply with such an outrageous demand."

She leaned forward, planting her hands on the table and staring him directly in the eye. "We are estranged spouses who've found themselves snowbound together. Who knows how long we will be trapped here together? If there is any time to be uncivilized or outrageous, it is now."

Claxton blinked. Exhaled. Indeed, he perspired on his forehead and upper lip. Were there that many names that he would become so discomposed? Apparently so. He lifted the pen and immersed the nib, only to abandon the quill to the jar and throw himself back in the chair in clear agony.

"Hell and damnation," he blustered. "I can't be expected to remember them all. That's almost twenty years of—"

"Quiet!" she blurted, silencing him with a hand, never wanting to hear the end of *that* sentence. "Limit the task, then, to those ladies with whom I might come into contact under social circumstances. At a ball, or at cards, or out shopping. That kind of thing."

"Good God, Sophia," he exclaimed hoarsely. "If you disliked me before, you will despise me now."

"I told you, this isn't about emotions or me liking you." She said the words to convince herself as much as Claxton. "It's about me being prepared to defend myself and your child in the future with dignity, no matter how unpleasant the circumstance."

"My child," he repeated quietly, closing his eyes. He breathed deeply. "My child."

With that solemn utterance, the child that had seemed so real and alive in Sophia's heart until the night before sprang to life again, even amid her self-warnings of caution.

By next year at Christmas, she might have a child of her own.

At last, Claxton appeared convinced. With both elbows on the table, he rubbed his hands over his face, looking suddenly very weary, with his jaw drawn tight and shadows beneath his eyes.

He took up the quill pen again. Sophia experienced a moment of pity. He looked so tortured and earnest, as if he *wanted* to please her. The pen's tip moved over the page, bleeding its indigo ink to form one name. Then two. Three. *Four.* Sophia closed her eyes, but the scratching sounds continued, forever it seemed.

At last, he stopped writing.

"Do you have another page upon which I can write additional names?"

Chapter Nine

Sophia's eyes flew open. "You can't be serious."

He glared at her darkly. "Of course I'm not. But you deserve a shock for forcing me to this."

"Give me the list." She extended her hand.

His eyes narrowed. "One moment, please. I just remembered another."

With dramatic flair, he scrawled one more name at the bottom of the list before handing the sheet to her. "Merry Christmas, darling."

"Are you certain that is all?"

"Quite certain."

Sophia cleared her countenance of all emotion and inhaled deeply. It was important that she distance herself from the intelligence on the page and not lose her head if she recognized any of the names, for most assuredly she would.

If she was truly going to forgive and forget, for the

purpose of endeavoring to have a child, she must learn to mute her emotional reactions.

Sophia looked at the paper. Her eyes moved over the first assemblage of letters written in her husband's hand. Then the next. As her mind registered each name, little explosions went off inside her head, powder kegs of alarm. Each one growing larger. Louder. More catastrophic. Her eyes widened. A jagged breath escaped her lips.

Vane muttered a low curse. *"I knew it."*

Before his very eyes, the lovely Sophia transformed into a dragon, complete with red glowing eyes and flames shooting out her nose. At least that's how she appeared to him. And she'd never been more beautiful.

"You despicable man," she shouted.

In that moment he knew without a doubt he'd lost whatever ground he had gained. Tenfold. For a moment, he felt guilty. Contrite. But then anger rippled up from inside him, ablaze. He launched up from the chair, coming to stand just before her. "You forced me to write the names, assuring me there was no other way to preserve our marriage. Now you call me despicable?"

"Yes," she railed, shaking the list at him so violently the paper made crackling noises. "I am acquainted with each and every one of these ladies. Mrs. Pettijohn. I sit beside her at tea and cards every Tuesday afternoon. Lady Gatcombe. She sits in the opera box next to my grandfather's all season long."

"I cannot believe I agreed to this loathsome folly," he muttered.

"Lady Noord—"

"Give me that." He reached for the list—

"No!"

She twisted, holding it just out of his reach. He caught her around the waist, pulling her close against him. With her elbows and her back, Sophia attempted to push away, planting her buttocks—*hell on fire*, her sweet round buttocks—firmly against his groin. Which she seemed to realize the same moment he did.

She gasped and jerked round to face him, her arm bent behind her back in a vain attempt to keep the list from him, but with his arms, he crushed her against his chest and groped behind her—

"Claxton!"

Clearly not the list. He chuckled wickedly, low in his throat.

—until he found her wrist…her hand…and the damnable list clenched inside.

"Let go of it," he uttered, his fingers prying at hers.

"I won't."

"I'm going to burn it."

For a long moment they stood thusly entwined, pushing and pulling beside the fire, dancing an intimate dance. He felt her tremble against him and then sweetly… slowly…go limp in his arms, sinking against him. A little sigh of surrender broke from her lips.

"You just don't know how it hurt to read those names," she whispered.

Her capitulation transformed their struggle into an embrace. Her breasts, round and soft, pressed against his chest. His brain went instantly fuzzy. He didn't release her because he very much liked her breasts exactly where they were, but he did ease his grip on her, sliding his hands over her back to hold her more gently. From somewhere in the fog of his desire, he realized if he wished her to stay there, he ought to cobble together some sort of soothing verbal response.

"I didn't mean to hurt you," he assured. Well, he hadn't. "You insisted."

"I know, Claxton," she murmured, peering up at him from beneath thick lashes. Her lips were parted and damp. Her silky hair hung down her back to graze the top of his hands.

He lowered his head nearer to hers. "Sophia."

She sighed and relaxed.

In the hazy recesses of his mind, he contemplated sweeping her into his arms and carrying her upstairs. No, too fast. Soon, though. Soon. He skimmed palms upward over her torso, savoring the slide of the fabric beneath his palms. He slanted his face to kiss her—

"Ha!" she exclaimed, leaping away the moment he released her.

"*Ha*" was right. He stood, arms empty, feeling as if he'd taken a bucket of cold water to his face.

She put a few more paces between them before pivoting around and pointing at him. "Knave!"

Her lips emitted a sound, something between a shriek and a bellow. She crushed the paper in her hand and hurled it toward him. The missile bounced off his forehead. Turning on her heel, she quit the room.

Only to return. She leveled him with a merciless glare, and while he stood like a senseless dullard, she snatched up the list and left again.

Moments later, her door slammed.

Vane dropped into the chair. He squeezed his thumb and forefinger on the ridge of his nose and let out a low, wry chuckle at the absurd turn of the past half hour. He had been trying only to satisfy Sophia's wishes. He'd glimpsed the path to victory, but had somehow fallen short. For all his experience with women, it seemed he'd never really had a clue how to handle a wife.

With the memory of her lush body still imprinted in his mind, he tore his cravat free from his throat. Crushing the cloth in his hand, he almost threw it into the fire, but he stopped himself, throwing the linen to the settee instead, where he would spend another lonely night. Not coaxing more kisses from his wife. Not stripping each layer of clothing from her body until she stood naked and bared to his hungry gaze. Not making love to her.

How bewildering to discover that shouting and arguing with Sophia only made him want her more. Once while hunting in Austria, he'd come across a male wolf separated by a high stone wall from its mate. Drawn by the sounds of her voice, the animal had paced and snarled and panted, desperate to rejoin her, until Claxton took pity on the poor animal's desperate condition and opened a gate. He felt much akin to that animal now, only he was separated from Sophia by a wall of his own making.

At least, as consolation, a goodly portion of Mrs. Kettle's plum cake remained. He unbuttoned his shirt at the throat and tugged its hem free from his breeches. Taking up his fork, he sectioned off a substantial bite.

That's when Sophia screamed.

Not a furious sort of scream, a *terrified* scream. He dropped the fork and sprang to his feet, nearly upending the table in the process.

When he reached her room, Sophia, garbed in only her short corset and chemise, crouched just inside the door, both hands over her mouth. Her attention appeared fixed on the bed, where her nightdress lay.

"What is it? Are you hurt?" He stepped inside.

Seeing him, she sprang into his arms. For a moment he was too dazzled by the contact of her body, the soft crush of her breasts against his chest, the intimate flex of her thighs at his waist, to process her words. Oh, God, the memories. The sudden rush of lust. They scrambled all rational thought from his brain.

Sophia shouted something about the bed. Yes. God, yes. He wanted to take her to bed.

She jumped off him and punched his arm.

"Claxton," she exclaimed. "There is *an animal* in my room."

"An animal?" he asked dazedly. Did she mean him? "Where?"

She ducked behind him and pointed to the far corner. "I told you. Under the bed, I think. It moved so fast, jumping off the walls."

"What did it look like?" Claxton advanced in the direction she indicated, crouched low, prepared, if necessary, to kill with his hands. She followed, a few steps behind, clutching his shirttail.

"Like a large rat. White with dark spots. And teeth." She pointed at her mouth. "Sharp teeth."

He lifted the coverlet and peered under the wood frame into the shadows. Two mirror-bright eyes peered back at him.

"I believe it is only a stoat."

"Bloodthirsty creatures!" she wailed.

"Indeed, if you are a rabbit or a chipmunk."

Claxton snatched up a blanket from the end of the bed,

but determining the swath of wool too cumbersome for his purposes, he shrugged off his coat. Holding the garment before him, he rounded the corner.

Sophia retreated to the door to watch in safety. Vicious snarls arose from the creature in the corner—and Claxton. He shoved a wooden chest across the floorboards. He stomped. Muttered an oath. Scrambled and crawled.

But at last, he arose with his bundled coat clasped in his hands, churning with contained movement.

"Give me that candlestick if you will," he ordered with a jerk of his head. "The large one."

"The candlestick? Why? Oh no." She scowled. "I will not. Don't hurt the creature." She rushed forward.

"Don't hurt the creature?" His eyes widened.

"He did not intend to do wrong." She clasped her hands together as if in prayer, just in front of her nose and mouth. "You must spare him. Please?"

"A moment ago you were terrified." And jumping all over him. He considered "accidentally" releasing the animal again.

She rolled her eyes. "A moment ago he was snarling and baring his teeth."

He lifted his unruly burden, one that emitted snaps and growls, careful to hold the creature far from his body. "He is not now?"

"Just put him out the window." Sophia waved her hand toward the draperies, trying not to think of how thankful she was Claxton had been here to help her.

He let out a sound of impatience, but conceded to her request, elbowing back the weighty crimson brocade. There, he paused.

"The window is already open. Did you unfasten it earlier?"

"Why would I do that? It's freezing outside." Sophia followed him, near enough to feel a gust of frigidity, one that sent the hair on her arms straight. Open by nearly three inches and rimmed by a white border of thick frost, the window provided a glimpse straight into the black pitch of night.

"Are you certain the window wasn't open last night?"

"Not that I'm aware, but I didn't look." It had been terribly cold in the room, but to a normal degree for a country house in winter. Certainly she would have perceived the movement of the curtain or the sound of wind unhindered by stone or glass. "I would have noticed."

Claxton bent through the opening and hurled his coat into the darkness, yanking back the unoccupied garment by its sleeve. With the heel of his hand, he pounded the frost free from the window and pulled the narrow frame closed. In the process, his linen shirt tightened, revealing the wide breadth of his shoulders and a powerful flex of muscle. Sophia swallowed hard, wishing she hadn't noticed, wishing the sight hadn't awakened something hungry and needful that had laid subdued, deep inside her, for so very long. She'd touched every part of that body. Memorized every indentation and plane.

"Perhaps it was closed but not fastened," he mused, oblivious to the lustful turn of her thoughts.

He turned toward her, cheeks ruddy, his blue eyes as cool and arresting as frost. Absent his cravat, the neck opening of his shirt revealed the firm golden skin at his throat and, tantalizingly, a glimpse of his upper chest striated with muscle.

Sophia's mouth went dry. Claxton really was the handsomest man. She could think of no one who compared.

She stood there transfixed as he blathered on.

"A change in the direction of the wind or pressure from the frost may have pried it open, allowing the creature to—"

He met her eyes and froze. Like weighted stones, his gaze dropped.

"Good God, Sophia," he said softly. "You always did have the loveliest breasts."

A glance downward revealed that in the activity of the previous moments, her breasts had spilled from her corset and now crowded the upper portion of her chemise. Her nipples, aroused by the chill in the room, jutted hard and plainly visible against the thin batiste.

She gasped and covered them with her hands.

Claxton's gaze intensified. "I can do that for you if you like."

She should have shouted *no*. She should have ordered him out and blistered him with a scathing set down.

Yet a paralyzing sort of bewilderment kept her silent.

He closed his eyes, his expression tortured, and exhaled through clenched teeth. When they opened again, they were lit by a predatory gleam she recognized from the first months of the marriage as a certain prelude to lovemaking. Every inch of her skin came alive, and the room around them dissolved to nothing, leaving only a woman and a man.

Despite every rational thought insisting *no*, her body begged *yes*. She wanted him to kiss her. Heavens, she

wanted him to do much more than that. If the thick ridge
at the front of his breeches was any indication, he wanted
more than kissing too.

Quite suddenly he advanced, every bit of the warrior,
a towering fantasy of long, muscled limbs and bristling
intensity. A dark fall of hair tumbled across his forehead.
Blue eyes, edged by dark lashes, thrilled her with their
appreciative glow.

"Don't tell me to go." He reached to touch her bare
arm, drawing his fingertips over her skin. That faint tracery of warmth in the chill of the room sent a shiver
reverberating through her body.

Her feet remained rooted to the spot. Her tongue
darted out to dampen her bottom lip.

"You don't know how badly I need to touch you." His
voice mesmerized her, spoke promises she wanted to believe. He cupped her cheek.

"Let me make love to you again."

Overtaken by a sudden fever, she turned her face into
his palm, savoring the controlled strength of his long fingers against her skin, their calloused warmth. So familiar,
but strange. So welcome, but forbidden. Every particle
of her went molten and surged toward him like an ocean
wave in worship of the moon.

"I've never begged any woman," he said fiercely. "It's
only right that you should be the first."

And the last. He was supposed to be hers. No one
else's.

Her breasts swelled, suddenly heavy and full, begging
for his touch. The place between her legs grew damp and
throbbed, aching to be satisfied.

"I'm begging you," he murmured. "Ask me to stay."

His hand moved behind her head, closing on the nape of her neck, a gesture of possession. Staring down, he pierced her through with his gaze.

"Sophia, say you want me to stay."

She glanced toward the bed, imagining herself there, spread beneath him. Already she felt his weight on top of her.

The power of his thrusts.

The salty tang of his skin—

But at the center of the mattress lay the list, stained with the names of his lovers. Familiar faces flashed in her mind, painted in vivid color. He'd shared *this* with all of them, this intensity of feeling. In the end, it must have meant nothing because he'd left them, just as she knew in her heart he'd leave her again too. Her name might as well be on that list, just one of many.

She wasn't strong enough, not yet. Her heart still felt too much.

The fire in her veins dimmed and flickered out. In an instant, the room grew immeasurably colder, and his touch on her skin, rough and foreign. She flinched.

"Please," she whispered. "I want you to go."

His hand flexed against her skull, gathering a fistful of her hair in his hand. He bent just enough so that his breath teased her temple. "You insisted on that damn list. Not me."

He released her. Malice radiated from him so intense she recoiled as he brushed past her into the corridor.

She gripped the doorframe, listening to the sound of his boots as they descended the steps. From there, she listened to him mutter. Storm about the great room. Curse. Her chest tightened. Something crashed.

"You could have at least left me the *damn key* to the *damn wine closet*," he thundered.

Her heart implored her to go to him. Instead she walked to the bed and took up the list and recited each of the names aloud. Her defenses renewed, she crossed the room again, closed the door, and backed away.

* * *

The next morning, after determining from the window that there would be no miraculous break in the weather, Sophia, armed with the ring of keys that Mrs. Kettle had given to her, located the upstairs storage room and linen closet.

There she found the necessary items to outfit a bed for Claxton, a sturdy bottom mattress of wool flocking, a softer upper feather mattress, and of course linens. Though old, everything was meticulously stored and in good condition. It was best, she determined, to do her good deed now, for if the events of the previous two days were any indication of how the third would unfold, she and Claxton would be on the verge of murdering each other by nightfall, and neither of them would make it to Christmas.

Five days remained. She wouldn't panic just yet. She would remain optimistic that the weather would be clear and she'd soon return to the comfort and strength of her family. Until then, she would devote her energies to defining a new and different relationship with Claxton. Whether that meant their proceeding with a formal separation, she did not yet know. By her way of thinking, that all depended on her and her ability to break free of the emotion and expectations she'd previously held of marriage and of Claxton.

After completing the task, she went downstairs, which remained very much under the cover of darkness. Frost covered the windows, dimming what was already a meager winter light from outside. Neither she nor Claxton had been in the habit of wasting precious candles or oil when it was only the two of them, and she did not undertake to prepare a lamp now. All in all, the dreary lighting very much represented her mood.

After the way things had ended between them the night before, she felt no small amount of trepidation at seeing him again. How close she had come to capitulating. How angry he'd been when she hadn't. Thank God she had come to her senses. Falling into bed with him in a fit of misguided passion would only complicate an already complicated matter. Absent the sort of love her parents had enjoyed, successful marriages weren't based on temporary passions but on enduring mutual respect and common goals, and she and Claxton had not yet achieved that venerable state. If she hoped to retain any power at all in their present negotiations, their child must not be conceived until after she came to a decision about their separation—a decision she'd come to believe would be best delayed until they returned to London.

Oh, but London. She'd slept fitfully, the names on Claxton's list pealing out like church bells inside her head until the early-morning hours. The truth stung. She felt wounded and betrayed, not just by Claxton, but by all the women on the list that she knew. How could she ever return to life in town and look any of them in the eye without giving in to the urge to lash out at them, and at Claxton as well, every time they crossed paths?

Even so, this morning she'd renewed her vow to move past the hurt. All emotion aside, she had forced her husband's hand, and to his credit, he had complied with her demand for a list of his lovers' names in an effort to appease her. She no longer doubted he wished to remain married, most likely for the same reason as she. They both wanted a child.

If the two of them were to proceed, Sophia would have to come to terms with the realities of her husband's emotional limitations. That meant, on a more practical level, that she must arrive at a place where she could sit at a banquet table with any one or *all* of those women without crashing into despair, without shedding a tear, even in private.

As she told Claxton the night before, their estrangement wasn't even about the women, but her doubt over his ability to *stay*. To love her. Because if he'd truly loved her before, he would never have left her. He would never have sought out his old way of life and the companionship—however limited—of those other women. She feared it was only a matter of time until he grew bored or some new difficulty arose between them, and he'd leave her again, in one way or another, whether for another woman, another diplomatic assignment, or some other life. She'd been unrealistic to expect more from a man of privilege, especially one with his libertine past. Despite her parents' happy history, love matches were rare in their circles. Men were raised with the understanding they could do whatever they wished, just as long as they acted with discretion. And yet knowing this, it still pained her to settle.

So perhaps childishly, as a reminder of his truer nature, she'd tucked the folded list inside her corset as a ward over her heart. If she did ultimately withdraw her demand for a separation, she would be wise to never forget that theirs must in the future be a marriage based on honesty and truths, not romance. Theirs, like so many other *ton* marriages, must be a partnership, rather than a love affair. Perhaps one day they could even be friends.

Her only hope was that at some point in these unbroken, snowbound hours spent with Claxton, he would somehow lose his shine. At her own peril, she remained much too fascinated by the duke. Sophia prayed that at some moment he would sneeze untidily and wipe the resulting snotty mess on his sleeve. Or burst out with a sudden battery of flatulence. If he would only voice some heartless opinion about widows and orphans or confess to despising puppies, chicks, and kittens. Of course, he had never exhibited any of those oafish habits before, but now that her eyes were wide open and looking for flaws, she felt quite certain they would become apparent.

She would just be patient and give him time to reveal his true loathsome self. Only then, when she saw Claxton for who he was—just a man, like any other—could she chance proceeding to the next level of intimacy without endangering her heart.

On the threshold of the great room, she perceived two things in the dim morning light. Firstly, one of Claxton's boots hung upside down from the center of the kissing bough. Secondly, the third Duke of Claxton's portrait had gone missing from above the mantel. The portrait now occupied the corner, upside down and curiously misshapen. Sophia ventured inside for a closer inspection, which revealed a gash at the center of the elder's painted face, the approximate size of Claxton's foot. Now she realized what the crashing sound had been last night.

A rustle of movement sounded behind her. Turning, she found his Grace sprawled on the settee, clothed in his shirt and breeches, covered only by his coat. Curiously, his feet were raised to a slight level over his head, as one of the wooden legs of the settee had fallen out. He appeared terribly uncomfortable and just a little amusing because his stockinged feet jutted more than a foot over the end.

Now she felt truly guilty for having enjoyed the comfort of the ducal bedroom for the duration of their stay. Overwhelmed by the desire to just look at him, unguarded and unaware, she moved closer, quietly, so he would not awaken.

If providence could see to start her day on a good note, she would find him in an unforgivable, slovenly state. His face would be swollen and puffy with sleep, and there would be drool. Lots and lots of drool. The more excessive, the better. But curse her foul luck, there wasn't a drop. He hadn't been a drooler before either, but one could always hope.

Despite herself, she sighed. In repose, he appeared a younger, more boyish version of himself. Yet he'd not shaven in two days and the evidence of his maturity shadowed his jaw.

Fearing that any moment he would awaken and catch her admiring him, she quit him for the kitchen, where she warmed some of Mrs. Kettle's rolls. After preparing a pot of tea, she made up a tray, the final touches being small dishes of the marmalade and honey she'd discovered in the pantry. Conveying all this to the great room, she set the tray on a table beside Claxton.

He exhaled and shifted, but did not open his eyes. No matter, he could sleep as long as he liked. She would return to her room with a cup of tea and read for the remainder of the morning once she removed the portrait, which seemed the conscientious thing to do as Claxton's frustration with her had been to blame, at least in part, for its destruction.

She grasped its frame and lifted.

"Burn it."

She turned and found him watching her, sleepy eyed and flushed. Inside she melted. How seductive he looked, with his hair tousled and his eyes heavy lidded. She blinked and glanced away, mentally shaking off her attraction.

"I was going to put it in the attic," she said. "Perhaps the canvas can be repaired."

"Repaired?" he muttered, righting himself on the cushions. He scowled. "Whatever for?"

"You'll regret this one day, the destruction of your familial history. Have you any other portraits of him?"

"I do believe that was the last." He smiled wickedly, an indication he may have disposed of prior paintings in the same manner.

"But, Claxton, whatever your feelings about your father, your mother clearly believed he deserved some measure of respect or else she would not have hung his portrait in her home."

His eyebrows shot up. "You believe she hung that portrait? She didn't. There's a reason I didn't know what he looked like until I was ten. Likely he hung it after her death, when he had the house shuttered. The bastard would have done that." He spoke quietly, but bitterness roughened his voice. He rubbed his hands over his face. "I'm sure he came here after and cleaned out everything that had made Camellia House hers, like so much refuse, and hung a picture of his own damn self on her wall. Try to find her likeness anywhere, Sophia. You won't find it. He had every portrait and miniature of her destroyed, and I've done everything I could to repay him in kind." Sitting up, he reached for his Hessian. "He might as well have pissed on her grave."

Sophia flushed at his crudity. "You seem as if you are only supposing what he did. Weren't you present when all this occurred?"

He stood and with the assistance of the fireplace poker extricated the second boot from the bough. "No, I was gone by then."

"What do you mean gone?"

"When I learned he'd dismissed the Kettles, I left." He balanced on one long leg, tugging on the boot. "I enlisted in the army."

"How old were you then?"

"Hmm? Oh, I was sixteen."

She set the portrait down. "Claxton, when was the last time you spoke to your father before his death?"

"You mean directly? Not through representatives?"

"Yes, talked to him face-to-face."

He circled the settee to stare out the window. "Sixteen."

Sophia's mouth fell open in shock. "I'd always assumed you entered the service in the same manner as other titled gentlemen, with a purchased commission. No one recognized your name?"

"Well, I lied about that, of course, and they shipped me straight off to India. It took the duke's investigators three years to find me too. By then, my general had purchased my first commission for me, something he did from time to time based on merit. Merit, Sophia. Not that damn bastard's name." He laughed. "The duke was so furious when he found out he told them to leave me there." He fell silent for a long moment. "He summoned Haden home from school then, just in case I ended up dead. I hated myself when I found out."

Looking at Claxton now, turned from her, his stance was invincible and strong. Yet her imagination showed her another picture, that of a proud young boy. She wanted nothing more than to ease the pain that the man in the portrait brought him. Since she could not do so with an embrace or a kiss, she offered the only other reasonable response.

"Well, then, let us burn this awful thing."

He continued to peer out the window, as if he refused to commit another word to the discussion of the cursed portrait. Or perhaps it was Haden of whom he thought.

She again lifted the destroyed canvas by its frame, prepared to condemn the despised countenance to the flames.

Only then did she see the pale rectangular object affixed to the back. A piece of parchment. No, an envelope, fragile and yellowed with age. Setting the lower edge of the frame on the floor, she tilted the destroyed surface back for a better view. Across the front of the envelope written in a beautiful script was the name—

"Claxton, look." She propped the frame against the wall. "There is an envelope with your name on it."

He turned from the window with a dubious look.

She tugged the envelope free from where it had been wedged into the frame. He met her in the middle, eyeing the object in her hand.

His expression softened. "That's my mother's handwriting."

"Open it," she urged.

He made no move to accept the object. "You may do so."

"What if she wrote something private?"

"You are my wife," he answered quietly, the look of sleepiness he still wore an unintended seduction. "What could she possibly have written that I would not want you to read?"

You are my wife. The words branded her. Took her breath away. She calmed the racing beat of her heart and slid her thumb beneath the seal. From inside the envelope, she removed the folded sheet of paper.

"Well, it's not a letter." She turned the open page for his view so that he could see the hand-drawn pictures of smiling pixies and curlicued words. "I don't know what it is."

Claxton threw a cautious glance at the paper. After a moment, relief eased his features and a faint smile turned his lips. "It's a quest for a game of lookabout."

"Lookabout?"

He exhaled, and his skin flushed a shade deeper. He nodded. "My mother used to write quests for my brother and me. Boons, if you will. There were usually four or five tasks or trials that we would complete here inside the house or outdoors or even at times in the village, and once we'd located all the quests and completed whatever requirements, we would receive a reward."

"So this quest will include instructions to find the next, and so on?"

"Yes." Again, he glanced at the paper. Quickly. Then looked away. "She's written a number one up in the corner. This is the first boon in a series."

"Claxton." Excitement bubbled up inside her to spread a smile across her lips. "How special that we found your mother's note. To think I was only moments away from burning it."

"It's just a child's game," he said quietly from where he situated himself beside the woodbox at the far side of the hearth.

Her mind buzzed with curiosity. "But if we so wished, we could find the second quest, and so on?"

"I don't know." He crouched, his muscular thighs flexed, to lower a large log on the steel frame atop the dying fire. Sparks spiraled up as the heavier wood invaded the embers and ash. His response lacked Sophia's enthusiasm. "So many years have passed. No doubt she wrote it up to keep Haden and me occupied, but forgot about it."

"But how would the quest have come to be on the back of your father's portrait, which you yourself said did not hang here while she was alive?"

"I—I don't know." His eyebrows drew together.

"Strange also that Haden's name does not appear."

He raised his shoulders. "We did not always play together."

"Twenty years," mused Sophia softly. "It's almost magical to find her quest now and so close to Christmas. Oh, Claxton, let's read her instruction and see where to go next."

His lips drew into a wan smile, and he shook his head.

"I told you, Sophia. I'm not that boy anymore. It's like finding a note she wrote for someone else."

Sophia's heart softened. "You think she would have been disappointed in the way you lived your life, but you're wrong. Mothers love their children unconditionally. They forgive."

"But wives don't?"

Flustered by the sudden intensity of his gaze, Sophia waved the paper about. "This isn't about you and me; it's about your mother's quest. Come now, how else shall we occupy our time?" she implored, desperate for any activity that would provide distraction.

"I can think of plenty of ways to occupy our time," he murmured, coming to stand behind her back. "You just refuse to oblige."

Sophia's cheeks filled with heat at his bawdy suggestion. The list of names she carried between her chemise and heart provided a convenient reminder that she wasn't ready for such ease of familiarity. When she could think of the names on that list and feel nothing—no anger or hurt—then she'd be ready.

"And I don't intend to cooperate. Please, Claxton, the last two days have been emotionally taxing." She shook her hair back from her face. "I hope you can appreciate that I need a bit more time. Which makes the idea of playing a game perfect."

"Do you intend to proceed with a separation or not?" he demanded with sudden vehemence.

"I don't know," she exclaimed. "And I don't appreciate being pressed on the subject."

At that moment, a solid rapping came from the front vestibule. Claxton pivoted toward the sound.

"Oh, dear Lord, yes, thank you," she whispered.

"I heard that," he growled.

With a step in the direction of the door, he tucked his shirt into his breeches and jerked his shirtsleeves and collar into place.

"There." Combing his hair with his fingers, he inquired, "Do I look presentable, as the lord of the manor should?"

"For a lord of the manor who is without a decent valet to tend to his appearance, yes."

"Or a decent wife, for that matter."

Sophia watched him go, knowing he had intended the last comment to cut.

She retrieved his coat from where it had fallen from the settee and draped it over the back of a chair. Fastidiously, she straightened the cushions. Hearing the door open and voices, she waited to welcome whatever visitor might accompany Claxton over the threshold.

He reappeared alone.

"Who was it?" she inquired.

"A young man from the village. Mr. Kettle sent him to deliver the horse and sledge for us to use at our convenience."

"How thoughtful of Mr. Kettle."

"Well, it is our sledge and horse after all."

"I assumed that. You gave the man a shilling, of course." The words slipped out before she'd given them any thought, reminding her disturbingly of the way her mother used to speak to her father.

"Don't play games with me, Sophia," Claxton warned quietly, sending a chill through her. "Either you are my wife or you are not."

"I'm not playing games," she said. "Not the sort of games you imply. All I'm saying is there is no reason we must rush into a decision. Perhaps we should separate. Perhaps not. I don't claim to know the answer, but there's no reason we have to decide at this very moment."

"Perhaps you're correct," he muttered darkly. "Heaven forbid we actually enjoy a pleasant Christmas together."

"That's not fair. Don't use Christmas against me."

"Better you learn now; I don't play fair." He lifted the teapot. Removing the lid, he peeked inside and sniffed suspiciously.

"It's just tea," she advised.

"Yes, that's what I'm afraid of," he muttered.

"What is that supposed to mean?"

He leaned toward her and with a wicked grin said, "It means I'm dumping out this swill and making a new pot."

She'd known full well her tea wasn't as good as her maid Mary's at home, but for him to label her efforts as *swill*? She frowned in consternation but returned her attention to the quest.

"Claxton, where is the Evil Dark Spirit Room?"

He set down the teapot and tilted his head. "What did you say?"

Chapter Ten

"Did you even bother to read what your mother wrote?" She held up the quest, exasperated. "The Evil Dark Spirit Room. It's all in capitals, as if it is a rather formal designation. The. Evil. Dark. Spirit. Room."

"If I told you, then I'd have to kill you." He sauntered closer, looking dangerous and handsome. "I am rather inclined to strangle you right now."

She threw him a distancing look. "I beg your pardon."

"It's quite the family secret."

"Well?" she demanded urgently. "Tell me."

"It's all right here in front of you." He rested his hand on the mantel.

"The great room is the Evil Dark Spirit Room?" She harrumphed, lowering the quest in disappointment. "That's not very interesting."

"No?" His hand moved to the right side of the mantel where the wall was overlaid with wood paneling. With his fingertips, he applied pressure to a narrow bit of decorative framing. With a click, a man-sized section of the wall released and shifted inward to reveal a darkened space behind.

"A secret passage," she exclaimed. "Or a priest hole?"

"It's the Evil Dark Spirit Room," he quipped. Then more dramatically, "Enter if you dare."

"Aha! That's how you got inside the house the first night."

His wry smile confessed all. How delightful! Of course, she hadn't thought that the first night, but she did now.

"You go first," she said, after lighting a lantern and handing it to him. "I'll follow."

Oh, how she wished Clarissa and Daphne were here to see. Her sisters shared her appreciation for games and adventure, and she'd much prefer their company to Claxton's. Well, that wasn't necessarily true, but it felt right to think it.

"Why me first? Are you afraid?" His query held a hint of the nefarious, as did his wicked expression.

A little ripple of excitement traveled through her at being the recipient of that wolfish stare. "Just cautious. Given our present circumstances, I wouldn't be surprised if you wished to murder me." Or seduced her. "I don't want to find myself shut up in this wall."

"Wouldn't that be convenient?" He smiled devilishly. He stepped into the dark and disappeared. She followed him and bumped straightaway into his shoulder. "Careful, there are steps here, rather steep."

His hand caught her arm just above the elbow, and she allowed it, appreciative of his guidance in the dark. Here, frigid air chilled her skin. Extremely narrow, the passage forced them to sidle along in close proximity, the duke a tall and tautly muscled presence beside her in the dark. He put off the most delicious heat, which kept her close. After just a few feet they arrived in a tiny, slightly more expansive space crudely finished and with a tiny door that she knew would lead to the outside of the house.

"This is it. The Evil Dark Spirit Room." He crouched, because if he stood full upright, his head would strike the low ceiling. His breath puffed like smoke from his nostrils. "I could be wrong, but I believe we are looking for a loose stone, but please don't get your hopes up. There may be nothing here for us to find."

He stood behind her and directed the lamp's light over the wall. Keenly aware of every brush of his clothing and his body against her, Sophia's hands moved over the cold stone and mortar, seeking movement or imperfection. Her heart beat faster, nearly bursting with curiosity.

"Here, I think," said Claxton, his voice low and sensual. His arm came around her, half of an embrace, to press his fingertips against a stone level with his chin. The rectangle shifted, emitting a soft grinding sound. "You do the honors."

Sophia caught the edges of the stone and carefully pulled it out. Claxton lifted the lantern outside the resulting space.

An envelope lay inside, very much identical to the first.

Sophia gasped in pleasure. "How exciting. It's like a voice from the past, Claxton, your mother's. I've got chills. Don't you?"

"Yes," he answered quietly. "I do."

"Aren't you going to take it?" she asked, glancing over her shoulder. He stood close enough to kiss.

"You." He did not smile. "You are the one who insisted on searching for the next quest, when I would have preferred other activities. It seems only right that you should claim it."

Sophia ignored his comment and reached inside. After replacing the stone, they returned to the great room. She sought the warmth of the fire, relieved to again put a bit more space between herself and her maddeningly attractive husband.

Sophia peered down at the envelope. "When you and your brother played the game together, did you compete against one another or work together to complete the quests?"

Claxton crouched beside the settee and located its errant leg underneath. "It depended on our mood, really, whether we could suffer one another's company for the day."

"Oh, Claxton, let's play lookabout. Let's accomplish the quests and claim the treasure."

He lifted the legless corner of the settee, and for the second time since arriving at Camellia House, he affixed the missing post into place. "Convince me."

"I shouldn't have to." Sophia's eyes widened in dismay, as if he were a clod for not immediately agreeing.

"After the state you left me in last night," he muttered, but playfully, hoping to extend the agreeable mood between them, "I'm not inclined to do you any favors."

Sophia's lashes lowered against her cheeks and she blushed. "You wouldn't be doing me, but yourself, a favor. Your mother wrote the clues. I think it would be wonderful to finish the game, no matter your age. As a tribute to her."

He sank into the tufted armchair, extending his legs. "Likely we'd go through all the trouble only to find the next clue missing or destroyed. It's been twenty years. Why don't you come over here and sit with me." He threw a wolfish glance down at his lap. "And we can discuss it."

"As if I would truly come and sit in your lap," she retorted, but softly and without anger.

"I have my own game of lookabout that I'd like to propose. One that involves you and me and a bed—and the only quest that in this moment I'm hoping to accomplish."

There, he'd coaxed a smile. A big, shocked one with blushing cheeks to match.

"I want to play this version of the game," she said, flapping the envelope in her hand.

He shrugged. "A man can hope."

She glanced down at the quest. "We've already found the second quest. How will we know about the existence of the next if we don't at least try?"

"For what reward? A petrified piece of peppermint or a shriveled orange? It's cold anywhere but here beside the fire. Again, it's been—"

She walked the perimeter of the room. "Twenty years, yes, I know. Come now, it is better than sitting here in this dark room all day dancing around the subject of things we've already discussed to death. It also takes my mind off worrying about Christmas and that we might not make it back to London in time."

The corner of his mouth bent into a smile. "You're just afraid I'll seduce you."

She threw him a warning glance. "You won't, because

it's not allowed. I'm telling you that now I need time to clear my head and to think."

He watched her move, admiring the way her gown clung to her curves.

"I know you're attracted to me," he drawled. "Don't try to deny it."

She glared at him. "Lots of ladies are attracted to you."

He scowled and let out a growl of displeasure. At every corner she sought to drive a wedge between them.

"I'm finished talking about any other lady but you."

"I'm tired of talking. I want to play the game." She shook her hair back from her shoulders, for a moment thrusting her breasts forward. She didn't even know how she tortured him. "I think you're just afraid I'll win the game."

"Win? You?" His brow went up. Deep inside his chest, an old competitive flare snapped to life. "So you would choose to compete against me, a master of the game, rather than work together?"

"I would."

He shrugged. "Be forewarned, I'm highly competitive."

"So am I," she claimed. "Daphne and Clarissa complain that I always *must* win."

"Just so you know, there are no rules."

She tilted her head, green eyes sparkling. "You mean to say that you cheat?"

"I *strategize*."

"So be it," she said, opening the envelope. "Let's read the next quest."

Claxton remained in the chair, watching her. She stood

between the fire and the window, painted two shades of light—one golden, the other frost. If he were a painter, this would be how he would capture her for the ages. Ideally with her clothes off. Instead, he had to commit the image to memory. That she could speak to him in so light and friendly a manner about something as inane as a game, when so much between them remained unresolved, frustrated him beyond bearing. Had the hurt he'd submitted her to pushed her too far away to ever truly win her back?

She read aloud. "Make with your own hands twelve iced plum cakes. Deliver them to Mrs. Kettle, who will determine whether your efforts are worthy of the next quest."

Claxton held silent, waiting for whatever she might say.

"Oh, my." She lowered the parchment. "Twelve iced cakes. I hadn't anticipated that as a quest for two little boys. I'd rather expected climbing a tree or crafting a man-of-war out of sticks."

"Most often the tasks were very much so," Claxton explained. "But other times my mother encouraged my brother and me to learn a broader array of skills, those of self-sufficiency." He shrugged. "And humility."

"Humph." She sniffed, one slender eyebrow lifting archly. "Humility, you say."

He ignored her jibe. "My mother believed it important for us boys to assist with the more menial tasks that kept the house in order so as to understand the difficult demands placed upon the Kettles, both of whom she adored, and the servants we would certainly one day employ. Sometimes her quests were intended to teach us empathy for a scullery maid. Other times, the groundskeeper. In this case, a cook." He chuckled, remembering. "She or Mrs. Kettle would have helped us bake the cakes, so we did not burn the house down."

She perched on the edge of the settee, glancing suspiciously at the suspect leg as if to be certain it did not fly out from under her.

"I think that's wonderful. Indeed, I admire your mother more and more the more I learn about her." She made a silly face. "Although I wish she would have chosen a different task, as baking is not my strongest talent."

"Nor mine, but no matter." He shook his head. "While it has been highly diverting to find this second quest, I don't believe the game can proceed further. Too much time has passed. Mrs. Kettle won't remember the details, and even if she did, I can't imagine that she held on to a meaningless scrap of paper for this long."

Sophia nodded, extending her arm to trace her fingertips over the carved leaves on the upper frame of the settee. "I understand your reluctance. Neither do I wish to subject myself to an hour or more of efforts in the kitchen when they may only result in disappointment. But we ought to try. You owe that much to your mother's memory."

Vane did not wholeheartedly agree. As much as the quest had brought back happy memories he'd not recalled for a very long time, what they had stumbled upon were the remnants of a child's diversion, not King Arthur's tomb. Yet he found Sophia's excitement in the game undeniably intoxicating. More so, the discovery gifted him with a glimpse of the young woman she'd been before his past had driven them apart. She'd actually smiled this morning, and he did not want her to stop.

He stood with sudden conviction. "I had thought to go down to the village this morning for a bit of tobacco. While there, I will inquire with Mrs. Kettle."

"Yes, let's do pay a call."

"You need not accompany me." He would almost prefer that she did not. Though the game had inspired an easier manner between them, he knew the list of names he'd written out at her behest the night before remained in her thoughts. She did not trust him. He saw that in her every wary glance.

"Of course I will accompany you," she said. "You made clear you don't intend to play by the rules. I'll not forget that warning. Do you think I would allow you to achieve an unfair advantage by proceeding without me?" Her eyes sparkled like emeralds ablaze in candlelight.

She came to stand beside him at the fire, an oblivious seductress. Firelight deepened the shadowy crevice between her breasts. His body thrummed with the primal urge to stalk and seduce.

Yet she only blabbered on about the game, suffering no such distractions.

"But we cannot go to Mrs. Kettle empty-handed," she said. "To do so would be contrary to the spirit of the game, even if our efforts advance no further. Certainly there's a baker in the village. Couldn't we simply purchase the plum cakes or something similar and present them to Mrs. Kettle?"

Resigned, he answered, "I'm happy to humor you in any way."

* * *

They arrived at the Kettles' cottage after leaving the sledge at the nearby livery stable so that the horse could be tended to. Moments later, installed in the tiny parlor, they sat in comfortable chairs warmed by tea and news of the Martindale child's arrival early that morning. News of the birth inspired a pang of wistfulness in Sophia, but joy for the parents as well. She borrowed pen and paper from her hosts and penned a short congratulatory note from herself and the duke, something Mrs. Kettle assured her would become a treasured family heirloom for the Martindales.

As for her and Claxton's news, Sophia could hardly wait to share the discovery of the Duchess Elizabeth's quest and learn whether Mrs. Kettle remained in possession of the third boon.

"Do forgive us Mr. Kettle's present state," said Mrs. Kettle. "As you'll remember, your Grace, he suffers terribly from chilblains."

Mr. Kettle sat beside the fire, a blanket over his shoulders and his feet ankle deep in steaming water.

"Indeed, I do," said Claxton, looking elegant and huge in a patchwork chair much too small for his muscular frame. "One of the officers with whom I served had some success with porridge."

"Really," exclaimed Mrs. Kettle.

The duke nodded. "He would prepare a large pot and, once it cooled a bit, immerse both his feet in the stuff."

"That's very interesting."

Mr. Kettle nodded. "Something we shall have to try."

Sophia sat quietly and listened to the comfortable conversation between Claxton and the Kettles. She found the exchange unexpectedly heartwarming, and yes— entertaining. She for one would never have thought to ask the duke about remedies for chilblains.

"Has Haden paid a call?" he asked. "He is at the inn."

"No, he hasn't, but he was younger when the two of you left Lacenfleet. I'm certain a reintroduction is not foremost in his thoughts. Mr. Kettle will venture over in a bit and invite him to visit."

Claxton nodded toward the fireplace and grinned. "You still have naughty Lord Misrule, I see." He stood and from the mantel carefully lifted a wooden doll dressed in the green-and-gold costume of a jester. Little bells, sewn at his toes, jingled at the movement.

Mrs. Kettle responded, "I only just let him out of his box."

"You always were more trusting than me. Better keep your eye on him." Claxton winked at Sophia. "Every Christmas he causes all sorts of mayhem. I remember one year he hid all the spoons in the tea jar, and until we found them, we had to eat our custard with forks."

Mrs. Kettle snorted and clasped a hand over her mouth. "Yes! Yes! I remember! The custard had not set, and we all had such a time getting it to our mouths."

Beneath his blanket, Mr. Kettle nodded and smiled.

Claxton returned the doll to his perch. "Another time, the sneaky wastrel poked holes all over a sack of sugar that had been left on the kitchen table, creating quite the mess. Haden and I caught him red-handed too, with a skewer clutched in his little hand."

"What a wicked fellow." Sophia laughed.

At that moment, three small faces appeared at the

window, bright cheeked and topped by winter caps. The muffled voices of children carried through.

"... Y'see? I told you. That be the duke, 'imself!'"

"Robert won't believe us when we tell 'im."

"Go get 'im then!"

"You go get 'im. I'm stayin' 'ere."

Claxton gave a quiet laugh and a flush rose up from his neck, going as high as his cheeks. Sophia watched, transfixed by his discomfort at being so admired by three little boys.

Mrs. Kettle sprang from her chair, an index finger held in the air. "Forgive me. I just remembered something."

She disappeared into the kitchen and a moment later returned with two small china dishes, the first of which she pressed into Claxton's hand and the second into Sophia's.

Claxton peered down into the dish. A smile curved his lips. If possible, the blue of his eyes became bluer. "I can't believe you remembered."

Mrs. Kettle's face lit up like a candle.

"Sophia, Mrs. Kettle makes the most delicious sugarplums." Claxton's gaze found her. Sophia caught her breath at the quiet emotion she observed there. "They were always my favorite at Christmas."

Mrs. Kettle, with a glance at Sophia, explained, "I use more apricot, less prune—" She counted out each alteration to the traditional recipe on her fingers. "And I always leave out the caraway seeds." She reached out to pat Claxton on the arm. "His Grace never did care for caraway."

Claxton chewed thoughtfully.

"Just as I remember them," he pronounced, smiling.

"Only better because they are real and not just a fantasy. I used to dream of these, you know, every Christmas Day."

"Delicious," Sophia agreed, her mouth filled with pleasurable spice and sweetness.

Mr. Kettle leaned forward in his chair. "You know, she made them every year to have on hand, on the chance you might return—"

"Oh, hush, Mr. Kettle." With a hiccup, the elderly woman pressed a handkerchief to her eyes.

"Did you?" Claxton asked quietly, obviously moved. A flush rose into his cheeks and he smiled a very different sort of smile than she'd ever seen on his lips—one of boyish, unrestrained joy. "Thank you, Mrs. Kettle."

Sophia dabbed her eyes as well. It felt good to see Claxton happy. Things had been such an ugly mess these past few days. How heartening to enjoy a moment of such cheer.

When Mrs. Kettle calmed, she tucked the handkerchief in her bodice. "I would offer buttered muffins as well, but I see you have brought something wonderful from Mr. Woodall's shop for us to share."

She lifted the box from the little table beside her and, opening the lid, peered inside.

Vane explained the discovery of the envelope.

"Where did you find the envelope, you say?" said Mrs. Kettle, smiling faintly.

"Affixed to the back of Lord Claxton's portrait," said Sophia. "The one over the mantel."

Beneath the lace frill of her cap, Mrs. Kettle inhaled sharply, her eyes awash with another surge of tears.

"Yes, actually." She took another deep breath. "I do recall something about that." She waved a wrinkled hand in the air. "Have you the quest with you, written out by her ladyship?"

"Indeed." Claxton produced the envelope from his coat pocket and handed it over.

Staring down into her lap, Mrs. Kettle drew her finger-tip along the upper edge of the envelope and smiled. "We all used to have such fun, didn't we?"

Sophia caught Claxton's sudden downward glance and drawn mouth. Compassion flooded her. Mrs. Kettle's tender words clearly caused him pain. Once, he had been just a boy, and in that moment she glimpsed the magnitude of the hurt he must have felt at being torn away from such loving circumstances. The memory of that difficult time had never receded. Yet at the same time she cautioned herself against feeling too deeply and allowing her softer emotions to be confused for something else.

Unfolding the paper, Mrs. Kettle read the contents, nodding slightly and lips twitching into a broader grin. Setting this and the envelope on top of the baker's box, she stood and lifted a black-and-gold tin from the mantel. Fingering through its contents, she produced an envelope identical to the first.

"I am indeed in possession of the next quest."

Claxton uttered a low exclamation and leaned forward in his chair. Sophia laughed and clapped her gloved hands, thrilled that the diversion would continue.

Mrs. Kettle's sparkling gaze narrowed with sudden discernment. "However, these are not plum cakes; they are queen cakes."

"Queen cakes and plum cakes are almost the same," Claxton argued softly, brows gathered in protest.

The housekeeper snorted mirthfully. "Not at all 'almost the same.' Nor were these prepared by your own hand as the quest specifies."

Claxton eased back in his chair, throwing Sophia an amused glance. "With the weather being so terrible..."

Sophia lifted her teacup for a sip. "We've none of the necessary supplies."

"Poor excuses." Mrs. Kettle *tsked* and shook her head. "And until you present suitable replacements, the next quest in the game will remain unopened. Those were your mother's own rules." She tucked the envelope into her apron pocket. "That doesn't mean we can't enjoy these. My lady?" She extended the open box to Sophia, who after glancing at Claxton selected one. "They are very good." But Mrs. Kettle slyly added, "Though mine are better."

Claxton stood. Three pairs of eyes at the window widened beneath winter caps. "We had best be on our way if we are to complete this task before nightfall." To Sophia, he inquired in a deliberate tone, "Unless you would like to forget the matter altogether."

Sophia's eyes widened with offense. "No, I don't wish to forget the matter altogether. I am consumed with curiosity over the contents of the next quest. We must find them all before the frost recedes and we are obligated to return to London for Christmas."

Mrs. Kettle asked, "Will you work together or compete against one another?"

Sophia looked at Claxton, nodding. "We will compete."

"The lady's choice," said Claxton with a sigh, spreading his upturned hands in surrender.

Mrs. Kettle winked at Claxton. "Very well. I look forward to your presentations, at which time I shall judge which are the best, showing no favoritism to either one of you."

Mr. Kettle dried his feet and found his boots. "I have sat too long in this chair. Sir, if you would allow me to accompany you to the livery, I've a bit of business to attend to with the hostler."

"Your Grace," Mrs. Kettle called. Following them to the door, she produced three brightly colored penny trumpets from her apron.

She pressed them into his hand. "For the three rascals out there. Can you imagine being their age and receiving a trifle from the Duke of Claxton? Give them a memory they'll never forget."

Claxton peered down at the tiny woman. "Thank you for thinking of it."

Moments later, a cacophony of cheers and honks could be heard from outside. Sophia and Mrs. Kettle watched from the window as the boys followed Claxton and Mr. Kettle down the lane.

Sophia said to Mrs. Kettle, "I cannot tell you how pleased I am to have met you and Mr. Kettle."

Mrs. Kettle reached for her hand and squeezed. "Likewise, my dear."

Sophia said, "Seeing his Grace with the two of you . . . well, it's allowed me to see an aspect of him I've not seen before."

"He's quite imposing isn't he? More like his father, in that respect, than I expected. But may I say, madam, that the two of you seem very well suited." Mrs. Kettle crossed to their chairs and refilled both of their teacups.

"His dear mother, the duchess, could not have hoped for better."

"Thank you for saying so." Sophia bit her bottom lip and lowered herself into the chair. A sudden rush of tears stung her eyes, and she attempted to blink them away before Mrs. Kettle saw.

"Oh, my dear." Mrs. Kettle sat down beside her, her brow creased with concern. "That doesn't appear to be a wholehearted expression of agreement."

Sophia cleared her throat. "Things have been difficult of late."

"The marriage is still young." Mrs. Kettle nodded reassuringly. "And from what we've read in the papers, his Grace has traveled much this past year. That can't have been easy, being apart."

"We lost a baby last March," Sophia blurted out, then covered her mouth with her hand. "Forgive me for being so familiar, but being that you are a midwife, I thought perhaps—"

"No apologies, please." Mrs. Kettle reached for her hand and gently squeezed before releasing her. "I'm so sorry to hear. The loss of a child is never easy."

"Afterward everything became strained. We've never quite recovered." Sophia looked into her lap, tracing the seam of her glove with her index finger. "I don't know how things will turn out."

Mrs. Kettle's eyebrows went up. "He would not have learned gentleness or sensitivity from his father."

"No, he wouldn't have, from all I've heard."

A long moment of silence passed, during which myriad emotions passed across Mrs. Kettle's face. "I'll never forget the looks of bewilderment on those boys' faces the day he took them away after their mother's funeral. Even now that memory haunts my dreams. I knew if their lives were anything like what the duchess suffered in the first years of her marriage, they'd be forever changed. The duke might have boasted the finest address in Mayfair, but there were nights when that house saw more depravity than the lowest of dockside bawdy houses."

Sophia felt as if she might be sick. She'd known Claxton hadn't told her the worst of it. She supposed now she could at least imagine.

"It must have been terrible for you and Mr. Kettle to lose the duchess and the boys all at once, and likewise for the boys to lose you. Claxton told me that sometimes he snuck away to visit you and Mr. Kettle at Camellia House."

Mrs. Kettle's gaze held hers unwaveringly. "Then you also know that after his father found out about those visits, he terminated our employment and boarded up the house." She laced one of her wrinkled hands over the other and sighed. "Not long after, we learned Vane had disappeared. Run away! His father's investigator came here looking for him, and I told the man all for the better, that if that dear boy came here, no, thank you very much, I wouldn't be so kind as to let him know." She rocked back into her seat. "He thought I was a horrible woman, but what did he know of the duke and his cruelties? From the time Vane was sixteen, we never saw him again. Until yesterday."

Sophia nodded jerkily. "He seems to believe that he changed in such a manner that he couldn't come back. That he no longer belonged here because he isn't the same person. I think also, in some way he believes his mother would have been disappointed with the life he lived and the man he turned out to be."

"She raised them to be sensitive, caring boys. The duke would have done his best to destroy that." Mrs. Kettle glanced down and shook her head. "But what I would like to tell you, madam, is that within one week of the duke's death we received a letter from the *new* duke's land manager reinstating us to our positions as house- and groundskeeper." Mrs. Kettle pressed her hand over her own heart. "The letter also contained a draft for the full amount of our wages for the years in between."

Sophia's heart swelled with a sudden rush of emotion. "Mrs. Kettle—"

"All that time, you see, he'd waited until he could make things right. As right as he could. He is still that same dear boy at heart." The handkerchief again appeared for a swipe to both eyes—and then across for a dab at Sophia's. "He just needs time to remember."

The sound of a door and men's voices ended their conversation. Mrs. Kettle gave her hand another squeeze before disappearing again into the kitchen.

Vane entered the room and the first sight of him took Sophia's breath away. Snowflakes glistened in his hair, but warmth glowed in his eyes as he laughed in response to something Mr. Kettle said. Even if she and the duke never found true happiness together, she hoped their time in Lacenfleet would bring him some peace from the difficulties of his past.

"Duchess," he said upon seeing her. "We'd best be on our way if we hope to complete this quest of baking cakes today."

Mrs. Kettle emerged from the kitchen, a small bag in her hand. "More sugarplums for the trip to the house! And your dear mother's book of cookery, where you can find the recipe for the cakes."

Before traveling to the house, Vane steered the horse and sledge to the village grocer for the purpose of purchasing the necessary ingredients listed in the recipe book. Outside the shop, furrows from other horses and wagons marred the snow, as did a host of footprints coming from all directions in the village.

When they crossed the threshold, the grocer, a Mr. Gilmichael, left the customers he had been assisting, two elderly ladies, and rushed forward to welcome the duke and duchess and introduce himself. Everyone else present gave a respectful bow or curtsy.

"How may I help you today?"

"Please do complete your business with your customers," Vane insisted. "We will wait until you are finished."

The two gray-haired ladies, dressed in heavy caps and dark wool clothing, nodded their thanks, and the grocer returned to his place behind the counter.

In a low voice, he counseled, "Now, you must understand, this is the last I can offer to you on credit with your account being so much in arrears."

"Yes, Mr. Gilmichael," one of the ladies answered with a nod. "We thank you for being so generous today."

Vane sensed Sophia's rapt attention to the conversation, and indeed, when he glanced down, he discovered her green eyes to be twin reflections of sympathy.

A moment later, the grocer presented the two old

women with a small crate of coal, which they struggled to lift from the counter.

Sophia jabbed him with an elbow. "Offer to deliver the crate to their home."

"Me?" he inquired. He was not in the habit of playing delivery boy.

The ladies held the crate between them and struggled with its weight toward the door.

"Don't be haughty. Just do it," she urged.

Just then, the door opened and damn his eyes if Lady Meltenbourne did not enter.

Sophia nudged him. *"Claxton."*

"Ah—pardon me, ladies." He stepped toward the two, which appeared to startle them because their eyes widened and they dropped the crate to the wooden floor with a loud *thud*.

"Yes, your Grace?" they responded in unison, voices hushed.

"It would give the duchess and myself great satisfaction if you would allow us to convey your purchase to your door."

"Oh no," said the taller of the two, clearly mortified. "We couldn't ask it of you."

Sophia stepped forward. "It's no trouble. We've a sledge, you see. If you'll just provide us with your address, we'll bring your parcel around once we've finished our shopping."

The two glanced at each other. Again, the same woman spoke. "We'd be very grateful, then, if you'd deliver the crate to the orphan house."

She provided them with detailed directions. After a profuse round of thanks, the two ladies disappeared through the door. Lady Meltenbourne, by now, had wandered off to the opposite side of the establishment and presently perused the offerings there.

"The orphan house," whispered Sophia, her gloved hand rising to her mouth. "What a paltry bit of coal on a cold day such as this."

She turned with brisk efficiency toward the grocer. "Mr. Gilmichael, could you please pull your account ledger? The duke and I would be interested in satisfying the outstanding debt for the orphan house and creating a satisfactory line of credit so that they can obtain the coal and food they require at times such as this."

"We would?" said Claxton.

She threw him a sharp glare. "Yes, we would."

Mr. Gilmichael presented the ledger for their review, and Claxton negotiated with Sophia a suitable settlement toward the cause. They also quadrupled the ladies' purchase of coal for that day and purchased several bags of apples and oranges to add to their delivery so the children would have a special treat.

"Now, your Graces, what can I help you with as far as purchases?"

Sophia glanced into the recipe book. "Let's start with citron."

The grocer turned from her and selected a small parcel wrapped in brown paper and string, which he placed on the counter between them.

"My only package." He smiled. "Not much demand for citron in Lacenfleet with the ingredient being so expensive."

A short time later, when their purchases had been loaded onto the sledge and the grocer returned inside, leaving them alone, Claxton assisted Sophia into the seat. "For barely being my wife, you're quite free with spending my money."

"You've an estate here, which makes Lacenfleet your village, Claxton. It's only right that you take an interest in its people. I'm certain the duchess did when she was alive. Not only that, but it is Christmas. If we don't see to the orphans having what they need, who do you think will?"

Sophia was correct, of course. His mother would have done just the same. He could not help but admire her for her generosity. Such charity hadn't occurred to him, not here in Lacenfleet or in the villages near any of his other estates. Which made him a selfish, arrogant ass, didn't it?

"Mrs. Stone, the innkeeper, told me the people here have seen very difficult times over the last several years." She spoke with quiet passion. "You have in your possession the power to change that."

"Ah, but what you suggest now goes beyond simple charity," he answered. "Once the river thaws, I've no plan but to shutter the house again. It's not as if you and I would ever live here for any real length of time. I will, however, speak to Mr. Kettle over how to make better use of the land for the benefit of the village."

Just as Claxton took his place on the blades, the grocer emerged from the doorway in a flustered rush. "Oh, your Grace, I'm so glad to have caught you before you departed. I've more gifts for the orphans." He held two large paper sacks. "Peppermints. From the Countess of Meltenbourne inside. She asks that you deliver them with all the rest."

Claxton observed a warm blush brighten Sophia's cheeks, one he could only interpret as pleasure. She took the bags and settled them onto her lap.

"Please tell her thank you," said Sophia as Claxton snapped the reins.

After a brief trip, they delivered the coal, fruit, and peppermints to the orphan home and remained for the next hour as honored guests, drinking tea and visiting with the children. The two widow caretakers could only press their faces into handkerchiefs when informed of the duke and duchess's generous financial bestowal. Only then did Vane return with Sophia to Camellia House as a fresh layer of snowflakes fell.

Their morning had passed in pleasant companionship, the ugliness of the days before, while not forgotten, at least dimmed. Still, Sophia's words of that morning sounded over and over again in his mind, that perhaps a separation remained the best decision for their marriage. But for his part, he could only see how well they got along together, just as they had before tragedy had pulled them apart. He had enjoyed their morning and could not be more pleased at how she and the Kettles had taken to one another. And their good deed for the orphans. He'd never been so moved by the simple act of giving a gift. And yet the gift would have gone ungiven, if not for Sophia.

In the kitchen he laid the fire while Sophia opened packages.

"Remember, the shopkeeper recommended that we dry the flour well." Sophia placed two pans, in which she'd spread the powdery stuff thin, on a small table near the stove. "This will be your flour, and this will be mine."

Vane, at Sophia's direction, searched the cabinet for baking tins. "How very good of him to realize neither of us are experienced bakers."

"Don't try to throw me off, you sneaky devil," Sophia teased.

He glanced over his shoulder, his attention immediately snagged by the velvety tone of her voice. "Sneaky devil?"

"I haven't forgotten your words of warning this morning." She turned toward him, her hair gleaming darkly in the lamplight. Her eyes narrowed, but playfully. "You aren't to be trusted when playing this game. You likely have some knowledge of cookery from helping your mother and Mrs. Kettle."

She wiped her hands on a linen towel.

He shrugged and shook his head. "That was ages ago."

"Whatever you say." She pointed at him and squinted. "I've got my eye on you."

"Likewise, Duchess," he drawled, his gaze slowly traveling down the length of her luscious body. "Though perhaps for entirely different reasons."

"Claxton, now none of that," she chastened, throwing the towel at him.

"You say that as if I can help it."

Next, she placed two bowls of similar size beside each other on the large table at the center of the room. Standing face-to-face, they broke sixteen eggs into each. When that was done, Vane removed his coat, waistcoat, and cravat and rolled his sleeves high. Turning back, he caught Sophia studying him and was struck by an ache so strong the force of it stole his breath. Did he inspire admiration or dislike in her? He wished he knew what she'd done with that deuced list of names he had written out. If he knew, he would find it and burn it; then they could go on as if it had never existed.

"If you don't mind waiting, I'm going to change," she announced. "The dress I wore yesterday is much more serviceable than this one."

"Go on. I'll wait." He could not help but add, "Unless you require assistance?"

"I'll pretend I didn't hear that," she said, disappearing through the door.

A smile turned his lips. Despite the fragile state of their marriage, he liked being here in the kitchen with her. Many of his most vibrant memories of his mother had taken place here. On cold winter nights, she had read books to him and his brother beside the stove. They'd played games such as hoodman-blind or Shoe the Wild Mare until their eyelids drooped, the loser always insisting on one more round. No one wanted to be the last to lose before being sent off to bed. He and Haden as boys had always taken games and winning seriously.

As for the game of lookabout, they'd refined that particular competition to a higher level. Sometimes the contest became downright ruthless but all in good fun.

Should he play in a similar manner against Sophia? No.

Claxton smiled. Or perhaps...yes. He was, indeed, a sneaky devil.

Ah, the dark arts of kitchen sabotage. He chuckled, pulling one tray of flour away from the fire's heat, so it would not dry as thoroughly as the other. Damp flour would ensure a most disappointingly dense cake.

Now that he'd decided to take such a tack, he did not think it prudent at this juncture to tell Sophia just how much experience he had in the kitchen. After marrying, they'd enjoyed the benefit of a talented cook and kitchen staff, and somehow the subject had just never come up.

His father had granted the duchess only two servants, Mr. and Mrs. Kettle, so oftentimes meal preparation required more hands, and countless times as a boy, and especially around holidays like Christmas, he'd been drafted into service by Mrs. Kettle and his mother to turn the beef roast on the spit or to pound almonds for a cake. He'd observed and learned much.

Later in the military, he'd employed those lessons often while he traveled and lodged in rustic circumstances without benefit of staff or servants. Often he'd found himself with the barest of ingredients, with only his creativity to produce palatable results. Quite simply, he liked to eat, and eat well, and if there was no one to prepare a meal for him, he would prepare a reasonably fine one of his own.

Taking one bowl of eggs—the one he intended to be Sophia's—he proceeded to the servants' door, where, with the help of a wooden spoon, he disposed of *one, two, three, four* into the snow. With the toe of his boot, he covered the evidence of his misdeed. Returned inside, he located a whisk and set about beating the hell out of his perfectly portioned bowl of eggs.

Some quarter hour later, he heard her footsteps. Fireside, he slid the much-cooled tray of flour again toward the stove. He returned his bowl of eggs to the table.

As soon as she entered, he smiled. "Good. You are

here. Let's get started." He picked up the same bowl and circled his whisk round the inside of the bowl. "I've set out a whisk for you as well."

"A whisk? What is that?"

He lifted his. "It looks like—"

She waggled hers at him. "I know what a whisk is. It's just very telling that you do as well. That's all. Ages ago, indeed."

He winked at her, and she looked away.

"Too bad for you, though," she continued. "I do believe women have an innate talent for baking and sweets, regardless of experience. It's all about following instructions precisely."

"Instructions, yes." Claxton took up the recipe book. "This recipe says to take care not to overbeat the eggs." He read the words aloud. Or pretended to.

She halted, examining the contents of her bowl. "Well, then, I think they are beaten well enough."

"Mine as well," he said.

Any good cook knew eggs needed to be beaten relentlessly so the batter would rise properly. It was right there in the recipe, if she cared to look. Really, it was astounding the mischief one could do right in front of another person when that person was not in possession of a suspicious nature. He almost felt guilty. Almost.

"Baking is a messy business," she muttered, dabbing a cloth at the front of her dress.

In the cabinet he found a length of linen, the sort Mrs. Kettle had always used as an apron, and came behind her to drape the fabric about her waist. She stiffened in the circle of his arms, and for a moment, he considered pressing a kiss to the side of her neck...

But instead he quickly tied the ends into a knot and proceeded to cover his own clothing in a like fashion.

Sophia exhaled, as if relieved, and lifted her arms to adjust one of the pins in her hair, the movement stretching her bodice over her breasts, revealing all their glorious rounded splendor.

She caught him staring and froze. Yet she said nothing as the blush suffused her cheeks. She only turned back to her bowl, which in his mind gave him permission to stare some more.

Claxton suffered both a love and a hatred of women's fashion. While the simple dresses displayed a woman's breasts most attractively—his lovely wife's a perfect example—they concealed the remainder of her shape within the classical column of her high-waisted skirt. One could only guess as to the true slenderness of a woman's waist or the lushness of her bottom. However, the makeshift apron, tightly cinched, confirmed what he already knew. Sophia was a goddess.

Two hours later, his goddess stared woefully into her bowl. White powder mottled her cheeks, and her hair had half fallen from its pins.

"I have a renewed appreciation for Cook and her staff," she said wearily. "Really, Claxton, this is a ridiculous amount of effort for twelve little cakes. I have had quite enough of creaming, beating, combining, and pounding. Not to mention all that miserable mincing. Will this task ever end?" Her shoulders slumped.

Even exhausted, she had watched him like a hawk, and he'd not been able to sabotage her cakes further. But he thought his luck might be about to change.

He leaned forward. "You've a piece of citron in your

hair." He plucked the sliver free. She looked more delicious than any cake and he wanted very badly to eat her up.

"How many more ingredients are there?" She groaned.

"Just one." He smiled, having waited patiently for this very moment. He lifted a bottle from the table and pried the cork free. *Pop.* "The brandy."

Chapter Eleven

$\mathscr{I}$ found four in the basement from which to choose," the duke announced, lining the bottles up beside one another. "Each very old, but I think this one may best suit our purposes. May I have your opinion?"

Sophia approached, standing on the other side of the table. She felt safer doing that, placing some piece of furniture or fixture between them. Not that he would reach out and grab her, but she had started against all good sense to wish that he would. They were having altogether too much fun together.

Accepting the bottle he offered, she held the opening below her nose and sniffed. The strong scent of spirits momentarily dizzied her.

"Oh, come now," he chided with a grin that made her heart jump in her chest. "You've got to taste it."

She stole another glance at him. The light from the stove painted his features in contrasting strokes of gold and shadow, defining his imperfect warrior's nose and broad cheeks framed by three days' worth of unshaved whiskers. For the hundredth time in the past hour, she noted how handsome he was.

"You know that I don't make a habit of drinking brandy," she answered playfully.

Yes, of course, he would know from before. They'd known each other so well. But then in the end—they hadn't. She tried to remind herself of that.

"But is it because you don't like spirits?" He smiled at her, a flash of white teeth. She'd become quite obsessed with his lips, the one on the top being rather thin, but the bottom one, full and sensual in contrast, a rather perfect pair. She'd always found him attractive, but somehow now that they were estranged, he had become even more so.

The more fascinated she felt by him, the more irritated she became.

"As a mannered lady, I've little exposure to spirits," she retorted. "No doubt the *ladies* with whom you are familiar make a regular practice of—"

"Shush, goose." He reached to press a fingertip to her mouth.

She blushed and pulled away, embarrassed by the unexpected touch and his use of an endearment. He'd never had a special name for her before. Just *Sophia* and *darling* and *dearest*. Why now?

He splashed a bit into the first of four little beveled liquor glasses. "Neither of us will feel any effect from this inconsequential bit, if that is your concern."

"Of course not," she scoffed, staring at his lips. *Heavens.* To think she'd kissed them just yesterday, and with such passion. "I wasn't saying so."

She sipped carefully from the first cup. Though she did her best to do so without any reaction, her throat tightened against the liquor's fiery path. She cleared her throat and softly wheezed her next breath. He did the same with the next three brandies, pouring a sample from each and setting the bottles down behind their representative glass. Soon, they had sampled all four. Or so he believed. She had dumped the last two samples into the refuse bucket beside her feet.

"Which one do you believe is the best quality?" he asked.

"Clearly I am no connoisseur," she said, smiling widely. "It's my opinion that one tastes just as fine as the next." At imbibing just that spare amount, everything inside her went warm and relaxed. Licking her bottom lip, she impatiently shrugged off her spencer. "As long as we are baking, I don't think it matters which one we use."

"I disagree," he said rather earnestly, picking up the second bottle in the row. "Sample this one again."

Sophia stared at Claxton, keeping all evidence of emotion from her face.

How stupid did her husband think she was? Now he was trying to get her drunk, all to win a child's game? Did he truly believe she was so unobservant as to not realize he'd removed four eggs from her bowl?

But she was more observant than he, apparently, because the moment he'd turned his back she had dumped a cupful of salt into his bowl. Unaware, when he'd turned back to the task he kept right on stirring. She giggled.

Claxton smiled across the table. "What are you laughing about?"

"Nothing." She giggled again. "Just a little thought

here inside my head that I don't intend to share with you."

His eyes widened. "Now I really want to know."

"I don't think you do," she assured.

Really, how many dukes ever used the words *whisk* or *sift* in conversation? She'd been instantly suspicious upon hearing such domesticated words from his lips. Thankfully she'd had the sense of mind not to voice her accusations. If he knew she was keen to him, she would not be able to beat him at his own dastardly game.

"I don't need to sample the brandy again. I trust your judgment." She smiled brightly. "Let's use that one."

Disappointment momentarily soured his countenance. With a sigh, he lifted the glass and downed the contents himself. The urge to laugh overcame Sophia and she snorted into her apron.

"What was that?" he asked sullenly.

"A sneeze. I'm sorry. A bit of flour must have got up my nose."

He licked the damp residue of the brandy from his lips, something she would have liked to do herself, if they were on kissing terms.

Had she really just thought that? Two little splashes of brandy had affected her mind, which was why she never drank it. She ought to have known better. She needed all her wits about her so she'd know when her wicked husband attempted another trick.

They each measured a cup of brandy into their respective bowls of batter, and after stirring the batter one last time, they filled the individual cake tins. Sophia's cakes would be shaped like hearts, and his, fluted spheres. When at last the tins had been conveyed into the oven, they looked at each other.

"Not long now," said Claxton, rubbing his hands together.

He washed the bowls and pans and assorted other whatnot and Sophia dried. When they'd finished, she moved about the kitchen, returning spices and utensils to their places. With a broom, he swept clean the oilcloth that covered the floor.

"I'm too tired to do any more," said Sophia, collapsing, exhausted, into a chair.

"Then let's sit." Claxton dragged a chair to the space beside hers and sat so close his thigh brushed her skirts. "We can tidy the rest later."

Sophia sighed, her cheeks flushed, feeling languid. "One benefit of brandy, it certainly warms one from the inside out."

He looked back at her, heavy lidded and intent. "Indeed, it does."

With just that look, a sensation of heat and excitement formed in her lower belly. She stared at his lips, remembering a time when she'd kissed them whenever she liked.

As if he read her thoughts, he lifted his hand and touched her face, tracing a fingertip along the outline of her cheek and jaw. "I want to kiss you."

He'd spoken her thoughts aloud, which pleased her more than it ought to. Yet she had to keep her head because she had so much to lose. "You and I kissing would be ill-advised, considering everything."

"I know things aren't perfect between us." The smile fell from his face. Leaning forward, all sudden seriousness, he brushed his knuckles along her lower lip. "But there's no rule that says we can't be fond of one another, goose."

"Fond," she repeated. Such a nice word, and yet it implied a certain contentment and peace of mind. No, fond did not describe her feelings toward Claxton. Her feelings were very much tumultuous and confused. And passionate.

"Why have you been calling me goose?" she asked, hopelessly flustered, thinking to lighten the subject and cool the dangerous heat building between them.

"I've always called you goose inside my head." He drew his fingertip down the center of her throat, a path toward her heart. "It's because you have such a lovely… long neck."

She'd been wound as tight as a spring all day. For nearly a year, there had been only the sweet embraces of her family, the affectionate pats of friends on her hand or back. Her body recognized the difference and reacted as if starved.

A small sound burst from her lips. The duke's eyes fixed on hers, glazed over.

"Sophia—"

Needing space, if only to breathe, she stood and crossed to the window. Lifting the curtain, she stared out at the falling snow. "How much longer do you think we will be trapped here?"

Anything more than a half hour and she feared she'd be lost. Claxton, in close quarters, had proved too magnetic to resist. If only they were in London, she could secure herself behind the protective wall of her family, of her own private rooms, until she was ready.

He came to stand behind her, a mere inch away, so that his heat warmed the skin of her back. Little prickles of desire danced across the lowermost part of her spine, weakening her legs.

"Impossible to say." His voice, low in his throat, vibrated through her, and she shivered as if from the sensuous brush of a feather. "Right now, I can't bring myself to care. I can't think of anyplace I'd rather be than here with you."

He rested his hands on her shoulders and smoothed them down over her arms before sweeping her hair aside at her nape. She exhaled, unwilling to move or twist away. "You have such beautiful hair. For so long I've imagined touching it again." He inhaled, his mouth and nose pressed against her bare skin. "I've imagined smelling it, remembered the slide of it across my skin."

This was Claxton. *Vane.* The old desires were there. They had never gone away.

Her heart ached from wanting him for so long, and now that he touched her like this and talked to her so sweetly, she found it nearly impossible to remember why she ought to say no. He pressed his lips to the side of her neck. The sensation of his lips, his warm breath, and the friction of his whiskers on her skin sent jolts of pleasure into her breasts and deep into her belly. A sensation much like being tickled, so delicious her toes curled.

Unsteady, she leaned back against his chest and gripped the window frame. The room had filled with the scent of baking cakes. Snow fell outside the window. Everything seemed so right.

"Sophia," he whispered, as with his hand he lifted her chin back to rest her head against his shoulder. The same hand descended again, lightly stroking the exposed column of her neck and collarbone. "Dearest goose. I've missed you."

"I wish you... wouldn't say things like that."

With a low growl, he wrapped his arms about her waist, enveloping her body in sinew and heat. "Why not?"

She melded against him, like a drowsy cat seeking warmth. "I like them too much."

"I like you too much."

He placed one kiss on the side of her neck, then another on her cheek... and her temple, her hair falling over them both. With each press of his lips against her skin and each stroke of his hand, desire coiled up inside her, tightening with each kiss, so much so she had to clench her teeth not to gasp or cry out.

"Your skin is so soft," he murmured.

His warm breath on her skin tantalized and made her squirm. His hands moved over her clothes, touching her everywhere, sweeping up her torso to cup and squeeze her breasts—

"Ah," she gasped, seizing them in her own, intending to stop him.

"Shhhh," he soothed.

She did not stop him. She did not want to. Her hands slid up his neck into his hair, while his descended in a pleasurable downward sweep to the indention between her legs, where with the heel of his palm he massaged her until in a sudden rush of need she twisted in his arms, meeting his devouring lips with her own. They did a slow little dance across the floor until her bottom bumped the table.

"Just kissing," she whispered against his lips, seizing him tight. He was so much larger than she, a difference that had always pleased her. "Nothing more."

"Kissing. Is that what this is?" Vane's breath filled her mouth in warm, brandy-sweet bursts. He thrust his fingers into the hair on either side of her face and cradled her skull, trailing kisses along her jaw, her chin, her nose, her mouth, and eyelids. "Very well. It's enough. For now."

There was a place against his neck that always intrigued her whenever he talked or turned his head. Sophia's mouth found that place now, where his skin tasted of salt and citron and sugar. In the back of her mind, a faint voice, perhaps that of her sensible self, told her she really ought to stop this now because all this kissing and touching and teasing would only lead to—

"Stop thinking," he murmured, coaxing her mouth open with pressure from his tongue. Her legs ajar just enough, he eased between them, his hands planted on the tabletop at either side of her hips. Gently, with only the pressure of his face and lips, he urged her head back and left a trail of kisses along the same path down the center of her neck as his fingertip had taken moments before. She arched backward, lost to sensation.

Taking full advantage, he again cupped her breasts and squeezed them together. She moaned, and her hands clenched his torso, a response that only aroused him further. What had he been thinking when he'd claimed to hate women's fashions? Everything about her was *more* than he remembered. More alluring. More fragrant and intoxicating. And her breasts, so soft and round and plump. He slid her gown from her shoulders.

"That is not kissing." She pushed his hands away and jerked the garment back up. But she did not push *him* away. Instead, she lay halfway across the table, her eyes sleepy, her lips swollen and parted. An alluring pagan offering in want of more kissing.

"But it would be." He smiled. His fingertips traced the

edge of her neckline downward, daring to slip to the plush flesh beneath, grazing over her nipple. "I want to kiss you *there*."

"Claxton." She gasped and jerked in response. Her cheeks flushed a deeper shade of pink.

His blood pulsed *forward*, like a team of horses hell-bent on one destination. Kissing most certainly was not enough.

He dragged his palms upward over her knees and across the tops of her thighs, ruching her skirts at her hips, exposing her stockinged legs and their black garters. Reaching behind and beneath her buttocks, he seized her, dragging her bottom closer to the edge of the table so their bodies joined more closely.

She stared up at him, eyes wide and expectant. Heat bathed the confines of the kitchen and a hazy golden glow from the stove. Behind her lay a sturdy table, the perfect height upon which to make love. The thought of her stretched beneath him on the aged wood, of rutting into her on a surface still strewn with flour and sugar, sent his already hard cock to twitching with impatience. Bloody hell, she was his wife and they ought to be—

He bent to kiss her—

"The cakes," she exclaimed and twisted free of him. Her hands went to the place between her breasts, where she pinched and adjusted her corset. With a flutter of her hands, she cooled her cheeks. "How much time has passed?"

"Let them burn." The way he burned. He groaned, suffering a physical pain at her sudden absence from his arms. "I'd be more than happy to forget the game. I propose we occupy our time in other ways."

Wicked ways.

"Your lack of competitive spirit disappoints me," she called without looking at him.

"Disappointed... you may be that," he muttered, thinking how unhappy she was going to be once she saw the difference in their cakes.

"Let yours burn if you like. I am more than happy to claim the prize."

Prize? His erection throbbed, dissatisfied. He'd almost won the prize. Primitive male rationale told him if he could only make love to her and pleasure her enough and get her with child, she wouldn't ever leave him again.

She prattled on, taking up two thick woolen pads and approaching the oven. But her eyes were glazed and her cheeks flushed, proof she'd been just as aroused as he.

"I can't wait to see them," she declared shakily. "Don't be envious when mine turn out better."

"I'll try."

She bent and pulled her tins from inside the stove. He bit the side of his thumb. Certainly there would be no more kissing allowed after this. Hell, it might be days or even weeks before she allowed him to touch her breasts again. For that reason, if no other, he now felt a staggering degree of remorse for what he'd done.

"Hmmm." Her cheek twitched, and she glared at him. "I expected them to rise more. But perhaps this is how they are intended to look?"

"Let me pull out mine, and we can compare." He took the rag from her and carefully removed his cake tins, which boasted twelve perfectly plump, rounded tops.

Her mouth fell open. "Yours turned out completely different. I wonder why."

Of course they had. His flour had been dry and he'd used the proper number of eggs.

Did he detect a note of suspicion in her voice? Too late for that. He tried not to appear smug. He'd also buttered his tins while she searched the cabinet for the missing twelfth heart-shaped tin, which he had strategically hidden behind the farthest row of pots.

With ease he turned his cakes out of their metal forms and sifted powdered sugar on them. Their heat instantly glazed the sugar into a thin icing.

Sophia, however, hadn't managed to remove a single one of her cakes. Dismayed, she exclaimed, "They are hopelessly stuck."

Of course they were stuck. After drinking that brandy, she'd completely forgotten to butter her tins. She knew better! But at some point, in *stealth*, Claxton had buttered his.

"Something stinks," she muttered.

He did not glance up from the plate, where he arranged his cakes with meticulous care. "Probably just some crumbs burning in the oven."

No, that's not what she meant. That isn't what she'd meant at all. With a knife, she at last chiseled one cake free. Or part of one. Half the heart remained in the tin.

"Don't worry about the ragged edges. They'll look grand once you sift them over with icing," he assured.

"Yes, I am sure Mrs. Kettle's decision will be determined *on taste*," she said, eyes narrowing. Even without the proper number of eggs, hers would taste much better than his overly salted cakes.

"*I strategize*," he had said. Well, Claxton, so did she.

She proceeded to chisel out the remainder of her cakes.

He had plied her with *brandy*, and worse yet, she now realized, *kisses*. If she hadn't been so befuddled by brandy, she wouldn't have been such a willing participant. That probably wasn't even true, but she felt better thinking it. But she wasn't done yet.

Shoving the broken pieces together, she sifted sugar over them and did her best to arrange them in an appetizing fashion. Soon they were both bundled up, and Sophia seated in the sledge with their cakes held in her lap in two baskets so he could drive.

"Oh, dear," she cried. "I've forgotten my mittens."

He stepped down off the blade. "I'll go back for them."

How very gallant he was, for a *charlatan*. She gave him instructions where to find them, and as soon as he disappeared inside the house, she scrambled out from the sledge, pausing only long enough to secure her plate of cakes in the soft nest of the blanket. With a wicked laugh, she tossed his basket aside into the snow.

Mittens drawn from her pockets, she yanked the reins free and climbed onto the blades. She was much better at driving carriages and handling horses than baking cakes. She'd never driven a sledge, but how difficult could it be?

The first bend in the road answered her question. When the sledge swung wide into a deeper snowbank, the vehicle and animal leading it lurched to a stop.

* * *

"I couldn't find your mittens, but I—"

Claxton's voice trailed away at finding only the deep groove of the sledge's blades in the snow to greet him.

Not just that, but his cakes lay scattered in the snow beside his upended basket. Bells jangled in the distance.

A glance down the hill revealed the horse and sledge with Sophia expertly poised on the blades, reins in hand, her dark hair streaming out behind her.

Laughter welled up from inside his chest. "You little minx!"

Of course he hadn't found her mittens. She'd tricked him. All along, his spirited young wife had been playing the game just as hard as he. Of course she had.

But the game wasn't over yet. Grinning, he grabbed the basket and tossed his frozen cakes inside.

* * *

A flicker of movement at the corner of her eye caught her attention. Claxton raced in the opposite direction of the road, churning across the paddock, snow flying up in his wake. Amazingly, it appeared he carried the discarded basket of cakes. Curse his long legs and boots.

He proceeded past the place where they had crossed the frozen riverbed the day before. From a distance, voices shouted and laughed. On the hilltop that overlooked the village, children played. Several boys threw snowballs while another group raised a small army of snowmen. Still others streaked on sleds or barrel lids down the snow-covered hill.

"No," she wailed, realizing his intent. Snapping the reins, she urged the horse to resume its forward motion. With a shrill whinny, the animal plowed forward, high stepping through the snow, yanking the sledge free.

But it was too late. Claxton commandeered a sled and

barreled down the hill, his coattails rippling on the wind. Sophia urged the horse onward, down the public road and through the village, where at last she slid to a stop in front of the Kettles' cottage.

The basket had tipped during travel, and several cakes had rolled across the floor of the sledge. Retrieving them, she blew them off and hastily returned them to the basket.

Claxton was nowhere to be seen, but a downward glance revealed fresh boot prints on the steps. Her spirits sank. Mr. Kettle opened the door and conducted her into the parlor.

"I'll see what's keeping Mrs. Kettle," he said, disappearing into another room.

Claxton turned from the fire, where he stood warming his hands. A mirthful smile broke across his face. "Oh, Sophia." He chuckled, his eyes lit with humor and admiration. "How delightful. I'd never have expected it of you."

She stormed across the carpet. "You deserve being left for sabotaging my cakes."

"I told you there were no rules." He met her halfway, his wicked smile all the confession she required.

"You tried to get me foxed."

He moved closer still. "I told you I played hard. That I would do anything to win."

"You *kissed* me."

He growled low in his throat. "I did more than that."

She held on tight to the cakes for fear he would snatch them from her hands.

"I might eventually be convinced to apologize for it all." He bent and seized her and kissed her hard on the mouth. "Except for the kissing and touching you. Never that."

Footsteps sounded on the threshold. He released her and with a wink stepped back.

"I am told we have cakes," said Mrs. Kettle.

"Yes, here," said Sophia dazedly. Claxton threw her a smile of pure sin.

"May I see them, then?"

Sophia handed them to the older woman. Claxton did the same, retrieving his basket from near the fire.

"Dear, take her ladyship's redingote. It's become overly warm in this small room."

Mr. Kettle assisted her in removing the garment. Unlike Mrs. Kettle, Sophia didn't feel overly warm. Indeed, without her coat, she suffered a distinct chill. She crossed her arms over her chest and sidled a few inches closer to the fire.

The elderly woman examined the cakes. "Oh, my. The hearts are falling to pieces, and the medallions appear to be crusted with snow."

Claxton glanced to Sophia, then back to Mrs. Kettle. "Perhaps taste will distinguish one from the other."

Mrs. Kettle did not appear convinced. "Perhaps."

She tasted Sophia's offering first. "The texture is a bit disappointing. Very hard and dense." With a shrug, she popped a pinch of Claxton's into her mouth. She blinked, coughed, and swallowed. "Salt. Far too much salt. Mr. Kettle, where did I set my cup of tea?"

"Salt?" exclaimed Claxton. "No, that can't be, I followed the measurements precisely—"

His gaze shot to Sophia. *"You."*

"Shenanigans!" declared Mrs. Kettle. "No surprise there. I do believe we must declare this particular effort a tie."

"No matter." Sophia glanced at Claxton and back to Mrs. Kettle. Her arms dropped to her sides. "I believe we have decided to work together to complete the subsequent quests."

Mrs. Kettle looked up with a smile. Her gaze, however, veered in another direction. Downward to the front of Sophia's dress.

"Yes, your Grace, I can see that you have," she replied tartly. She burst out with a delighted laugh.

Looking down, Sophia saw the reason for Mrs. Kettle's mirth. Each of her breasts bore a white, powdery imprint in the distinct shape of Claxton's hand.

* * *

Vane could not help but delight in Sophia's mortification, which he found no less than adorable. She had hardly been able to enunciate the words *good night* to the Kettles, let alone walk a straight line from the cottage to the sledge without his arm for assistance. Even so, they had completed the second quest to Mrs. Kettle's satisfaction and were in possession of the third, which they had decided to open upon their return to Camellia House.

Though the sky already dimmed into a lavender twilight, once arriving at the top of the hill, on impulse Claxton drove out to where several village boys still sledded and urged Sophia to disembark the sledge.

"Wait here," he said.

"Where are you going?" she asked, frowning.

He left her there without further answer. Returning the sledge to the bottom of the hill, he secured the horse and climbed the incline. From the edge she peered over, watching him make the ascent. Perhaps he was wrong, but he believed he saw a begrudging admiration in her eyes, an appreciation of his physical strength and his capability. Like a fool green boy, he very much liked the feeling of impressing her.

Still, to say she was happy would be a vast misstatement. Something was wrong, and he could not help but feel that that something had nothing to do with the handprints he'd left on her breasts and everything to do with their marriage. He didn't know what to do. He knew only he'd had the most wonderful time with her today. Still, he knew the existence of that damn list hovered over them like a dark cloud. He'd do anything to make her forget.

"I'm weary and cold, Claxton. I don't want to wait here while you sled with the boys."

"I'm not going to sled with the boys." He laughed. "I'm going to sled with you."

"Me?" The stolid expression dropped from Sophia's face. Her green eyes sparked with interest.

"I thought you might like to try."

Sophia did want to try. He could tell by the way she peered down the slope and the small smile teasing the corner of her pretty mouth.

"What if I fall off? What if I go tumbling and my skirts fly up in front of those young boys and I humiliate myself worse than I already have today?" She closed her eyes. "Oh, Claxton. What must the Kettles think of me?"

He chuckled, pleased that she cared. Taking a chance, he slipped his gloved hand into hers and lifted her knuckles to his lips. "They think you're delightful."

"I've never been more embarrassed in my life."

Her eyes fixed on his lips. He kissed her and then she

met his gaze. She let out a shaky breath and bit her lower lip. Her cheeks pinked, and he knew she was remembering, as was he, their passionate—yet unfinished—interlude in the kitchen.

"You shouldn't be. We are married. They want us to be happy." He pulled her into the circle of his arms and lowered his head—

Sophia paled, and she averted her face. "Not in front of the children."

He glanced over his shoulder to find they had an audience of at least seven, all gaping at them with wide eyes and open mouths. Reluctantly, he released her and drew back but retained possession of one of her hands.

"What can I say?" he murmured intimately. "You make me forget myself."

"Claxton—" Still, she refused to meet his gaze.

And he knew with a sudden intensity, he did not want to hear what she had to say.

"Sophia, I'm going to go get on that sled and go over the edge." His thumb rubbed the underside of her wrist. "Even though I'm not certain what's on the other side. Perhaps the ride will be bumpy and rough at times, but for the most part it will be exhilarating. I promise."

"You know what's on the other side," she said in a low voice. "You sledded down the hill not even an hour ago."

He blinked. "I was speaking metaphorically."

Beneath the brim of her hat, her lashes lowered, hiding her reaction.

"I know that," she answered softly.

Turning sideways, he coaxed her toward the sleds. "Come on. We'll go down together. There will be no tumbling and no skirts flying. I won't allow it."

At last, Sophia nodded in assent.

Claxton signaled to the same boy as before. Eager to earn another coin, the child pulled his sled to the ledge. Closer now, she saw something she hadn't from a distance. The boy's trousers and coat had holes in them, and he wore tattered boots.

"Thank you, young man," said Claxton, pressing a coin into his hand—one Sophia recognized on the boy's open palm to be a half crown.

Her throat constricted with a sudden onrush of emotion. Just that morning, Claxton had seemed so oblivious to the idea of charity, of giving to those less fortunate. But he had just given the boy enough to warmly clothe an entire family.

Claxton removed his hat and handed it off to the boy. He then sat on the small wooden platform, planting his boots at the forward end. Looking toward her, he beckoned with his hand. "Sit here, between my legs."

In that moment, Sophia's heart opened another small bit. Perched on the edge of this hillside, Claxton extended an invitation to her, one that had nothing to do with seduction or producing heirs or winning a game, and everything to do with creating a memory. Claxton might not realize it, but she did.

How could she explain to him that she wasn't perturbed about the cakes or even those appalling handprints? Rather, her mood stemmed from the certain fear that she was falling in love with him, head over heels, all over again. And that the only reasonable response was for her to pull away, to protect herself from the pain that loving him would most assuredly bring.

When she loved, she loved completely, yet given all

she'd learned of Claxton over the past three days, she now understood why his heart might never be capable of returning that love to the same degree. It wasn't his fault. His father had done everything to destroy the gentler side of him.

But while to her, love and lovemaking were entwined into one experience, the same wasn't true for her husband. He hadn't loved any of those other women any more than he loved her. She feared more than anything the most he would ever be able to offer her would be fondness—however sincere—and the carnal offerings of his body. The same thing he'd offered those other women before their marriage. It wasn't enough, but if she wanted a baby within the legal bonds of marriage, she had to find a way to come to terms.

She took his hand, climbed onto the sled, and sat.

A flush rose into her cheeks at the easy familiarity of settling so intimately against him, of the sensation of his muscular legs bracketing her safely in place and his warm chest against her back. She tucked her skirts underneath her legs.

"Wrap your arms around my legs and hold on tight." Sophia did as Claxton instructed, his roughened voice in her ear. His arm came across her abdomen, a solid band of wool-covered muscle.

"Are you ready?" he asked quietly. "You know that once we go over the edge, there's no turning back."

"That's what I'm afraid of."

"Don't be."

At his encouragement, the boy gave them a running push. The blades *swooshed* over the snow, and at the precipice the sled tilted downward—

Cold air streamed against her face, blowing Sophia's hair free of her hat. *Faster.* The sled rocked and rattled as the landscape flew past. *Faster!* A wild, billowing pleasure spiraled up inside her, the purest sensation of joy, returning her, for the briefest moment, to the happiest days of her youth when her heart carried no fear or premonition of hurt or tragedy. She laughed, then screamed, as Claxton held her tight, his face pressed close beside hers. His laughter rumbled against her back.

Sophia regretted when all too quickly they arrived at the bottom. The sled bumped and skidded to an eventual stop. The euphoria in her chest calmed, and when the boy bounded down behind them to return the duke's hat and to reclaim his sled, she almost begged them both for another turn at the hill. Instead she remained quiet. Dragging his sled, the boy returned to the top, where his friends cheered.

Sophia straightened her redingote and laughed. "I feared that rickety thing would fall to pieces beneath us. It shook and rattled so!"

"You enjoyed it then." Eyes bright, with his hair blown straight back from his face, he looked very much in his element, like a Russian prince, alive and glorious, against the backdrop of winter.

"Yes. Oh yes," she exclaimed. "Thank you for taking me down."

With his hand at the small of her back, he led her toward the sledge, their boots crunching over the snow. Fat, fluffy snowflakes fell all around them, and the cold worked its way through the soles of her boots and through her clothing. She shivered.

"You're cold." He wrapped an arm around her shoulders, and with a twist of his other, he removed the scarf from his own neck and draped it round hers. "I apologize. I shouldn't have pressed you to—"

"No," she interrupted. "The best sort of cold. What fun! And I saw what you did up there."

She glanced at his profile.

"What is that?" he asked, his cheeks ruddy and handsome against the stark white background of the hillside. The wind ruffled his hair. She avoided looking at his lips in a failed effort to forget their passionate embraces in the kitchen.

"That boy," she said. "Quite different from the others, with threadbare clothes and his boots in pieces. You made sure to use his sled, the most dubious of the lot, and gave him a half crown."

"A half crown?" He glanced down at her from beneath dark lashes. "Surely not. Only a shilling."

She pinched his sleeve. "A half crown, Claxton."

"Purely by mistake." He returned his hat to his head. "He was merely the closest and most eager."

"I don't believe you."

His eyes burned into hers with a sudden flare of intensity. "Is it so difficult to believe there is something good inside me?"

"No, Claxton," she answered softly. "Not at all."

A slight pause followed.

"It is almost Christmas," he said, jerking his chin aside and peering out over the village. "Perhaps he will purchase new shoes or a coat. But more likely, I expect, he will feed his family."

He extended his arm, and she grasped it, climbing into the sledge.

After a short ride, they arrived to a darkened Camellia House. A half hour later, a blazing fire and the careful placement of screens vanquished the chill from the great room. There, in the same place where they had partaken of Mrs. Kettle's wonderful meal, they ate the guinea fowls given to them by the innkeeper the previous day with bread, cheese, and some Christmas beer they'd purchased in the village.

"You play chess, don't you?" he asked when they were done, setting up a board with the proper pieces. Having removed his coat but not his cravat, he looked very much like a gentleman at ease.

"It has been a long time. I'm certain I've forgotten how." Sophia had intended after the meal to immediately retire to her room.

"Oh, I can't believe that," he answered wryly, tilting his head downward and giving her a suspicious eye. "One doesn't forget how to play chess."

A familiar heaviness filled her chest, one formed of hurtful memories.

"Perhaps that is true," she agreed. "It's just that I was the only one in my family who would play with my father. Neither Daphne nor Clarissa could sit still and pay attention for that long. I haven't undertaken the game since his death."

She and her father had shared a love of chess and books and had spent endless hours together, just the two of them. Those were special times that she'd always remember. She could not help but wonder for the thousandth time what he would think of her present difficulties with Claxton. She often yearned for his gentle advice.

"It was a terrible thing, your father's death," he said quietly. "Such a terrible stroke of chance."

"Who would ever have thought? Struck down by a rearing horse. He was always so good with them."

Claxton remained silent, watching her intently. "You told me, after we first met, but we've never talked about how it happened. I always felt that even after two years, the tragedy was still too fresh in your mind. For all of you, including Wolverton, of course. You were there, weren't you?"

With careful precision she arranged the white pieces on her side of the board, so as to disguise the tremble in her hand. Claxton was right. A stroke of chance. More than three years had passed, but it still felt as if the tragedy had struck just yesterday.

"We'd been outside for hours, watching Daphne and Clarissa at their riding lessons when the skies suddenly darkened." Sophia paused, remembering the fateful moment that had changed her life and the lives of her mother and sisters forever. "Daphne was having so much fun, she didn't want to ride in. She told us later that she pretended not to hear us calling. So my father walked out to fetch her. At the first faint rumble of thunder, the animal went skittish. Daphne couldn't control him, and so my father reached for the harness. That's when an enormous thunderclap seemed to break the sky in two." She closed her eyes and exhaled. "It wasn't Daphne's fault, but I know she's never forgiven herself. She's never ridden again."

"I'm sorry it happened." He shook his head. "And just two years after Vinson was lost on the *Charybdis*."

"Yes." Her eyelids lowered at the mention of her elder

sibling, who had been lost while on a scientific expedition to the South Seas. "I don't believe I ever told you, but Havering was on the same expedition. The night Vinson died, Havering was ill and kept to his cabin. It's why he hovers about so. He believes things would be different had he been there." She shrugged. "As if he could have done something to stop the sea from claiming my brother."

"Do you find your cousin, Mr. Kincraig, a worthy heir to your grandfather's title? I met him only briefly at our engagement ball and had no opportunity to form any sort of opinion as to his true character."

Inwardly she flinched. Mr. Kincraig was a sore subject in the family since being named heir to the Wolverton title and estates. Until then, he'd been a stranger to them all, and to their dismay, he seemed determined to remain so. The idea that he should take possession of the ancestral history that they had all for so long tended with honor and revered seemed a travesty.

"Hmmm. What a question." She threw a glance at the ceiling. "Shall I answer with diplomacy or with truth?"

"Always truth with me, Sophia," he answered solemnly.

She ran her fingertip over the crenellated crown of the king. "He strikes me as arrogant and cold, and he has made no effort whatsoever to seek my grandfather's good graces or approval or to become part of our family, though we have sought on numerous occasions to make him welcome. He just seems to be waiting. Waiting until—" She could say no more, for a sudden rush of emotion closed her throat. She exhaled miserably and lowered her lashes to conceal her tears. "I just wish my father was still alive and my brother. Once my grandfather is gone, everything will change."

"Yes, I know."

"It is his greatest wish that his two remaining granddaughters marry before his death so that their futures are secured."

"Oh yes." Claxton sat back in the chair and glared into the fire. The leather of his Hessians glowed like onyx. "Because marriage will solve everything. You and I know that better than anyone."

She sighed again. Oh, the folly of words and falling into traps laid by one's self. Their marriage. She had thought all day on the subject in the back of her mind, while they were visiting with the Kettles, and shopping, and baking, and sledding. Oh, and while they were kissing too.

He tilted his head aside and peered at her. "I apologize if I have pressured you too greatly to accept me. I believed we were growing closer. Enjoying our time together. Clearly this afternoon I overstepped. I could sense your discomfiture when I touched you, and after all my silly talk about going over edges—"

"Claxton, I have come to a decision about our marriage."

He blinked, then straightened, instantly serious and attentive. His expression conveyed a mixture of dread and hope. He was afraid, she realized. Afraid of what she might say. "A decision. Yes?"

"I will agree to withdraw my demand for a separation."

"Sophia." He leaned forward, his long legs bending between them, his larger boots planted on either side of her smaller ones, and grasped her hands in both of his. "You don't know...I can't explain what that means to me." He exhaled sharply, as if suddenly unable to form words.

"You are happy with my decision?" she asked.

"Yes." His eyes widened. "*Yes*. And you?"

"I am content." She wouldn't lie. *Happy* wasn't a word she could use to describe her feelings on the matter. Since last night, she'd felt as if she were standing on the edge of a dangerous precipice—with the growing desire she felt for her husband threatening to drag her over to a place from which she could never return. She had to step back.

Making love to her husband wouldn't be like before, when she'd given herself to him freely. It couldn't be. Rules had to be put in place, so as to safeguard her heart. She wouldn't be able to proceed with having a child otherwise.

"Only content?" He leaned closer and with his hand brought her face to his for a kiss.

She gave him her cheek before his lips could touch hers.

"But this should stop," Sophia said.

He froze. "What should stop?"

"The kissing. The efforts to seduce me."

"You're my wife. I want to seduce you." He reached out to touch a tendril of her hair. "More importantly, goose, you're the only woman with whom I've ever sledded."

"Don't tease."

"Who is teasing?" he asked incredulously, his eyes widening to reveal a glimmer of temper. "I'm half out of my mind with wanting you. I want you in my bed. I want to make love to you."

"Truly, Claxton, there is no need to say such things.

I've agreed to remain in the marriage, and yes, to have a child, and we shall do what needs to be done—" She blushed and primly averted her gaze. "In a straightforward fashion. However many times it must be done, and hope for the best."

He sank back against the cushion, his expression mulish. "How utterly romantic."

"Don't you see? That's what I'm saying. While I had such a nice time this afternoon—" The memory of what had taken place in the kitchen between them even now made her cheeks go hot. "—and I'm glad we can enjoy each other's company, I don't require romance or wooing, or even kissing." It was that degree of intimacy that terrified her. That took away her ability to reason. "A parody of falling in love, just because we happen to be married. Indeed, I don't want it."

"That's what you think this is between us?" He pointed to the narrow space between them. "Even before we lost the baby, a parody?"

She closed her eyes. "I don't want to talk about before." She'd lost a baby before, and she'd lost Claxton. She couldn't exist in a constant state of fear that she'd lose them all over again. She needed distance. Security. That was the only way she could have peace. "Let's leave all that ugliness behind. I'm talking about now. And please don't misconstrue my words. They aren't intended to in any way offend."

"You just want the baby, don't you?" he said, his voice thick with anger.

"I've been very clear about wanting another baby."

"But you don't want me."

Sophia's mouth fell open. What did he want her to

say? That she loved him? So that he could kiss her and make her body burn with desire... only to tell her he'd always feel fondly toward her?

She couldn't expose herself that way. She didn't want to hurt again. Never that deeply.

No, she couldn't bear it.

At last, she answered, "I don't want to confine you."

"Or yourself, I don't think," Claxton muttered.

Sophia exclaimed, cheeks hot, "Don't be cruel."

"It is you who is being cruel," he retorted, standing from the chair with such force the wooden legs rocked off the carpet. He strode away—then returned, making a circle around the space where she sat. He rubbed a hand over the lower half of his face for a brief moment, concealing his scowl. "Denying what happened between us today. Yesterday. And then asking me to conceive a child without passion. God, I don't even know if it's possible."

"It must be possible." She kept her tone light and her expression placid, though inside her heart pounded like a drum. "People in our situation, of our station, do it all the time."

"So really what you're proposing is an informal separation. Isn't that it, Sophia? Once we have a child, we'll go our separate ways, even if it's just to opposite ends of the house? Without any true obligations to one other. Only to the child?"

"You make it sound so cold when really I've agreed to everything you want."

His eyes widened, and he answered with a derisive curl of his upper lip. "You're correct, I think. The sooner we get started, the sooner we'll be done with this unpleasant business of procreating." He bowed, his dark head low, and with a courtly bend of his arm, said, "Your Grace, I would request your company in my bed tonight for the purpose of attempting to conceive my required heir."

"Now you're being hurtful. You can't be serious."

Only moments ago, she shared her intention to remain in their marriage. Now, at the first sign of difficulty, he was already striking out to hurt her and pushing her away.

"I apologize." He stood, his dramatic air falling away. "I don't have a secretary presently in residence, or I'd submit my proposal for your approval in writing—" His voice rose to a thunderous volume. "And have it delivered by official courier under the duchy's wax seal."

"Have some respect for my concerns," Sophia cried. "I've agreed to remain in our marriage, but that does not mean I'm prepared to jump straight into your bed."

"Ah, it would be *your* bed, as I don't have one." The dark slash of his brow arched upward. He took several steps toward her, leering. "Though the settee certainly has its allure."

Sophia answered quickly, contriving to look composed. "No, actually, I made up a bed for you this morning in the room where I found your boyhood things. You can sleep there tonight. Very nice linens and several blankets and even a bed warmer. I know you'll be comfortable," she babbled, attempting a return to normal conversation. To ease the intensity she saw in his eyes. "Doesn't that sound comfortable?"

He stared at her, his body tense, his eyes hard.

"Don't shut me out," he said, his expression suddenly desolate. "Sophia, I don't understand why you are doing this. What are you afraid of?"

"And I don't understand why you're so unhappy," she

said. "You've won. Why don't you see that? There will be no separation, and we'll have a child. I just need a bit more time to grow accustomed to the idea."

"The idea of what?"

"The idea of *you*."

"You've had seventeen months," he said quietly.

"No, Claxton, I've had three days."

Chapter Twelve

$\mathcal{I}$t's that damn list, isn't it?" Claxton hissed through gritted teeth. "I told you once I wrote out the names, you would despise me."

"I don't despise you," she said. "I don't even dislike you."

"Once a rake, always a rake. That's it, isn't it?" With a jerk of his head, Claxton's chin rose a notch higher. "I'm soiled goods. Ruined. Too dirty from past exploits to share your snowy-white bed—"

"*Claxton.*" Her eyes widened, the acidity of his words like a blow.

Suddenly, he was there beside her.

"Don't pretend to be shocked when it is exactly how you feel," he said roughly, pulling her to her feet and into his arms. "What is that you want? A promise that I'll always be faithful?" He tilted his face in mock affection and brushed his fingertips along her cheek.

"Don't be cruel," she warned, the intensity of his ridicule stealing her breath.

"Then I'll say the words. Lots of men do." He pulled her close, hands gripping her hips. He ground himself against her, making her unavoidably aware of his manhood, which he wielded like a weapon between them. "One look and I knew, Sophia Bevington, you were the only woman for me. I'll never leave you, dearest. I'll never so much as think of another woman for as long as I live—"

"That's not what I meant," she cried. Cheeks flaming, she broke away, removing herself from the anger in his touch. A few more steps placed the settee between them. He was trying to provoke her, but she wouldn't lose control of her emotions and strike back with the same bitterness—though he very much deserved a set down. She wanted a child just that much.

"Then tell me what you did mean," he demanded.

"That I don't expect you to change. We are who we are, Claxton, made up of hurts and memories and disappointments and desires. We can't help what we've become, you and I. We can only own up to our faults and accordingly make smarter decisions and move forward."

"How very mature of you." Claxton's lips curled, his compliment clearly not a compliment at all.

Stung, she blurted, "Don't belittle me for being *mature* enough not to demand from you a promise you could likely never keep."

He laughed, an empty sound that filled the darkness.

"The awful thing is, Sophia, that maybe you speak the truth." He turned from her suddenly. His head falling back, he stared at the ceiling, legs spread into a wide stance. If she didn't believe in him—if she saw no honor in him—what hope was there for any sort of a future together? Hopelessness flooded his veins like ice. "God, yes, the truth. Any other man in his right mind would have stayed, but like a coward, I left you. I left you, and for that you will never forgive me. Even if you did forgive me, you'll never forget."

His shoulders heaved, but he did not turn back in her direction, still requiring that bit of privacy in which to compose himself.

After a long moment, she said, "So please stop getting angry with me when I am only trying to be realistic. We will endeavor to have this child, and once the task is accomplished, we will both be free to continue on with our lives as we wish."

Now he did turn—a smooth pivot on the heel of his Hessian.

"But we will remain married," Claxton confirmed in a low voice. The light from the fire painted the gentle curves of her face. "There will be no separation even then."

"That is my hope," she said. "Many couples remain married but lead completely satisfying separate lives. I could name five such pairings right now if I had to. I'm certain you could as well."

He could, indeed, but that didn't mean he liked her tidy little plan. He didn't like it at all. If they had a child and went on to pursue separate lives, she might take a lover. His mood turned decidedly sour at the thought. Worse yet, her lover might seek to become some sort of friend or mentor to *his* child. A child that was part him and part

Sophia, theirs alone. Such scenarios occurred all the time in their landed society, but no, he would not stand for it. Possessive rage took to simmering in his blood. He would be the only father his child knew from the first day of its life and each day forward.

He would remain by Sophia's side, whether she wished him there or not.

He scowled. "What about another child? Wouldn't we want two? Or three?"

Or four? Or six? Or eight? If he kept her pregnant, would that be enough to bind her to him?

She blinked rapidly, and her lips formed a thin line.

"Speaking of three, where is the third quest?" she asked quietly. "Let's read it so we know what is in store for us tomorrow."

So she was finished and ready to change the subject. What if he wasn't ready? He was still trying to figure out what had changed between them this afternoon and transformed her from a warm and delightful woman who welcomed his kisses into someone cold and distant who forbade his touch.

"I liked the other Sophia better," he growled.

"What other Sophia?"

"The one who dumped salt into my bowl and absconded with my cakes. The one who rode on a village boy's sled with me. The one who isn't afraid."

"That was child's play." Her brow gathered. "The matter of my heart is not. Please don't kiss me again."

He grabbed his coat, and scowling like the devil, he delved into its pocket for the envelope, which he promptly dropped into her lap. Sinking back into the cushions, he sulked. "You read it."

She looked at him overly long, but in the end she opened the envelope and the note inside.

"Sir Thomas has a bee up his nose." She blinked. "That's all it says. Sir Thomas has a bee up his nose. Do you even know what that means?"

He barely heard the words, for the dark cloud crowding the inside of his head.

"Yes." He stood, going to the table, where he lifted the bottle of claret, but tilting it to its side, found it disappointingly empty. "It means we are going to church tomorrow."

"Very well, then." She stood, retrieving her redingote and folding it over her arm. "I will see you in the morning."

He rested his elbow on the mantel and rubbed his jaw, growling, "I suppose."

"You needn't be so surly about my simple request for time." She stopped at the foot of the stairs, her hand on the newel post. "Your life will go on exactly as before, unchanged. For me, everything will be different. You don't have anything to be afraid of. I do."

Oh, but she was wrong. She terrified him each time he looked into her eyes. Miss Sophia Bevington was the only thing he'd ever really wanted, and he feared that while he'd won this battle, he would never win her heart.

"Go, then." He waved his hand dismissively.

She fled up the stairs, abandoning him for the third night. At least he had a bed. Unfortunately, all this talk of heirs and boundaries had him wound tight. He would never be able to sleep.

* * *

An hour later, he hauled the third steaming bucket up the stairs. If he couldn't convince Sophia to spend the night with him, at least he would provoke her envy by preparing a nice hot bath. Without closing the door, he dumped the bucket into the hip tub, ensuring she heard the crash of water against the metal.

No doubt she stood with her ear pressed to the door at this very moment, coveting the luxury only he would enjoy just as soon as he could get his clothes off.

He closed the door rather loudly and stripped naked. Sinking into the water, he eased back, relaxing into the delicious heat.

There, as steam bathed his chest, shoulders, and face, he fumed, wishing *she* was there naked across his lap, her golden skin slippery and wet. For nearly a year, such fantasies had tormented him, although in reality he'd never enjoyed her in such a manner. In those early months of their marriage, he'd taken immeasurable pleasure in their lovemaking, but the nightly act had always occurred in the very respectable paradise of their marriage bed. She'd been so young and inexperienced. He had thought to take things slowly, assuming there would be plenty of time later to teach her other pleasures and to explore more daring settings.

For nearly a year he had been a dedicated onanist. Only in the vivid imagination of his mind, in the silent privacy of his rooms in Vienna or Töplitz, had he taken her against a wall as she cried out his name or thrust into her from behind as she bent over a chair, her long hair tumbling to the floor.

The idea of not pulling out of Sophia, his beautiful wife, at the moment of completion had become a constant fantasy in his mind. That she had now agreed to intimacies but *held him at a distance* made the anticipation all the more torturous. When he'd told her he was half out of his mind for wanting her, he had not been exaggerating.

With his hand clamped on his cock, he held a vision of her riding him in the bath, her glistening breasts bouncing in his face. Candlelight bathed her skin, and she smiled as she leaned down to kiss him, long and hard on the mouth, with no trace of doubt or mistrust on her lips.

Vane, his imaginary temptress whispered against the skin of his throat and down his chest, until with a sudden cry she arched back, bearing down with her hips so forcefully her movement sent water splashing to the floor.

With a groan, Vane closed his eyes and reclined his head, rhythmically sliding and squeezing his hand along his rigid length until he exploded, her name an agonized whisper on his lips.

* * *

Sophia paced in her dressing gown and slippers, unable to bear Claxton's cruel taunt any longer. The parading of the buckets. The sloshing of all that delicious hot water. *Bah!* She could practically feel its luxurious heat from here behind her very *cold* door, standing on her *frigid* floor in her *chilled* bedchamber.

That he would wield such an extravagance as a means of torment, to make her pay for displeasing him, proved what an insensitive lout he was. She intended to confront him and tell him exactly what she thought of his cruel games. Only she had to wait until he was finished with his infernal bath.

But no...just then she heard his footsteps in the corridor, stealthy ones, as if he were trying to sneak down the hall, outside of her hearing. Lucky for her the floorboards of the old house told tales.

Throwing open the door, she leaped out.

"Did you forget the soap?" she loudly accused.

Claxton barreled into her.

Only it wasn't Claxton.

Another man stared down at her, his eyes wide and his face pallid beneath a mountainous winter cap. A scarf covered his mouth and chin. Sophia shrieked.

The man plowed past and bumped her shoulder. Sophia went sprawling. He uttered some indeterminable exclamation and turned back toward her. Fearing violence, Sophia cowered against the wall.

"No, please," she begged.

Claxton's door flew open. "What is it? Another creature in your room?"

When he saw her, his query stopped short. His eyes fixed on the man, now a shadow in the darkness at the end of the corridor.

"Who are you?" he growled, his expression instantly murderous.

The man ran for the stairs, his boots pounding out each step.

"Stop there," Claxton roared.

But the man didn't stop.

Claxton lunged into the hall to crouch beside Sophia, unconcerned, it appeared, that he was almost completely naked, with just a towel across the waist, clutched at his hip. His thigh, dusted in glossy dark hair, covered the most intimate part of him.

"Did he hurt you?"

"Just a bump as he went past," she answered, dazed.

"Go in your room and lock the door." He helped her up. "There may be others."

From downstairs, there came the sound of a door slamming open in its frame.

Claxton lunged down the hall, a blur of long limbs and corded muscle. Sophia stared after him, the magnificent sight of him making her almost forget the intruder. Seconds later, her husband, the naked savage, returned.

"Damn it. I need clothes." He disappeared into his room. A moment later he barreled past her again, pulling on his coat. *"Lock your door."*

Sophia glimpsed a flintlock fastened to his side.

She did as he ordered, retreating into her room and locking the door, doing her best to remain calm, praying the man did not have a weapon or wish them harm. After what seemed an eternity, Claxton knocked, announcing himself.

Fresh snow encrusted his hat, shoulders, and boots. Exertion flushed his cheeks.

"He ran straight for the forest. I followed his tracks for some time, but did not wish to be drawn too far from you and the house. If only I'd not taken the time to dress."

"You had no choice. You couldn't go off naked into the snow."

He took another deep breath and flashed a grin. Again, almost instantly, his expression returned to serious. "Was the man someone you recognized?"

"His face was covered with a scarf, but from what I did

see, I don't recall ever seeing him before. Not at the village inn or elsewhere." She bit her bottom lip. "He was carrying something in his arms, but I didn't see what it was."

He scowled. "Doubtless he thieved something."

"What if that's how my window came to be open last night? That man coming or going?" The idea that an unknown intruder had been in the house, possibly while they slept, left her completely discomposed and no small amount terrified. What if the man returned? What if he was a murderer?

He nodded. "It's winter. He may be a pauper simply looking for shelter in the storm, in a house known to have long been empty. I did not undertake to inspect the premises after our arrival." Claxton glanced upward toward the floor above them. "He could have been here all along, and we did not know it. I shall go down to the village in the morning to report the matter to the watchman, though I'm not certain what good it will do."

"Could he have gotten inside through the priest hole downstairs?"

"No one knows about that passage but my brother and the Kettles and now you." He shook his head. "No one. My brother and I were sworn to secrecy over its existence, and the Kettles would never tell."

Beginning downstairs, they carried a lamp from room to room and confirmed all doors and windows were secure and that no one else lurked in the shadows. While they did so, they searched for any sign that someone had been living in the house beneath their notice. Three floors, countless rooms, and nearly an hour later, they returned to the corridor between their rooms. On the uppermost floor in a small stove, they'd found warm embers, certain evidence someone had indeed been in the house without them knowing.

"The house is secure," said Claxton. "There is nothing to do now but go to bed."

Sophia peered into the darkness at the end of the hall. "I don't know if I'll be able to sleep a wink, for fear I will awaken to that man standing over my bed."

His blue eyes flashed with heat. "I'd be more than happy to sleep with you."

Never before had she been more tempted. The discovery of a stranger in the house left her anxious and not wanting to be alone. In London, with a house fully staffed with servants, she would not be so unnerved, but Camellia House was located on a property set apart by itself and had so many rooms, all shrouded in darkness. It was just the two of them.

Claxton's physical competence and skill with a weapon added much to his attractiveness. Still, she ought not to invite her husband into her bed out of fear, but rather because she was emotionally ready to share such intimacies again. They'd checked all the rooms and found no one. She shouldn't be such a ninny.

"You have your own bed," she said, doing her best to sound firm.

He moved toward her with a sudden and purposeful intensity.

"There was a stranger in this house tonight," he said quietly. "I don't know how he got inside. I don't know if he'll return." Unshaven, with his shirttails hanging free beneath his greatcoat and no cravat, he looked more like a pirate than a duke. A swarthy, handsome pirate.

"Don't be ridiculous, Sophia. We're sleeping together tonight."

The determination in his manner sent a trickle of alarm down Sophia's spine and an undeniable thrill. She retreated into her room, but in the moment she could have closed her door against him, she did not. He followed, as she knew he would, pushing the door closed behind him.

He exhaled through his nose, his eyes gleaming.

"Very well," she said, endeavoring to keep the quaver from her voice. "Let's sleep together. I admit, I will rest more easily, knowing you are here." Clasped at the front of her dressing gown, her hands held the embroidered collar together primly over her breasts. "I—I think I might read for a while. What about you?"

He removed his coat and draped it neatly over the back of a chair. "I'm not here to read."

In one smooth movement, he removed his shirt over his head. Powerful muscles bunched in his shoulders. Firelight bathed his skin, revealing a deep striation of muscles along his torso, chest, and arms. Certainly he knew he was beautiful. That naked, he became temptation personified.

"I've been very patient," he said softly, advancing toward her. She backed away until she could go no farther, having come to the wall. His gaze traveled over her with an almost dispassionate ease. "I've tried, however ineptly, to be thoughtful. Sensitive. Understanding. Have I not?"

"Yes," she whispered. "I would agree that you have been."

"Good. I'm so relieved we finally agree on something." He lifted his hand to the back of her head, and eyes burning, slowly lowered his face toward hers. Every nerve, every muscle, every fragment of her body capitulated. She closed her eyes, her lips burning, tingling with anticipation.

He halted suddenly, exhaling against her cheek. "I almost forgot. No kissing allowed. That would constitute romance, which you specifically told me you don't want or need. We are here for the business of making a child, correct, Sophia? And only that." He drew back. "Your rules."

"I did say that," she breathed.

She had indeed said something like that, and it would look badly on her if she now told him to never mind. Inwardly, she shook of her regret. They were here for the purpose of conceiving a child. Not for any sort of . . . *frivolous* recreational activity.

"Yes, you did." He touched her hair. Her cheek. A look of puzzlement came over his face. "Working under such rigid strictures," he said, brow furrowed, "I'm not quite certain how to proceed."

He was being ludicrous, of course. Her husband was an expert and knew exactly how to proceed. Light as a feather, his fingertips traced a path over her collarbone. She forced herself to remain calm and silent, not wanting him to see how his touch affected her. But inside, oh, inside, every nerve burst out in flames.

"Clearly," he drawled, "I shall have to improvise."

The same fingers delved inside her collar to lift and push her robe from her shoulders. He tugged it farther, somewhere near the waist, so that the quilted silk fell to pool at her feet. The frigid air of the room chilled the bare skin of her shoulders and arms.

"Correct me if I'm wrong," he said quietly. He moved closer, backing her against the wall. His hands smoothed up her arms, feeling warm and strong and oh, so competent. "But I do not recall there being any limitations made on...*sucking*?"

Chapter Thirteen

She swallowed hard. Sucking.

Such a naughty word, especially when spoken from Claxton's lips.

Holding her arms just above the elbows so as to prevent her movement, he lowered his head, lightly brushing his nose and lips against her temple, her ear. *Not* kissing her. Instead he caressed her with his breath and skin and texture.

She shivered, taking pleasure from that barest touch.

He exhaled and nuzzled her cheek and neck, leaving a path of heated breath and friction on her skin, one that ended at her breasts. She still wore her short stays over her chemise. The undergarment lifted her breasts, displaying them as if for a feast. She sighed. Exhaled. For feast Claxton did.

Legs bent and openmouthed, he explored her breasts, dampening the fine lawn that covered her skin with his heated breath. Exploring the plump underside and the crevice between. At last he took an erect tip in his mouth. Her eyes rolled back and she sighed, her legs instantly weak.

Oh, but then he *sucked*.

"Claxton," she cried, her hips bucking off the wall.

He held her there, unrelenting, as with his teeth he tugged the lace edge of her chemise low, until one breast popped free.

"Very nice," he murmured, his breath tantalizing the nipple.

"I told you before, I don't...need to be seduced."

"You've made that perfectly clear," he murmured against her skin. "So I suppose it's not necessary to say you're the most beautiful woman I've ever seen...even though you are." His heated gaze met hers, and he worshipped her with his hands. "And I won't tell you that the first time I saw you I knew...I knew...there would never be anyone else."

Lips parted, she whispered, "Claxton—"

"Instead I'll do my best within the boundaries you yourself laid out." His hands skimmed down the length of her torso to her hips, which he planted firmly against him, before seizing her arms again.

"Very well." She gasped, feeling the distinct outline of his member against her belly. "If you must."

"As I recall," he whispered near her ear. "Neither was there an edict against licking."

Oh yes. Licking.

"Ah...correct." She sighed.

His head swooped again, this time to her bare breast, his tongue licking up from the underside to encircle and lave her nipple. His unshaven jaw abraded her skin. She watched, transfixed, until she could bear it no longer. She needed completion now or she would go mad.

"Claxton, I'm ready."

"No, you're not." He chuckled. "Not just yet."

Oh, but she was. She knew what body parts went where, and she was ready for *all of that* to take place *now*, but he refused to relent, fixing her helpless against the wall, like a quivering butterfly, pinned. He caught her nipple between his tongue and teeth. Everything inside her went wet and slick and hot.

"And biting," he murmured. "Not forbidden."

She whimpered when he sank to his knees, releasing her arms at last. He shoved the hem of her chemise above her waist, exposing her. With his teeth, he nipped the sensitive skin at her waist, her hip, and her thigh, sending off little shocks of sensation along her spine. She moaned, half-senseless. Such an indelicate response, but she could not help herself. Refusing still to touch him, she pressed the flats of her hands against the wall. Reached to grip the drapery. Thrust her fingers into her hair.

With a curse, he unfastened his breeches. No drawers encumbered him, and his member sprang free, magnificently aroused.

His hands swept up her legs, again lifting her chemise, rubbing her thighs, urging them apart until at last, his hand was *there*, stroking, massaging, one finger slipping inside to glide against her slickened center. Without preamble his mouth joined his hand.

"Claxton, please," she cried. "I can't bear it." Sophia's breath caught in her throat. Her legs almost failed her. "Oh, my, that's sucking again."

"You smell good," he murmured. "Taste so divine.

Sweet. Better than sugar. I knew you would. Mere obser-
vations of fact, of course, naught to do with romance."

In the next moment, the room spun around her, he carrying her to the bed, where he dragged her chemise up her
body and off, leaving her naked.

He'd been playing with her before, but now a different
expression ruled his countenance, one of controlled reverence.

"Are you cold?" he asked softly.

"Yes." She shivered, crossing her arms over her
breasts, miserable without his touch, conscious of his
gaze always on her body. He did not deny her long.
Divesting himself of boots and breeches, he joined her,
stretching across her, pulling a blanket over them both.

Surrounded by shadows and firelight flickering on the
bed hangings, they seemed in a place removed from the
rest of the world. A haven of warmth, linen, and naked
skin. She lay beneath him, half-drunk in anticipation. She
remembered how he would feel inside her and knew she
would cry out from the pleasure.

He lifted her hair, fanning it out over the pillow.

"Beautiful," he whispered. "Like chocolate silk."

He disappeared beneath the blanket, suckling her
breasts and spreading her thighs to again taste her there,
squeezing the swollen part of her with his hands and
mouth. He'd never kissed her there before. Made love to
her in this way. She hadn't known such sensations were
possible.

Stretching, she gripped the headboard. She felt languid
and beautiful. Like a wicked goddess, taking pleasure at
the hands of her immortal lover.

When his tongue went suddenly deep and flat, massaging the most intimate part of her with quick, rhythmic thrusts, she felt herself slipping into a sort of delirium. Forgetting her own promise not to touch, she grasped his head, fingers staving through his hair.

"Claxton, I want—"

She couldn't say it. She'd never been one to speak her desires aloud.

"Please," she begged, awash with a sudden fever. She lifted her hips, seeking. "I need—"

Suddenly, he was there, massive and strong, his breath on her cheek. His sex lay between them, pressed into her stomach, as large and pleasing as she remembered.

"Tell me, Sophia. Tell me what you need."

He lifted his weight from her and readjusted so that he nestled against her more intimately. She gripped his arms.

"I need this," she said.

"Show me," he murmured.

She had to. She couldn't wait. She'd never touched him so brazenly, but she did so now. She gripped him, savoring the hot, velvet-over-steel texture of his member against her palm. She guided him until she felt him against her entrance, a sudden, probing pressure.

He shifted, cupped her buttocks, and entered her several inches.

She gasped.

"Oh, God." His arms came round her, his face stark and tortured, and his eyes glazed. "Just let me—" He moved, pressing further inside her. She forced herself to hold still, not to scream. Her body for so long unused to such invasion cried out in pleasure and discomfort. He let out an agonized groan. "I can't *not* kiss you."

His hands crushed in her hair. His lips pressed against

the corner of her mouth, tentative, a passionate request for her permission.

"Please," he said.

That he would take her body so unapologetically, but beg for the kiss she'd so pettishly withheld broke one of the bars she'd installed around her heart and she relented.

"Kiss me," she whispered.

His mouth captured hers, his lips and tongue claiming her with such fervor, she could hardly breathe. With a growl, he eased even deeper inside her. She arched against him, all discomfort slipping away.

"Kiss me back," he said against her mouth.

She did so, meeting each turn and slide of his lips with equal passion. His hips pumped, slowly, then faster. Amid the discomfort came the return of pleasure. She thrust her feet into the mattress, lifting her hips, seeking it, wanting it.

Her movement pleased him. He grunted, and his movements became more urgent.

"I can't be gentle," he whispered against her throat. "Please forgive me. I've waited so long."

With a groan, he rose up on his knees. The blankets slid from his body. He lifted her buttocks and speared her deep.

A sudden pulse of pleasure erupted at the center of her womb to crash outward through her body, all the way into her toes and fingertips. His head fell back, and he rocked into her, hissing between his teeth. She cried out, never having expected such power. Her heart stopped beating— certainly it did—and she glimpsed a paradise created of violet and velvet and stars.

He throbbed deep inside her. With a groan, he collapsed over her, his arms braced on either side, his blue eyes staring down into hers.

In that moment, the look he gave her, she could almost believe he loved her.

* * *

Claxton's first awareness the next morning was of an uncomfortable chill. Without opening his eyes, he pulled Sophia close and tugged the blanket over the both of them. To his irritation, she'd donned her night rail, which come to think of it, was fashioned of a rather crisp and unwieldy fabric. Her perfume clouded his nose.

All wrong.

He opened his eyes to find himself in the midst of a living nightmare.

Annabelle stretched and yawned, giving the appearance that she'd only just awakened. "Good morning, Claxton."

The sudden realization came over him as to why he'd been so cold and devoid of a blanket. Annabelle hadn't been asleep at all.

"Bloody hell."

He shot across the bed, as far from her as possible, snatching a pillow over his nakedness. She, thank God, was fully clothed, wearing even a heavy pelisse and matching hat tied under her chin. An enormous fur muff lay discarded on the chair.

"Where is the Duchess of Claxton?" he demanded.

He'd only just managed to seduce his wife into his bed. He did not need *this* to frighten her away again.

Annabelle looked about, wide-eyed, as if she'd only

just realized Sophia was not present. "I don't know. She was here when I fell asleep."

"More importantly," he growled, eyes narrowing. "What in the devil are you doing here?" He slid backward off the mattress, pulling the bed curtain across his hips.

She lolled languidly, smiling like a naughty cat. "Things have become unbearable at the inn. Meltenbourne is being very bad tempered. It's so very disconcerting. Your brother and I made our way here early this morning while everyone was still asleep."

Of course, the house had been made secure last night, safe against all intruders except the one other person in Lacenfleet who had a key.

"I mean why are you *here*?" he snapped. "In my bed?"

She blinked innocently. "I was so cold and exhausted once we arrived. I just wanted to get warm and go back to sleep. Why are there no servants to lay fires or make up rooms?"

"*This* bed was already occupied, if you did not notice. There's another perfectly good bed across the hall, or did you simply not look?"

She shrugged. "The common people do it all the time, sleep three or four or more to a bed, especially in cold weather when it's too cold to sleep alone. I don't see why we can't as well when circumstances warrant. It is the country, after all."

Claxton thrust his shirttails into his breeches. Boots. Coat. Walked toward the door.

He glared down at her. "You overstep, my lady. Quite deliberately, I believe. Don't do it again."

Her smile faded into a pout.

He found Haden, not Sophia, in the great room,

sprawled and snoring on the settee. One firm kick collapsed the leg, sending the oblivious sleeper atilt. His brother's eyes popped open.

Vane glowered down from above. "What in the hell are you doing here, and why did you bring that doxy with you?"

Haden rolled onto his side and with gloved hands pulled his coat over his face. "I didn't really have a choice about bringing her. I can't seem to get rid of her."

"Lord Meltenbourne is coming up the hill with a young boy."

Vane jerked at hearing Sophia's voice.

She stood at the window, a cup of tea in her hand. Fully dressed in dark blue wool, she'd pinned up her hair and looked nothing like the temptress of the night before.

"Indeed, I believe half the village is following him." She sipped. "Oh, Claxton. I do believe I've at last prepared a respectable cup of tea."

Her tone was suspiciously unaffected and underscored by a distinct coolness.

Vane strode toward her. He spoke softly so that his brother would not overhear. "I'm so sorry."

"For what?" Her smile, her eyes, shined too bright.

"For Lady Meltenbourne in our bed this morning."

Sophia's eyes widened. With an angry flare of her nostrils, she said, "No matter. What happens in your bed is your affair."

"What? No," he sputtered, hating the tone of her voice, the implication of her words. He grasped her arm and pulled her against him. "You can't honestly believe—"

To his surprise, she softened and leaned in to him. "No, I don't believe, but tonight, Claxton—"

"Tonight what?"

"We'll be sure to lock the door."

Relief spread through his chest. "Yes, we will."

He pressed a kiss to her lips.

"What is that infernal caterwauling?"

The question came from the settee. Vane turned. He'd been so focused on trying to mend things with Sophia, he had not heard the other sound, the one coming from outside.

"I told you. It is Lord Meltenbourne," said Sophia, having redirected her attention out the window again. "I do believe he is shouting something about a duel."

"Oh, *that*," arose the muffled response.

Vane stormed to the settee. He gripped the upper frame and gave a fierce shove. Haden tumbled onto the floor, a tangle of arms and legs.

"*Oh, that*?" Vane growled. "What do you mean by that?"

Clothes and hair in disarray, Haden scowled up from his new position on the carpet. With obvious reluctance, he said, "That's why I came here this morning. I didn't take him seriously, though. I thought he'd settle down once I removed myself from the premises. Only the countess insisted on coming along."

Vane tamped down his first instinct to explode. This was not at all how he had imagined his and Sophia's morning to begin. They should have awakened quietly in each other's arms so that he could reassure her that the night before had not been a mistake. Though heartened by her exhortation to lock their door tonight, he could not help but notice she'd not once actually met his gaze this morning. Perhaps she had regrets. Perhaps she had not been affected as deeply as he had. For the first time in his life, he doubted his ability to seduce, which seemed perfectly, disturbingly *right* given she was the only woman he'd truly ever wanted. What if the thaw came today, and she insisted on returning to London straightaway?

They needed more time. If only he could get the interlopers out of his house.

"You are the one who created this debacle." Claxton crossed his arms over his chest. "Don't expect me to be your second."

Haden shoved the tumble of dark hair from his eyes. "That's just it, your Grace. It's not me he wants to duel." He offered a sheepish look. "It is you."

"Why Claxton?" Sophia demanded from where she had come to stand at his side, one hand fisted at the center of her chest.

Vane pressed his fingertips against his eyes, almost certain that they were about to pop out of his head. "Yes, what her Grace just said. Please explain."

"His lordship is certain there is some scheme afoot, that I have merely been designated by you as a scapegoat to soothe difficulties at home with the Duchess of Claxton."

Vane's eyes narrowed on his brother. "Why would he think such a thing?"

Haden unfolded his long legs and stood, shaking out his rumpled greatcoat. "Perhaps because it is exceedingly clear that Lady Meltenbourne and I can hardly suffer one another's company." He exhaled and rolled his eyes. "Good God, Claxton. She is the most tiresome chit." He crossed the carpet and knelt to add another log to the hearth.

"I am not tiresome," said a voice from the stairs. Lady

Meltenbourne descended in her winter finery, looking like an affronted queen. But tears glimmered against her lashes. "The truth is, Meltenbourne has cast me aside. I didn't have anywhere else to go."

"This is your fault, Haden," Claxton said, storming back to the window.

"No, it is all my fault," said the countess. "I behaved abominably! I allowed the earl to believe I'd been un-faithful, when I hadn't been, not really. It's because I *wanted* him to cast me off. I never saw myself married to such an old man, but my father insisted. Now that I have, I'm s-s-so very miserable." She burst into tears.

Claxton glared at Haden. "You should never have brought her here."

Haden interjected, scowling, "Yes, yes, I understand that now, but what are we going to do about the earl? He seems quite intent on shooting someone."

"Yes, *me*," Claxton retorted.

"Just apologize to him," said Lady Meltenbourne. "That would settle everything, I feel quite certain."

Vane pivoted toward her in outrage. "Apologize for what? An affair I did not have with his wife?"

"It's ungentlemanly to shout at a lady," the countess wailed.

"I wasn't aware I was shouting at one." The words were out of his mouth before he could stop them, but once gone, gave him no small degree of satisfaction.

"I don't know what I ever saw in you." Annabelle buried her face in a handkerchief. "Horrible man!"

Haden called from the window, "The boy is bringing a note. I can only assume he is acting as his lordship's sec-ond."

Vane marched through the vestibule and wrenched the door open. With a growl, he snatched the folded paper from the boy's hand and slammed the door closed again.

Opening the missive, he read aloud, "No need for negotiations or false apologies. Just die. Die. Die." He tossed the paper into the air. It fell in a zigzag fashion to the floor. In exasperation, he fisted his hands on his hips. "That's all it says."

"What do you propose to do?" asked Sophia, her lips thin with apprehension.

He glared out the window, assessing the gathering crowd, all knee-deep in the snow and bundled up so that only their eyes gave evidence of their humanity. "I suppose there is nothing left to do but to fire a shot at the old bastard."

Lady Meltenbourne's eyes widened. "You're going to agree to his demand for a duel?" Her expression became frantic. "But he is *elderly*."

He advanced on her, herding her into the corner, she backing away, nearly tripping over her ermine hem.

"You should have thought of that long ago before you started playing games with people's lives." He uttered each word with blistering heat. "It is not I who issued the blasted challenge. I am in no position to deny his demand."

God, he just wished they would all disappear and leave him alone again with Sophia. Could a man not be snowbound with his wife without half of England arriving to interfere?

He hissed, buttoning his collar. "It is the only way I can see to get us past the present crisis. Years ago I attended a hunt with the earl. If memory serves, the earl is a dreadful shot and could not hit the side of St. James's if he was standing five feet from it. Haden, you will act as my second."

"It is the least I can do," Haden answered wryly. He buttoned his greatcoat and smoothed his hair into a more decorous appearance.

Vane tied his cravat at his throat. "Please inform the gentleman on the front steps that I will agree to the duel, and indeed that I wish to issue my own challenge based upon the earl's continued false and unsupported aspersions against my character, which have deeply offended me and the duchess. One-shot only terms."

Lady Meltenbourne burst out in a sob and clasped a handkerchief to her nose: "Please don't hurt him."

Vane looked at Sophia, his expression grave. "Please know if the duel goes unexpectedly awry, everything is in order to see that you are well taken care of. You should never need to marry again, unless you should so wish."

Sophia's face drained of color, and at last, yes, her green eyes met his.

"Why would you say something like that?" demanded Haden, frozen in place. For a moment, Vane had to blink, because his brother didn't even look like the same person, devoid of his humor.

Moisture glistened on Sophia's lashes, and her lip quivered. "I don't want you to go out there."

Her tears unsettled him but also gave him hope, even more than their lovemaking the night before. Could it be that she truly had feelings for him? He drew her aside, a hand at her elbow. "I didn't mean to frighten you. It's just that you never know what will happen. I'm certain all of this will be over in a moment."

He kissed her forehead. Then he opened the door and followed Haden outside.

Sophia turned to Annabelle, who sank down onto the bottom stair. "I love Meltenbourne. I don't want him or anyone else to die."

"If that's true, Annabelle, then you have to do something. And you have to do it now."

Chapter Fourteen

Annabelle, you've got to hurry," said Sophia, urging the countess toward the distant field. Together they ran through the snow.

The countess stumbled, struggling with the cumbersome magnificence of her cloak.

"It's too late," she sobbed. "I can't stop them now."

"Yes, you can, if you hurry."

Despite the frigid temperatures, Vane had removed his coat. Wind swept across the field and ruffled his hair. Standing boot deep in the snow, he handed his two-barrel flintlock to Haden, who marched forward to meet the earl's young second. Each confirmed only one ball occupied the chamber before returning the weapons to their masters.

With that, the seconds moved aside to join the silent crowd of spectators who had drawn back to provide wide berth for errant shots. Sophia was abruptly consumed by a wild terror. Not for a moment did she believe that Claxton would actually shoot the earl. What she had feared, with a sudden and overwhelming certainty, was that by some chance of fate the earl's bullet would find its mark in her husband's heart.

If Claxton died—

The world spun around her, a kaleidoscope formed of stone, gray sky, and ice. She couldn't breathe.

On the snow-blanketed lawn, the two duelists stood back-to-back and at Haden's count began their paces.

She turned to the countess. "If the earl shoots Claxton, God forgive you, because I never will."

Annabelle dropped the cloak from her shoulders and broke into a run.

"Meltenbourne," she wailed.

Sophia followed, but over the countess's head, she saw the pistols raised and cocked.

"Stop, darling!" screamed the countess. "Don't do it. *I love you.*"

The earl turned his head to her. "Annabelle? Are you talking to me? Or him?"

"You!"

Suddenly, the snow upon which he stood collapsed.

With a bellow, the old man disappeared, until only his arm remained visible above the surface, his knobby hand clutching the pistol. The weapon discharged into the sky. The crowd roared with laughter and approval.

Claxton, expressionless, fired his pistol into the snow, several feet to the side of his boot.

"Oh, thank God," Lady Meltenbourne sobbed, rushing toward the men. Sophia followed, but slower now, each breath painful, as if chilled by frost.

Striding forward through the snow, Claxton wrested the gun from the earl's hand and peered into the hole.

"Now, enough of this nonsense. I will suffer no more of your unfounded accusations, as they highly offend not only my sensibilities, but those of her Grace."

"Here, here," shouted several villagers.

Reaching into the hole, Claxton hauled his lordship out by his arms. Red-faced and clearly abashed, the earl sputtered out complaints about the weather and the misfortune of faulty firearms. Lady Meltenbourne collapsed, embracing him.

Sophia reached them just then. "Lord and Lady Meltenbourne, please come inside and out of the cold. I'll make tea."

Claxton's head swung toward her, eyes wide and blazing. "What did you just say?"

"Lady Meltenbourne has something to say to her husband." She looked at the countess. "Isn't that so?"

Annabelle lifted a tearstained face from Lord Meltenbourne's neck. "So much to say. And to you as well, your Graces. I have been the most foolish woman, and I beg you all to forgive me."

Inside, Sophia saw to the tea service. Afterward, she fled the house. Emotionally raw and unable to remain inside for another moment, lest she burst into tears in front of everyone, she made her way through the snow toward the cemetery. Alone at last, she exhaled the breath she had been holding for what seemed an eternity. Her breath puffed out, white vapor against white snow, and she pulled her cap down over her ears.

Thank God Claxton had not been killed. Tears blurred her vision. She'd danced along a dangerous cliff for the past two days and had at last tumbled down, head over heels. Her neat little plan to wait to make love with him, until her heart could be held separate, lay burned to ash at the bottom of that pit.

Now, as a result, her heart felt as if it had been torn out of her chest and put back in place, but upside down. If only she was not so physically attracted to his handsome face, his brawny muscles, and his magnificent—

"Oh!" She kicked the snow and muttered a very unladylike curse. He was an indulgence she'd found herself unable to resist.

But if she were honest, her feelings went much deeper than that. These past several days she'd seen something else in his eyes, an openness she'd never perceived in him before. He'd always been so cool and imperturbable before, his ducal façade never wavering. It was as if Lacenfleet had unlocked some hidden part of him, a missing piece that completed the puzzle of him.

Did that make him a *better* man, one capable of constancy, no matter the trial or misfortune?

What would happen after Christmas, when the magic faded? What if she became pregnant only to lose the baby again, like her dear friend Lady Peyton, who had endured not one, but four miscarriages over the past three years? Without a child to keep them together, what would happen to their marriage? Would it dissolve into the same sad state as before?

This morning, after waking to the shocking realization of Lady Meltenbourne snuggled up asleep beside her, she'd quickly gathered up her clothing to dress in the next room. And yet, for some reason, she'd hesitated at taking Claxton's list. She had even considered throwing the despised piece of paper on the grate to curl, blacken, and dissolve into ash.

But…what had changed between them since last night? Nothing, other than she'd surrendered a large measure of the power she had battled so fiercely to assert and now felt weaker for the loss.

No matter how much the earth had trembled for her when they'd made love, she could not be so foolish as to believe some magnificent transformation of her husband or their relationship had occurred simply because they were again sharing intimacies. To do so would return her to the same indefensible position in which she'd been before.

In the end, she had snatched the folded paper up as well, a reminder to keep her heart in its rightful place, behind its safe little wall—not in her lover's hands.

"My lady," a voice called, drawing her attention.

Haden rode horseback toward her from the stable.

Quickly she wiped her eyes. "Lord Haden."

He dismounted smoothly, his boots crunching on the snow, and removed his hat. Drawing the animal by its reins, he walked toward her, cleared his throat, and laughed.

"Well. Thank God things turned out as they did."

Beside him, the animal stamped and snorted.

"Indeed." She smiled, struck in that moment by Lord Haden's similarity of appearance to her husband. The stark winter light revealed the younger man's hair to be a shade lighter than Vane's. While they shared the same startling blue eyes and height, Haden's face and physique were decidedly leaner, more leonine, and elegant than Claxton's muscled stature.

"I—ah—well—" he stammered handsomely, peering at her with an almost boyish shyness. "I have already

apologized to my brother. I wished to apologize to you as
well."

"You already apologized inside."

"Insufficiently." He rotated his hat in his hands. "If not
for me bringing Lady Meltenbourne here that first night,
this duel and all the rest would never have happened."

"You certainly added excitement to what could have
been four dreary snowbound days."

"You are too kind, I'm afraid." He glanced down at his
boots. "My behavior of the last week, and indeed, for the
whole of my life, has been nothing short of reckless." His
lips twitched. "And thoughtless. At some time we must
all come to the realization it's time to become an adult.
I am twenty-eight years old. I suppose I'm long past due
for that, and it is time for a change."

"Thank you for saying so, Haden, and of course I accept your apology."

He nodded again and shifted his stance. His gloved
hand tightened on the reins.

"My brother is fortunate to have married a woman
such as you."

"That's very thoughtful of you to say."

"No, not thoughtful." He shook his head and winked
at her. "Just true. I can only hope that one day I will be
as fortunate. I know I've been very much absent, but I'd
like to be a better brother, not only to Claxton, but also to
you."

The earnestness with which Lord Haden spoke earned
him a very immediate and solid place in her heart. "It
would make me very happy to see more of you."

His cheeks flushed. "Wonderful. And I say that not just
because you have two very lovely, ever-so-charming un-

married sisters. Daphne and Clarissa—they are both well and . . . remain unattached?"

"Indeed." Sophia laughed. She would not tell Lord Haden that he was too much of a rake for her to ever recommend him as a match to either of her sisters or anyone she considered a friend. Even though she would never play the part of his matchmaker, she liked him very much.

He chuckled. "Well, then. I ought to go." He returned his hat to his head and retrieved the reins from where they trailed in the snow. "Wouldn't want to be here if things go badly between Annabelle and Lord Meltenbourne." He chuckled. "If anyone is looking for me, except either of them, mind you, I'll be on the pier, waiting for this damn frost to break so I can get on the first barge out. See you in London, then?"

"Indeed."

Boot thrust into the stirrup, he swung onto his mount. The animal pranced, hooves crushing through snow and ice, and set off a few paces.

"Lord Haden," she called after him.

He drew on the reins and circled around. "Yes, my lady?"

"We'll expect you for Christmas Eve at my grandfather's home."

"I'll be there." He smiled warmly. "Thank you for including me."

Left alone, Sophia trudged on to the cemetery. Numerous gravestones emerged from the snow, some leaning and others pockmarked by time. At the farthest patch of ground, nearest the forest, stood a bell-shaped mausoleum bearing the words ELIZABETH. MOTHER. DAUGHTER. WIFE. A sudden wistfulness weighted Sophia's heart. The three simple

words seemed insufficient to describe the legacy of a re-
markable woman whose influence still marked the lives of
her sons and her village. At the same time, she prayed she
would be blessed enough in life so that her grave marker
carried the same three words.

An unexpected blur of color on the steps of the mausoleum caught her eye. At first she thought a bird perched
there, but no. Moving closer she found three butter-
yellow roses, with a distinctive shading of pink along the
edges, almost perfectly preserved by frost.

"There you are." Boots crunched in snow. "I have been
looking everywhere and was about to set off to the village
in search of you."

Sophia turned.

He stood on the path behind her, concern muting his
smile. "Is everything well?"

She hoped he couldn't tell she'd been crying. She
smiled. "That was not your first duel, was it?"

"May I decline to answer that question?"

"Yes, you may." She turned back to Elizabeth's grave.
"Did you leave these beautiful roses for your mother?"

He came to stand beside her. His gaze moved over the
monument with reverence. "Roses?"

She pointed to the flowers, not wishing to disrespect
the memorial by touching them.

"I don't know anything about them. Curious. I'm not
sure who would have left them."

"I just saw Haden coming from here. I thought perhaps
he left them, but they are frozen to the stone. They must
have been here for several days." Sophia looked at the
roses again. "It's a lovely monument. You haven't visited
since we arrived, have you?"

He traced a leather-encased fingertip in along the letter E at the beginning of his mother's name.

"Why? Tell me," she implored softly.

"She'd have been disappointed in the way I lived my life after leaving this place. She raised me to be stronger. She would most certainly have chastened me over the way I handled the loss of our child, leaving you the way I did when you needed me most. Duty to the Crown be damned; that's what she'd have said." He offered a little smile, chuckling softly. "Only she wouldn't have said 'damned.' I never once heard her curse."

"Disappointment is one thing, but she was your mother. It's not as if she would have stopped loving you, no matter what."

He looked back at the house, his gaze extending down the vale toward Lacenfleet. "I don't deserve all this."

"Camellia House?"

"Everything."

"Why would you say something like that?"

He looked up at the very top of Elizabeth's monument. "It is cold," he said. "You ought to come inside."

She held back, reluctant. "I don't wish to eavesdrop on whatever Lord and Lady Meltenbourne have to say to one another. I know I'm a terrible host to say so, but I've had rather enough of the both of them for one day."

"And yet you invited them into our home?" He reached out to tug on an escaped tendril of her hair. "Why?"

Our home. The words sent a shiver through her, very different from one inspired by the cold. A pleasant sort of shiver that she decided to allow herself. She explained to him Annabelle's explanation for her dalliances, or rather, her flirtations with other men.

Claxton grunted and frowned. "I don't much care why she does it as long as they leave us alone. She is a spoiled woman who cares nothing of the damage she inflicts on others. Once we are free of this frost, best neither of them cross my path again."

"Lady Meltenbourne will find her way. She just needs to know she's not invisible, that she's valued as his wife."

He answered dryly. "She could certainly find other ways to gain notice."

It would be easy to smile and say nothing more. To simply walk along beside him as if she had nothing more to say. But silence had caused such difficulties between them.

"I don't want to be like that, Claxton," she burst out. "Like Annabelle."

"You?" His eyebrows went up in dismay. "I don't see how in any circumstance you could ever be compared to her."

"I don't want to be perceived as grasping. Of begging for your attention."

His eyes widened as if in disbelief. "I assure you, you'll never have to beg."

She joined him, and together they walked toward the house. "It's easy to say that while we're here, cut off from the world as you and I know it. You don't have any choice but to see me." She hated speaking these words and voicing her doubts aloud. Lady Margaretta had taught Sophia and her sisters very early in life that much of a woman's beauty came from confidence and a respect for one's self. It had never been Sophia's nature to plead for anyone's reassurances. "When we return to London, everything will be different. There will be all the same people. All the same challenges as before."

He pulled her to stand in his shadow, blocking the brunt of the wind with his body. The next gust sent his hair curling around his ears.

"After last night, you wish to paint our future with dread?" He reached for her hand and lifted her palm, spreading it over his heart. He frowned. "Don't do that. Let me be your husband again. Give me the chance to make you happy."

At his mention of the night before, she blushed. "You never used to say such romantic things."

"I'm saying them now," he answered fiercely, spreading his hand over hers.

And just like that, her resolve faltered. "How can I refuse you with my hand pressed over your beating heart? Yes, I will. I will let you make me happy." She offered her bravest and most sincere smile. "I will strive to make you happy as well."

She *would* be happy, even if that meant one day giving him up. For now, this was enough. It had to be, if she wanted a baby. Perhaps even now she already carried their child.

He rubbed both of her shoulders before grazing his fingers over the collar of her redingote. Gently grasping each side, he pulled her toward him for a kiss. His lips plied her gently, sweetly urging hers apart, purchasing entrance for his tongue. His hands framed her face, while his slanted, deepening the kiss. Just like that, like magic, her body responded. And not just because she wanted a baby. Because she wanted him.

"Let's go upstairs," he suggested against her lips, nipping the bottom one. "This time we'll lock the door."

"Yes," she agreed, wanting nothing more than to be

buried beneath a paradise of warm blankets with him, at least until Christmas Eve when she hoped they could emerge and travel all the way to London and surprise her family for the singing of carols and decorating of the tree.

They arrived at the kitchen stoop. "You go on inside and see if Lord and Lady Meltenbourne are finished," she said. "I wouldn't want to interrupt if things are not settled between them."

He passed her on the steps and reached for the door. "We should have made them talk this out on the front lawn, or better yet, at the inn," he muttered darkly. "I want them out of my house." He bent to kiss her again, open-mouthed and urgent. "I want everyone out but you and me. Once they're gone, I'm going to shove all the furniture in front of the doors and perhaps even nail them shut."

Cheeks flushed, she waited for him. It was not a minute before she heard his footsteps on the kitchen floor, and he came rushing out again, wearing an odd expression. "Ah . . . we can't go inside just yet."

Sophia's hopes fell. "They are at odds again?"

Claxton's eyebrows shot up. "From the sounds of things, they are very much in the midst of reconciling."

"Oh, splendid." She rubbed her hands together to create a bit of warmth. "At least they are still talking."

"I wouldn't call what they are doing 'talking.'" He paled and flushed all at once. "I can't honestly say what's going on in there, but whatever it is, I don't think we can interrupt without one or both of us being scarred for life."

"Oh," she said in sudden understanding. "Oh, my."

"And no, I didn't see. Thank God." He laughed. "I only heard. I was too afraid to look."

Sophia bit her bottom lip. "Clearly they need more time."

"But who knows how much longer it will be?"

Disappointment cooled her ardor. That and the freezing weather. "How to pass the time?"

He pivoted on his heel, coming to stand side by side with her. Though he did not put his arm around her, warmth emanated from his coat where his sleeve touched hers. "With all the excitement, I've almost forgot that we have the third quest to complete. Sir Thomas still has that bee up his nose. Would you care to accompany me to the church?"

Sophia smiled and nodded. "Perhaps this will be the last one."

The words inspired within her an unexpected sadness. She could not help but wish the game would go on forever.

Claxton set off for the stable. "I'll bring the sledge around."

* * *

In a silence broken only by the steady trod of the horse's hooves and the *swoosh* of the sledge, Vane pondered the subject most prominent in his thoughts. His marriage to Sophia.

He should be satisfied. He'd won the return of her smile. They'd made love and would make love again. They even talked in pleasant terms about the future. But the pensiveness he'd glimpsed in Sophia at the cemetery troubled him. Had she agreed to the idea of future happiness only to appease him? If so, he would not press her further. He could not help but suspect she held some part of herself back. Could he blame her when he had done the same for so long?

Vane looked down at Sophia bundled up tight in the seat of the sledge, her gloved hands folded in her lap. He wished he knew what thoughts occupied that complicated little head of hers. Even though he knew he had no right to demand her unquestionable trust, he desired that prize no less, but he counseled himself to be patient. To simply enjoy this day together because it might possibly be their last before leaving this place and returning to their lives in London.

After the wide curve in the road, they arrived at the parish church, a place his mother had loved. He and his brother, not as much. Everything was just as he remembered—an impressive, Gothic structure with long windows, pointed arches, noble pilasters, and a spire that as a child he'd believed reached halfway to heaven.

"Let us go over our plan once more," he said, assisting Sophia from the sledge.

In the spirit of subterfuge, Sophia glanced around to be certain they were not under observation. "I am to act as the distraction. The rector will be immediately suspicious of you because of the dreadful pranks you and your brother undertook when you were boys."

"Correct," Claxton said, chuckling rather subversively under his breath.

Claxton had also told her that in addition to Mr. Burridge being the rector, his mother had also, on occasion, retained the older man to be their tutor in various subjects. He and Haden had apparently been very naughty boys.

She recited the instructions he'd given earlier. "The key word to employ in distracting Mr. Burridge is *history*."

"Very good."

Together they entered the narthex, a narrow room formed of shadow and stone, where Claxton removed his hat. Upon their entrance, a heavily bundled, quill-thin man paused in his work stacking hymnals to shamble forth on knobby legs to call to another man who hung Christmas greens near the altar.

"Is that mistletoe I see mingled in with the greens? No, no, no, we can't have druid's weed in the church. Take it all outside, and remove every bit of it."

Seeing them, he came to meet them midway along the nave. With each step, his breath puffed out in a cloud, visible in the frigid cold of the cavernous space.

"Your Grace." The elderly rector gave a curt bow and peered down his prominent nose at Claxton, quite an interesting feat considering he stood a full two feet shorter than the duke. "What an unexpected surprise. I had heard you were in residence. At last you've returned after all these years."

Claxton, looking every part the elegant nobleman, answered with all cordiality. "Temporarily at least, snowbound here by this uncommon winter frost."

"Incommodious weather indeed." Mr. Burridge sniffed. "Preventing all but three of my parishioners from attending services yesterday morn, the remainder confined to their homes."

"Mr. Burridge, may I introduce you to the Duchess of Claxton." Claxton brought her forward and introductions were made.

"What a lovely church," said Sophia, peering up into the barrel-vaulted ceiling. "So much *history*."

"Ah." Gray eyebrows ascended Mr. Burridge's wrinkled forehead. "You are a student of the arcane, then? Unlike his Grace, who as I recall, could never be persuaded to attend to his lessons." His gaze narrowed on Claxton, as if fixing upon an old, familiar foe.

"No!" Sophia exclaimed in faux surprise. "Claxton, tell me that's not true."

Claxton manufactured a sheepish look.

Sophia returned her attention to the rector. "As for myself, I am fascinated by our glorious past."

Mr. Burridge's eyes brightened and his cheeks flushed with pleasure. "Then please, my lady, if you will allow me the honor of showing you the chapel's most significant points of interest."

Behind the rector's head, Claxton nodded gleefully and gestured for her to continue.

Sophia bestowed an encouraging smile upon Mr. Burridge. "Nothing would delight me more."

He gestured with a gloved hand. "Then let us begin in the nave with the font, which is cut from Turkish marble. Note the cherubim embellishment."

It was too much to hope they would begin the tour with Sir Thomas, who according to Claxton's prior description lay upon a stone table in the opposite direction, nearer to the narthex.

Instead they crept along for what seemed an eternity, pausing to examine every monument, coat of arms, statuary, and epitaph until Sophia thought she would faint from the effort of remaining so endlessly engaged.

Claxton's attempts to wander away from them proved

futile. On each occasion that he fell behind, Mr. Burridge insisted, quite firmly, that he return to the tour so as not to miss details he'd certainly not retained from their lessons during his childhood. After several failed efforts, Claxton followed dutifully behind, scowling sullenly, his hands clasped behind his back.

"You are certain I'm not boring you?" Mr. Burridge inquired for the thousandth time. A most attentive individual, the rector required constant nods, smiles, and assurances to ensure their progression.

"Not at all," Sophia assured him, her throat parched from repeating similar niceties over and over again. "Why, each treasure is more interesting than the next."

He sighed, pleased. "My thoughts precisely. It is so rare that I'm able to share these artifacts with someone who appreciates them as much as I do."

Claxton, at last, came to stand beside her, so close she shivered from the heat he gave off. He touched her back and peered into her eyes.

"I do believe, my dear," he said with deliberate intonation, "you will find the next statuary the most fascinating of all. Mr. Burridge?"

Mr. Burridge tilted his head as if he was unsure whether to trust Claxton's sudden display of enthusiasm.

"Why, yes, I do agree," he said, nodding slowly.

At last, they approached the sculpture Sophia believed to be Sir Thomas, who according to Claxton's mother would have a bee up his nose. Whatever that meant, she could not wait to find out.

"This magnificent table monument fashioned of freestone dates from the sixteenth century. Upon it, as you can see, lie two figures, one an armed knight. Do examine the detail of his sword, as it is quite breathtaking." He extended a hand toward the center of the carved figure. "And there beside him is his lady. Is she not beautiful?"

"Just look at their faces. So lifelike." Indeed, the lord and his lady stared upward toward heaven, their faces forever preserved in placid contentment. Sophia could not help but notice the knight boasted a magnificent pair of cavernous nostrils. Above their heads were words etched in stone. Sophia read aloud. "Sir Thomas Longmead and his wife."

One glance toward Claxton revealed the same relief she felt. *At last.*

Sophia marveled over Sir Thomas and his bride long enough to avert any suspicion, then chose another point of interest to draw Mr. Burridge away. "Oh, look at that kneeling angel and the detail of its wings. What can you tell me about that sculpture?"

Sophia proceeded down the aisle, Mr. Burridge following close behind. Claxton, of course, lingered behind.

However, something made Mr. Burridge glance back. A lingering suspicion perhaps.

There, to Sophia's abject mortification, Claxton sprawled atop Sir Thomas's supine form, his fingers thrust inside his marble nose.

Chapter Fifteen

$\mathscr{I}$s there some problem, my lord?" barked Mr. Burridge. His narrow physique bristled with outrage.

Claxton jumped, his Hessians instantly returned to the floor with a resounding *thump*, his expression one of a schoolboy caught in a prank, eyes wide and lips slack.

Sophia, for her part, considered a dash for the door.

But a look of calm came over Claxton's features. "I—ah—was attempting to clean his nose. There's a bothersome bit of dust floating about his nostrils." From his coat pocket he produced a handkerchief. He reached again, re-creating the same awkward pose, and rubbed Sir Thomas's nose free of the imaginary dust. "It is our duty, after all, to keep Sir Thomas dignified. There. All tidy."

Sophia clapped a hand over her mouth, desperate to contain the bubble of laughter that crowded the back of her throat.

Just then, a young woman and a small boy entered the narthex, each carrying a wooden box.

Mr. Burridge glared at Claxton reprovingly. "If you will excuse me."

Joining the visitor, Mr. Burridge positioned himself with obvious purpose so that he could still keep his eye on Claxton. Under this scrutiny, Claxton joined Sophia, looking every part the guilty scoundrel.

Despite their peril, Sophia experienced the sudden, overwhelming urge to grab Claxton by the lapels and kiss him, which would be quite improper given their ecclesiastical surroundings. It was easy here, in the golden light created by the church windows, to believe that they would always exist in this blissful state of happiness.

She whispered, "So? Was there a bee in Sir Thomas's nose?"

A conspiratorial smile slanted his lips. "Indeed, something is there in the nostril on the farthest side, the one closest to his lady." He leaned closer to murmur in her ear, "But my fingers are too large to pinch the object out."

"Oh no. That means—"

"Yes!" Claxton's eyes glowed with delight. Clearly he welcomed this new complication, the higher stakes. "Sophia, you must get the bee."

"But how?" she asked desperately. "When Mr. Burridge refuses to leave my side? And yours because apparently you have a peculiar fetish for dusting and cannot be trusted unsupervised with the antiquities."

Claxton grinned. "For a moment I thought he would box my ears, just as he did when I was a boy."

"I don't believe he can reach your ears now."

Mr. Burridge approached, boxes stacked across his arms.

"Hurry," warned Claxton. "We must think of some new diversion."

"Pardon the interruption, my lord. My lady," said Mr. Burridge, his expression brittle with mistrust. "It is that time of year when villagers often bring Christmas tithes and other gifts to celebrate the season."

Tithes and gifts. It was, indeed, that time of year. Sophia knew from her review of the account books that Claxton paid tithes once a year through his accountants. Somehow, the villagers appearing in person bearing gifts of butter and jam and chickens—necessities very dear to them—seemed infinitely more personal. All at once, it came into Sophia's mind that she'd not heard a church bell ring since arriving in Lacenfleet.

On instinct, she inquired, "Mr. Burridge, tell me about the church bell. On what occasions do you ring it?"

"Ah." Mr. Burridge issued a little sigh. "Our bell cracked two winters ago, splitting quite nearly in half. No donor has stepped forward with the funds to replace it."

The perfect opportunity had just presented itself. How could she nudge Claxton in the proper direction without being completely obvious?

"Your Grace," she said with careful emphasis. "You and I were just pondering yesterday—"

"What could be done to honor my mother, yes," he said suddenly with a long glance at her. He'd stolen the words right out of her mouth, and she couldn't be more amazed.

He tilted his face upward, and his gaze moved over the arched beams above them. "She so loved this church. A new bell would be a perfect tribute."

She knew in that moment his offering had nothing to do with the game and everything to do with the memory of his mother and his growing affection for Lacenfleet and its people.

"Yes," she exclaimed softly, blinking away tears. "I agree."

The rector's eyes lit up like lanterns. "Your mother, a saint of a woman."

Sophia said, "Mr. Burridge, perhaps you could show his lordship to the bell tower so that he might understand the contribution that would be required?"

All of the rector's prior suspicion fell away. Indeed, he appeared on the verge of tears. "Why, a new bell would breathe new life into this old parish church."

"Wonderful," said Sophia. "I will wait for the both of you here. I would like to spend some time viewing the windows."

She moved toward the nearest stained glass window, one which bore a brass placard at its base engraved with the familial name GARSWOOD. Beneath that, on the floor, she discovered a porcelain bowl full of roses.

Ones with yellow petals and pink edges.

* * *

A half hour later, she and Claxton made their way through the snow to the sledge, Sophia still smiling from everything that had occurred. Their breath gusted out before them with each breath.

"Do you have it?" he asked.

"I do." She opened her hand. A tiny scroll, bound with a faded strip of fabric, lay on her gloved palm.

"You ought to be a spy in the service of England, goose." Claxton's arm came around her shoulder, the admiration in his gaze and in his words more warming than any fire. "You truly were quite exceptional in there. Mr.

Burridge, I must say, is smitten. Let us go to the inn for a quick meal. We can read our next instruction there."

Soon they were settled into a table near the hearth. Just as before, the room was crowded with villagers, today unabashedly impressed by the presence of the duke, who had just that morning dueled the inn's most infamous resident on his snow-covered front lawn.

Several of the ladies smiled at Sophia. There were even a few satisfied nods and winks. She could only assume they believed her the victor for her husband's affections over the determined trollop, Lady Meltenbourne. At that, she felt some degree of satisfaction. She'd enjoyed herself exceedingly this afternoon and purposefully forbade herself from pondering deeper thoughts about their future, or the implications of the night before, although memories of their lovemaking never drifted far from her thoughts. She just had to keep things in perspective, be forgiving of her husband's limitations, and continue to guard her heart.

As they waited for the innkeeper to bring their fare, Claxton drank ale and Sophia sipped from a steaming mug of tea.

"So let us see this bee that has been buzzing around Sir Thomas's nose for all these years." Claxton scooted his chair toward hers. They sat side by side, two conspirators discreetly examining their plunder. He rested his arm across the back of her chair, bracketing her between his body and the wall. Her skin warmed with awareness. She could see nothing beyond the high wall of his shoulder, cravat, and waistcoat, and an endless sprawl of finely turned male legs.

Sophia slid the fabric binding free and unrolled the little scroll on the table between them. He helped her spread the small rectangle, pinning two corners with long, elegant fingers while she secured the other two. His familiar scent tantalized her, made more complex by the lingering acridity of gunpowder.

Ah, but the quest. At the uppermost corner hovered a charming little bee boasting a wide, toothy smile.

"Oh, your mother." She did venture a glance at Claxton then, only to have her breath stolen by startling blue eyes, which studied *her* rather than the quest. "Quite the artist."

He agreed faintly, "Hmm, yes, she was."

Underneath the table, his hand found her knee.

Breathless from that mere touch, Sophia read the quest aloud. "The hungry huntsman clamors for more stew. And look." She turned the paper so he could see the drawings. "She's drawn a rather fearsome fellow."

"The huntsman," said Claxton.

"You know something about him, just as you did Sir Thomas."

He nodded. "There's an old cottage in the forest; in times long past it would have been occupied by the estate huntsman. My brother and I used to play there, and sometimes my mother would accompany us."

"And make stew?" Sophia leaned toward him, eager to hear more.

With a suddenness that stole her breath, his gaze went to smoldering, and he stared at her lips. His hand, still on her knee, squeezed. "Yes, actually, in an old pot, the ingredients being whatever we gathered. Stones, leaves, and sticks gathered from the forest. It was all very juvenile."

"And charming." She eased back in her chair, but he

followed, just those few inches, teasing the nape of her neck with an upward brush of his fingertips. "Could we go to the huntsman's cottage after we leave here?"

"I'd rather go somewhere else first," he murmured suggestively.

"After we find the next clue."

"The cottage was in terrible condition then. I'm not sure the roof has not fallen through. Our game may very well come to a disappointing end there. Time may have destroyed what was likely our final quest."

"I hope not," Sophia said. "Not when we have come so far."

A girl brought out their stew, placing two bowls before them, a fragrant, steaming mutton stew. Reluctantly, he removed his hand from where it had crept up Sophia's shapely thigh. Only after Sophia greeted the girl as Charlotte and made a fuss over her pretty hair did he remember seeing her before.

"Your Grace, the hairpins you gave me must have been magical ones." The girl touched the neat coil of hair above her nape.

"Oh yes?" said Sophia. "Tell me, why would you say that?"

"I've got myself a suitor." Her lips broke into a shy smile.

Sophia's face brightened with surprise. "The farmer in the tall boots?"

"No, madam, the chandler with the fine cottage." The girl's face filled with color.

They chatted for a short time longer until Mrs. Stone cheerfully shooed the girl away. After the girl had gone, Sophia dazzled him with a happy smile.

"That's wonderful to hear," she whispered, her cheeks fetchingly pink, a likely consequence of their proximity to the fire. "I do hope Charlotte finds a happily ever after."

Vane reached to touch her cheek, his tone solemn. "Happily ever after. A few days ago, I wouldn't have believed in such a thing. The words sound as if they only belong in a fairy tale, don't they? Not in the lives of everyday people. But I think I've changed my mind."

Sophia peered steadily back at him. "That's a wonderful thing to hear you say."

Vane could not help but think how perfectly Lacenfleet suited Sophia. Having seen her in London, so perfectly at ease with the most elevated members of society, he'd never expected her to take so easily to these simple folk and their quiet way of life.

When they were ready to again be on their way, Vane left coins on the table in payment of their meal, and he followed Sophia toward the door. Only at the center of the room, he impulsively caught her by the sleeve and slowly pulled her back around. Her eyes flew wide at the suddenness of his mouth on hers, but she softened in his arms and with a sigh kissed him back. Then, as if she remembered where they were, she broke away. Yet he refused to release her entirely, and he caught her hand in his.

"It's all proper," he said, pointing at the mistletoe above them.

From around the room came cheers of approval and laughter from the patrons.

"You see," he added. "I think all these good people agree."

Soon they traveled alongside the frozen river. Sophia

leaned out with interest, watching as villagers, mostly young people, glided across the surface. Claxton drew the sledge to a stop. Within moments, he'd lightened his pockets of several shillings and secured temporary possession of two pairs of skates.

He would not have to instruct Sophia as she already knew quite well what to do. A happy memory came to mind of last December as newlyweds in London, when they'd skated on the frozen Serpentine. She secured the blade to the bottom of her boot and left him still working to fasten his.

She executed a graceful turn and shouted, "Hurry."

Within moments, he joined her. He had not much experience himself with the sport, but being generally hearty and athletic and possessed of a solid natural balance, all such diversions fell well within his capability.

Together they stood side by side on the ice, Sophia peering away from Lacenfleet across the river. In the distance, the faintest outline of the spires and towers of London could be seen.

"We could probably skate all the way to the other side."

"No, it would be too dangerous. The ice isn't strong enough all the way across." Again, just the idea of leaving Lacenfleet sent an undercurrent of trepidation through his blood, as if London, like the Thames, was a fast-flowing river and would tear her from his grasp.

She glanced up at him. "I have never spent a Christmas apart from my family. I know it makes me sound like a child, but the holiday and togetherness became even more important to all of us after Vinson's and my father's death."

"It's good that you have each other. That you are all so close." He'd not been so fortunate in later years to have that sort of familial bond.

"It's not just that." With a turn of her ankles, she skated a small half circle around him. "As you know, my grandfather has been in ill health. It would ease my mind to see that he is well."

"I know it would."

"At the same time," she said softly, coming to a halt. "I'm not sure, if given the chance, that I would change a thing about being snowbound here. With you."

"Not a single thing?" he teased, reaching out to take her hand and spin her in a gentle pirouette beneath his arm. "Lord Meltenbourne shooting at us. Waking up to a lunatic woman in our bed. A duel on the front lawn?"

"Well, perhaps just a few things." She grinned.

She skated off into the center of a group of children, who formed a circle about her. How ironic that the idyllic scene took place on the exact path the barge would take as early as tomorrow, conveying them away from Lacenfleet, to the world they had left behind. A clock ticked off time in his head, growing louder and more threatening with each moment. He could not help but feel that things were disintegrating around him before he was ready, before they were strong enough.

Sophia returned to his side. "The boys appear impatient for the return of their skates."

Returned to the sledge, they traveled toward Camellia House, but instead of following the indentations in the snow indicating their previous travel up and down the hill, they continued along the public road for another quarter mile farther. At a break in the hedge, Claxton directed the horse onto a narrow path into the woods until overgrowth prevented further passage, requiring them to walk the rest of the way. The dense population of trees held much of the snow on their limbs, lessening the amount on the ground below.

"It's so quiet here," said Sophia, tucking her scarf at her neck.

"Not in the summer. Try to imagine sunshine and all the trees green and full with leaves. There are birds, and here below, creatures scurrying all about. Perhaps even your Mr. Stoat. It's better than Vauxhall, I tell you."

She laughed as if enchanted by the picture he painted. "I should very much like to see that."

"We'll visit in the summer, then."

Just then, she wobbled, her boot having slid on a patch of ice. She grabbed his arm, but he caught her by the waist to steady her. Surrounded by a sanctuary of tall trees and sparkling ice, he pulled her closer for a kiss, which she allowed with a complacent, hazy smile. Instantly after, however, she pulled away and removed herself from him by several feet.

A small fire, born of suspicion, rasped to life in his chest again, larger and hotter this time. Did she only allow his kiss and his touch to placate him? Because she felt as if she had no other choice? What if she only wanted a child, but not him?

For a man who'd never had one moment's difficulty attracting female companionship, the possibility left him dismayed. Clearly they got along very well, or had these past two days, and better yet, enjoyed each other's company in bed. Why did she continue to hold herself emotionally apart?

"Which way?" she asked.

"There." He pointed. "It's not far."

The obscure path all but disappeared into a dense tangle of trees. He recalled with vivid clarity every stone, every fallen tree and dip in the path. What joy he and Haden had once known here, with no fear or premonition of the pain their mother's death would one day bring. With a hand to Sophia's elbow, he led her forward over exposed roots and fallen trunks. At last he perceived a familiar shadow, the outline of the old structure.

"There, do you see it?" he asked.

As he'd expected, the cottage roof sagged beneath the weight of forest debris and snow. Strangely, though, it appeared that a faint tendril of smoke arose from the chimney.

A woman's voice pierced the silence, a strangled scream. The breath evaporated in his throat. He and Sophia looked at each other, the blood draining from her face.

"Claxton," she whispered. "What was that?"

It came again, a female's desperate cry, as if she were dying. Vane flipped aside his coat and drew his pistol.

He made efficient work of preparing the weapon's double chambers. "You return to the sledge. If I don't reappear in five minutes, leave without me."

"I won't leave you here."

"You will," he insisted fiercely. "You will go to the village and find Mr. Kettle. He will know what to do. Promise me."

With reluctance, at last she nodded. "I promise."

He left her there and crept from the shelter of one tree to the next, unsure of what he would face. The woman sobbed, begged for mercy. With all stealth he peered through the window opening unencumbered by glass or shutter. Therein, Vane made out in the dim light a man in a crouched position. He could only assume the woman was being held against her will and assaulted.

Vane crashed through the doorway and aimed his weapon.

"You there," he shouted. "Stop."

The man whirled. A man he recognized as the intruder at Camellia House. Before him lay a woman propped on her elbows. Despite the frigid chill, her face was flushed and she perspired. A small fire smoldered on the tiny hearth.

"My wife," the man exclaimed. "She is having a baby, but something is wrong. The child is not coming. Please help us."

Claxton lowered his pistol. "Oh my God."

Chapter Sixteen

$\mathcal{T}$en minutes later, Sophia paced the length of the sledge, whispering prayers for Claxton's safe return. In the distance, she had heard male voices raised but no gunshots.

All at once, Claxton burst from the forest. Behind him emerged a young man she believed to be the intruder from the night before. He carried a woman, whose head rested on his shoulder. Both appeared ragged and half-frozen through.

Claxton quickly explained in a terse, controlled tone. "This is Mr. and Mrs. Branigan. Mrs. Branigan is having a baby but with difficulties. We'll take her to Camellia House and I'll go for Mrs. Kettle."

Sophia tore the blanket from the seat. "Hurry."

Mr. Branigan lowered the woman, and Sophia quickly covered her.

"Take her," Sophia urged, backing away from the sledge. "Just take her and go. We will follow."

He growled and leaned close, snatching her by the wrist. "I'm not leaving you with him. I don't know who the hell he is. Get on the sledge. Stand here on the blades in front of me."

But they'd not gone far when it became clear the horse labored to carry the added weight. With a push against Claxton's arms, Sophia leapt from the blades.

"Go deliver her to the house," she insisted. "I'm here, just behind, and will be there momentarily."

She trudged up the hillside aware of Mr. Branigan behind her, closing the distance. When at last she reached the steps, she passed Claxton on the way out.

"I'll return as quickly as I can." He raced toward the sledge. "She is in my room."

To Sophia's surprise, Annabelle met her at the door. "I'm so glad you're here. I know nothing of delivering babies and feared I would be called into service."

"Who is with the girl now?" demanded Sophia, quickly removing her hat and scarf.

"Why, Lord Meltenbourne," she responded, as if the answer made perfect sense.

Sophia rushed up the stairs and indeed found the earl sitting beside the bed, one leg crossed at the knee, holding the girl's hand, looking very much the country physician.

"Now, dear girl," he said. "If you feel you need to push, then you must push."

The girl cried, "I can't. I can't. Something is wrong. My baby."

A moment later, her husband burst into the room.

"Lydia." He collapsed on his knees beside the bed. "His lordship has gone for the midwife. She will be here in a blink and all will be well. She will know what to do."

Just then, Annabelle peeked through the door. "Is the girl well?"

Sophia went to her. "Annabelle, could you please go to the kitchen and begin boiling some water?"

"Boiling...water?" she repeated, eyes wide and dismayed. "Using what, a-a pot? Where do I find the water? Is the stove already lit?"

Lord Meltenbourne stood and in a calm tone said, "I shall boil the water, your Grace. I assume there are linens in the kitchen?"

"Yes, in the large cabinet."

"I was present for the births of all five of my daughters." He offered a wise smile. Though his eyes were red from who knows how many days of drinking, he appeared quite a different man from the one who had that morning presented himself on the front lawn demanding a duel. "I am happy to do whatever I can to assist."

Given the present situation, Sophia was more than willing to forgive. Five daughters! Indeed, there was something reassuring and paternal about the earl's presence that reminded her, however fleetingly, of her own father, which made her feel sad and thankful all at once. The earl's calm demeanor provided a benchmark for her own. She exhaled and vowed to proceed without panic.

After he had gone, Sophia sent Annabelle down the hall with the key to the linen closet for more blankets, a task that she assured the countess she was more than capable of doing.

Left alone with Mr. and Mrs. Branigan, Sophia did the only thing she knew to do. She tried her best to comfort the girl, who screamed and cried intermittently, propping pillows behind her back and placing a cool cloth on her forehead. Given her inexperience, she prayed the babe would not come before Claxton arrived with Mrs. Kettle. Having experienced her own tragic loss of a child, she prayed Mrs. Branigan's complications would be resolved by the presence of a knowledgeable midwife.

Now was not the time for questions, but so many swirled unanswered in Sophia's head. Why had Mr. Branigan been in Camellia House that night? Had the couple lived undetected on the premises before she and Claxton arrived? What were their circumstances? Clearly they had nowhere else to go, having taken shelter in the huntsman's cottage. Could they be criminals? Dangerous even?

In that regard Sophia could not bring herself to feel any measure of alarm, not when the girl looked so young and vulnerable and clutched her hand so tightly. And her poor husband. He knelt beside the bed on his knees, a look of abject fear consuming his features.

Things went very much the same for the next half hour. Annabelle brought additional linens and blankets for the bed, and Lord Meltenbourne, pots of steaming water, though Sophia had no idea what to do with them. At last, Mrs. Kettle barreled through the door, a look of brisk efficiency on her face.

"Dear girl, I am Mrs. Kettle." She removed her cloak and rolled up her sleeves. "Let us see what we can do to bring this child into the world with as little trouble as possible."

Sophia nearly fainted with relief. Instantly, Claxton was there, his arm around her. "Are you unwell?"

"No, only relieved now that you've arrived. Or more specifically, Mrs. Kettle."

Mrs. Kettle immediately banished Claxton, Lord

Meltenbourne, and even the young Mr. Branigan from the room, saying that she, Sophia, and Annabelle were quite sufficient to do the job.

Annabelle appeared mildly traumatized. "I do believe there has been some mistake. I can't imagine I shall be any help at all."

"Nonsense, my lady. I'll need the both of you when the time comes to hold Mrs. Branigan's legs."

The countess blanched.

Though half-terrified herself at the prospect of assisting in the birth of a child, Sophia couldn't bring herself to shy away. If she were to have her own baby one day, perhaps soon, she wanted to know what to expect, so as not to be shocked when the time came.

Mrs. Kettle inspected the preparations already undertaken and deemed them well done. A gentle interrogation of the girl told them how far along she was and whether there had been any concerns about her or the baby's health before now. Then the housekeeper-midwife lifted her skirts and undertook to examine her.

When she was done, a worrisome frown turned her mouth. "We've a malpresentation. That much is apparent."

"What does that mean?" asked Sophia.

"If any other part of the baby besides its head appears, the birth will be breech. Let us undress her down to her chemise, then get her up and walking. Perhaps that will convince the child to turn."

The three of them took turns in pairs walking Mrs. Branigan around the room, with her arms over their shoulders. When her pains increased, they encouraged and cajoled and tried their best to make her comfortable, believing that birth was imminent.

But hours later, despite numerous attempts at various methods, there had been no progress, only pain and misery. Mrs. Branigan grew lethargic from exhaustion, eventually refusing to follow any instruction.

Sophia stood from the chair beside the bed, where she'd been holding the young woman's hand, and joined the others. An air of desperation weighted the room.

From the corner, out of hearing of the girl, Mrs. Kettle stared morosely toward the bed. "The baby has long stopped moving."

"What can we do to help them?" asked Sophia.

The older woman whispered, "I'm afraid there is nothing more to be done."

"What are you saying?" Her chest seized with dread.

Tears glazed the old woman's eyes. "That there shouldn't be such tragedies, especially not at Christmastime."

Annabelle pressed a hand over her mouth and whispered, "The poor girl."

"No," gasped Sophia. In that moment her heart shattered into a thousand pieces all over again. Her baby lost. Never to be held in her arms. Never to experience its mother's love or a father's pride.

More than anything, she wished she could spare the young woman in the bed that same pain. But what more could they do? She had never felt more helpless.

Mrs. Kettle pressed a handkerchief to her eyes. "Someone should go downstairs and fetch Mr. Branigan."

Sophia nodded, knowing it must be her. "I will go."

"Not yet, please," begged Annabelle. "I think we should pray for mother and child or speak our hopes for them aloud or *something*. We can't give up just yet." She reached a hand out to either of them.

"Yes, because I fear that only a miracle will save them now," said Mrs. Kettle.

The three of them stood in a circle, holding hands.

"Please," whispered Annabelle, tears streaming over her cheeks. "Let Mrs. Branigan and her baby live. Oh, please."

"Let there be a Christmas miracle," Sophia said fervently.

On the bed, the girl moaned and shifted.

Annabelle looked over her shoulder. "Mrs. Branigan?"

Sophia approached the bed and reached a hand out to touch her shoulder. "How can we help you?"

Mrs. Branigan cried out, grasping her belly with both hands.

Mrs. Kettle folded her hands together and looked pleadingly toward the heavens, then came bedside for another examination.

"Oh my goodness." Her cheeks flushed with relief. "The baby is coming. He's done a somersault for us. Your Grace, the towels. My lady, if you will please hold her hand and encourage her. It won't be long now."

Within the hour, the babe arrived, a big healthy boy.

At her first glimpse of the tiny, little body, Sophia burst into tears. Lady Meltenbourne sobbed. They embraced each other.

Mrs. Kettle exclaimed, "Ladies. Please. A handkerchief. Someone dab my eyes." Sophia hurried to comply. "It is a miracle, nothing less. The good Lord hath seen to intercede and bring the babe into his mother's arms."

The child squalled as Sophia bathed and swaddled him, according to the instructions she'd been given. Mrs. Kettle tended to Mrs. Branigan while Annabelle slumped in a corner chair, her usefulness having come to an end.

With the babe returned to its mother's arms, Sophia descended to the great room to find the girl's husband standing with Claxton, Mr. Kettle, and Lord Meltenbourne. A bottle of brandy sat on the table beside four half-filled glasses.

Seeing her, Mr. Branigan leapt forward. With that sudden action he caught the corner of the table with his leg. The brandy bottle tipped and fell, splashing a dark stream across the carpet and floor. Lord Meltenbourne threw a pillow atop the rampant liquid before it could reach the fire.

"We don't wish to ruin the occasion by burning the house down," he exclaimed, eyes bright.

Mr. Branigan asked of Sophia, "My dear Lydia? Is she well?"

He looked so afraid and hopeful and on the edge of tears.

"Very well," she exclaimed with a smile.

"And the baby?" His lips mirrored hers, forming a dumbfounded smile. "We thought we heard a cry."

She smiled. "Why don't you go see for yourself?"

"Thank you, my lady." He bowed his head. "Truly, thank you. I can't say it enough. And I'm so sorry, so very sorry for knocking you flat last night."

"No apologies are necessary."

He disappeared in the direction of the staircase.

"Oh, Meltenbourne." Annabelle glided into the room and threw herself into her husband's arms, dissolving again into tears. "I have never seen anything so ghastly and beautiful all at once."

He nodded and patted her back. "Yes, I know."

She led him away by the hand. "Come, you must see the baby."

When they were gone, Claxton drew Sophia into the circle of his arms.

"Are you all right?" he asked quietly.

She eased against him with a deep sigh, curling her fingers in the front of his shirt. In that moment she decided it was very nice to have someone to lean upon. With her sisters, being the eldest, she always provided the comfort, the calming words. In this moment, being in her husband's arms felt very right.

"For once, I agree with Annabelle." She chuckled. "Ghastly and beautiful all at once. It is true what they say, babies are miracles, and this one a Christmas miracle."

Claxton said nothing. Her chest rose and fell as she inhaled and exhaled—a more labored effort with each passing breath. How could she feel so happy and so sad all at the same time? The smile faded from her lips.

"I just wish—I just wish—" Emotion welled in her throat, so sudden her voice broke and she seized his arm with both hands.

"Yes, I do as well," he murmured near her ear and pulled her closer. She rested her head on his chest and in a ragged gasp inhaled his scent.

Tears overspilled her lashes. "Things should have been different for us—"

"Yes, they should have been." He pressed a kiss to the top of her head.

"I'm so sorry."

"I'm sorry too."

The words unlocked a floodgate inside her heart. As

she should have done those months before after losing their baby, she sobbed against her husband's chest, taking comfort in him as he held her, murmuring soothing words until his shirt was soaked through.

She drew back, wiping at her eyes with the handkerchief he'd given her. "Claxton, who are the Branigans?"

"We had a lot of time to talk while we were waiting," he answered. "They came from London, having both lost their employment there. Hers because her employer realized she was with child. And him not long after, when the cooperage in which he worked burned down."

She gasped, remembering. "Yes, the cooperage on Sagemont Lane. I remember last month when the warehouse burned. The fire lit up the entire night sky."

Claxton nodded and smoothed a loose strand of hair behind her ear. "It being November and a slow time to find work, they soon became destitute. Refusing to have their child born at the poorhouse, they spent their last shillings to pay for the ferry crossing over, where they hoped to throw themselves on the mercy of a distant relation. Only when they arrived, they discovered the old woman had died."

She tucked the sodden handkerchief in her pocket. "To be so helpless, with no one to turn to, while others such as ourselves enjoy such privilege." Sophia's heart broke for the young couple. "Why, it's unfair. They had nowhere else to go but here."

"But here's the deuced thing. I know Mr. Branigan, or at least I used to."

Sophia reacted in shock. "No!"

He nodded with a smile. "My mother employed his father and mother one summer for a brief period of perhaps two weeks to assist Mr. Kettle with the gardens and the stable. I remember, it was an expense the house accounts could ill afford, and she hated sending them away."

"And they had a son."

"Yes. I had little dealings with the parents. To be honest, I didn't even recall their family name, but their boy's name was Adam and sometimes he played with Haden and me. We ran all over this place and the village and the woods, causing all sorts of trouble."

"So he knew about the huntsman's cottage from playing there with you. And I'd venture to say you showed him how to get inside the house through the Evil Dark Spirit Room, didn't you?"

His lips gave a little twitch. "Yes, we did—I had forgotten all about it—and we were both sent to bed with no supper for doing so. We'd been warned by my mother countless times to keep the secret entrance to the house— well, secret. Living here very much alone and unprotected sometimes weighed on her mind, and if there'd been any sort of threat, we could have safely hidden there or escaped the house. Despite her generosity, the Branigans were little more than strangers."

"She didn't appreciate that you'd essentially given them a key to the house." She squeezed his arm.

He covered her hand with his. "He'd always remembered this place with fondness and came here. They slept several nights upstairs, going about during the day looking for work. They built only the smallest fire, and only at night, afraid someone would see the smoke from the chimney."

"Then we arrived," said Sophia.

He nodded. "They hid in the attic until the day before

yesterday but feared discovery. When we left for the village, they took refuge in the huntsman's cottage, only to realize in their haste they'd left a small box containing their personal papers. Necessary letters of reference and whatnot."

"Mr. Branigan came back for it, and I surprised him. I'm certain that given the situation, he was too embarrassed to introduce himself as an old acquaintance."

"That's what happened."

"We can't just turn them out, Claxton. Even if there is now room at the village inn, I can't see sending them there, not with a newborn. Not at Christmas."

He nodded. "In the morning we'll set them up in the old stable master's quarters. They can stay there until the storm passes and Mrs. Branigan has recovered enough for them to move on."

The remainder of the evening passed quickly. Only periodically did the silence break with the sound of a newborn's cry. When that occurred, Mrs. Kettle went to offer her assistance. Without specifically gaining permission, Lord and Lady Meltenbourne set up in one of the spare bedrooms. Mr. and Mrs. Kettle took their old quarters. Sophia produced keys to the storage rooms and closets, and soon all the necessary beds were made up and everyone had their place.

At last, late that night, Sophia and Claxton retired together to their room.

Claxton leaned against the inside of the door, his arms crossed behind his back. He watched her remove the pins from her hair, admiring the exposed curve of her neck, the pale skin there—

But, oh yes, her hair down was paradise. He swallowed hard, wanting nothing more than to drag her into bed.

"Mr. Kettle predicts that the frost will break tomorrow," he said quietly. "Are you ready to leave Lacenfleet?"

"I pray he's right. Oh, to be home for Christmas." Sophia smiled. "But we haven't finished the final quest. We can't leave until we do."

Relief crashed through him, knowing that she would not abandon him at the first opportunity. Though he felt they'd at last come to terms with the loss of their baby, a troublesome distance lingered behind her gaze and in her hesitant manner. Guilt struck him through. He ought to be grateful for all they'd achieved this past day. But he wanted more. He demanded more.

"We'll return to the cottage in the morning. The final quest shouldn't take long, being that all the duels and babies are out of the way."

Sophia turned to him. "To think that four days ago I imagined us snowbound, hopelessly cut off from the rest of the world. Since that time I have never in my life encountered so many memorable people, or been witness to so many uncommon events."

"Memorable people? Uncommon events?" He chuckled. "That's a very diplomatic way of describing things as I saw them."

Sophia brushed out her hair. "Looking back, I believe these have been four of the most entertaining days of my life. But I suppose it can't last forever. It is almost Christmas."

He went to the bed and lay back on the pillows, his booted legs extended to the side. "Your family will allow me in the door, I hope?"

"Of course they will. Just like last year, we'll spend

Christmas Eve at my grandfather's. We'll burn the Yule log, light the Christmas candle, and decorate the tree."

"What else?" He closed his eyes and listened to her talk, thinking no other sound had ever been so soothing.

"There'll be a roast goose and Cook's special plum pudding. Grandfather always does the honors, lighting it ablaze, and we always send half to the servants' quarters, where they are having their own happy celebration. We'll play ridiculous games like bob apple and snap dragon and sing songs."

"Sounds divine," he murmured, watching her through slitted eyes as she removed her spencer. "As long as I'm not required to sing. I'd hurt everyone's ears."

Sophia glanced over her shoulder to find him watching her intently. Turning back to the cabinet behind the screen of the door, she removed the folded square of paper from her corset and slid the list underneath her folded stockings. The list was the one thing that kept her from being swept away by a crushing wave of new and overwhelming feelings for Claxton. The list was her rock. Her anchor. The only thing that kept her grounded in reality.

But being present for the birth of the Branigans' child made her only more determined to have a baby of her own. Which meant making love, again and again, as many times as they could manage in these times spent alone.

Just the thought of him naked quickened the pace of her blood, dizzying her.

With yesterday's ludicrous theory that they should proceed without kissing or romance having been thoroughly blasted to bits, her way of thinking had altered. Wasn't it her right as a wife to *enjoy* the act of lovemaking for as long as life allowed and to embrace these memories in the making with enthusiasm?

She'd not brought any of her prettier sleeping gowns. When she'd packed for her stay at Camellia House, she'd expected to spend three days alone moping, crying, and writing a letter, all in dull gray flannel. She would have to make do.

For warmth, she undressed beside the fire, removing her gown, her stays, and at last, her chemise. Her nipples immediately hardened from the chill, but also from the knowledge that Vane watched from the bed. Completely naked, she rubbed a bit of scented oil into her skin, something she always did on winter nights to keep her skin soft. But tonight, the sensation of her own hands smoothing over her own skin while her husband observed took on a sensual pleasure. Feeling daring, she poured more of the glistening stuff into her palm and applied it to her legs, stomach, and torso. When she arrived at her breasts, she heard a distinct sound from the darkened recesses of the bed. A rough exhalation of breath.

She pretended not to hear, but what an unexpected thrill to realize the control she displayed over him, to make him react in such a way. If she wanted his baby, it only made sense that she should do everything in her power to keep his attention.

Emboldened, she rubbed the oil onto her breasts, making wide purposeful circles around her nipples, before at last dragging her palms across the distended tips. A low grunt came from behind the curtains and a creaking of the bed. As if in response to his arousal, the place between her legs grew damp and heavy, just as it had the night before when Claxton had tasted her there with his lips and his tongue. She hoped he would dare the same intimacies tonight. Last night's lovemaking had opened her eyes to the fact that her husband had held back in those early months of their marriage, no doubt out of respect for her innocence. The list she'd just hidden away, while still a sore spot, nonetheless testified to his vast experience in pleasuring the female body. She could not help but hope in this moment, as her hand briefly slipped between her thighs so as to scent herself there, that he would expand her experience even more tonight. Legs trembling, she knew that in a matter of moments she would find out.

Covered neck to toe in her flannel gown, she made no effort to tie the ribbons along the deep slit at its front, instead leaving the fabric agape so as to reveal the inner swell of her breasts. Crossing the carpet, she joined him on the bed. Her body already throbbed in anticipation for him, aching for completion. Yet he lay with his forearms crossed behind his head, atop the pillow, and barely spared her a glance.

Odd behavior when she knew he'd been paying rapt attention just moments before. Stretching out beside him, she waited expectantly for him to pounce on her. He only gave a little yawn and touched the back of his hand to his mouth.

"It's been a long day," he said in a gravelly voice. "I know you must be fatigued."

She blinked at him. "I'm not *that* fatigued."

"Well, then, perhaps I am." He settled even deeper into the mattress.

The skin at the nape of her neck prickled in alarm. Too tired to make love? Vane? He'd spent the last three days doing his best to seduce her. Why the sudden turnabout?

"Vane," she exclaimed.

"Vane, what?" He closed his eyes, as if prepared to drift off to sleep.

"You don't want to make love?" she demanded softly.

Did he detect disappointment in her voice? Or just irritation that he wasn't going to provide that which she needed to conceive a child?

"I don't want you to feel that making love is expected," he replied. "Something you have to do now that we are actively trying to have a baby."

"I don't feel like it's expected," she retorted. "At least not the way you imply."

"Of course you do," he answered. "You must. How could you not? I can't forget what you said last night about not wanting to feign passion or parody love just because we are married." He paused. "And then I lost all control and gave you no choice but to do so. But you shouldn't have to pretend only to please me. Perhaps we should just wait and see what the coming days bring. You could already be pregnant."

He peeked through slitted eyelids to find her jaw dropped and the light of temper in her eyes. Even in this dim light, he could see that her cheeks had brightened to a rosy pink.

"I'm not *pretending*." She reached out and pinched his arm. "*Claxton.* Now you're making me angry."

He glared at her. "Why are you angry when I'm only trying to be understanding?"

"Because I want to," she answered quietly.

His heart clenched. "You want to what?"

Her eyes widened, pleading. "I want to make love."

His body responded. Desire rippled like thunder

through every layer of his body, skin, muscle, bone, and marrow.

Even so, now that she'd said what he wanted to hear, somehow it wasn't enough.

"Because you want me?" he gritted out. "Or because you want a child?"

She did not speak for a long moment, but her breath grew labored. "Both."

He could take her now in this moment, and oh, how he wanted to. But throughout the course of the day, she'd given him a hundred little reasons not to believe. It took all his strength to feign disinterest and once again ease back against the pillow. "Perhaps it is I who require convincing."

A little huff of consternation broke from her mouth. After a long moment, she shifted on the mattress, rising up to sit on her knees. She reached out and lowered her hands against the tops of his thighs, spreading her fingers wide to grip him there, as best she could, being that her hands were small and his legs muscular.

Slowly...purposefully, she slid them upward, circling and massaging...until they came to rest on top of his swollen crotch. He swallowed hard, commanding himself to hold absolutely still.

As she leaned forward, the neck of her sleeping gown shifted, exposing one full round breast and its pink tip. "Pardon me for saying so, Claxton, but you don't appear to need convincing."

At her saucy tone, one he hadn't heard in a very long time, his mouth went dry. He curled his hands into fists against the coverlet to prevent himself from reaching out to touch her.

"There's a difference between convincing me," he rasped, staring down at her hands where she covered him, "and convincing my cock."

"Is that what you call it?" She licked her pink lips, her eyes bright and sparkling. "Your...cock?"

He let out a ragged breath. At hearing her speak the vulgarity, the appendage in question doubled in size, or at least felt as if it did. As if sensing his reaction, her hand tightened on him as best it could, separated from his pulsing flesh by the hide of his breeches. "Perhaps your cock and I, together, can persuade you to our way of thinking."

They already had, but he wasn't going to tell her so.

She leaned over his torso and kissed him, her lips and breath warming his mouth. Warmth from her body and the oil's complex floral scent emanated from beneath her gown. He felt dizzied. Intoxicated. Yet he enforced control over himself. While he did not reject the kiss, he did not respond with discernible passion.

"Still unmoved, I see," she surmised, a scant inch from his face. A determined gleam lit her eyes.

With a feminine little sigh of pleasure, her lips traveled down his neck to his chest, where with her hands she parted his shirt. Traveling lower, she lifted the linen, shoving the fabric against his skin. Her tongue touched the sensitive skin of his abdomen, awakening the flames he sought to keep confined. Vane almost seized her and dragged her beneath him, but he was enjoying her efforts too much to rush things.

Then, blessedly, her hand returned to the juncture of his thighs and the fastenings of his breeches, where she made fast business of the laces. He closed his eyes, feeling the invasion of cool air on his heated member. With bold precision, her fingertip traced his bare length before she gently eased him free and gripped him at the base.

Damn. Yes. He rose onto his elbows. *"Sophia."*

"Are all men as large as you?" she whispered, staring at the rigid monument in her hand.

"Of course not," he grunted, watching her.

"I was always too shy to look before," she said. She looked like a beautiful mermaid with her tail tucked round her, as she hovered over him, her breasts half-exposed. "I don't know why, because you're beautiful, like a watermelon ice from Gunter's, but hot. I think I'd like to taste him."

He exhaled raggedly, like a man in the throes of death.

Indeed, he could die now. He had just experienced the single-most sensual moment of his life. He would never forget those words for as long as he lived.

He watched, unable to breathe, as with a tilt of her head, she pushed the dark cascade of her hair back over her shoulders and slowly bent over him. "May I...taste him?"

Every ounce of his willpower collapsed.

"Don't let me stop you," he rasped.

Her small tongue darted out to lick his swollen head and the pearl of liquid that glistened there. His hands seized in the coverlet, grabbing fistfuls. Any timidity on her part quickly fell away, and she licked and tasted him more thoroughly.

He hissed a curse.

"I take it that if you're cursing that means you like what I'm doing?" she queried from behind the curtain of her silken hair, which had again fallen to pool against his abdomen.

"Yes."

Her hair rippled as she lowered her head farther. Warm, wet heat enveloped his crown. Every muscle in his body clenched and flared alive. His control, which he'd kept so tightly coiled, shattered, and with a groan, his head fell backward—but only for the briefest moment because, bloody hell, he had to watch. With each slow bob of her head, a new wave of pleasure crashed over him. Involuntarily, his hips bucked, but her jaw widened, and she accepted more of his length, the flat of her tongue sliding against his shaft.

She pulled up, lips glistening with moisture, her eyes glazed and bright.

"I don't want to waste the tiniest bit." She pushed his shoulders, easing him back on the pillow.

"How did you know to do that?" he asked hoarsely.

"I found those books in your library—"

"The books."

"So many interesting illustrations." With his help, she eased his breeches lower. "Like this one—"

He didn't even get them or his boots off before she straddled him. "Yes."

He'd been reduced to one-word syllables, like a Neanderthal.

"Show me how." Candlelight from the bedside lamp gleamed off her thighs and her face.

He shoved her gown up, bunching the flannel over her waist. The dark shadow of her mons hovered above his arousal. Sophia. His wife. His every fantasy come to life.

"Take me inside you," he commanded in a guttural tone.

"Yes." She gripped him again, directing him until his cock probed her warmth. The sight of their bodies joined proved too much. Impatiently, he thrust up, evoking a ragged cry from her lips and his own. His wife was as tight as a virgin. She adjusted her position and grasped his shoulders, gasping as her body stretched to accept him, inch by blessed inch, while he met her from beneath. When at last she'd taken all of him, he fisted his hand in her gown and dragged the flannel from her shoulders, baring her shoulders, breasts, and torso to his hungry gaze.

She bent low, pressing her mouth to his and staving her hands, fingers outstretched, across the plane of his chest. Through pink and swollen lips, she whispered, "This isn't about obligation. Certainly now you must know that."

He wanted to believe her. But did he dare? In this moment with their bodies so intimately joined, he knew only one certainty—that they would give each other pleasure.

His heart beating wildly, he kissed her back. Yet she pushed away, rocking back on her hips until her face tilted toward the canopy. The motion impaled her more deeply on his shaft.

"Sophia." He seized her breasts in his hands, dragging his thumbs across her nipples.

"Claxton, yes." Her inner muscles clenched him tightly.

She covered his hands with hers and with a flex of her thighs lifted herself up a few inches to sink down on him again. Gripping her hips, he encouraged her to ride him and they found a rhythm that pleased them both—one that started slow and sweet, but that soon had the bed creaking and swaying with the intensity of their efforts.

"Ah—" he groaned from deep in his throat. He wouldn't last another—

"Now," she cried.

Like the sudden strike of a flint against the frizzen, he exploded, his body reverberating with one earth-shattering report after another. She collapsed onto his chest, her hair strewn across his shoulder.

Afterward as they lay tangled in the sheets and each other's limbs, he silently prayed she would be as open with her heart and mind in the bright light of morning as she had been with her body in the shadowed privacy of their bed.

* * *

Sophia awakened to near darkness and the pleasure of a strong male body twined around hers. Just when she'd finally grown accustomed to sleeping alone, her husband had returned to her bed. She liked the feel of him behind her in the dark. The steady rise and fall of his chest against her back. His muscled thigh aligned with hers. His arm banded tightly over her body, as if he'd never let her go. In this moment, everything felt perfect. She felt protected and cherished. As if their marriage was meant to be. Yet like a dirty secret, the list seemed to whisper at her from its hiding place. She ought to get up from the bed right now and burn the hateful thing... only she didn't. The idea of leaving all this luxurious warmth made her snuggle closer to him, savoring Vane's even warmer body...

Only to feel the sudden press of something long and thick against her bottom. And hot.

"You're not asleep, are you?" she whispered.

"What gave me away?" He chuckled low in his throat.

His chest vibrated against her back. He shifted, and with a hand to her hip, gently settled her flat on her back. His eyes, black in the night, peered down at her intently. "I couldn't sleep. I couldn't stop thinking..."

"About what?" she asked softly.

She hoped he wouldn't press her about the future. Yes, things were changing between them, and so quickly. There were decisions to be made. Though she knew Vane wanted her and even cared for her, she realized he also sought to put his ducal house in order. Their lives as duke and duchess were very much scrutinized by all who surrounded them—peers, servants, and the public. There were details to discuss. Social appearances. Sleeping arrangements. But it would be unwise to make such decisions while lying naked in his arms. Though her body had been thoroughly seduced, her mind—and more important, her heart—still harbored reservations.

Why ruin the magic of their night with talk of reality, of tomorrow?

Yet she instantly forgot her concerns. Propped on one elbow, he slowly tugged the sheet downward, dragging the linen over her breasts, baring them to his gaze and the chill of the room. Her nipples stiffened into hard points. She shifted, deliciously tortured by being so exposed, and felt the blunt pressure of his sex against her hip. At the foot of the bed, the fire had burned low, and it now gave off only the glow from its embers.

"About those books from my library." Slowly his fingertips circled her breasts and teased her nipples. With a dip of his head, he suckled one, leaving it wet, glistening, and puckered. She squirmed, but he pinned her against the bed with his knee. "The naughty ones."

She sighed, wanting more and knowing with a certainty she would have it.

"They were very naughty books, indeed," she whispered.

His palm ventured downward over her stomach to slip beneath the sheet.

"Were you shocked by those books, Sophia?" Long, square-tipped fingers touched her, sliding between her legs to stroke and tease swollen flesh, already drenched with desire. Like a cat, she purred and stretched, parting her thighs just enough to grant them entrance—

She moaned the moment they entered her.

"Tell me." He stroked more deeply, and she lifted her hips off the bed, matching his tempo. "Were you shocked by the pictures?"

She panted. "Not as ... shocked ... as I ought to have been."

She'd never let go of herself like this, been so free in taking pleasure for herself. Nothing else mattered in this moment but these delicious sensations and the two of them. She moaned again, this time into his mouth when he dipped low to kiss her.

But he drew back. "When you looked at those pictures, did you think of me?"

Suddenly his fingers were gone, and in a blur of linen and darkness and ember glow, she found herself half turned on her side and propped against a pillow, with him behind her ... stroking again, probing with his fingers and then, blessedly, with his cock. "Did you imagine me doing this to you?"

His hand caught her behind the knee. He lifted her there, spreading her, entering her fast and deep.

"Vane!" she cried, shattered by the pleasure of being so completely filled and stretched by him.

"Did you?" he murmured in that low, wicked voice that she loved. He pumped his hips, but slowly in smooth, controlled thrusts.

"Yes, always." It was true. There had never been anyone but him, even in her most secret of fantasies.

Gently and without pulling out, he maneuvered her onto her hands and her knees. A glance over her shoulder revealed him reared back like a stallion, his torso tautly defined by shadow and muscle. But in the next moment, he came down, his body a cage around her, one arm coming up to band around her waist.

"From what I recall," he rasped into her ear. "There were many different pictures. You . . . weren't hoping to go back to sleep anytime soon, were you?"

Chapter Seventeen

The next morning brought no new snow and news from the village that the frost on the river had begun to disappear. Vane smiled like everyone else and pretended jubilance, but inside he cursed his miserable luck.

Selfishly, he had hoped for just a few more days. And nights if he had to be honest with himself. His luxurious house in London inspired the envy of many, but there were so many visitors and servants and expectations... while here at Camellia House, things were uncomplicated and warm and true. Only he couldn't keep Sophia here forever. She had a family to return to, one with whom she desperately wanted to spend her Christmas.

But this chilly December morning, for the first time in Vane's memory, Mrs. Kettle threw open the doors of the dining hall, a large and formal room never used by his mother. With just her and the two boys in residence, there had been no need.

However, Mrs. Kettle, declaring that all known babies

had been birthed, had thrown herself into the task of feeding the Duke and Duchess of Claxton and their guests in residence with unparalleled enthusiasm. Together they enjoyed a full sideboard of selections as fine as any grand London residence would boast, or better, Vane had assured her.

The only absences were Haden, who remained at the inn in the village, for the obvious reason of wishing to avoid Lord and Lady Meltenbourne, and the Branigans, who breakfasted in their room, insisting they could not further impose upon the duke and duchess, who had already been more than kind, given the circumstances of their initial introduction. Sophia had insisted on taking two trays up.

Afterward, Sophia helped Mrs. Kettle tidy the kitchen and discuss preparations for the house to again be closed for the next several months, at least until summer. Vane donned his coat, gloves, and hat and joined Mr. Kettle and Mr. Branigan in the snow-covered courtyard at the back of the house for an inspection of the old stable master's quarters. Despite the frost having subsided on the river, the air remained cold and the sky above them gray.

Inside the stable, they climbed a narrow column of stairs. Mr. Kettle unlocked a door, and together they entered the small apartment. Dust cloths covered a table and chairs, a bed, and numerous other pieces of furniture.

"Thank you, your Grace. I don't know quite what to say," Mr. Branigan said, an expression of hope returning a measure of youth to his features, some vestige of the boy Vane had once known. "Our lives had taken such a turn for the worse of late. That you'd offer something so generous to Mrs. Branigan and me, as a place to live, especially after we trespassed in your house and frightened you and her Grace—well, I'm overwhelmed."

Vane couldn't help but feel that the Branigans returning to Camellia House had been intended all along. Since his arrival on a cold, dark doorstep three nights ago, the old mansion had returned to life. He felt in some way that he had as well. "Your thanks is enough."

Mr. Branigan held his cap in both calloused hands. "I couldn't help but notice that there are repairs to be made in numerous locations about the house, starting with that settee leg that keeps falling out from under everyone. Like my father was, I'm very skilled with woodwork."

Claxton listened quietly, giving the man his chance to speak.

"Please allow me to undertake any repairs, under the supervision of Mr. Kettle, of course, in exchange for our being allowed to stay."

"That's not necessary," Vane assured him. "I'm pleased to have someone to live on the premises to keep out the vagrants and such."

Mr. Branigan's cheeks flushed; he was suddenly mortified. Vane grinned. Mr. Kettle clapped the young man on the back, and they all three shared a laugh.

"Thank you for your kind trust, but I must insist on providing something in exchange," Mr. Branigan persisted. "Please, sir, for my own pride."

At last, with an encouraging nod from Mr. Kettle, Vane agreed.

A flash of scarlet drew his eye to the house—and in that instant, everything inside him went warm with anticipation. Sophia waved, dressed for the out-of-doors, they having already agreed to this morning to complete the remaining quest. Mr. Branigan insisted on harnessing the horse to the sledge and, all in all, made fine and expedient work of the task.

Traveling over crusted snow, Vane and Sophia returned to the same thickly treed path in the forest that led to the huntsman's cottage. Vane lifted a frozen tree limb to allow Sophia to proceed underneath. Waning winter light illuminated the slanted, one-room structure.

"Careful," Vane said as they stood side by side on the threshold. "I'm not certain how reliable the roof or the floorboards are. At least there is very little area to search."

Sophia stepped cautiously over creaking floorboards. "We're looking for a pot, you say?"

"Cast iron, from what I recall, with a handle and a heavy lid." Even stooped, his large frame filled the small room.

Sophia looked inside a ramshackle cabinet. "Like that one?" She pointed far in the back.

"Yes." He crouched and hoisted the pot out. "Let's go outside and have a look."

An old stump served as a table. Vane tugged at the handle. "The lid is stuck."

"No, sealed with wax, I believe." She pointed out the darkened edge.

When their eyes met, she flushed, as she had done repeatedly that morning, no doubt because she revisited, as did he, the sensual pleasures they'd enjoyed the night before. In the shadowy privacy of their room, they'd lost all pretenses of propriety and inhibition and exhausted their mutual lust only sometime near dawn. While her insatiability had put to bed his concern that she did not feel desire for him, he suspected he had not yet won her love.

Vane ran the blade of his penknife around the circumference of the lid and pulled until the top popped off. Inside lay a small linen parcel bound tight with string. Vane cut it open.

"Hmm," he said.

"What is it?"

"A book of poems, it appears."

He offered the small leather volume for Sophia to see. Something fell out, falling like a dark moth to the snow below. She bent to retrieve it.

"It is a rose." Wide-eyed, she held the flower to the light. Pressed flat, mottled with age, and faded, its petals retained the barest vestiges of color. Yellow rimmed in pink.

"I've seen this rose, Claxton," she whispered urgently. "Do you remember? Yesterday on your mother's grave. I saw the same uncommon variety yesterday in the church."

Bewildered, Claxton shrugged. "I'm not sure what it all means. A book of poems. A pressed rose. There is no message, no instruction. Perhaps the book is the prize? She usually included a little note of congratulation."

"What was the name on that placard?" Sophia pressed the gloved knuckles of one hand to her forehead. "I'm certain the name I saw started with a G. Graham. Garnett. Garner."

Claxton looked up from the book. Holding it open to the front inside cover, he displayed to her a name, scrawled in faded ink. *Robert Garswood.*

"That's it."

"Again, what does it mean? Who is Robert Garswood?"

"There's no question," said Sophia. "You must go see him and find out."

Confusion dampened Claxton's response. The game of lookabout had taken a surprising turn, the most recent discovery not the sort of "clue" his mother would have left for Vane the boy. He had the strangest feeling she'd intended it for Claxton the man to find.

"Who is this man and what would he have to say to me, if anything at all? It's been years since these clues were left behind. Robert Garswood may not even be alive."

*   *   *

But Robert Garswood was, indeed, very much alive.

The rector, still aglow over the Duke of Claxton's promised gift of a church bell, provided the necessary information. A member of the local gentry, Robert Garswood resided on a small estate not far from the village.

Already midday, the snow had begun to melt, making for slower travel in the sledge. But at last they came to a gentle valley and an expansive country house fashioned in the Jacobean style.

"This is all very unsettling." Vane scowled.

"What's unsettling is that we've remained in this very same spot staring down the hill for at least a quarter hour. It's cold, Vane. Let us go to the front door and introduce ourselves." His manner perplexed her. Why did he exhibit such reluctance? Clearly his mother had wanted him to meet and speak with Mr. Garswood.

"Perhaps we should just go," he suggested darkly.

"Perhaps I don't want to know who Robert Garswood is or what he might have to say."

"Why would you even suppose that? I don't understand."

And yet he provided no explanation.

At last, at her gentle urging, Claxton agreed. After only a short wait, a footman led them down a brief corridor past a cloisonné vase full of familiar yellow-and-pink roses. A tall, dark-haired man with silver dusting his temples stood near the fire, dressed in a blue greatcoat, buff breeches, and tall boots, waiting to receive them. Sophia estimated him to be somewhere around the age of sixty. A dashing athletic figure and the epitome of a country gentleman, Mr. Garswood leaned heavily on a cane and peered at them with unconcealed surprise and delight.

"Your Graces." A warm smile spread across his face, and he bowed his head to each of them. Approaching, his gaze remained fixed on Vane. "Yes, the likeness is certainly there. Please, come inside."

Framed in rich burgundy draperies, large windows afforded them a view of the valley below and a large greenhouse on the distant corner of the snow-covered lawn. Numerous books lay around the room and lined the bookshelves, most sharing the theme of English flora and botany.

"You knew my mother?" asked Claxton in a solemn tone, one that contained, Sophia believed, a bit of dread.

"I did. And your father as well."

From the pocket of his greatcoat, Vane produced the book of poems. "She left this for me. Do you know what it means?"

"I do, indeed. When you were ten years old, my wife

and I placed that book of poems in an old black pot, just as your dear mother instructed us to do." Again he smiled. "But I must say I'm still very shocked to see you. After her death, when we received her letter, I'll admit to being doubtful you would ever cross our threshold. But those quests and you completing them—once you were grown, mind you—seemed very important to her."

Vane looked at Sophia. "After we discovered the first quest, my wife rather insisted we complete the rest. I wouldn't have otherwise."

Though his jaw remained tense and his shoulders, rigid, the look he directed to her conveyed gratitude.

"Then well done, your Grace," Mr. Garswood said warmly, nodding to her. His eyes sparkled with good humor. "Elizabeth would be very happy to know you are both here. I think somehow, even now, she does know."

"Why *are* we here?" Vane asked bluntly.

Mr. Garswood's chin went down, toward his chest, and he stared for a long moment at the carpet before returning his gaze to Vane's. He said in a voice softened by emotion, "Because your mother believed it important for you to know the truth. All of it. Once you were a man."

, The truth? A sudden, fierce protectiveness came over Sophia. What would this man tell Vane, and how would it affect him from this day forward? She didn't want him to be hurt any more.

"The truth," Vane repeated, closing his eyes. "Yes, whatever that means, I would like to hear it."

"You may wish for your wife to leave the room. Some details may be difficult to hear."

Again, Sophia tensed. Leave the room? Why? But of course, she ought to if Vane wanted her to—

"I want her to stay," Vane answered with firm conviction, though Sophia believed his color had paled a shade or perhaps two.

The words pleased her, in that they offered proof that the time they'd spent together here in Lacenfleet, and the intimacies they'd shared, had brought them closer together. Vane did not reach for her. He did not so much as glance at her. Still, Sophia felt compelled to move closer to him. To stand beside him while he heard whatever this kind-eyed stranger had to reveal.

"Very well." Mr. Garswood nodded in assent and circled round to walk the length of the windows. "Your mother grew up not far from here. Very close, in fact, on her uncle's property, which bordered this one."

"I did not know that," Vane answered, leading Sophia to the window where they joined their host in looking out over the winter landscape. "There is not much I do know about my mother's bloodline. She did not often talk of her girlhood."

Vane couldn't explain it. Despite a certain trepidation over hearing what Mr. Garswood would say, he felt welcome, even comfortable here, in this man's home. It was as if they were two old friends, reuniting after many long years for a warm and heartfelt reunion.

Mr. Garswood rested a hand on his shoulder and squeezed affectionately. "Let me tell you our story, then. I knew your father when we were young boys. Our fathers before us had been friends, and we were friends as well. True friends as only young boys can be. But then your father, Follet as he was called then, was sent away to apprentice in the navy at only eight years old, a traumatic thing, as he was immediately thrust into the midst of the conflict with France and Spain in the siege on Havana. His ship, the HMS *Stirling Castle*, was one of those heavily damaged by the artillery from the fortress Morro and subsequently scuttled."

"That's too young," interjected Sophia, her expression showing the same concern she would feel toward any child in the same circumstance. "I know it was done more often then, but eight years old. What horrors he must have witnessed. There must have been times when he felt so afraid."

"During those years he visited rarely, but when he did, he would always come round and we would have the most marvelous time," Mr. Garswood continued. "Only after the death of his father and brothers, from the same dreadful influenza that claimed so many lives that year, did he return to stay and to assume the title you, your Grace, now bear. By then, I must impress upon you, he was notably different. A man, of course, but darker somehow."

"Darker, you say?" Vane inquired, his gaze intent. He'd borne witness to his father's darker nature, but according to Mr. Garswood, that shadow hadn't always been there.

Mr. Garswood nodded. The gray hair over his ears shone like silver in the winter light. "Another naval officer of my acquaintance told me that as a young officer Follet had sustained some sort of injury while serving. A blow to the head, and that he'd not been the same after, but prone to long periods of moodiness and fits of rage. Of course, none of that mattered. I welcomed his return as a friend. We hunted together. Attended the same parties and balls."

"An injury," Vane repeated. As a boy, he'd tried so desperately to find some trace of goodness in his father, only to be disappointed time and time again. But perhaps an injury had long ago altered the elder Lord Claxton's mind and not evil as he'd always feared. The knowledge gave him at least a measure of the peace he'd craved for as long as he could remember. "This is the first I've heard of that."

"People don't talk of such things, of weaknesses in men from whom greatness is expected. What am I thinking? It is cold here by the windows." He pointed to two chairs. "The both of you, please sit nearer to the fire, where it is warmer. This may take a little time."

Vane complied, leading Sophia forward, where they took occupancy of two armchairs, while their host remained standing. He leaned toward them, speaking in the measured tones of a storyteller.

"Well, it wasn't long before, unbeknownst to each other, Follet and I fell in love with the same young woman." He turned to a small lacquered chest, and when he faced them again, he presented something small and round on his palm, a miniature portrait, encircled by a delicate gilt frame, which he urged Vane to take.

Vane's breath staggered in his throat. For the first time in nearly twenty years, he viewed his mother's likeness.

"There she is," he whispered solemnly. "Just as I remember her."

Where Vane and his father possessed dark coloring, Elizabeth had radiated light, not only in her golden hair, but in the sparkle in her eyes and humor on her lips.

"She was lovely," Sophia whispered, smiling at him through tears.

Mr. Garswood presented his hand for the return of the miniature, and Vane reluctantly complied. Of course, Mr. Garswood could not know he possessed no other likenesses of his mother.

The elder gentleman glanced at the miniature briefly but with clear affection before returning the memento to the chest. "When I made my interest in Elizabeth known and began to court her, it became very clear to me that he cared for her too. Elizabeth had no idea, and at the time, I did not tell her, not wishing to shame him by her declared preference for me. I attempted to speak to him about it, but by then he was the Duke of Claxton. He did not share his thoughts or feelings. He only made it clear our friendship had ended."

Mr. Garswood sank into the chair beside Vane's, holding one leg rigidly straight. "To my great honor, your mother and I became betrothed. Yet shortly after, my regiment was called up, I at the time being a proud and brash young captain of the dragoons. But your mother wanted a summer wedding, you see, and I indulged her, believing as all young men do that I'd return in a few months' time so that we could be married."

"Obviously that did not happen," Vane concluded.

Mr. Garswood crossed his hands over the pommel of his cane. "I sustained wounds. For months, I lay insensible in a German hospital, my family believing me dead." The elder man's gaze faded. "Pardon your Graces for my being so forward as to speak so familiarly, but unbeknownst to me, I'd left your mother in a...a delicate condition."

"Oh my God," Vane uttered. "It's true, what the duke said. You are my father."

"What?" Sophia gasped, her face gone pale with shock. Her hand found his arm, and she squeezed.

Mr. Garswood's expression softened, and he chuckled. "No, your Grace. I am not. Though I have often wondered what might have been if the story would have gone that way."

Abruptly, Vane left Sophia's side to stand alone near the fire, where he stared at the ducal ring on his finger, almost afraid to relinquish the doubt that had eaten away at him since the age of ten. He had lived with that doubt for twenty years. It had become a part of him.

"Are you certain?" A rush of emotion moved through him so fast it left him dizzied. He'd harbored that festering kernel of doubt inside him for so long. "He always told me I was another man's bastard, not his son. That he'd been forced to acknowledge me as his own because of what my whore of a mother had done."

Mr. Garswood's eyes flashed with outrage. "It's simply not true. Follet married Elizabeth, of course, to spare her the scandal, but she lost our child soon after. Lord Claxton, whether you like it or not, you are his spirit and image. When you walked into this room, the resemblance took the air from my lungs."

Claxton nodded. "I suppose, in some way, I wanted what he said to be true. I did not want to be his son, only hers. And yet the idea that I've been living the life of an impostor, pretending to be someone I wasn't—" He cast a deliberate glance at Sophia, to find her eyes glittering with tears. "That did not rest well with me either."

"He was wrong to have said it."

"You and my mother—" Vane couldn't bring himself to say the rest.

Mr. Garswood's cheeks pinked, but he shook his head. "We never resumed our affair. Her ladyship was too honorable a woman to betray her vows, no matter how badly your father tormented her."

"That woman in the portrait over there," inquired Sophia. "Is that your wife?"

His gaze joined hers on a richly painted portrait of a smiling, auburn-haired woman holding a bouquet of wild roses.

"Indeed. Viola was a wonderful woman and very understanding about a young man's first love. She actually sought out your mother, and they became friends."

Claxton leaned forward in his chair and shifted toward Mr. Garswood. "I thought she looked familiar. I remember her. She visited the house from time to time and always brought my mother flowers and a book to read."

Mr. Garswood nodded, a wistful smile on his lips. "She grieved Elizabeth's death as if she'd lost a sister." His voice softened. "I lost her in May of last year."

"I'm sorry for your loss, sir," Claxton murmured.

"I count myself among the luckiest of men to have known them both."

"Thank you also for telling me all this."

Mr. Garswood nodded. "It ate away at his soul. The jealousy. His love for your mother, however sincere in the beginning, eventually bordered along obsession. He could not abide the fact that she had once loved another, and the knowledge that it was me, a man he came to believe was a rival rather than a friend, tormented him."

With difficulty, he again stood, pushing up on his cane. Slowly he made his way to a side table, where he poured two brandies and a sherry, which he distributed among them.

"When I was recovered enough from my wounds to return to England, Elizabeth visited me here, only to wish me well and to explain in person what had happened with our child and why she had married another." Mr. Garswood emptied his glass. "The servants talked, and the duke immediately believed we'd resumed our affair. You, meanwhile, had already been conceived within the honorable bonds of their marriage. They reconciled to whatever extent, long enough for you and Haden to be born, but he never forgave her for her alleged betrayal. Their relationship was always stormy and he eventually set her aside. But almost as if to torture himself, he placed her there, in Camellia House, in close proximity to my home."

They spoke a while longer, talking over smaller details of those stories and lives forever entwined. At last Vane stood, raising Sophia by her hand.

To Mr. Garswood he said, "I cannot thank you enough. All these years I lived with that grain of doubt, one I carried with me always, believing in my darkest moments that I had no right to bear my ancestors' name. And knowing of this injury my father sustained...it gives me peace that he was not purely evil, but somehow changed forever quite against his will."

"I am glad to have set things right." Mr. Garswood's eyebrows shot up. "But this old man and his stories are not your reward. At least, not the best part of it."

From his desk he withdrew a small wooden chest and handed it to Vane.

"This was delivered along with the instructions for that game of lookabout. Among other things, there's a letter inside she wrote to you, just before her death, and one intended for your brother, Lord Haden, as well. I was only to give them to you if you completed the final quest."

*   *   *

Their return to Camellia House took nearly twice as long as the initial trip to the Garswood estate. The blades that had conveyed them so swiftly from place to place for the last several days now sank deep into the melting snow, even touching the earth beneath, requiring the draft horse to exert more effort than before. As Vane held the reins and urged the animal to continue, his gaze continually fell to Sophia's lap, where she held the precious box containing his mother's letters and mementoes of his past. In a matter of moments he'd be able to examine everything. He looked forward to sharing the moment of first discoveries with Sophia. How strange and wonderful it had been to realize, as Mr. Garswood had revealed one secret after another, that no matter what the man had said—no matter how it might have shocked Vane or shaken his foundations—as long as Sophia was there standing beside him, everything would be all right.

Once returned to the house, he rekindled the fire and they spread a large blanket before it and reclined there with the box between them.

Hours before, Lord and Lady Meltenbourne had returned to the village to await the first possible ferry passage to London. Mr. and Mrs. Branigan and the baby were comfortably settled into their new quarters over the stable. As for Mr. and Mrs. Kettle, the excitement of the previous days had resulted in considerable fatigue for them. At Sophia's urging, they rested in their old quarters adjacent to the kitchen, refusing to leave Camellia House until the Duke and Duchess of Claxton made their departure the next day.

Sophia removed the lid of the box and peered down at the envelope resting on top. "Don't wait another moment, Vane. Read your mother's letter."

Dearest Vane,

When was your mother ever predictable? Can you believe I myself undertook to have that awful portrait hung on my very own wall? When I am gone, he will destroy any remnant of me. But never a portrait of himself hanging on my wall. He is too prideful for that.

I am just as certain one day you will remove the painting, as only you would understand its offensiveness to me. In that way, acting as my champion, I feel certain you will discover the first quest that after all this time spent apart will lead you back to me.

This simple game is the only way I could think to prove to you that no matter what has happened, you're still my Vane. My gentle, loving boy and the honorable man I knew he would become.

I know that to be true, because that honorable man is holding this letter now and reading my words. Only the Vane I know would fulfill a silly game of lookabout for the purpose of honoring his dead mother's memory. Set your spirit free of the past, and live your future with all the hopes I had for you.

Your loving mother, always and forever,
Elizabeth

Vane stared at the letter, and at last returned it to the wooden box filled with old diaries, miniatures, and letters he had yet to examine but appeared to represent the history of her family, which had ended with her death. In his head, it was almost as if he could hear his mother's voice.

Sophia touched his hand. "This is all so wonderful. I couldn't be more happy for you."

Vane stood from the floor, eyes wide and amazed.

Sophia peered up at him. "How do you feel now after reading her letter?"

"Broken." He exhaled and straightened his shoulders. "Healed."

He pulled her up to stand beside him.

"Then it was all worth it. The ruined cakes." She beamed. "Lady Meltenbourne. The duel and the surprise Branigan baby."

He rubbed his hands down her arms. It wasn't a seductive touch, but one that spoke of affection. "Tomorrow we return to London."

"Yes. Just in time for Christmas."

"Before we go, I need to tell you something."

"What's that?"

Touching her chin, he lifted her gaze to his. He felt freed. Somehow the words that had seemed so difficult before weren't any longer.

"I never wanted anything more than I wanted you," he said quietly. "From the first moment I saw you."

She said nothing, but her eyes softened and she let out a little breath.

He continued, having so much more to say. "On paper, I had everything, a title and wealth, to be a worthy husband to you. But on the inside, here in my heart and inside my head, I felt like a fraud. For living the life I'd lived and for doubting who I was. I believed myself wholly unworthy of someone as lovely as you. I know it sounds strange to say, but the happier we were, the more fearful I became that one day you would see me for what I was."

She stared up into his eyes. "What you are is a good man."

"But not then. That day, everything came crashing down. We lost the baby, and I believed I'd lost you too. When I should have stayed beside you and held you and proved to you I was someone else...I didn't. I was wrong." He touched her face and looked down into the green eyes that had always enchanted him. "I can't take those memories and those hurts away, but I can tell you I love you. I have *always* loved you."

Chapter Eighteen

I love you too. The words hovered at the back of her
tongue. She did love him. Desperately. She always had.
But she hesitated. Why? When she wanted to throw her
arms around him and kiss him and cry yes to happiness.
Yes, to forever.

"It's all right," he said. "I don't expect you to say you
love me too. Not after these few days. I just wanted you to
know before we left Lacenfleet how I felt, now more than
ever. Sophia, I wouldn't have been the honorable man my
mother describes in the letter if not for you." He pointed
at the wooden chest.

"That's not true."

I love you too. Still, the words wouldn't come.

She wanted to cry because it hurt her to be so begrudging, that she couldn't simply let go of the fear that had
consumed her for so long.

She'd forgiven him, but why couldn't she forget?

"It is true." He took her in his arms, embracing her

tight, the naked admiration in his eyes almost more than she could bear, because she craved it so deeply, but feared once they left this magical place, that light would fade. She wouldn't be able to survive losing him a second time. She needed more days like this one with Claxton before she could at last say good-bye to her doubts. A history. Then she could finally surrender everything. She could again give him her heart. "If you'd not been here, goose, I would have thrown that first quest on the fire with his portrait without ever having read it, a coward from my pain."

She shook her head. "You're the furthest thing from a coward. To hear what you have suffered at the hands of your own father, a man who should have treasured you. I can hardly bear it."

"No pity." He mouth found hers, breathtakingly ardent.

"Vane." She sighed. "No, never pity."

He had fought his battle and won.

"I need you now," he murmured. His mouth burned a hot path down her neck to her breasts.

Sophia stared into his eyes, her heart swollen with a love she couldn't express in words, so strong and consuming she felt terrified from the immensity of it. "Claxton, I—"

He touched his fingertips to her lips. "I told you. You don't have to say anything. Not until you're ready."

Sophia melted in his arms, lost to his touch. He scattered kisses along her temple and cheek. Down her throat.

"Let me make love to you now," he rasped against her skin. "One last time before we go . . . then again in our bed in London."

"Please," she begged, grasping fistfuls of his shirt and tugging the linen free from his breeches.

"We've got to be quiet." He laughed, a chuckle deep in his throat. He cupped her breasts in his hands and squeezed before plucking at the tiny pearl buttons at the center of her bodice. "The Kettles—"

"Yes, quiet." She tugged his shirttails from his breeches, tilting her head, so he could kiss her neck.

Suddenly, he stilled in her arms. A low, jagged breath issued from his lips.

"Vane?"

She felt something there at her breast. The brush of his fingertips, the sensation of—

Oh no.

He tore the folded page from her bodice.

"What the hell is this?" He held the folded square of paper in her face. "That damned list? You wear it here against your heart, a ward against me?"

He paled, his face having gone devoid of emotion. A sudden flick of his wrist unfolded the page with a snap.

"Vane, don't be unfair. And please don't misunderstand. Everything happened so fast, and I felt so scared. I just needed to keep my head in the right place, my heart—"

"Unfair?" he roared. "After everything? After *last night*? Don't you know what that meant to me? Don't you understand what we did? And you still woke up this morning and thought *this* of me?"

"I just—I just need more time. It's only been four days, even less really...and I felt so overwhelmed—"

He trembled with rage. "Do you think I don't feel? That I can't love?"

He lunged forward to toss the list on the fire.

"No," she wailed for some inexplicable reason, not ready to let go of the one thing that had given her power when she'd felt so powerless. It should be her choice when to burn it, not his. Once it was gone, she'd have no choice but to love him completely, to take the terrifying chance her heart might get broken again.

With the poker, she fished out the curling rectangle, an impulsive move she regretted instantly, for the page, already consumed by flame, floated on the air, an ashen wraith, to flatten against her skirt.

She beat it away with her hands, but too late. The flames latched onto the muslin. She screamed. Claxton cursed, throwing her to the floor, where he tore her skirts from her legs.

"There's more," she shrieked. "There."

Flames rippled across the carpet, devouring old threads and the ancient wood beneath, but most horrifying of all, the little wooden chest containing his mother's family treasures and Lord Haden's letter, still unread.

Vane threw her a glance, one that in the brief second it lasted, screamed betrayal.

I gave you my love, and you give me this?

In that moment, she knew. She loved him more than anything. *I love you. I take it back. Please forgive me.*

But it was too late. She had doubted not only him, but herself, and in doing so destroyed everything she'd ever wanted.

Mr. and Mrs. Kettle rushed into the room, their faces transformed by fear. Sophia's nose filled with smoke and her heart with frantic dread. How quickly the fire grew out of control. All she could think was that she had done this to them. Camellia House was on fire, a place she had so come to love now destroyed by her petty insistence on keeping a meaningless list.

Vane lifted her, snatching up her redingote. He carried her away from the horrible heat and light through the vestibule and out the door until his boots met snow and he flung her from his arms.

"Go," he ordered, his eyes wild and furious. He threw the garment at her. "Stay out and don't return."

*   *   *

Sophia did not return. She waited with Mrs. Branigan in the stable, the both of them inconsolable until the fire had been put out. By then, villagers crowded into the yard, having come from the village to offer help. Boots trampled the melting snow, turning the grounds into an ugly mud bog.

Mr. Branigan eventually returned, his skin shadowed by soot and his eyes with regret.

Still, he explained to them one bit of good fortune. The frost, having thawed earlier that day, allowed Mr. Kettle to install a hose on a functional pump. The availability of water, combined with Lord Claxton's quick action in smothering the flames with the heaviest draperies, allowed the fire to be extinguished. Although he described the great room as severely damaged, the remainder of the house had been largely spared.

"But no one was hurt?" Sophia demanded softly through tears.

He shook his head. "No one hurt."

Thank God. But she could never face Claxton again, not after what she had done. He had given her the gift of his love, and in return, she'd continued to harbor secret doubts, ones that had brought about the destruction of not only the new trust between them but also his mother's home. A place that had inspired his sweetest childhood memories. Just as heartbreaking, he'd lost the treasure chest of mementos, of a family he had never known. Such precious items could never be replaced or rebuilt. She had taken all those things from him.

All for an imbecilic list she ought to have burned the same night it had been written, committing its sins to the past. Claxton's stunned look of betrayal would forever be preserved in her mind.

How would he ever forgive her? How could she ever expect him to?

She'd never felt so choked with sadness, so dead inside.

"Mr. Branigan," she said numbly. "Would you please take me down into Lacenfleet?"

The young man displayed reluctance, clearly in fear of provoking the duke's displeasure, but at last, when faced with her tears, he took pity on her. She would indeed be home for Christmas, but with her spirit broken and more hopeless than she'd ever imagined.

They arrived at the village inn a short time later, she with no possessions other than the clothes she wore, ruined by soot and flame.

"My lady," exclaimed the innkeeper. "What a relief to see you in good health. We all saw the smoke. This gentleman who says he knows you had just inquired as to your residence. I was just about to tell him the terrible news."

Only then did Sophia look at the man who stood beside him. She recognized the familiar face and golden hair of a childhood friend.

"Oh, Fox," she exclaimed, dissolving into tears and collapsing into his arms. "Please take me home."

Within moments his carriage conveyed them toward the Mowbray ferry landing, where the vehicle paused to await the disembarkment of a wagon and horses that had just come over from the other side. The river, swollen from melted ice and snow, nearly overwhelmed the dock.

"I came on behalf of your family, of course," Fox explained from the seat opposite her. "They, having heard nothing from you since the night of your grandfather's party, wished to confirm your well-being as soon as the river became passable."

Her *well-being*. She would never be well again. What she had told Claxton last night was true. The past four days had been the most uncommon of her life. Now forever, they would be shadowed in darkness. She grieved their loss and Claxton's loss like a death.

"Sophia." He extended a handkerchief, which she gratefully clutched to her eyes. "You must tell me what happened."

"I can't," she rasped. "It's all too terrible."

He pulled aside the window curtain, an action that provided a direct view of Camellia House high upon the hill over Lacenfleet. Even from this distance, Sophia clearly saw the gaping hole and the cloud of soot that smudged the lovely façade. She moaned and buried her head in her hands.

It was then that Fox's composure fractured.

"Why is he not with you?" he demanded ferociously. "Why have you left in this fashion, unescorted, with only the clothes on your back? As if in secrecy. As if in *escape*?"

She shook her head, unable to respond for a sudden eruption of tears. He lunged across the carriage, taking her in his arms. Sobs racked her body.

"Tell me, Sophia, what did he do to you? If Vinson were here, he would demand to know. Since he is not, then I will."

Just then the door of the carriage flew open. Claxton's face appeared in the door opening, his eyes cruel and his skin and clothing blackened by soot. He breathed heavily and his features were strained, as if he'd run all the way on foot. His boot slammed onto the step and he gripped the handle, for all appearances prepared to hurl himself inside.

"You would leave me now?" He uttered the words hoarsely, his gaze only briefly veering to Havering before returning to her. His body shuddered with some emotion, his expression grew hard, and he fell back to simply stand and stare. "I was a coward for abandoning you before, for not fighting harder for us. But make no mistake. It's you, Sophia, who are the coward today."

Nostrils flaring with rage, he slammed the door.

"Oh, Fox," she cried. "It's not what he did to me, but what I did to him. He will never forgive me."

* * *

Two days later, upon returning to town, Vane took residence in his London house instead of his club. He had no fear of crossing paths with Sophia because from what he could surmise, she had not spent one moment in their marital home, but had flown straight into her family's waiting arms. He expected it was just a matter of time before Wolverton summoned him to discuss their separation.

"It's officially 'eve,'" Haden said, looking at his time-piece. "Christmas Eve, that is, which means it's almost time for me to depart."

Vane didn't bite. Haden had been dangling some supposed invitation in front of his nose all evening. As if Vane had ever cared about society or parties before, and he most especially did not now.

"Where will *you* go tonight, Claxton?" asked Rabe, who also made ready to depart, donning his hat and gloves.

"To bed, I suppose." Vane had given the servants two days' leave in honor of the holiday. He wanted to be alone. He had not slept in two days, not since the fire. Not since Sophia had left Lacenfleet in the company of Lord Havering. If he could just force himself to fall asleep, he might stay there forever.

"To bed? But it's Christmas Eve." His cousin frowned.

"And?" Vane answered stolidly.

From outside came the sound of waits singing on the pavement outside his window, a song of hope and good-will toward one's common man, two sentiments he could not summon within himself.

"Come with me to Mother's," Rabe insisted.

"Thank you," Vane answered. "But no."

Haden jumped in. "I, for one, have accepted an invitation to participate in one generous family's traditional holiday festivities."

Vane spread the morning's newspaper on the table and pretended to read. It wouldn't do to murder his only remaining immediate relation on Christmas Eve. Perhaps, though, tomorrow.

"Well?" demanded Haden.

"Well, what?" Vane responded darkly.

"Aren't you going to ask who invited me to spend Christmas Eve with them?"

"No," Vane growled, his head feeling as if it might just explode.

"The two of you are imbeciles." Rabe rolled his eyes. "Tell us, who invited you, Haden?"

Haden puffed his chest out and smiled. "The Duchess of Claxton."

Rabe whistled through his teeth.

Vane glared at his brother, his hands seizing the paper. "No, she didn't."

Haden's eyebrows jumped with mischief. "Yes, she did. That morning after the duel. I can only assume the invitation still stands." Turning to gaze into the gilt-framed wall mirror, he whistled cheerfully and pinned a sprig of holly to his lapel.

"If I were you, I would assume," Vane seethed, "that the invitation has been rescinded."

"Last I checked I was still her brother by marriage. You might do well to—"

"Don't say it," Vane warned.

Haden's good humor dimmed. "Suit yourself. But you can't stay here forever being miserable. I think if you would only talk to her—"

"I hope you choke on mistletoe," Claxton growled.

He wasn't trying to be funny. Mistletoe's knobby thin branches would be exquisitely painful if thrust down one's throat, and as an added benefit in his brother's case, poisonous.

"Hmm. Mistletoe," Haden mused. "Her Grace has two lovely sisters."

"I'll visit tomorrow, Claxton," said Rabe.

"Don't bother. I plan to be asleep." Or drunk.

Haden and Rabe exchanged looks of exasperation. A moment later the door closed behind them. At last. Silence.

Damn, and the memory of Sophia's beautiful face. He curled his fists and pressed them against his forehead, aching for her with such a sudden miserable intensity he—

A sudden rapping came on the door.

Damn it, Haden. He waited for his footman to answer, but then remembered...he had no servants. The rapping continued unabated, driving a nail straight through his skull.

Unlocking the door, he bellowed, "Next time remember your key—"

A different face waited there. Vane snarled, for there on his doorstep stood Lord Havering, his eyes ablaze, as if prepared for battle.

"You and I are going to have a talk," he said.

But puzzlingly...behind him stood Haden and Rabe.

They all, in a rush of tall hats, shoulders, and winter scarves, pushed past him into the vestibule. He considered walking straight out the door into the night without his coat or hat. He'd just keep walking until he could walk no more and spend the night, or maybe a month, at some anonymous inn.

But this was his house, and he wasn't leaving. He firmly shut the door on the cold and proceeded to return from whence he had come. They all waited for him beneath the arched threshold of his study, doffing their hats, with expressions of grim-faced determination. He could only assume that Havering had been sent as Wolverton's representative to present the terms for a separation and that his own blood relations had been recruited to bear witness and to intercede, as necessary, if Claxton did not take the proposed provisos well. No doubt Havering would *talk talk talk* and expect him to listen.

"Listen here, Claxton," declared Havering, proving his point. "This nonsense between you and her Grace is going to stop right here, tonight."

"It's Lord Claxton to you," Vane said, striding past. "And I don't see that 'this nonsense' is any of your business."

Of course Havering followed, practically riding on his back. "As the duchess's friend, I'm making it my business. If Vinson were alive, he'd be here. But since he's not, I am."

"But you aren't her brother, are you?" Vane snarled. "Are you happy now that our marriage has fallen apart? Don't think I don't know you've been waiting in the wings all along for that to happen."

He dropped into his desk chair and snatched up a stack of correspondence, which he pretended to peruse. He'd been gone for months and had so much catching up to do. Didn't they realize he was busy?

The other man snatched the envelopes out of his hands and tossed them to the desk. "Nothing matters to me, but that Sophia is happy—and she loves you."

Vane barked out a laugh, shaking his head.

"I was there the night the two of you were introduced," Havering said, his voice lowering to a low hush. "She was smitten from the first moment. After you, I never had a chance."

"You never had a chance before that, Havering, from

what I heard," murmured Rabe, who walked slowly along the bookshelf, reading the spines. "Claxton, I can't believe you still have these naughty books. How old were we when we purchased them in that back-alley shop? Thirteen?"

"Did someone say naughty books?" Haden inquired.

"They are right here."

"What did you say?" Havering demanded.

"I told him where the books are." Rabe pointed to the second shelf from the floor.

"Before that."

"Before...oh. It's just that I heard that Wolverton forbade you from marrying any of his granddaughters."

Havering's stance went rigid, and he crossed his arms over his chest. "That's a fine detail for you to throw out now when we're supposed to be working together." He clenched his teeth and growled, "Tell me, where did you hear that?"

Rabe merely shrugged and raised his eyebrows as if his words were the undisputed truth.

"If Sophia loves me," Vane muttered, "she has a fine way of showing it."

"Havering says she's destroyed," Haden interjected. "Her Grace told him you have every right to despise her, not just because of the damage to the house, but because of whatever happened in the moments before the fire."

"She told you about that, did she?" he growled at Havering. Just the mental image of the two of them sitting alone and talking and Sophia confiding to another man about her unhappy marriage drove him half-mad.

"Not really," Havering answered. "Whenever she gets to that part of the story, all she can do is cry."

Vane closed his eyes, doing his best to shut down the onrush of emotion and his regrets. He'd never wanted to make her cry.

"So why did she leave?" he said. "When she ought to have stayed?"

"A fine question, coming from you," Havering retorted.

"Gentlemen," said Haden, who looked at his pocket watch. "I really have somewhere I need to be. If the two of you will excuse us, I would prefer a word alone with my brother."

"I could use a drink," gritted Havering, scowling at Claxton.

Rabe grinned. "Good thing I know where he keeps the liquor."

Together the two men disappeared into the corridor.

When they were gone, Vane exhaled through his nose. "There is nothing you can say—"

"Of course not," Haden snapped. "Not if you're too obstinate to listen."

"I'm not being obstinate," he argued. "Things have just gone too far off course. I tried to win her back, and I failed. No doubt she's already instructed Wolverton's lawyers to draw up a formal proposal for our separation."

"Oh, good. Then you can get on with the business of growing old and bitter and being just like him."

What a low thing to say to him right now, but nothing he hadn't already said to himself.

"Don't bring our father into this." Vane strode past his brother to flatten his palms against the surface of his desk.

"Vane, it is almost Christmas," his brother said in a quiet voice. "Which hasn't meant anything to me in a very long time. But those days we spent in Lacenfleet, however unintended, brought back such memories from when you and I were younger. When we were closer. We spent so many years apart I almost forgot I had a brother."

Vane closed his eyes.

Haden continued. "Do you know I can't remember her face anymore? I haven't been able to for a very long time. But there, in Camellia House, I could almost see her again."

"That's not fair," Vane said.

"I'm so very thankful you thought to put the letter she wrote to me in your coat pocket, so her final words to me were spared from the fire." Haden rounded the desk and faced him squarely. "But you didn't ask me about it. Don't you want to know what her letter said?"

"I don't know." He straightened. "She didn't write the letter to me."

"She wrote that I must help you to forgive him." His brother's gray eyes shone in the lamplight. "And I think she's right, you know. Perhaps it is as Mr. Garwood told you, that our father suffered that strike to his head, and the injury forever changed him. Vane, we've spent our entire lives hating him. Trying to beat him and to prove we were stronger. When really, what we need to do is forgive."

Vane exhaled and closed his eyes.

* * *

Morosely, Sophia descended the staircase, having been forced by her mother to get out of her bed an hour before and dress for Christmas Eve, when all she wanted was to remain abed until she was an old woman, when hopefully, at last, she'd forget the reasons for her sadness.

She wore a gown of deep plum silk with ruched sleeves that were puffed and pleated at the shoulders. The garment had given her such joy during her fittings at the modiste's shop. Everyone had marveled over the fine sheen of the fabric and declared the hue a perfect complement to her complexion. She might as well have worn sackcloth for all the joy the pretty dress gave her now. Daphne and Clarissa had made a fuss over her hair and tried to cheer her, until at last she had gently shooed them away.

Familiar voices, just around the corner from the lower landing, made her pause near the bottom of the stairs. She made out two figures in the dim lamplight.

"You're still carrying that wilted thing around?" said Lady Dundalk a bit grumpily.

Beside her stood Sir Keyes, leaning on his cane, with a much decreased ball of mistletoe suspended from his hand.

"There's one berry left," he answered cheerfully. "I saved the best for last."

"Who is the lucky young woman this time?" asked her ladyship drolly.

"Why, you, my dear." Slowly he lifted the mistletoe above her head. "If you will have me."

"Oh, Alfred," she whispered softly, reaching up to pat her gloved hand against his cheek. "What took you so long?"

He bent and kissed on her lips, and the two embraced.

Moments later, Lady Margaretta found her sitting on the stairs. "Sophia, more tears?"

"Lady Dundalk—" Sophia choked. "Sir Keyes. It's so wonderful that they have found each other."

"Isn't it?" A dreamy smile spread across her mother's lips. "One never gets too old for love."

"I'll never have that." Sophia sighed. "Someone to grow old with, who will love me until the end of our days."

Her mother tilted her head and let out a low breath. Sophia's heart shattered a fraction more. Of course her words wounded her mother, whose one true love had been taken from her.

"Oh, Mother. I'm so sorry. I shouldn't have said it. It's just that I don't deserve it. You did. You do!"

"I don't believe you are undeserving, not for one moment." Margaretta patted her back, as if Sophia was a small child crying over some disappointment. "Things aren't irreparable with Claxton. The two of you just need to talk."

"I can't ever face him again." Sophia shook her head and wrapped her arms around her knees. "Not after what I did. He showed me in every way that he loved me, and I just couldn't let go of the past. In doing so, I betrayed him, Mother, in the most horrible way, and now I fear it's too late."

"That you feel that way means that you still care deeply for him," her mother counseled sagely. "And dare I say, that you love him? Otherwise, hurting him wouldn't hurt you so much. Now wipe your eyes, dear, and join us downstairs."

Margaretta left her there. Moments later, after composing herself, Sophia peered into the drawing room. Sir Keyes and Lady Dundalk sat on a green velvet settee beside the fire conversing with her grandfather. At a nearby table, Daphne and Clarissa arranged apples, oranges, candy, and cookies that would later be placed on the tree. She continued to the dining room, where the table had been set for their Christmas Eve feast. Her grandmother's crystal, silver plate, and porcelain gleamed atop the snowy-white tablecloths. Marvelous smells wafted down the hall from the direction of the kitchen.

The perfect Christmas! And yet the scene provided her with no comfort. Nothing would ever be perfect without Claxton at her side.

"Everyone," exclaimed Daphne, rushing out from the drawing room. "There are waits at the door."

Clarissa pushed their grandfather's bath chair in the same direction. Wolverton, finding Sophia, winked. Lady Margaretta accompanied them, reaching to wrap a wool scarf around Wolverton's shoulders.

Glancing back, she called, "Sophia, could you bring the oranges?"

Oranges, yes, which her mother always insisted on giving to carolers, being that they were so rare and she so loved the tradition. From the table in the corridor, she listlessly lifted the basket by its handle and followed everyone else to the front doors.

Arriving at the door, she hovered behind Daphne, but Clarissa elbowed her forward. There were four carolers, but she could see none of their faces. Only the back sides of their sheet music. Really, who didn't know the words to Christmas carols? What was the world coming to?

"Ready?" she heard one of them murmur. "One, two, three."

What followed was the worst cacophony of male voices she'd ever heard, no clear tune among them.

"...Snow!"

"On a sleigh!"

"Bells ringing."

"Angels singing."

The centermost caroler lifted his music suddenly. "Christmas Eve surprises! It is I!"

At realizing his identity, the air left her lungs. Lord Haden. Yes, she'd invited him, but no, she'd not expected him to come, given present circumstances. Certainly he had every bit a right to despise her as Claxton.

Clarissa laughed delightedly. "Lord Haden."

Daphne giggled as well. Sophia couldn't blame them. Next to Claxton, he was probably the most handsome man in London.

"And also *this man*!" Haden grabbed the music from the caroler beside him, revealing—

Lord Havering? Sophia blinked in shock. She wasn't even aware that the two men knew each other, aside from being introduced the morning of her wedding to Claxton.

"So sorry for the deception." Haden laughed. "We can't sing, and we don't really have sheets of music, and none of us could remember the words to any carols. We just wanted to be certain you'd open the door because some of us don't have proper invitations."

He swiped the sheet of paper from the third male caroler, who turned out to be Mr. Grisham, Claxton's cousin. "This fellow in particular."

"You're all very welcome here," her grandfather announced magnanimously.

The blood drained from Sophia's face as she realized with a sudden dread certainty the identity of the very tall, broad-shouldered fourth caroler. Though he still held the sheet over his face, she would recognize those fingers anywhere and the square, masculine shapes of his finger-nails. She'd studied the man with such intense fascination for four days, she'd probably be able to recognize his ear-lobe if necessary.

She made the sudden decision to flee. To back away into the house, but suddenly Clarissa was there, and Daphne, pushing gently, taking the basket of oranges from her hands—

Everyone jostled past her. Perplexingly, Haden pressed a brotherly kiss to her cheek as he did the same. "Merry Christmas, your Grace."

She turned to follow him, but the flat side of the door closed in her face.

Slowly she turned back around.

Vane stared at her in silence, tall, beautiful, and ele-gant. She flushed all over, no longer aware of the chill.

"Hello," she whispered morosely. "Happy Christmas Eve."

"It wasn't your fault, Sophia." He spoke all in a rush, his breath puffing, visible on the night air. "The day before, don't you remember, after the Branigans' baby was born? That whole damn bottle of brandy tipped over and spilled across the carpet and the floor? I'm a lazy, slovenly man, and I didn't think to clean it up. There was just so much happening. It was enough to help the fire along."

"No." She shook her head, imagining for the thou-sandth time the ravenous path the flames had taken. If only she could go back and do things differently. "It was not the brandy's fault. Not your fault, but mine. I'll never forgive myself."

He shrugged. "The house was old. Neglected. In need of repairs. Mr. Branigan, it seems, is a skilled carpenter, and being that he's in need of employment appears the perfect candidate to undertake them. In the spring, he'll enlist help from some men in the village."

The stone in her chest did not grow any lighter.

"Mr. Branigan can't replace your dear mother's letters, yours and Haden's." Just speaking of those treasures lost renewed her regret. Her voice became so thick she could hardly speak. "Your precious box of memories. All destroyed because of me."

"Oh, that. I had already placed Haden's letter in my coat pocket and gave it to him the next day. As for the rest, we managed to save the most important thing here." From his pocket he pulled a small rectangular box tied with gold ribbon. He shook it gently. Inside, something slid back and forth, bumping the sides. "It is my most precious treasure, really. But you can look."

An overwhelming curiosity overcame her, a desperate need to see the item in the box, to know that something had been salvaged. Anything to lessen the smothering guilt she'd carried since that day.

"You're certain?" She stepped closer.

"Yes, look." He rested the box on his palm.

She fell back. "No. I don't deserve to see."

He shook the box again. "I insist."

With the box rested upon his open hand, she slid the ribbon free and lifted the lid.

A small mirror lay faceup in the box. Her own face peered back at her.

"A mirror," she whispered, not feeling much better after all. All those letters, the miniatures. Lost. "Not the slightest bit of charring. Now, to whom did this mirror belong? Your mother?"

"No, silly," Claxton murmured, his gaze steady and somehow questioning. "The mirror I bought from a trinket vendor for twopence on the ride over."

Her thoughts buckled, making no sense of his words. "I don't understand."

"It's not the mirror that is my most precious treasure, goose. *It is you.*"

She must have misheard him. But no, because the words he'd spoken still echoed in her ears.

She backed away. "Don't say that."

He followed, the house lamp illuminating his face and hair and the snowflakes falling to dust his shoulders. "Not that you're a possession, mind you, but you are my most special thing. The box that burned held my past, Sophia. So be it. It is gone. You are my future."

She could only listen, stunned and uncertain of what to feel or say.

"By the way, it is Christmas Eve. There is a gift in this box for you under the mirror." Again, he lifted the box, holding it between them.

She shook her head. "I don't deserve a gift."

"Well, too late," he asserted crisply. "If you don't at least look at it, you'll hurt my feelings."

She frowned and lifted the mirror. A folded piece of paper lay concealed beneath.

No, not the list. The list had burned and destroyed Camellia House, along with her dreams.

"What is that?" she asked warily.

"It's a list. I wrote you another."

No. Her breath evaporated in her throat. He wouldn't be that cruel. Would he?

"Open it," he urged.

"No," she said, too afraid, turning away from him, preferring instead to face the stone wall.

She heard a sound behind her, the soft shuffle of the box against a twopence mirror and paper.

He cleared his throat. "Reasons Vane loves Sophia. That's what this list is called."

Sophia fisted her hand against her mouth. Vane loves Sophia. How could he love her after what she had done?

"That Sophia snores, and I do not." He paused and inhaled sharply. "That Sophia has such pretty toes. That she docs not complain when I call her 'goose.'"

She whirled toward him, eyes wide and filled with tears.

"I'm not finished," he said, holding up two pages. "You see, this list is much longer than the other one."

His eyes shone with such earnestness, she gasped. "Vane."

"I could have written more, of course, but those idiots made me get in the carriage before I was finished." He reached to brush her tears away. "Havering feared we'd miss the games."

She turned her cheek in to his hand. "How can you forgive me?"

"I already have." Eyes damp, he shoved the box into his pocket and pressed the pages into her hands. "The question is, my darling, can you forgive me?"

"There is nothing to forgive," she cried. "I would change nothing about you, not now, not before. That horrible list I forced you to write. I'll never think of it again."

Grasping the same hands, he kissed them. "Sophia, please come home. I haven't slept. I can't without you."

"Home?"

"Yes, our home here in London. In Lacenfleet. Wherever I am, be there with me. Always. I love you, Sophia. I love you." His hands came up, framing her face, and he kissed her. "You."

"You asked me that night if I would choose you again, if I had the chance. I never had the chance to answer." She hiccuped, laughing. "Yes. Oh yes, Claxton. A thousand times, I would choose you again." She threw herself into his arms. "Always. I love you too."

He pressed his lips to her nose. Her cheek. "Merry Christmas, darling."

"Reasons Sophia loves Vane," Sophia exclaimed into the night. "He is mine. All mine."

Epilogue

One Year Later

"Merry Christmas morning, darling."

Sophia awakened to a kiss on her nose and a paradise of warm male skin and layers and layers of blankets.

"Mmmm." She smiled. "Merry Christmas."

She stretched across the bed, then suddenly remembered. "We're not late, are we?"

"No, it's still early yet. We've plenty of time."

Her entire family, including Wolverton, had traveled to Lacenfleet to observe the dedication of the new church bell, to be rung for the first time on Christmas Day in memoriam of Claxton's mother. Afterward, she and Claxton and the family would host lunch and games at Camellia House for the children of the orphan home, with Mr. Burridge and Mr. Garswood and numerous others from the village as invited guests.

Relaxing again, she sighed happily. "Could you bring Vinson to me, please? He must be hungry."

The bed creaked as Vane left her to bend over the

cradle. Dim morning light filtered through the draperies to define the deeply cut muscles at either side of his abdomen, above the waist of his low-slung linen drawers. Though she'd given him a nightshirt as an early Christmas gift, he'd worn the garment for only a blink the evening before. Remembering the pleasure he'd brought her after discarding the linen shirt on the bedside table, she reconsidered and wished she hadn't asked him to bring the baby, who from his lack of noisemaking seemed to be perfectly content.

"If he's sleeping, don't bother him and come back to bed," she hastily amended.

She heard the movement of the baby's bedclothes and her husband's low chuckle. "I was just thinking how quiet he's been and that we'd been allowed to sleep uncommonly late." He lifted a tightly swaddled bundle and turned the opening so that she could see within. Lord Misrule's painted wooden face peered back at her. "Now I know why."

"Daphne!" they both exclaimed.

All week her sister had taken immense pleasure in planning Lord Misrule's next act of mischief.

A half hour later, with the flush of passion still on his cheeks, Vane brought Sophia her dressing gown. "Let's go rescue our baby from your sisters."

Though Camellia House, returned to its intended glory, had required a full staff hired from the village to tend to the house and the grounds, they met no one in the corridor outside their chamber, only polished wood walls and new carpet. The Duke and Duchess of Claxton had given their new retainers two days off to celebrate Christmas with their families in the village, in what they intended to be an annual tradition. The Branigans remained in residence, but they, like the Kettles, had become something closer to family.

Holding hands, Sophia and Vane descended the staircase, pausing for a brief moment midway to simply observe their well-loved guests and listen to their lively chatter. Sophia gave a sigh of happy contentment at seeing Wolverton in a chair beside the fire, holding three-month-old Vinson.

Fresh-cut laurel adorned the mantel behind him, verdant and glossy. The day before, they'd all ventured into the forest in a big raucous group to gather greens and cut a Christmas yew.

The house itself glowed with new life. Mr. Branigan and the other skilled carpenters from the village had made the necessary repairs in the spring, and no trace of last December's fire remained. But more important, new life had come to Camellia House when Sophia had given birth to Vinson in the ducal bed in early October, with Mrs. Kettle and Mrs. Branigan acting as midwives.

"Merry Christmas, Grandfather," she said, dipping to press a kiss to his cheek.

"Merry Christmas, dear," he said. Vinson, at seeing her, began to wriggle. Wolverton's old eyes opened wide, and he lifted the baby against his shoulder for a soothing pat on the back. "I've already got my best present. Here he is. That's a good boy."

But the round-faced child started to fuss.

Daphne reached up from where she sat reading a book at his feet. "I'll take him again, Grandfather. I think he wants his auntie Daphne to sing him a Christmas carol."

Clarissa turned from where she played with William,

the Branigans' one-year-old little boy. "Sister, dearest, your singing will only traumatize the child. Clearly he's asking for his auntie Clarissa."

Claxton kissed Sophia's temple and murmured, "Best you rescue the poor boy now."

And indeed, Sophia reached—

But Margaretta swooped in and took the baby in her arms. "He only wants his grandmamma." She kissed the baby's nose. "My sweet little Vinson. How your grandpapa and uncle would have adored you."

"Breakfast is served," called Mrs. Kettle from the direction of the kitchen. "Mrs. Branigan has made her special Christmas morning meat pie."

"But we're still missing several gentlemen!" called Clarissa, her eyebrows furrowed.

"More of Mrs. Branigan's pie for us!" Daphne declared with a mischievous grin.

A tall figure turned from the nearby wall, where a large portrait of the Duchess Elizabeth hung, and joined them as they all made their way to the dining room.

"I'm still amazed, every time I look at it," marveled Lord Haden, his hair still tousled from a night's sleep. "The likeness is astounding. Sophia, I can't thank you enough for thinking to have the portrait done."

The painting had been Sophia's birthday gift to Claxton the previous July, created by an artist who utilized Mr. Garswood's miniature as inspiration. As for the damaged portrait of the old duke that Sophia had hidden away in the attic months before, the canvas had been painstakingly repaired and now hung in the cavernous gallery of their London home between a portrait of Vane's great-grandfather and himself.

In the dining room, Daphne crossed to the window, where she peered out through the new peacock-blue draperies Mrs. Branigan had finished and hung with pride just the week before. "At last! Clarissa, our handsome husbands have returned from their walk about the property with Mr. Kettle and Mr. Branigan."

Clarissa joined her, William perched on her hip. "They are handsome, aren't they? And look, they've brought more mistletoe."

The two of them broke into a round of delighted giggles.

"Girls!" chided Lady Harwick, momentarily looking up from Vinson's laughing face. "Not at breakfast."

Claxton pulled Sophia's chair from the table, and she stood beside him, reveling in the familiar banter. To have her family here, at this happy place with her and Vane, meant more to her than anything. He moved to stand behind her, his arms encircling her waist and pulling her close.

"I believe my mother would be very happy if she were here to see," he said, nuzzling her cheek.

"Of that, I have no doubt."

"This is the best Christmas ever," he murmured.

Sophia smiled. "You said the same thing last year."

"Every Christmas will be my best Christmas as long as I have you." He pressed a tender kiss to her temple. "I love you. Merry Christmas, goose."

Miss Daphne Bevington will do anything to help a friend...even masquerade as a dancer at a house of ill repute for a night. But when a police raid threatens to expose her identity, she finds help in the arms of Cormack, Lord Raikes, a sinfully sexy man with a secret all his own...

Don't miss the next enthralling book in this sizzling series!

Please turn this page for a preview of

Never Entice an Earl.

Chapter One

$\mathcal{D}$aphne Bevington smiled at her sister's obvious excitement for the Heseldons' ball. Clarissa looked like a princess in blush-pink silk, a color Daphne would never, as long as she lived, choose to wear. She'd developed an aversion for the color in her youth, when Lady Harwick had oftentimes insisted on dressing her and her sisters in matching pink dresses. Daphne shivered at the memory but reminded herself not to lose focus. She had to get her sister and her mother out of the house as quickly as possible.

"I wish you were coming." Clarissa pouted. "But I understand how fond you are of Miss Fickett. I do hope she improves very soon. You're such a dear to offer to stay and nurse her and the others. I wish I'd thought of it first. They are all going to like you better now!" She laughed, and merriment lit her eyes.

"I only want to keep an eye on Miss Fickett and the others, Clarissa. Will you keep an eye on Mama? She didn't want to leave me here alone." At Clarissa's nod, Daphne continued, leading her closer to the front door. "The physician believes the illnesses are the result of tainted sausages on the servants' midafternoon tea sideboard and that's why those who had chosen to eat mutton suffered no symptoms. You should have seen Cook when he came back from confronting the butcher." Daphne laughed despite herself. "Steam was shooting out of his ears. But at least this time it didn't require an intervention from the authorities."

Clarissa waved a gloved hand. "I'll tell you all the on-dits tonight when we return—what everyone wore and who asked me to dance."

"I can't wait to hear, but tomorrow at breakfast, perhaps," Daphne responded. "Most likely I'll be asleep when you return." Balls always ran late, and it would be two or three o'clock before they arrived home.

"Come along, Clarissa," called her mother. Behind her, the footman opened the door.

In a shimmer of pearls and diamonds, her sister and mother were gone. Daphne breathed a sigh of relief. Finally—time to help Kate! Thank heavens Wolverton had decided to make an early evening of it and take dinner in his room. She'd glimpsed O'Connell, his valet, descending the servants' staircase some thirty minutes before, having already been dismissed for the night.

"Now, what next?" she whispered to herself, as she rushed down the stairs, returning again to the servants' corridor.

Daphne's mind raced and her heart pounded so hard and rapidly she could scarcely breathe. How unjust that a girl like Kate, who worked so hard day to day as a lady's maid, should have to bear the dreadful burden of her dead father's unpaid debt.

She had told her friend—*her dearest friend!*—not to worry, that she'd take care of everything, and poor Kate had been too exhausted by illness to do anything but collapse into an exhausted sleep.

She had to come up with a plan. There wasn't much time. She could no more allow Kate's elderly grandmother and siblings to be turned out into the streets or sent to the workhouse than she could allow the same misfortune to befall her own family.

But she'd already considered every option. For Daphne, simply paying off the debt wasn't possible because despite her privileged life, she had no access to money of her own, not of the magnitude required. She couldn't sell her dresses or her jewels. Anything of value that went missing would be noted immediately either by her mother or the keen-eyed housekeeper, Mrs. Brightmore, and the loss construed as theft. The servants would be questioned, and she would be forced to step forward and declare herself the guilty party in stealing from… well, from her own self. A strange predicament but true.

She alighted on the lower landing and gripped the banister. If only she could go to her grandfather or her mother and simply ask for the money, but she knew from experience their rule about lending money to servants. Her grandfather, no matter how generous he might be, would soundly reject the lending of money to a servant. The problem had presented itself before, and she had heard his reasoning. What he did for one, he must do for all. There would be no loans granted, only fair wages earned, and never in advance.

Likely by opening her mouth she would only find herself on the receiving end of a lecture about proper behavior and boundaries—and Kate in search of a new position.

She could only imagine her grandfather's explosive reaction to learning that she'd involved herself in the financial affairs of a servant. Her mother's dismay. She couldn't even go to her older sister, Sophia, who very well might take pity on Kate's plight, because the Duke and Duchess of Claxton had not yet returned from Vienna, where his Grace was deeply involved in diplomatic affairs related to the war.

Daphne hadn't felt this helpless since the day of her father's death.

Hurriedly, she spoke to the nurse who had been brought in to tend to those servants who had been stricken ill, and afterward, she visited each of the female staff, where she fluffed pillows and coaxed spoonfuls of weak beef tea through unwilling lips. All the while, her brain churned out one useless idea after another. At last she returned to Kate's door, having arrived at no useful resolution. Inside, thankfully, Kate still slept, her face pallid against the linen pillowcase.

Hands shaking, she took up Kate's reticule from the table and searched inside until she found what she wanted—a scrap of paper upon which all the necessary particulars had been, in her friend's familiar handwriting, neatly inscribed. There was no other way.

*   *   *

"Cheatin' nob!"

Cormack intercepted the fist, which had only a second

before been drunkenly presented to his face. Grabbing the red-nosed fellow by his shoulders, he spun him round and shoved him in the direction of his intended opponent.

Lord, he despised bawdy houses. Having only just passed through the well-barricaded door, he elbowed aside the threadbare velvet drape and ventured inside. If only vengeance had not commanded him here tonight.

Tobacco smoke clouded the air, dimming his view of the men who crowded around the faro tables, gentlemen in evening dress intermingled with tradesmen in dark suits and rough-hewn men off the wharves. Gilt-framed mirrors cluttered the walls, and lopsided chandeliers hung from the ceilings, trappings of faux luxury. A ramshackle quartet assembled in the distant corner. The establishment had the feel of transience, as if every fixture, table, and drape could be snatched up at any moment, thrown in the back of a wagon, and installed elsewhere for the same effect. Understandable, as Cormack's source had warned him the club changed locations often, so as to avoid discovery by the constables. Predators with painted lips and rouged cheeks circled him, already taking note of the newcomer in their midst.

"Looking for a bit of company t'night, good sir?" inquired a redhead, boldly assessing him with kohl-lined eyes.

"Two is good company. Three is a party." The brunette sidled closer, offering Cormack an unrestricted view of her breasts, only barely constrained by a bodice of sheer muslin. "You look like the sort of man who likes more than just one."

Hmmm...perhaps. But his tastes were far more refined than what he would find here.

As far as London brothels went, the Blue Swan was the seediest he'd visited thus far, though he'd paid a handsome bribe to the bully at the door for the pleasure of entering without the required referral. But he wasn't here to drink, gamble, or to whore. He was here to find the man he had sworn to destroy. If only he knew who the hell he was looking for.

His hand passed over his coat pocket, confirming the existence of the hard lump within—the gold amulet he'd taken from Laura's hand in the moments after her death, one bearing a severed Medusa's head and the Latin word *Invisibilis*.

Three years had passed. At last, he felt...close.

His hatred renewed, Cormack made his selection carefully and caught her wrist as she moved past, a woman in a jade-green gown. Older than the others with a faded complexion and dull hair, perhaps she would be more eager than her competitors to earn a bit of coin in exchange for a whispered, forbidden secret.

"'Ay!" The harridan's eyes widened in outrage, but upon assessing him, they softened into heavy-lidded seduction. "Well, 'ow do you do, 'andsome?" she breathed. "'Aven't seen you 'ere before. I'm Nellie. What are y' lookin' for tonight?"

"I'm looking for you, Nellie." He took care to remain in the deepest of shadows. Though few would recognize him in London, he expected that might change, depending on how long this business of retribution kept him here.

In the crush of the crowd, she pressed against him, curling her hands into his lapels. "I've a room upstairs, nice and cozy. What do you say? I'll get us a bottle, just for ourselves."

"Actually, I've become separated from friends and would like to rejoin them. I was hoping that perhaps you know them?"

"Friends?" Her eyes narrowed. "What sort of friends?"

He pressed a crown into her palm.

After a quick glance to assess the coin's worth, a smile eased onto her lips. "Per'aps I do know them. I've known everyone 'ere at one time or another, it seems."

He murmured near her ear, "They follow this club from place to place. Meet here on occasion." He did not know that to be certain, but he had a strong hunch that's how the men he sought remained . . . well, invisible.

"Oh . . ." Her face went slack. "Indeed. A mysterious lot, they are. Don't come here for the entertainments, for the most part."

The beat of his heart increased. "Can you provide their names?"

She glanced over her shoulder before whispering, "Never actually seen their faces, but gentlemen they be, all of them, with fancy clothes and carriages. They've not yet arrived, but soon, I think. Keep an eye over there beside the stage. They'll come through the back."

He stepped away, and her hands fell from his coat. "Thank you, Nellie."

"Wot, that's all?" She pouted, a saucy smile tilting her carmine lips. "You paid for better than just a bit of chitchat."

"Forget about me, if anyone comes asking later. That's all I ask."

"Beshrew me, forget that 'andsome face?" Her gaze traveled over him longingly. Regretfully. She sighed. "Don't think that's possible, but Nellie don't tell tales on her favorites, and you'll forever be one of mine." She came near, her voice lowered. "But be careful with those ones. They're dangerous men."

"How do you know I'm not one of them?"

"I know," she answered softly, and with a shrug of her bare shoulder, she disappeared into the crowd.

Just then, the musicians struck up a tune. Beside them, curtains jerked apart on ropes to reveal a makeshift stage made out of wooden shipping crates, a common sight on the nearby quay. On each of the four corners stood a young lady, frozen in a dramatic pose. Elaborate scarlet carnival masks studded with paste jewels concealed their faces above their painted lips. Close-fitting, flesh-toned body stockings conveyed the illusion of nudity. Those men not otherwise engaged at the gaming tables surged forward to jostle for position along the edges of the stage, shouting out expressions of vulgar admiration. The stage rocked and several of the girls wavered from their poses.

A bulldog-faced man in an ill-fitted greatcoat and top hat strutted to the center of the stage and bellowed, "Gentlemen, gentlemen. Do control yourselves!"

Hands held high for quiet, he waited for the clamor to subside.

"We have assembled here for your personal erudition and viewing pleasure, four of the foremost actresses of Drury Lane presenting the finest in *tableaux vivants*." He gestured toward the young women. "For your eyes only they will enact the most memorable scenes of the classics, the first being the story of Electra and the grievous murder of her father, the king, Agamemnon."

Cormack chuckled. Actresses, indeed. Having studied

the classics intensively at university, he could not discern what any of their poses had to do with Electra or Agamemnon, but he supposed that wasn't the point.

Though he could not claim to be an expert on strumpets, these four were clearly of a higher quality than the others who crowded the room. Young and pretty, at least from this distance, they had bodies to match with high breasts, pinched waists, and flared hips.

His attention lingered on one in particular, a young woman with blonde hair and luminous skin. Something about her engaged him and refused to let go. Perhaps it was the bright blue flash of temper in her eyes or the querulous set of her pretty mouth. He could not help but feel he'd caught sight of an angel who had unknowingly alighted among lesser mortals and who, now entangled in mankind's sin, had become helpless to escape.

Apparently he wasn't the only one who had noticed her, for suddenly the young woman yelped and smacked the hand of the patron closest to her, a man who, after being so rebuffed, snatched his hand away from the girl's well-turned ankle. The collective thunder of male laughter shook the floor beneath Cormack's boots.

Cormack did not laugh. Instead, he maneuvered closer to the stage, fixated. Inexplicably smitten. A bright flush moved up the girl's throat into her cheeks to disappear beneath her mask. She resumed her pose, and yet... her hands trembled.

He knew in an instant she didn't belong in this place.

With each step forward, a tangle of memories and regrets welled up inside him, along with a sudden impulse to protect her, to make whatever had gone wrong right. Something he'd been helpless to do for Laura.

So distracted by the girl was he that he almost... *almost* missed the man ducking down the back corridor, dressed in the clothes of a gentleman, his top hat tilted so as to conceal his face.

* * *

Daphne cast another glare at the filthy creature who had grabbed her leg and resumed her pose. Was it only her imagination, or did her skin now *itch* where he had touched her? *Ugh.* A shiver of revulsion rippled through her.

Perhaps it had been unwise to take Kate's place after all. Not that Kate even knew she was here, of course. The girl would never have allowed her to walk out the door if she'd realized Daphne's intentions. Unwise decision or no, she wouldn't change a thing. Given the urgency of the situation, taking Kate's place had seemed the only alternative. A true friend would never balk at doing the same.

She simply had to be home by the time Clarissa and her mother returned from the Heseldons', else her intricate tangle of not-necessarily-untruths would fall to pieces.

"Pirouette."

Mr. Bynum's command jerked Daphne into the present. She mimicked the movements of the young woman on the stage beside her and twirled like a ballerina. More like a *drunken* ballerina. She had been the only one of the four who had declined to imbibe from the fortifying bottle of gin that had been passed from girl to girl in the moments before the curtain was drawn. While spirits would no doubt take the edge off her present humiliation, she believed it best to keep her wits about her. To her good fortune, no one seemed concerned about talent or proper form, only that they prance around under the pretense of being actresses, wearing unseemly costumes for the illicit pleasure of the men salivating at their feet. Coming to a stop, she sashayed to the next corner and took the place of the girl who had just vacated the spot.

According to the foul-mouthed bully of a stage master, Mr. Bynum, who was also the very same sot who had threatened Kate, they would perform the same salacious rotation ten times before taking their leave of the stage. Only then would Kate's debt be satisfied, at least for the evening. Given a day or two, Daphne was certain she could come up with some other solution for satisfying the remainder.

Mr. Bynum shouted a French command. *"Parader!"*

Truly, he displayed the most appalling accent. Daphne executed a different "classical" pose.

He blathered on, this time about Helen and Paris. In that moment, she desperately tried to forget where she was and imagined herself as Helen, the face that had launched a thousand ships. Why, she had always had a flair for the dramatic. She and her sisters had always put on productions for the family, and in secret she had dreamed of a life onstage. In some ways, tonight's daring venture was exceedingly diverting, and she might actually enjoy herself if not—

If not for the fact that she, Daphne Bevington, the Earl of Wolverton's granddaughter and quite possibly this season's declared incomparable, was at this moment standing on a stage in London's most notorious bawdy house, half-naked and making a naughty spectacle of her jiggly bits for the entertainment of strangers.

Daphne bit down a gasp. *Not all strangers*, for *there*, having just come through the doorway, was Lord Rackmorton, a hopeful suitor who had sent her flowers just yesterday, two dozen perfect white roses. He'd seemed like such a nice gentleman. Obviously, she'd been fooled, and she would rebuff him at the earliest opportunity now that she had seen him here in this palace of iniquity.

She couldn't shake the feeling of terror that had chilled her blood from the moment she'd stepped through the door of the Blue Swan. What if, even though her face was half-concealed by the mask, Lord Rackmorton saw and recognized her? What if her mother and grandfather learned of her not-very-smart, but well-intended adventure?

Yet in a blink, two women plastered themselves to his lordship's side and escorted him off, laughing, into the shadows, past *another* gentleman she also recognized, sneaking in the back—

"Pirouette!"

Just then, a big hand smacked her buttocks, latched there, and squeezed.

Daphne squawked and jumped. A glance over her shoulder confirmed her assailant to be the same cretin as before, looking rather pleased at getting such a solid handful of her. Indeed, in the next moment, with the help of a friend's knee, he hurled himself half on the stage, reaching for her, his tongue hanging out of his mouth like a hound on the street. "Come on, sweet. How about a little ballum-rankum?"

Lunging away, she somehow managed to twirl like a ballerina—

Only to crash into the girl behind her. The room erupted in laughter. In her discomposure, she'd gone the wrong way. The girl shouted a vulgarity a lady ought not to even know and gave Daphne a shove in the opposite direction—

Just in time for her to see the most *attractive* gentleman plant his fist in the face of the man who had affronted her.

Looking up, he glared at her rather ferociously, something that ought to frighten her but instead inspired everything inside her to tingling. Yes, he had to be a gentleman because he looked so very fine with his cravat so perfectly tied and his dark blond hair so neatly cut, somewhere between short and longish, the ideal frame for his broad cheekbones and astonishing gray eyes.

"Thank you," she shouted, though she knew he couldn't hear her for the din of the room.

The gleam in his gray eyes intensified. She'd never had anyone look at her like that, so blatantly, without the filter of decorum, as if she was not a girl or even a lady, but a *woman*.

"You're welcome." Or at least that's what his mouth appeared to say. She couldn't hear him either.

A large crash sounded from the direction of the entrance. A woman screamed. The music trailed off. An enormous man in a black suit and top hat appeared on the threshold. Patrons scrambled away from him, pushing and shoving.

Bracing his legs wide, he bellowed, "Under his majesty's authority, this bawdy house is hereby closed for the crimes of lewdness and common nuisance." Lifting both hands high, he displayed what appeared to be a constable's blazon and piece of paper that could only be a warrant. "You are all under arrest."

A swarm of men rushed in behind him, wielding batons.

Daphne stood paralyzed for a long moment. She? Daphne Bevington, under arrest?

Like everyone else, she dashed for the door.

THE DISH

Where Authors Give You the Inside Scoop

From the desk of Jennifer Delamere

Dear Reader,

One reason I love writing historical fiction is that I find fascinating facts during my research that I can use to add spice to my novels.

For Tom Poole's story in A LADY MOST LOVELY, I was particularly inspired by an intriguing tidbit I found while researching shipwrecks off the southern coast of Australia. In describing the wreck of a steamer called *Champion* in the 1850s, the article included this one line: "A racehorse aboard *Champion* broke loose, swam seven miles to the shore, and raced again in the Western District." Isn't that amazing!? Not only that the horse could make it to land, but that it remained healthy enough to continue racing.

Although I was unable to find out any more details about the racehorse, as a writer this little piece of information was really all I needed. I knew it would be a wonderful way to introduce the animal that would come to mean so much to Tom Poole. Tom and the stallion are the only survivors of a terrible shipwreck that left them washed up on the coast near Melbourne, Australia, in early 1851. Tom was aboard that ship in the first place because he was chasing after the man who had murdered his best friend. By the time he meets Margaret Vaughn in A LADY MOST LOVELY, Tom has been involved in two other real-life events as well: a massive wildfire near Melbourne, and the gold rush that would ultimately make him a wealthy man.

As you may have guessed by now, Tom Poole is a man of action. This aspect of his nature certainly leads him into some interesting adventures! However, when he arrives in London and meets the beguiling but elusive Miss Margaret Vaughn, he's going to discover that affairs of the heart require an entirely different set of skills, but no less determination.

Jennifer Delamere

♥ ♥ ♥ ♥ ♥ ♥ ♥ ♥ ♥ ♥ ♥ ♥ ♥ ♥ ♥ ♥

From the desk of Erin Kern

Dear Reader,

There are two things in this world that I love almost as much as dark chocolate. One of them is a striking pair of blue eyes framed by thick black lashes, with equally dark hair just long enough for a woman's fingers to run through…Excuse me for a moment while I compose myself.

And the other is fried pie.

Okay, I just threw that last part in as an FYI. But what I'm really doing is tucking that useless tidbit away for a future project. That's just how my weird mind works, folks.

But in all seriousness, while I really do love a blue-eyed man, even more than that I love a wounded soul. Because I love to fix things. In my books. In real life I kind of suck at it.

Way back when I first started writing the Trouble series, as was kicked off with *Looking for Trouble*, I had an atypical wounded soul already forming in the cavernous recesses of my mind. I just needed to find a home for her.

Yes, I'm talking about a wounded heroine. I know that sounds kind of strange. Most romance readers love a scarred hero who gets his butt kicked into shape by some head-strong Miss Fix-It. Not that I don't love that also. But I also knew *Looking for Trouble* wasn't the place for her.

Lacy Taylor needed her own story with her own hero. And not only her own hero, but one with an extra tough brand of love that could break through her well-built defense mechanisms.

But make no mistake. Lacy Taylor isn't as much of a tough cookie as she'd like everyone to think. Oh, no. She has a much softer side that only Chase McDermott could bring to the surface. Of course, she tries to keep Chase at arm's length like everyone else in her life. But he's too good for her defenses. Too good-looking. Too loose-hipped. Too quick with his melt-your-bones smile. Not to mention his blue eyes. Gotta have those baby blues.

But Chase underestimates Lacy's power. And I'm not talking about her tough-girl attitude. Never in Chase's years as an adult would he have expected Lacy Taylor to get under his skin so quickly. Not only that, but nothing could have prepared him for his reaction to it.

Or to her.

You see, Chase and Lacy have known each other for a long time. And that's another one of my weaknesses—childhood crushes turned steamy love stories. And Chase and Lacy can cook up steam faster than a drop of water on hot pavement. But it wasn't always like that for these two. You see, Lacy blew out of Trouble years earlier, and after that Chase hardly gave the tough blonde a second thought.

But then she comes back. Now *that's* when things get interesting.

Mostly because Lacy had to all but beg Chase for a job, which, in Lacy's opinion, was almost as painful as a bikini wax. So then they're working together. Seeing each other often. Subtle brushes here and there...you get the picture.

It gets hot. *Real* hot.

But the most fun part is seeing how these two wear each other down. Lacy thinks she's so tough, and Chase thinks he can charm the habit off a nun. Well, actually he probably could.

Needless to say, heads butt, tempers flare, and the clothes, they go a-flying.

But which of these comes first? It's all in HERE COMES TROUBLE. Because every woman needs some Trouble in her life.

Especially the blue-eyed kind.

Steamy readin',

Erin Kern

♥   ♥   ♥

From the desk of Lily Dalton

Dear Reader,

History has always been my thing.

Boring? Never! I've always viewed the subject as a colorful, dynamic puzzle of moving pieces, fascinating to analyze and relive, in whatever way possible. I used to have a history professor who often raised the question, "What if?"

For example, what if Ragnar Lodbrok and his naughty horde of Vikings had decided that they adored farming, so instead of setting off to maraud the coast of England in search adventure and riches, they had just stayed home? How might that omission from history have changed the face of England?

And jumping forward a few centuries: What if historical bad boy Henry VIII had not had such poor impulse control, and had instead just behaved himself? What if he'd tried harder to be faithful to Catherine? What if he'd never taken a shine to Anne Boleyn? There wouldn't have been an Elizabeth I. How might this have changed the path of history?

At the heart of history, of course, are people and personalities and motivations. *Characters.* They weren't flat, dusty words in black and white on the pages of a textbook. Instead, they lived in a vivid, colorful, and dangerous world. They had hearts and feelings and suffered agonies and joy.

Just like Vane Barwick, the Duke of Claxton, and his

estranged wife, the duchess Sophia, who stand on the precipice of a forever sort of good-bye. Though the earlier days of their marriage were marked by passion and bliss, so much has happened since, and on this cold, dark night, understanding and forgiveness seem impossible.

Of course, in NEVER DESIRE A DUKE, the "what if?" is a much simpler question, in that the outcome will not change the course of nations.

What if there hadn't been a snow storm that night?

Hmm. Now that I've forced that difficult question upon us, I realize I don't want to imagine such an alternate ending to Vane and Sophia's love story. Being snowbound with someone gorgeous and intriguing and desirable and, yes, provoking, is such a delicious fantasy.

If there hadn't been a snow storm that night...

Well...thankfully, dear reader, there was!

Hugs and Happy Reading,

Lily Dalton

www.lilydalton.com
Twitter@LilyDalton
Facebook.com

♥   ♥   ♥   ♥ ♥   ♥ ♥

From the desk of Debbie Mason

Dear Reader,

So there I was, sitting in my office in the middle of a heat wave, staring at a blank page waiting for inspiration to strike. I typed Chapter One. Nothing. Nada.

And the problem wasn't that I was writing a Christmas story in the middle of July. I had the air conditioner cranked up, holiday music playing in the background, a pine-scented candle burning, and a supply of Hammond's chocolate-filled peppermint candy canes on my desk. FYI, best candy canes ever!

No, the problem was my heroine, Madison Lane. I didn't get her, and honestly, I was afraid I wasn't going to like her very much. Because really, who doesn't love Christmas and small towns? At that point, I was thinking of changing the title from *The Trouble with Christmas* to *The Trouble with Madison Lane*.

It took a couple of hours of staring at her picture on my wall before Madison finally opened up to me. Okay, so I may have thrown a few darts at her, drawn devil horns on her head, and given her an impressive mustache before she did. But she won me over. Once I found out what had happened to her in that small Southern town all those years ago, I fell in love with Madison. She's strong, incredibly smart, and loyal, and after what she suffered as a little girl, she deserves a happily-ever-after more than most.

Now all I needed was a man who was up for the challenge. Enter Gage McBride, the gorgeous small-town sheriff and single father of two young girls. A born protector, Gage is strong enough to deal with Madison and smart enough to see the sweet and vulnerable woman beneath her tough, take-no-prisoners attitude. But just because these two are a perfect match doesn't mean their journey to a happily-ever-after is an easy one. The title of the book is THE TROUBLE WITH CHRISTMAS, after all.

I hope you have as much fun reading Gage and Madison's story as I did writing it. And I hope, like Gage and Madison, that this holiday season finds you surrounded by the love of family and friends.

Wishing you much joy and laughter!

Find out more about Forever Romance!

Visit us at
www.hachettebookgroup.com/publishing_forever.aspx

Find us on Facebook
http://www.facebook.com/ForeverRomance

Follow us on Twitter
http://twitter.com/ForeverRomance

NEW AND UPCOMING TITLES

Each month we feature our new titles
and reader favorites.

CONTESTS AND GIVEAWAYS

We give away galleys, autographed copies,
and all kinds of exclusive items.

AUTHOR INFO

You'll find bios, articles, and links to personal websites
for all your favorite authors—and so much more.

GET SOCIAL

Connect with your favorite authors, editors, and
other Forever fans, and share what's important to you.

THE BUZZ

Sign up for our monthly romance newsletter,
and be the first to read all about it.

VISIT US ONLINE AT

WWW.HACHETTEBOOKGROUP.COM

FEATURES:

**OPENBOOK BROWSE AND
SEARCH EXCERPTS**

•

AUDIOBOOK EXCERPTS AND PODCASTS

•

AUTHOR ARTICLES AND INTERVIEWS

•

**BESTSELLER AND PUBLISHING
GROUP NEWS**

•

SIGN UP FOR E-NEWSLETTERS

•

**AUTHOR APPEARANCES AND TOUR
INFORMATION**

•

SOCIAL MEDIA FEEDS AND WIDGETS

•

DOWNLOAD FREE APPS

BOOKMARK HACHETTE BOOK GROUP
@ WWW.HACHETTEBOOKGROUP.COM